ALSO BY PIPER CJ

a Frozen Pyre

PIPER CJ

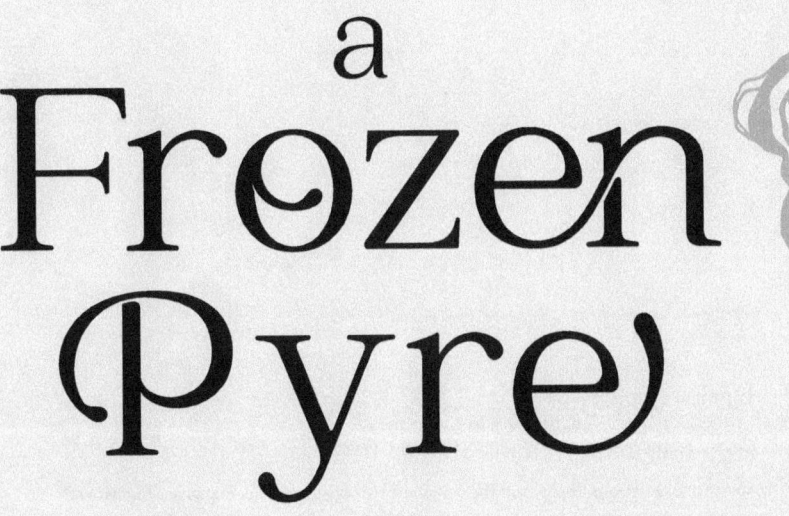

Bloom *books*

Published by Bloom Books, an imprint of Sourcebooks
1935 Brookdale RD, Naperville, IL 60563-2773
(630) 961-3900
sourcebooks.com

Cataloging-in-Publication Data is on file with the Library of Congress.

Printed and bound in the United States of America.
POD

For the villains who deserve happy endings—
and the tragedies that made us villains

Continent of Cyrradin

Pact Encampment

western Red outpost

Sulgrave Mountains

the unclaimed wilds

the Frozen Straits

the Etal Isles

Raascot

Gwydir

the university

Uaimh Reev

Stone

Raasay Forest

Yelagin

Farleigh

Farehold

Priory

Aubade

the Temple of the All Mother

Henares

Amurah

Tarkhany Desert

the Zatra Oasis

Kafarem

Valor Mast

the Dying Sunset

Midnah

LISTEN ALONG WITH OUR
villains

THE BEGINNING

Holy - Zolita
Hanging On - Ellie Goulding
Devil's Playground - The Rigs
Monsters in My Mind - Cloudy June

THE MIDDLE

Throne - Saint Mesa
Castle - Halsey
Monster - Victoria Carbol
Venom - Little Simz

THE END

Toxic - Anthony Willis
Seize the Power - YONAKA
Cult Leader - King Mala
Dangerous Woman - Power Haus, Future Cello

PRONUNCIATION GUIDE

CHARACTERS

Anwir—AN-weer
Berinth—BEAR-inth
Caris—CARE-iss
Ceneth—SEEN-eth
Eero—Arrow
Guryon—GER-yon
Hassain—HAA-sin
Ophir—oh-FEAR
Firi—FEAR-ee
Onain—oh-NANE
Sedit—seh-DETT
Suley—SOO-lee
Tyr—TEER
Zita—ZEE-tuh

PLACES

Aubade—obeyed
Gyrradin—GEER-a-din
Gwydir—gwih-DEER
Henares—hen-AIR-ess
Midnah—MID-nuh
Raasay—ra-SAY
Raascot—RA-scott
Tarkhany—TAR-kah-nee
Yelagin—YELL-a-ghin

CONTENT WARNING

Turn to the Afterword for a complete list of content and trigger warnings.

PROLOGUE

✦   ✦   ✦   ✦

MIDNAH, TARKHANY

"IT CAN'T BE OPENED. WE'VE TRIED EVERYTHING." THE ADVISOR wrung his hands uncertainly as he eyed the monarchs.

"Destroy it," Tempus urged, voice ripe with irritation.

The queen sighed, gliding from where she'd rested to pour herself a glass of wine. The sharp scent of citrus filled the room as she moved, accompanying the gossamer, weightless fabric that floated behind her. Zita shook her head, bored with the men and their outbursts. "What advice is that? We destroy what we don't understand? We don't know where it leads. We don't know what it offers. You'd have us eliminate all possibilities?"

"Spare us your righteous monologues," Tempus said.

She took a slow sip of her wine, expression cool as she savored every drop. She lowered the glass and relaxed her weight against the table. She addressed the advisor when she spoke, though her eyes did not leave Tempus. "Give us a moment, will you?"

The advisor nodded nervously as he exited the room.

The palace had been spared from the calamity that had claimed scores of lives. The winged demons hadn't just claimed those caught in the collateral damage as the enormous beasts had touched down, nor the ones lost to the stomach of the dragon. The true death toll had come when the royal guard had dispatched to fight the creatures. Tar-like blood had filled the courtyard, intermingling with the sulfuric stench that rolled off their amphibious skin. Strike after strike, blow after blow, fallen man after fallen man, the body count had grown into the dozens before a valiant warrior had hacked the final, decapitating blow through the elongated, serpent-like neck of the monster. The victory had been enthusiastic, raucous, and short-lived. A hush had pressed on the guards as the fallen creature had begun to twitch, its body rolling toward the severed head. Smoke-like tendrils had emerged, knitting the parts together before the men had realized the unspeakable, nightmarish truth: the creature could not be killed.

The retreat had been challenging and tinged with the sort of shame that clouded the soul from failing at an unwinnable game. Tarkhany was under siege from atrocities that had spilled over from the darkest and most depraved of night terrors, and there was nothing they could do.

"Did you hear what they're calling it?" Zita asked.

Tempus made a scoffing noise as he crossed to a chair. He sat and looked away.

"Ag'drurath."

"Winged death," he said. "I'm aware. The dragon of winged death and its winged reaper. The people make it sound like we're at the end of times." He looked at her then. "I suppose you want to blame me for this, too? Do you think I had something to do with it?"

She arched a brow. "You did."

He clenched his fist, then resumed looking at the wall. "You could express gratitude for what I did on the morning of the execution. If you hadn't thwarted—"

"I am Tarkhany's queen, and you locked me in my chambers at sunrise like a common prisoner. You assumed my form, took my place, and set forth to murder Farehold's princess. And I am to be grateful?"

2

His eyes flashed red. "You would have been safe from the dragon's attack if you had remained in the palace. Farehold would have gotten what it deserves."

"If you had killed their only remaining heir, you would have brought war to my doorstep after I've moved heaven and earth to escape the grasp of that blasted kingdom's overreaching fingers. You are a blight, Tempus."

His lips pulled back, baring his sharpened fangs. "I am not the one who brought demons to our home."

Zita took another slow drink of her wine. She lowered the glass and ran a finger along the rim. "I'm not a fool. I know you can't create or summon hell. You have no command of death. But you have attempted to take justice into your own hands against my wishes on more than one occasion. You attempted to poison our guests, including a monarch and friend to the continent to whom I'd extended clemency and intended to help with her retribution. And you would have seen her dead with a thousand witnesses."

His twitch of anger betrayed him.

"I think you should know something," she said.

He exhaled slowly before looking at his wife once more.

"Not only will I never love you"—Zita stared at him while he absorbed each word—"but I will never forgive you. You are no friend to Tarkhany. And I don't care if you're in the form of a man, a bird, or wearing my crown and dressed in my finest attire, impersonating me before my people: You are not welcome. I will give you until tomorrow to leave of your own volition, and then I will have the guards escort you."

Tempus wore his emotions on his sleeve. He sounded crushed, then confused, betrayed, shocked, and furious—dominoes of emotion as he sputtered. He was on his feet in an instant, crossing the room quickly as he headed for her. "I'm king!" he shouted. "No! You, you can't—"

Zita raised a hand and wiggled her fingers.

Tempus froze. The halted sound of his advance echoed

off the smooth marble walls as a stifling fear descended upon him. She held his eyes as his gaze flickered between her face and her fingertips. The anger leached from his face as a new emotion entirely replaced it. "You wouldn't."

They both knew she wasn't talking about her shield. She possessed a great and terrible power that would bring all of Tarkhany to its knees in an instant.

Zita looked at her hand, then back to Tempus. "I would. But you know how reluctant I am to use it. Don't force my hand, Tempus. Be gone by the morning."

He swallowed as if choking down the sound of his name.

She remained expressionless. "Please send the attendant in as you leave."

"Zita, I—"

"I said: You have until morning. I don't care where you go or where you live, but you won't be welcome in Midnah. Do you understand?"

The man stared despondently at her, still frozen where he stood. His eyes raked over her, and she spied the expression of a man in love. She knew he saw the ageless elegance of the fae, and if he were wise, he would also see the stoic, unimpeachable regalness known only to true monarchs. Today, he would see her eyes and lips were painted gold, as though she'd chosen to adorn her face with the sun itself. Perhaps the metallic sheen had seemed unusual when he'd first entered the room, but now, surely he saw it for what it was.

She was sovereign. She didn't need a crown. She *was* the crown.

"Where will I go?" he asked, shoulders slumping as he absorbed the fullness of her words.

Zita allowed her hand to drop to her side, finishing her wine. "You loved Aubade so much that you made an unsanctioned trip once before. Why don't you return to the land you've been so desperate to reclaim? Live in the sand. Sail to the isles. I don't care. So long as it isn't here."

Tempus idled on the marble floor for a long time. He took slow inventory of the room. She watched as he examined the high, arched ceilings, the impeccably smooth pillars, the scented bouquets of orange, lemon, and lime, the things he'd never see again.

"I love you," he said helplessly.

Zita turned her back to her husband as she began to pour another glass of wine. Without looking at him, she said, "I know."

She kept her back to him until she heard his long, slow breath. He'd crossed the room, hand on the door, perhaps waiting to see if she would turn for a final goodbye. She did not.

The door opened, and with it came the flood of sound that had been withheld by the dampener. The palace was still a flurry in the wake of the chaos. Servants, advisors, nobility, and guards had flooded into the safety of the palace walls.

She didn't turn until the door clicked shut, dampening the noise of the outside world.

"Your Grace?" the servant asked nervously.

Zita turned her attention once more. "The door is not locked, correct? The one Princess Ophir created?"

He blinked at her repeatedly, perhaps shocked that she wouldn't be addressing the king's sudden exit. "No, Your Grace. The knob turns."

She continued, "And those present? They saw three exit through it?"

"Yes, Your Grace. Princess Ophir, plus an unknown man and woman escorting her, both of whom appeared to be from Sulgrave."

She chewed on this. "I'd heard the rumors. You'd think we'd notice if a Sulgrave fae were wandering our streets. And yet, I'm to believe they made it into the palace and onto the breakfast table the morning of the banquet without being noticed?"

"Well, the woman—"

"Exited the palace with Ophir. Yes. Do we not have guards? Do we not have centurions? Has anyone addressed this breach in security? Or perhaps more than Tempus need to be held accountable for how things unraveled."

"I'm sorry, Your Grace, I—"

Zita persisted. "Back to the door. The knob turns, so it isn't locked, and yet it does not open. Are we to believe it's magically sealed?"

He shook his head. "It moves slightly, it—"

She cut him off once more. "If you open a door in the palace, and it moves slightly but won't open, what would you assume is wrong with it?"

He frowned at her. "Well, I suppose someone would have put furniture in front of it."

She nodded. "They've blocked it."

"Your Grace?"

"Fetch me someone who can speak to stone."

PART I

A Loose Thread

ONE

✦ ✦ ✦ ✦

CASTLE GWYDIR, RAASCOT

OPHIR'S EYES FLEW OPEN AS UNSEEN ARMS WRAPPED around her between the silken sheets, pinning her to a body. She gasped against the sudden motion. It took a moment for her eyes to adjust before she could make out the shape of a woman silhouetted against the gloom. Dwyn was turned away from her, draped in an inky pool of her own long, dark hair. Ophir breathed in her crushed mint scent. Dwyn was the only familiar piece of her surroundings. The rest was cold, dark, and strange.

She sucked in a surprised breath when she inhaled leather and smoke. Tyr was here.

She began to squirm, and his strong arms tightened around her.

"Shh," he whispered. She scanned the shadows for the invisible arms that held her. His power was both blessing and curse. She'd understood why Tyr hadn't wanted Ceneth to spot him, but she didn't fully understand his insistence upon remaining unseen even when they were alone.

"I want to see your face," she whispered, careful not to wake Dwyn.

"Trust me," he said against her hair, breath warm on her ear.

He was firm: She couldn't tell Dwyn that he'd come with them from the desert to the northern forest. Dwyn had slumped into unconsciousness in the chaos that was their escape from Midnah. She'd remained dead to the world as Tyr had flung her over his shoulder and carried her through Ophir's door to the northern kingdom. By the time Dwyn had opened her eyes, Ophir and Tyr had discussed their next steps and come to an agreement.

Still, she ached to watch her fingers run through his dark hair, look upon his amused smirk, gaze into eyes as rich as the earth, trace lines along the gilded chisel of his jaw. Ophir had taken numerous men and women to her bed in her time, all fawning and grateful to be there. Perhaps she was beholden to his elusiveness.

In his absence, she was trapped, reliving the last time she'd fully looked upon him. She was flung back into her first days in the north as if experiencing them for the first time.

One week ago, she'd awoken in Midnah.

She'd stared down an ag'drurath. She'd watched a shape-shifter impersonate the Queen of Tarkhany. She'd tasted the barest edges of vengeance against her sister's murderer. When chaos had descended, Tyr had begged her to make a door so they might escape.

And so, she had.

RAASAY FOREST, RAASCOT

The wind left her lungs as she sprinted from the hot desert air into freezing rain. She was dressed for the dunes—a sheer gown that was soaked to the bone in an instant. Her teeth chattered as she struggled to fling out her hand, spread her fingers wide, and manifest something, *anything*, given the terrible command she had of the power. She envisioned a castle, a mansion, even a cabin, but only a rickety shelter sprung forth so they might escape from the storm.

She made a cot, a few tattered blankets, and succumbed

to exhaustion before trying and failing to fix their surroundings.

Tyr plopped Dwyn's lifeless shape on the cot as if glad to be rid of her.

Given his hatred for the siren, she supposed she had to be grateful he'd thrown her over his shoulder in the first place. Perhaps he knew enough to understand that she wouldn't forgive him if he let her lose someone else. She needed Dwyn, for better or for worse.

The defeated growl that tore from her throat made her want to summon a hole to fling herself into if she couldn't do anything right.

"You're going to freeze to death, Firi," Tyr said. He knelt in front of her, tipping her chin to look up at his face. His black hair was inky with raindrops that dropped onto the floor. The sharp, angled tattoo cut above the soaked collar of his tunic. He chafed her arms for warmth. "Summon your flame."

"And do what?" she managed through her shivers. "Burn down the shack?"

He leaned forward and crushed her into a hug, wrapping his arms around her. It was the only thing that kept her from falling apart. He had no wisecracks about getting naked for body heat or jabs about manifesters. He simply held her until she stopped shivering.

"Where's Sedit?"

He pulled away but didn't meet her prodding gaze. It was big of him, she thought, given his feelings for the manifested canine. He loved animals—a quality that had driven him to his murderous hunt for revenge over the fate of his hound—and her demons could hardly be considered living things. His restraint on the issue was the only thing keeping him from being banished to the arctic downpour. Ophir could cry over how much she missed her dog—the first and only good thing she'd ever manifested. She'd commanded Sedit to remain in the forest, far enough from them so he would neither be persecuted nor rouse suspicion.

She should have been the one left behind to wander the desert, she thought. Not her creations.

Dwyn made the first noise she'd made in hours.

Tyr looked over his shoulder, then back at Ophir.

"I'm going to need to shift back into the space between things before she wakes up," he said.

"What?" Ophir leaned away so she could look at him fully. She squinted at him through the dim light filtering between the cracks in the boards. "Why?"

Tyr sucked in a breath. She didn't understand his expression.

"So many reasons," he said after several long moments. "I think we're in Raascot. Based on the trees and mountains, I assume we're just outside of Gwydir. You're going to need Ceneth's help. You're his betrothed. He won't want another man sniffing around you."

Ophir was incredulous. "Neither of us want to be in this arranged marriage! He loved my sister. He barely tolerates me. The feeling is mutual."

"He's a monarch, as are you," Tyr argued. "Appearance is everything. We can't humiliate him by having a lover move in with you the moment you arrive at his castle."

Ophir's eyes became slits. "Dwyn and I have fucked," she said. "Shouldn't I get rid of her, too, by that logic?"

"Trade on their assumptions. Let sexism work in your favor so you don't lose both of us," he sighed.

Ophir could barely whisper the next two words. "Lose you?"

"No, no, I'm sorry. I shouldn't have said it like that. I'm not going anywhere. But for all intents and purposes, I need to appear gone, and..." He cleared his throat. "I'm not sure if Dwyn can lie. She's too blunt, too confident to play it close to the vest."

Her eyebrows bunched. Something was odd about his delivery. His tone landed false, though she couldn't explain why.

"You already have a mission for vengeance. You need to garner favor while you can if you hope to get away with whatever schemes will get you vengeance for Caris's murder."

Ophir struggled through his words. A headache bloomed as she tried to make sense of them. She drove her fingers into her temples to massage the tension, barely managing to shake her head.

While she tended to the throbbing between her ears, he added, "Can you say with certainty that Dwyn wouldn't let something slip through a snide comment or sarcastic remark? We have to assume his walls have ears. Dwyn and I would need to remain peaceable within Castle Gwydir or we'd raise suspicion, and the two of us have never gone an hour without fighting. Could she be trusted to be convincingly amicable, no matter what happens? Could we trust her acting skills under Ceneth's watchful eye?"

The pounding subsided as the topic changed back to Dwyn. Deceiving monarchs was an easy pastime. She understood the game.

Ophir's face softened as she leafed through her memories. He had a point. She'd seen Dwyn and Tyr interact countless times, and the only constant in her life was how antagonistic they were toward one another.

Ophir shifted out from under Tyr's hold and knelt beside Dwyn. The tips of her index and middle fingers found the weak pulse on the siren's throat.

"She's fine," Tyr insisted.

But he didn't know why she was so worried. How could he? She hadn't seen Dwyn at all in the moments since Dwyn had fallen unconscious. Instead, she'd seen sister's lifeless form. She'd smelled roses and tasted bitter drinks.

"There's one more thing. I know this doesn't need to be said, but you know what you are. I know what you are. The others..."

The swallow caught in Ophir's throat. She was a manifester. She'd created a venomous snake the size of a horse. She'd made dripping black hounds, rotting horses, and a dragon and its rider that had thrust an entire city into a spiral of madness and death. Anyone who learned what she was would be terrified.

"Who would I tell?" she said, heart aching at the question. Her sister was dead. She'd fled her family. Her only friends were inside this shack.

They were quiet until Dwyn showed signs of waking.

"Please don't go," Ophir asked of him.

"I won't," he said, still holding her hand as he disappeared before her eyes.

She steeled herself against the loss she felt, even knowing he was in the room with her. She helped Dwyn into a sitting position, manifesting her new clothes, helping her warm by the fireplace she summoned. Ophir told a flimsy lie about how she'd dragged her through an unknown door, and Dwyn was too groggy to question the story.

She slept. She woke. She planned.

Tyr slipped his hand into hers as they carved through the forest to let her know he was there. She and Dwyn didn't exchange more than a few words as they picked their way between the enormous fir trees. She asked Dwyn if the siren could use a borrowed ability as a tracker, but Dwyn sadly informed her that she had nothing left.

Tyr tugged her slightly, and she turned her head to look through the empty space where he walked. He'd been right to get her attention.

"Dwyn?"

The siren stopped in her tracks. "Where the hell are we?"

They peered through the break in the trees, over the dripping, dew-soaked ferns, and beyond the craggily broken rocks to a distant blue-black city.

They made it to Gwydir by nightfall, sweaty, cold, and filthy.

Between Midnah and Gwydir, she was making a habit of unceremonious arrival, but so far, it had gotten her where she needed to go. They were escorted to rooms and closely guarded until news came from the king. Dwyn remained uncharacteristically quiet, citing sickness after the drugging, which Ophir understood. They bathed separately, they ate, and they crawled into bed.

The gemstone castle was a far cry from their shack in the woods, but she was more terrified now than she'd been when wandering through the wilderness.

CASTLE GWYDIR, RAASCOT

Ophir was restless.

"It's bedtime, Princess," Tyr said quietly. She'd believed him when he'd said he'd be there, but it was still a relief to hear his voice. "Who knew she was such a good sleeper? Isn't there an adage about villains sleeping well at night?"

"I know you hate her..."

He waited, then stifled a laugh. "Here I was thinking you were about to argue her case."

"I can't make you two like each other. But she saved my life. We're...*important*...to each other. If you care about me, you owe her, and I think you know it."

It was his turn to be silent.

She ran her hand up Tyr's unseen arm, rolling around to face the space where he should be. He pressed her body in closer, keeping his arm to her back as he tucked her face against his chest.

"Are you anxious to see your fiancé?" he asked.

She nodded. She was.

He brought his hand to the back of her hair and began stroking it comfortingly. She nestled into him and was surprised to feel her breath catch. It was so intimate. Something about the safety choked her with the urge to sob against his neck. He held her so tightly, she almost felt as if she weren't alone. It was nearly as if she wasn't in Castle Gwydir, sharing a roof with the man her late sister had been set to marry. She almost

15

felt as if she hadn't been poisoned, as if her parents hadn't attempted to send her to Raascot to take Caris's place, as if her world hadn't fallen in around her, disintegrating like paper under water.

But the nightmares were real.

She shifted against him and slipped her leg over his, hooking him even closer. She closed her eyes against the unseen wall of strength and the warm, masculine scent of campfire smoke. She lifted her mouth, searching for his. Her lips parted slightly, eyes closing against the darkened shadows of the night as his kiss found her. She melted into him, relaxing her body as he held her.

"I'll do anything I can," he promised. "And even some things that I can't."

She wasn't sure what that meant, but she understood the intention. He'd be there. He'd be with her when she woke up to meet Ceneth. He'd be there in her meetings, in her uncertain moments, over the next few hours, days, weeks. She wasn't exactly sure how he managed to stay unnoticed, but Tyr had more than enough experience navigating the spaces between things to remain unseen. If he'd maneuvered through Sulgrave and Aubade without detection and spied within Tarkhany's palace, then Gwydir was sure to be no different.

Ophir slid her hand over chest, down his stomach, traveling lower to the space where their hips met. She fought a triumphant smile at his quiet, controlled exhalation the moment her fingers grazed the leather south of his belt. Her fingertips continued to move against him, but he snatched her wrist lightly in one hand. She frowned through the darkness at where she knew his face would be, hoping he could read her expression through the midnight gloom.

"You don't want to?" she asked.

She savored the vibration of his low growl. "You have no idea how badly."

"Good," she said, pressing her hips into his. "Me, too."

16

"Listen—"

"I want this," she said. She didn't care that they were only a few rooms away from the man she was to marry or that Dwyn slept beside her. Dwyn had proven on more than one occasion that she could sleep through an invading army. The only thing that had ever successfully roused the siren from her slumber was the flame of Ophir's long-forgotten night terrors. Tyr had once said he'd love nothing more than to slip inside her while her favorite witch slept inches away.

He released his hold on her wrist and brought his hand to her face, cradling it gently as his thumb and forefinger moved against her cheek, tucking her hair behind her ear. "I want to do right by you."

"And you have," she said. "So do it again."

He pressed a kiss to her hair.

Her frown was deep. "Don't make a girl feel rejected. I won't be able to fall back to sleep."

She could feel the warmth of his breath as he chuckled lightly beside her. "Well, far be it from me to keep you from sleep," he said, rolling her onto her back with a quiet, gentle motion so as not to wake the woman beside her.

She bit her lip as she felt his mouth begin to move against her throat, then her breasts. There was a quiet, sucking sound before she inhaled sharply. A tingle went down her spine as warmth flooded her. He'd slipped one, then two fingers within her. Her back arched off the bed. One knee bent upward while the other stiffened, outstretched. His opposite hand returned to her hair, bringing his face close to hers as he whispered, "If you can't stay quiet, I'll have to stop. Understood?"

She nodded, biting her lip until it nearly drew blood as he slowly filled her.

Dwyn turned over in her sleep, and they stilled. Tyr's hand covered Ophir's mouth as she turned to watch the half-asleep shape of the woman beside them.

"Firi?" Dwyn asked through a nearly delirious haze of

17

sleep. Her eyes remained closed as her hand stretched out, seeking Ophir.

Ophir slipped her hand up and their fingers intertwined.

Satisfied, Dwyn snuggled back into her pillow and returned to her deep and restful slumber.

It was all Ophir could do not to squeeze down on the fingers that held her as Tyr moved within her. Her free hand dug into his back, channeling all her building tension into the skin beneath her nails. She tore five achingly slow ribbons into the man above her as his fingers continued to work within her. His lips, his tongue, his mouth moved over hers, kisses wet, hot, and silent.

Fuck, his hand moved with rhythm, with power, with authority.

She sucked in a breath and held it as she crested climax. She squeezed her eyes shut so tightly, not understanding why he stopped moments before orgasm. She cracked her eyes open, releasing the breath she'd been holding, only to see where her hand sparked with embers against his back.

Horrified, she yanked her hand away. She immediately extinguished the early signs of her uncontrolled flame and searched for his face.

"Are you okay?" she breathed.

His laugh, though quiet, was unmistakable.

"Hang on. Ask me in twenty minutes."

"Twenty min—"

He slipped out of her slowly, and she was instantly worried that she'd injured him more than he'd let on. But rather than return to the space next to her, she felt his body move farther and farther down the length of her until his lips grazed her inner thighs.

She would be sleeping very, very well that night.

TWO⊙

✦   ✦   ✦   ✦

TYR SMILED TO HIMSELF AS HE WOKE, THE TASTE OF SUNSHINE still on his tongue. He'd learned at a young age how to stay between things even while sleeping—an ability that had come in handy on more than one occasion. His smile faltered at the sight of Ophir's fingers still interlaced with Dwyn's. He knew that Ophir cared for Dwyn, and that in theory, she was safer beside Dwyn than anywhere in the world.

He was sure that Dwyn had feelings for Ophir, too, but not in the way that a human or fae cared for one they loved. It was the sort of care a goblin might have for their gold, or a viper might have for its lair. He also knew that he would trade almost anything to be able to slit the witch's throat where she slept and put an end to her wretched life. But if Dwyn hadn't found a way to break the bond that prevented them from ending one another, then it couldn't be done.

He hated lying to Ophir, even more so when it came in the form of lying to protect Dwyn's agenda.

He wasn't staying invisible because Dwyn couldn't tell a convincing lie.

He had to stay out of sight because Dwyn had told a series of lies so sinister, so manipulative, that they'd never get out from beneath her cobwebs of deceit if they couldn't gain the upper hand.

For a little while, that meant she had to believe she'd successfully done away with him.

The frown stayed on his face as he slipped out from underneath the sheets and assessed the room. Though they'd arrived in the light of day, the siren had spent too much time shrewdly inspecting the women's newfound quarters for him to truly investigate the space without risking detection.

He brushed strands of hair away from Ophir's face with unseen fingers, sighing as he looked down at her.

How was he supposed to help her?

He'd expected to aid in her quest for vengeance against those responsible for Caris's murder, but after Berinth's death, Ophir had gone uncharacteristically silent regarding her original mission. No talk of finding and destroying killers. No schemes for bringing the responsible parties to justice.

At first, he'd wondered if Ophir only remained quiet in Dwyn's presence, but Ophir hadn't spoken about it when the siren slept, either.

His frown deepened as he stared at the princess. She was perhaps the most powerful person on the continent. Maybe she'd ceased speaking of such things because she didn't need his help. Perhaps all she needed to solve things on her own was the complete picture. But how could Ophir possibly be safe from the siren once Dwyn knew that she was no longer in control? He wouldn't gamble Ophir's safety against Dwyn's impulsive, greedy rage, especially if the only toll was his own suffering conscience.

He'd scarcely slipped into the hall when a sound drew his attention.

Perhaps the servants were already stirring. It would be useful to monitor how they readied the castle for the day. He'd gain a better understanding of its inner workings, its layout, and the culture of the people within.

Tyr hurried down the hall, keeping his footsteps light.

Just because they couldn't see him didn't mean they couldn't hear him. He slipped around the corner and nearly ran into a straight-backed woman, legs apart and arms at her sides as if confronting an enemy. His heart spiked with his near-brush mistake. If it weren't for years of careful training, he would have given himself away on sheer surprise. Instead, he swallowed the emotion and examined his unexpected find.

The woman stood several arm's lengths away from a closed wooden door. Her hair was so tightly braided on each side, he'd nearly thought it had been shaved. The rest of her dark hair ran down her back, ending somewhere between her shoulder blades. She didn't possess the telltale wings so common among northern fae, but everything from her ears to her gold-brown skin suggested that she had to be from Raascot. Either that, or there were entirely new kingdoms beyond the continent to be discovered, which was a thought too exhausting for him to entertain.

She twitched, looking over her shoulder ever so slightly, most definitely in reaction to the gentle noise of Tyr stopping himself from impact. He held his breath as he waited for her to shake off her paranoia, as they always did. He counted on fae and humans alike to ignore their gut. They chose to only believe what they could see with their eyes, and one day, their presumptions would be their undoing.

Of course, this morning was not for undoing.

He'd never expected to visit Gwydir. He'd also never expected to bed a princess, join a blood gang, or witness a dragon slaughter masses, but life had a funny way of changing one's plans. He released his expectations and prepared to do what he did best: gather information.

The woman was waiting, but why?

Tyr kept perfectly still, as the pewter skies barely offered enough light through the arched corridors for him to see her. Her shoulders slumped as she relaxed her posture at long last. The woman leaned against a wall but did nothing more. He didn't know enough of Raascot's culture to know how one normally dressed, but from her leathers and the snug fit of her clothes, he assumed she must need the freedom of movement typically required by those who served as centurions or military. She released the last of her tension, resting her head against the stone.

It was a strangely intimate sight, unintentionally peering into a stranger's private moment of exhaustion in the pre-dawn hour.

The moment a new set of footsteps sounded in the distance, she snapped from the wall and tightened her shoulders. A winged man strode around the corner, dipping his head from the distance down the hall to greet her.

"Onain," he said, raising a friendly hand in greeting.

"Evander," she responded, posture rigid.

It took him a few more steps to reach her. His hand went directly to the doorknob. It turned easily in his hand. He looked over his shoulder as he said, "You could have gone in. It wasn't locked."

"It wasn't my place, sir," she replied.

"I'm not military," he responded. "You're an equal here. Come in."

"With skin as hard as diamond, you would have been unbeatable in the military. Your powers were wasted," she said.

The man chuckled. "If you say it, then I know it's so. Surely, being impenetrable will benefit my king in closer corridors."

"If you say so," Onain replied.

Tyr hugged the empty space at her back as the door closed behind them. Once again, she flinched, her gut doubtlessly sensing something unusual. Women were particularly adept at feeling eyes on them or bodies near them. He'd once thought this might pose a problem, before he'd learned a more important truth: Women had been conditioned to ignore any such instinct that couldn't be confirmed with firm, physical evidence. So, despite the way her chin jutted toward him,

Tyr knew that if he remained still, she'd shake off the feeling once more.

She turned toward the empty room. One large table, decorated with a map and pieces that may have belonged to a chess set, dotted the surface. Tyr realized he was in Gwydir's war room. It was quite the find for someone who'd only intended to tail maids and servants for his first morning in the castle, but he'd be foolish to question the goddess for her gift.

"Sit, sit." Evander gestured as he slid into a tall-backed chair that had been specifically carved to accommodate wings.

Her expression remained impassive. "I'm more comfortable standing, if that's okay."

He sighed as he looked up at her. Purplish bruises smudged beneath his eyes, which Tyr rarely saw in the fae. He wore signs of stress and age, irrespective of his blood. He asked, "Do people tell you that you're difficult?"

"Often, sir."

Evander touched the map. He dragged it from Aubade, to Tarkhany, to Gwydir. "Princess Ophir is under our roof. Have you been briefed?"

She dipped her chin. "I was told that she arrived. I've also been told you'd be filling me in, sir."

Tyr fought not to suck in an audible breath. This was a strike too fortunate. A debriefing on Ophir's arrival was a far sight better than following the laundrymaid as she tucked clean linens into spare rooms around the castle. These must be the king's advisors, if they were here at the crack of dawn to discuss official messaging. He moved as close to the table as he dared.

"Her presence is not the problem," Evander began. "Raascot's known there would be a union between Gwydir and Aubade for decades. Of course, she was never the intended, but an advantageous marriage is still an advantageous marriage. The issue is that the princess stumbled in from the forest, soaked to the bone, accompanied by a girl from Sulgrave and unable to tell us how she'd gotten here. Then, after receiving Eero's message regarding Tarkhany—"

Onain's lips turned down. "I've heard, but I'm not sure I understand."

"None of us do," he agreed. "Queen Zita is calling for a summit. I'm sure her raven will arrive any day, but given Ceneth's direct quill to Eero—"

"Yes, it's not the communication that's troubling me," she said, pinching off a glare. Tyr had the impression that she was both disciplined enough to control her emotions, and important enough to not tolerate perceived disrespect. "What I fail to understand is why we're hearing from Tarkhany for the first time in six hundred years. They abandoned their coastal hold without contest to the usurpers five centuries before my time, and their inactivity within my life has more or less precluded our consideration of them as a superpower. If it weren't for our sources in the region, I wouldn't even know if Zita were still on the throne. Explain to me what Ophir has to do with Tarkhany. Why was she there? Why are three kingdoms holding a summit after all this time?"

Tyr held his breath.

He had to believe that the summit was not the result of Harland and Samael betraying Ophir's gift to the queen. Last he spoke to them, the three were in Palace Midnah, and they'd reached a consensus on Ophir's gifts and the dangers of manifestation to understand the consequences of Dwyn's manipulation. If King Eero's advisors had counseled Queen Zita of the true state of affairs, they may have forced everyone's hand.

Tyr waited on bated breath, praying that nothing would confirm his fears.

Evander's shoulders slumped. "Why don't we send messengers to the corners of civilization and see if Sulgrave and the Isles will join us while we're at it?"

The man paused to appreciate the sorrow in his joke.

24

Tyr found it quite funny, too, as it were. Crossing the Straits would have been impossible if he hadn't possessed a gift that had allowed him to stow away, undetected, with the only capable crew in Sulgrave. No, there would be no representative from Sulgrave at this or any meeting, and they were all better for it.

"Does this change things?" Evander asked. He looked at Onain seriously.

She folded her arms across her chest and sank into one hip. She stared down at the map for a long while before saying, "We should move forward with the summit, and welcome the princess. She arrived as a drowned rat, not as a clandestine spy. My primary concern comes not with her character, but with her mode of travel. She's covering a lot of ground in an unprecedented amount of time. We know Ophir wields flame. What of her Sulgrave companion? Could this be the fae's gift?"

Evander rested his chin on his fist thoughtfully. "Traveling through space like it's a folded map? I've never heard of such a gift."

Onain didn't appear perturbed as she said, "I wouldn't immediately meet the companion with distrust. New gifts are discovered every day. And as we know—"

"There are no dark gifts—"

"Only dark practitioners. Yes, sir." She looked around stiffly before asking, "Will His Majesty be joining this morning?"

Evander's expression softened. "You know he doesn't want us to call him that."

Her spine remained rod straight. "I'm aware."

Evander expelled a long puff of air. "I know you have your reasons. We all understand that this is your gift… Even if we don't *understand*. So, I won't press you further on the issue. But no, Ceneth won't be joining us. This morning was just for me to catch you up to speed before the castle rises so that you have everything you need to…make decisions.

Once the world knows Ophir is under our roof, there's sure to be an uproar. I believe he's already informed Aubade's king. We needed to get ahead of the turmoil of the day. It was important for me to hear firsthand that you don't feel she's a threat. I'm sure as the next few days progress, you'll be summoned."

"I'll be ready." She dipped her head.

Evander made a sympathetic face. "You could make yourself more at home at the castle."

Onain shook her head, and he didn't press her on the issue.

"Is that all, sir?"

He patted his leg before rising. "It's all until we know more. Or, unless you come to a different conclusion. Of course, if you feel anything—"

"I will let you know," she supplied.

Evander led them from the room. Once again, Tyr scarcely slipped out before the door closed behind them. Onain stiffened again at his nearness but did not press the issue.

"What was that?" Evander asked.

Tyr took a noiseless step into the far wall.

"It's nothing you should concern yourself over."

Evander looked at her gravely. "Onain, with you, it's never nothing. Please, speak your mind."

She appeared to chew the inside of her cheek. "What I mean to say is, it's nothing I can name. Something is off." She looked up at Evander's concern, then returned her gaze to the middle distance. "Nothing regarding Ophir, so far as I can tell. I appreciate your belief in me. When I have firm details, I will inform you."

"I—and Ceneth—have bottomless faith in you, Onain. Please, feel at home here."

"I do consider Raascot my home, sir," she said. But his answering look of disapproval over the cordial term implied that no, she had not yet made this her home, wherever she was from. Tyr couldn't imagine where that might be, if not here, though he supposed she could have been born in Farehold. Perhaps it was a mystery for another day.

He watched as she gave a tight bow and departed. Evander loitered for a moment, waiting for her to leave before he walked down the corridor. Tyr trailed him only to find the man had simply returned to his rooms. He didn't follow the advisor into his chambers. He saw enough from the unmade bed, the half-drawn curtains, and the bare back of a sleeping partner to know that Evander was returning to the comfort of his sheets. The door clicked behind him softly, and Tyr didn't bother to wait around.

He wandered down the hall to see if Onain was anywhere to be found, but the castle was too big, too sprawling, to pick up where he'd left off. Through the arched windows of the corridor, the first piercing orange lights of day breached the shelter of distant stone buildings and stung his eyes. The world would wake and ready itself for the day. He briefly considered returning to Ophir's room, but if the rest of the world was stirring, then Dwyn would be waking, too. He couldn't risk being around the witch any more than necessary if he hoped to stay concealed. Dwyn had barely tolerated him before. She'd skin him alive if she realized he'd been present without her knowledge.

After their fight in Tarkhany's dungeon, they'd struck a bargain.

She'd teach him how to drain, and in exchange, he wouldn't tell anyone that she'd orchestrated the downfall of kingdoms. He hated her for it, and by extension himself, for not forsaking his mission against Svea's killers to slay Dwyn before she knew he was present. Tentative alliances could be easily shattered by soured tempers, and he didn't trust Dwyn any farther than he could throw her. He amended to himself that he could probably throw her even farther than he could trust her, given that he didn't trust her at all.

His thoughts were interrupted by the scents of sizzling breakfast meats and the waft of fresh biscuits from a distant kitchen. He decided that whatever he had to learn, it could be learned on a full stomach. He'd be no use to Ophir if he died from starvation. Even well-fed, he wasn't exactly sure what he'd learn. For now, he'd play the waiting game—but he'd play it with a mouth full of bacon.

THREE

✦   ✦   ✦   ✦

I T FELT LIKE YEARS SINCE OPHIR HAD BEEN AWOKEN BY THE
incessant, cordial rapping of knuckles at her door. Her eyes
flew open. Grumbling at her side, Dwyn threw the sheets
over her head. She couldn't quite make out the siren's irrita-
ble string of curses beneath the comforter, but she felt the
same. Neither of them was a creature of the morning. She'd
neglected to pull the curtains shut, and the first bright, golden
beams of day pierced through the room. Metallic flecks of
dust caught in the light. It would have been peaceful, if not
for the banging.

Ophir struggled to slide out from between the sheets.

"Princess Ophir?"

"I'm coming," she said through a yawn.

Dwyn flopped dramatically in bed behind her.

"Should I kill them?" Dwyn asked.

Ophir paused with one leg dangling over the bed. Images
of dried husks, of murdered bodies, of papery, drained carnage
flashed before her eyes. Dwyn's handiwork was brutal, and it
could not follow them to Gwydir. She faced the sleep-drunk
siren. "No. You can't kill whoever's at the door—you can't
kill *anyone* in the castle. Do you hear me?"

"Goddess's sake, Firi, I was joking." She grabbed a pillow and shoved it over her face as if smothering herself would spare her from the agitating early-morning wake-up call.

"Well, I'm not. I mean it, Dwyn. No murder." Ophir shrugged into a robe. She twisted the doorknob, expecting to see a meek, apologetic servant. Instead, her chin tilted upward as she took in the tall, lithe form of a woman more fit for war ballads than for attendance as a maidservant. Her black, angelic wings were tucked politely behind her as she stared down at the princess.

"Yes?" Ophir asked.

"His Royal Highness has requested your presence for breakfast," she said.

Ophir did little to conceal her skepticism. "Ceneth expects me at breakfast when?"

The woman replied, "Thirty minutes from now in the dining hall. Shall I send attendants in to help you bathe and dress?"

She blinked. "Are you not an attendant?"

The woman smirked. "No, Princess Ophir, I am not. I just happened to be heading in your direction. You'll find things in Raascot operate a bit differently from Farehold, I expect. I won't be returning your word to the dining hall for the negative or affirmative, so do me a favor and don't make me look bad. The servants will lead you to the dining hall to help you find the way."

The woman hadn't offered her name, nor did she say goodbye.

Before Ophir had the ability to process the strange messenger, two attendants curtsied politely before pushing past her and entering her room. She remained gaping in the doorway, clutching her robe while the servants opened the curtain, shuffled through the armoire, and began drawing a bath. Dwyn grumbled her string of obscenities with abject obstinance from beneath the feathered pillow. The servants didn't bat an eye, laying out clothes for both the princess and for Dwyn.

"How are you dressing me to meet your king?" Dwyn asked from beneath her pillow.

"Princess Ophir," said one, ignoring the lump in the bed, "you're the only guest expected at breakfast."

This snapped Dwyn to attention. She finally removed the pillow from her face as she sat up in bed, allowing the sheet to fall away from where it had been covering any semblance of modesty. Dwyn glared at the attendant. To the servant's credit, she returned the look, unfazed.

"In the future," said the other servant, "you'll be able to ring this bell if you need us." She gestured to a small rune-engraved bell near the door. "I'm sure you have something similar in Farehold. It'll ring in our rooms, and we'll come right to you."

She did not have something similar in Farehold.

"We'll wait in the hall to show you the way," said the first. They shut the door behind them as they exited. Ophir hadn't moved from her place near the wall.

"Make a replacement," Dwyn said. "You're a manifester, after all. A goddess shouldn't have to do something that displeases her."

Ophir looked at her five fingers, heart sagging. She dropped her hand. "If I tried to make a fae who looked like me, I'm certain the beast would come out with four heads and twenty eyes and tentacles for arms."

"Then we put a toffee-blond wig on it and make it wear a crown," Dwyn said with a smile.

Ophir wasn't ready to joke. "I've never made anything good."

"Nonsense," Dwyn said. "Everything you've made has been spectacular. You're a being of sheer power, and your creations reflect that. Maybe the world doesn't understand them yet, but they will. You're making history, Firi. Now, should we manifest a doppelgänger?"

Her silence was answer enough.

To her credit, Dwyn dropped the issue. "Come on, then;

let's get you ready for your husband, *His Royal Highness*," she said, no hint of reverence to her words.

A chilly sort of heaviness weighed down Ophir's shoulders at this.

Dwyn motioned as if she were a dog shaking rainwater from her fur coat. She discarded the sleep, the unpleasantness, the angst from her skin as she looked Ophir with new, alert eyes. "I'm sorry," she said. "That wasn't fair. You're going to be the queen of Raascot. Of course, I don't want you to be forced into a marriage. But if you're here and this is the path you want, I'm here to support you. Let's get you in the bath."

Dwyn hopped up from the bed and headed toward the bathing room as Ophir asked, "Are you being supportive, or do you just want to get me in the water?"

"Are the two mutually exclusive?"

She would have been clean, dressed, and ready to meet the king within thirty minutes, had it not been for the twenty-minute distraction that occurred in the bath's warm waters. That being said, it put a smile on both of their faces, relieved immeasurable tension, and sent her off to breakfast as if she were tipsy from a strong glass of whiskey.

"He's not going to be happy you're late," said one servant quietly as Ophir slipped out the door. She shot a parting glance at Dwyn's smug, still-naked form as the siren leaned against a bedpost. Dwyn flicked two fingers in a salute as the princess disappeared around the corner.

"I'm sure His Majesty is magnanimous enough to understand that life can't always happen on a schedule," Dwyn said.

That, and that many of us are more amenable after we've climaxed, she thought.

A distant pocket of her brain understood that she was skating on very thin ice. One did not disrespect a king. Then again, a princess did not run off from her kingdom and shirk her royal responsibilities. Furthermore, no decent fae conjured demons, murdered people, and took multiple lovers in the same night without either knowing of the other's pleasure. Perhaps she would not make history for being the most virtuous monarch, but at the very least, she would be the most satisfied.

Her room had been tucked deeply into the Castle of Gwydir. Within a few moments, a door opened as a servant ushered her into the dining hall. Ophir had hoped that others would join them but was dismayed to find Ceneth at the table, alone. Every chair had been carved to accommodate large black, angelic wings. Ceneth's were folded behind him in the kingliest way as he tilted his head in greeting. He wore a tailored navy-blue dress coat that seemed to have captured the very stones of the kingdom around him. Given that she had generally only seen him at the gates of Farehold before immediately disappearing to the wall to drink her weight in wine, she'd expected him to wear a crown of some sort, as he always had upon his arrival in Aubade. Perhaps such showmanship was only for when he made diplomatic appearances or sat on his throne. She idly wondered how often he'd worn it around Caris and then swiftly decided she didn't want to know.

Ophir swallowed as she approached the table, unsure of where to sit.

He offered her a grim smile and patted the seat nearest to him.

"Please," he said, "let's talk."

She didn't want to, but that wasn't his fault. She didn't want to do anything. She'd never wanted to do anything. The sliver of soul that recognized her selfishness forced empathy to the forefront as she sat gingerly in the seat beside the king. Ophir frowned at the unfamiliar food, but her grumbling stomach urged her to take her chances. She scooped a number of aromatic fruits, meats, and pastries onto her plate. Ceneth ate quietly beside her until she'd had time to digest her food. Once she slowed to sip her tea, he was ready to break their silence.

"Ophir, I think we should respect one another enough to be honest."

Ophir's fingers went motionless against her teacup. She shifted under the intensity of his stare but resisted meeting it until it became clear that he would not continue without her acknowledgment. She fought the grimace as her eyes slowly rose to his. Their gazes touched, then softened as they truly saw one another. She'd known he wasn't her enemy—not truly. She hadn't hated him. She hadn't even been angry with him. To her knowledge, Ceneth had never done anything wrong. His crimes were that he'd loved her sister and desired a better future for the continent. Her reluctance to be in his presence stemmed from somewhere much deeper.

"May I go first?" she asked, surprising even herself.

His eyebrows lifted. Clearly, he'd expected to do most of the talking.

"I'm not Caris," she said, stating the obvious. "But I also don't think you expect me to be. I blame myself for her murder, and it would be right for you to blame me, too. I accept that. I miss my sister more than words can say. And I'll..." She stopped herself from telling him that she'd always blame herself for Caris's death. She bit her tongue before saying she'd spend every waking moment avenging her sister. Now, anytime she tried to think of her mission of vengeance, her thoughts ran off a cliff and tumbled into a black abyss, ending with a throbbing headache and the image of Berinth's face.

It was hard to think about her purpose, if she was born for one at all. Caris had known her life's calling. The eldest princess was born to bring the kingdoms together. Ophir, however, was caught in the terrible, tar-like nothing of uncertainty. If she pulled herself out of the goopy pit and forced the world to see Caris's vision, perhaps she could mend things and bring the land together. If rage found her again, and she prayed it did, she might claw her way ashore and leave the pit behind only to tear the world apart.

Maybe she would sink into the blackness and do nothing at all.

In lieu of a migraine, she said, "I'll do what I can, as your political bride. For her."

His face softened, and for the briefest moment, she saw the true well of his heartache.

"I love her," he said.

"So do I," she replied.

They stared into their drinks for a long, quiet moment. She hadn't missed his verb tense, nor he hers. Caris had left a wound that would not heal. Sitting in Ceneth's presence made her feel the droplets of blood as they leached through the fissures in her heart, as if sitting near Caris's beloved was the cruelest reminder of the life she'd been denied.

The distant sounds of servants in the kitchen and castle attendants in the hall were friendly noises. Humans and fae were awake. The castle was alive. The world went on. Yet at the dining table, they sat alone with their pain.

Ceneth cleared his throat. "I think there are some things we need to make clear long before any of our arrangement takes place. Namely, I don't expect an heir. I'll never approach you—understand me, I don't mean this as an insult, I mean—"

Her relieved exhale was nearly laced with tears. "I do understand."

"Perhaps in a human lifespan, we wouldn't have such a luxury. I just want you to know that I'll continue to see you as Caris would have wanted me to see you: as my sister, and my family. You'll have an ally in Raascot, which is what she would want, too. The best way I can protect you is for us to move forward with the wedding," Ceneth said.

She was speechless, though perhaps she shouldn't have been. This was a man who seemed truly worthy of her sister.

He was right. She'd be safer from the other kingdoms under Ceneth's literal and metaphorical wing of protection. That's what Caris would want. He was offering an olive branch that she didn't deserve. He extended titles and coverage and the promise of expecting nothing. Perhaps she'd been right to come here. Perhaps the door that had opened to

Raascot's forest had known more than she could have possibly understood. She'd manifested escape, and it had delivered. This had been the only true path forward.

"What does this mean?" she asked. She gulped a breath before clarifying, "Practically speaking. What does this look like for us?"

"There will be a wedding, of course." He took a sip of his tea. "Before that, we will formally announce our marriage before Raascot's court. Our kingdom is not as formal as Farehold, as I'm sure you'll notice, so it should not be a particularly stifling affair. We show face, we state our intent to join our kingdoms, and they give us our blessing before both kingdoms come together prior to the formal event in the southern kingdom. But there is something more pressing."

Ophir arched a brow. "More pressing than the wedding?"

He leaned back in his chair and frowned at her.

"Ophir, you arrived on foot, soaked from the rain. Within a day, a summit was called between Farehold, Tarkhany, and Raascot. I need to tell you two things before this conversation continues. The first is that—and please, take this in the best way possible—I don't care. If you've made enemies across the continent, I don't care. I'm dedicated to pursuing the goal of unity and honoring Caris's wish of offering you shelter."

Ophir examined him. "You mean, what you *believe* would have been Caris's wish."

He cleared his throat once more. "Yes, of course," he said. He moved on before she could consider his words further, saying, "The second thing is, I can't go into this meeting ready to defend you, prepared to be your advocate, if I'm playing catch-up with the other monarchs. I'm going to need you to both believe that I'm on your side and trust me enough to tell me whatever it is I need to know so that I don't walk into a summit blind."

Ophir forgot how to breathe. She was certain her expression was anything but subtle.

She saw how Ceneth absorbed the way her lips parted

slightly, her intake of air, the way her face tightened as she flicked through the events of the recent past. What could she tell him? How much could she share? What was worth concealing? What would come out?

He didn't push to break the silence, and for that, she was grateful. She drained the now-bitter dregs of her lukewarm tea before she told the story of how she'd pursued Lord Berinth to Tarkhany. She explained that Zita had accepted her into the palace, offered her sanctuary, and had then been betrayed by a shapeshifter. She watched Ceneth's face as she described the events of that morning, from Tarkhany's imposter queen, then her intent to murder, to the arrival of great winged beasts. It was within Ophir's best interest, she believed, to be as ignorant about the demons as everyone else in the kingdom. Anything the witnesses reported would support the same shock, surprise, and horror that she conveyed in her retelling over almond pastries and now-cold eggs.

"And your travel?" Ceneth pressed. "How could you get from Tarkhany to Raascot so quickly? Is this your companion's gift? Is that how she was able to travel from Sulgrave?"

Without realizing it, he'd provided her the perfectly logical excuse she needed.

"Yes," she said. "Her name is Dwyn. Her secondary ability is one of travel. It's made her an invaluable companion. She's my dearest friend, and I would be devastated to be separated from her. Also"—Ophir paused for importance—"her primary ability is to summon water. It's been very useful when flame has come in my nightmares. It's why we mustn't sleep apart. She was tasked to share my room before we left Aubade. Given the night terrors, following what happened… If it weren't for Dwyn, Castle Aubade would be little more than charred stones by the sea. I know it's not a conventional arrangement, but…"

Ceneth looked unperturbed at the thought of his fiancée sharing her bed with another. "I understand, and am happy to grant you any ally, comrade, or partner, should that be your wish. I'm confident the All Mother will forgive us for anything we must do to move through Caris's…"

The king did not finish his sentence.

She stared at the man, and for the first time, she understood what her sister had seen in him. This was him presumably at his worst, and he was still wonderful. He deserved the throne.

With her tea empty and her food cold, Ophir didn't know what to do. She wasn't sure how much longer she was expected at his table. She fidgeted before asking, "How will I spend my days? I have the dinner with Raascot, and the summit, and the wedding? Are those the three events expected of me?"

Ceneth's eyes glazed over. He didn't bother looking at her as he said, "I'm sure there will be things here and there, but yes. Those are expected. You're not a prisoner, Ophir. You're to be Raascot's queen."

His eyes refocused, but he was not looking at her. She felt as though he was searching her face for any sign of her sister. She could tell from the disappointment smeared across his expression that he found none.

"Spend your days as you please," he said finally. "Send word if you need me, and I'll do the same. Please, ask the servants for whatever you like. No one will bother you or your companion. Thank her for preventing Castle Gwydir from becoming embers. Do let us know if there's anything she needs as a water elemental, though I'll tell the servants to fill the bath each night and leave the door open, just for preparedness."

Ophir stood to leave, but Ceneth stopped her with a sound.

"Dwyn? Is her name?"

Ophir nodded.

"How much time does she take to recover? For her secondary ability, that is?"

Ophir hoped her face remained blank. Neither she nor

Caris possessed secondary abilities. At least, none that the public was privy to. Caris's perfect memory had been her only known ability. Ophir was... Well, no one could know what Ophir was. She tried to think of anyone in the castle with secondary abilities but struggled to recall a reasonable recovery period.

Ophir shook her head finally, saying, "She's still quite sick. She'll undoubtedly remain in bed for a few more days."

He nodded absently before offering a wave in farewell.

Ophir managed to turn her back to the king before showing her true suppressed panic to the wall. She let herself outside of the dining room before she felt a hand on her back. Her pulse spiking, Ophir jumped and turned to see...no one.

"Tyr?"

"Hush, Princess, you did great in there."

She wasn't sure if she was grateful or frustrated. "Do you spy on everything?"

He ran hands down her arms to let her know he was there, saying, "I try. I slipped out this morning to follow servants around the castle to gather the layout. They seemed to be bringing too much food for one man, so I loitered."

"I hated it," she said quietly.

Tyr said nothing. He squeezed her arm gently.

"Not him," she clarified. "I hate being around someone who loved her so much. I hate—"

"He's your ally," Tyr whispered, "and my intelligence from this morning suggests that everyone else in the castle is, as well. They have their reservations about Dwyn, but you handled that perfectly. Water and travel? All their questions will have been answered satisfactorily. No one on the continent, aside from Dwyn and I, has any reason to believe you can manifest."

Ophir made a face.

"What?"

"Harland knows," she said quietly. Her memories flashed to the crashing waves, the way Dwyn had slapped her, had kicked her, had forced her to the brink of panic before she'd created the demonic snake to defend her. He'd beheaded it, shoved it into the sea, and cleaned up the evidence. He knew everything. "He was there when I first manifested. The three of us were on the cliff when I made my first serpent."

She expected Tyr to react with something akin to shock or disdain, but he did not.

She prodded him. "You don't believe this is a setback?"

He pursed his lips. "People will begin to find out one way or another, though I respect the wisdom in keeping your gifts close for as long as we can. Gods can't hide for long."

It was her turn to look at her feet in silence.

"Tyr?"

"Yes?"

She moved uncomfortably in the hall, fully aware that it would look to any passersby that she was touched by the sun and chatting to herself. Fortunately, there was no foot traffic in the early-morning corridors of the castle.

"I don't like that I can't find you if I need you. I hate that I have to just wait and hope and—"

His mouth met the soft place on her temple, dragging his kiss onto her cheek. He waited until she parted her lips, inviting his mouth, before turning her so that her back was flat against the stones. Tyr wrapped his body around hers, enveloping her in his warmth. With her eyes closed against the morning light pouring through the windows, she could pretend that they were a normal couple stealing moments in the hall. As long as her lids remained tightly squeezed against reality, she didn't have to face the painful layers of complexity that made up their relationship.

He broke the kiss first, raking his fingers roughly into her hair on one side. His weight continued to crush her against the wall, and the pressure made her feel safe, secure, and whole. It was almost as if the physical presence filled a spiritual ache.

"I'm sorry I can't be present," he said, voice quiet and slow. She believed his sincerity.

"It's okay." She swallowed. "I know what it's like to love a ghost. It's not this."

He rested his forehead against hers, and she let her eyes flutter shut once more. No, Tyr wasn't gone. Tyr was like the All Mother—present and helpful and listening in ways that even you didn't know you needed. Tyr pressed a kiss to her forehead before saying, "I'll be there for you more often than you think. I'll whisper in your ear or touch your back whenever I can, okay? Only if you can promise me you won't jump. You can't give me away, Princess."

"I promise."

He chuckled quietly. "Maybe soon I'll have to start calling you Queen."

She looked away from his voice, face angled toward the distance.

"I just… I called Svea 'Princess,' and…ah, shit. That wasn't the right thing to say at all. I meant that I cared so deeply for her, and with you—"

Ophir didn't meet his eyes. "Your dog. I get it. Your hound is dead, my sister is dead, we all have death in common."

"I'm sorry." He ran a hand along her arm, squeezing her elbow. "Maybe it doesn't mean to you what it does to me when I make that connection. But Ophir: I care so deeply for you. You've derailed the reason I traveled south in the first place. You've become the center of my universe. You've—"

"Ruined everything. I heard you."

"Hey." He tilted her chin up with the lift of unseen fingers.

She looked through him into the warming morning light of the trees, the river, the city beyond the castle. It was easier to be around him with her eyes closed, and so she allowed herself the darkness once more.

"Let me walk you back to the room," he said. He swept his hand between the wall and her back before she had time to respond and began ushering her toward the chambers where Dwyn would be waiting. "I'd ask you to tell the siren I hate her, but for all she knows, I don't exist. Did she ask how I died? Or if you left me in Tarkhany?"

Ophir's forehead creased. She stopped in the middle of the hall. "No, in fact, she hasn't."

She lifted a hand as she searched for Tyr's face. She clutched the side of his neck.

"What is it?"

Ophir shook her head. "Why didn't I think of that? She should have asked. Even if she hates you, even if she wants you gone, she should have asked. Does she know something?"

Tyr made a quiet noise. "It's possible that she doesn't care."

Her look was perplexed enough to prompt his explanation.

"What I mean is, it's possible that she doesn't care to bring up anything that might trigger you. She wouldn't want to remind you of anything potentially unpleasant, as it would upset you. She's invested in keeping you happy."

Ophir chewed on the thought, releasing the space where her fingers had wrapped around his neck. She squinted, trying to see if she could distinguish anything in the space around her. She almost felt as if the light caught on a pair of eyes, though it seemed to only be from her peripherals. Whenever she turned her head to look fully into them, they were gone once more.

He finished escorting her to her room and brushed a final kiss against her hair. She almost caught the outer edges of an annoyed, masculine scoff from the closing door as Dwyn called out to her from under the covers. "I've been keeping the bed warm for you, Firi."

Ophir was exhausted. After her discussion with Ceneth, most of her fears had been soothed. She'd be allowed to spend her days in bed and drink herself to sleep. Perhaps she could find a lookout tower and mimic her old life perfectly, exchanging only the bodyguard, as her present escort was substantially prettier.

"Help me get out of this?"

Dwyn made a fuss of leaving the bed as she got up from the cozy nest of blankets and undid the top button of Ophir's dress. The gowns didn't possess the constrictive bodices and lacing like the ones of Farehold, but it was still rather difficult to fetch that button by oneself. Presumably, she was meant to stay clothed until nighttime, when servants would help her out of her gown. Instead, she left it in a crumpled pile on the floor as she interlaced her arms and legs with Dwyn's and told her everything about breakfast.

"I wish I could tell you I was impressed," Dwyn said once she had finished, "but truth be told, I expect there's nothing you can't do. You're unstoppable. The only disappointment of the morning is that there's no food for me. How can we fix this while both remaining naked? Is it too early in your reign to scandalize the servants? Shall we test it?"

Ophir found her robe once more and rang the enchanted bell. She waited by the door so she could keep it cracked to prevent any invasion of privacy as she asked for food and tea to be sent to their room. The servant managed to keep her face neutral while still expressing amusement and disapproval in equal forces, all behind the flickering of her eye. The woman was back at their door within fifteen minutes, knocking politely, lest she interrupt whatever sort of indecent activities went on behind closed doors.

Ophir had thought she was full, but joy had returned her appetite. She found a delightful, chocolate-filled bit of fried bread and let out a sound that she'd only made during sex. Dwyn was outright offended. Ophir finished chewing, her smile fading as she studied the siren's face. Swallowing, she asked, "Do you ever think about what happened in Tarkhany? After we left?"

Dwyn shrugged. "No."

Ophir frowned in clear disapproval.

Dwyn extended a hand and gave it a squeeze. "Patience pays off in dividends, dear heart. It only took a few decades for me to realize that worrying about things I couldn't control

43

would not change them. Thinking about people I couldn't control would not alter their courses. Expending my energy on anything beyond my own thoughts, my own actions, was a waste of breath and joy and life. I'm not thoughtless, Firi. I've just learned where to channel my thoughts."

Ophir considered this. On one hand, she saw the wisdom in Dwyn's words. On the other, she knew she was personally and unforgivably responsible for every stone, every piece of rubble, and every life lost outside of Tarkhany's palace.

FOUR

+   +   +   +

VALOR MAST, TARKHANY

THE CONSISTENT CRASH OF WAVES WAS A WELCOME RELIEF. The woman closed her eyes and let the sound wash over her like a lullaby against the cool, dark night. She sipped on the salt and dust in the air, appreciating each night away from the city. She pretended the ceaseless noises made by others were little more than specks of flotsam, whipped by the wind and obliterated by the cliffs. She pictured each sound shattering as it broke against the red rock and smiled.

She hadn't known what to expect when she'd abandoned the capital and joined a caravan bound for the seaside. Life was harder here, as were its people. She was sick of eating fish. With nothing else to do, she'd run out of books far sooner than anticipated, which was fine. It encouraged her to return to her writing. She used the noise to make art, crafting stories from the lives that flowed in and out of her. Pages, scrolls, leather-bound books, and loose papers filled her modest home. She wasn't content with her life, but it had nothing to do with the fish, the tiny village, or the lack of entertainment. Maybe it would have been enough of a life— at least, enough of what she could hope to expect, should she be forced to go on living—if there had been drinking water.

She wasn't religious enough to pray for rain, yet she regularly found herself begging the All Mother to send in fresh water when the days grew long and the village was thirsty.

Water wasn't the only thing they craved.

Her arrival had been met with excitement akin to blood-lust. It was rare to meet travelers, let alone have a beautiful new fae move into one of the cliffside dwellings. A few women had remarked that she'd draw less attention if she dressed differently—if she took the gold cuffs from her arms or the piercings from her nose. She advised that she'd have a better chance at going undetected if she covered herself from head to toe and became one with the cliffside rocks.

She'd kept her gold, her bangles, her piercings. She wore what she pleased. Even with a scarf and every inch under wraps, they'd still have spotted the tattoo masking her jagged scar. There'd be no way to slip between the cracks of society unnoticed.

Some men had met her with kindness, advances, and courtship. She'd turned them all down, of course. Then there had been those with less pure intentions. Times like that, she didn't mind the noise. It kept her safe. It kept her distant. It kept their greed, their entitlement, their fingers, their force as far from her as possible. Her noise was both gift and curse.

She heard something.

It was not her noise.

She tilted her head and listened to the strange sound as it grew louder. This wasn't the familiar, goddess-awful noise. This was wind, and compression, and…something. A jolt of panic hit her the moment before the screech confirmed her fear. Her heart caught in her throat as chaos unfolded, ears ringing, cold sweat clinging to her brow as the noise flooded her.

A scream tore through the village.

She jumped from the bed and ran to the window just in time to see moonlight glinting off an enormous black shape as it shot over the cliff. With the inky shape came the suffocating stench of sulfur, a mist of rot and decay in its wake choking out the scents of fish and sea. Her mouth dropped open in silent shock. She barely had time to react, barely had time to feel fear before the shape lunged for the cliff opposite her own. The moon lit the cliff with metallic clarity, showing her each unholy movement, each unbelievable sight, each nightmarish lunge. Her lips parted in a scream as sound and noise overlapped, both the sounds of screaming, of crunching of clawing and dragging, and the noise, the terrible, endless noise of the others. Half the cliff disappeared behind the flexing, flapping, membranous wings of a serpent the size of a mountain. It dug its talons into the windows and doors in the cliffside dwellings and struck its great head.

The first lunge was unsuccessful. The creature shook the impact from its reptilian head like a dog attempting to remove rain from its hide. Then, it slithered into the house with serpentine slowness, head and neck twisting and bending while its body remained lodged on the cliff. She heard the bloodcurdling cry and knew her neighbor was gone. She clutched her heart and stumbled backward from the window.

Her heart thundered. There was nowhere to run. Nowhere to flee.

She caught movement as a neighbor jumped from her house onto the little ledge at her doorstep. She knew this woman—she was the newest mother in the village. The wrappings secured against her body betrayed the tiny shape that clung to her, freeing her hands. The woman grabbed the ladder and began to ascend with spider-like speed.

The snake saw it, too.

The mother hadn't stood a chance. In a single moment, it had woman and child in its teeth. It tore into her from the side, teeth crunching her torso as it ripped the woman from the ladder. Anguished wails of body and bone ripping filled every nook, every crevice, every hiding place within the village.

Taking her from the side had been a mistake. Unable to

throw her back in a single bite, and with nowhere to set its kill, the winged snake wasted its meal. It released her from its jaws, and her now-limp body tumbled from its teeth to crack against the salt-slick rocks at the base of the cliff.

She stumbled back from the window, hand flying to the muscle skittering arrhythmically in her chest as she begged it to calm. She would have time to grieve later. She wanted to vomit, but her sickness would not serve her survival. What would she do? Where could she go? She'd meet the same fate if she went for her ladder. Even if she made it to the top and ran from the cliffs and into the desert, she'd be exposed. If the winged monster didn't consume her, the sand and the sun's baking rays surely would.

She pressed her back to the far side of her small stone home, gaping at the tiny window to the carnage as villagers were devoured one home at a time. She sank slowly to the floor and brought her knees to her chest as cries, pain, blood, and the unholy wail of a demon consumed the night.

A choking, sulfuric wave rolled from the square window, vanquishing the scents of dust, salt, and blood until death and hell were all she smelled.

She closed her eyes against the horrors until she felt something.

A push of air filled her small home. A breeze ruffled her loose hair. A roll of carrion on a new wind forced her to open her eyes just in time to see a set of horrible wings keeping the creature aloft as it hovered just outside her window. The enormous black eyes of a nearly human face peered through the window as it looked directly into her soul.

FIVE

+ + + +

MIDNAH, TARKHANY

"HE'S GONE, YOUR MAJESTY," THE ADVISOR PROMISED. HE looked around the marble room for effect. "We've secured every entrance and exit. No one is getting in or out without our permission."

Zita waved a hand. "That's not enough, Hassain." She addressed the man directly. He'd served within the palace for decades for his strength, loyalty, and cunning. His ability to speak to stone—the man's secondary gift—had never been of relevance to her before the incident. She examined him as she said, "We've thought Tempus was gone ten thousand times before. You've seen what he can do. The man can glide past you wearing my face. We need to be sure. Where is Suley these days?"

Hassain winced at the name. "You wish for me to fetch Suley? She went a long way to escape the city's noise. She won't be happy."

Zita's lips pursed at the doubt in his voice. "Please do not defy my judgment again. Summoning Suley is the only way to know. If she takes residence in the palace, Tempus won't be able to return unnoticed."

"We will tighten our guard, Your Majesty. We will increase patrols. We—"

"You can't secure the skies, Hassain. I will not hold my breath around every little bird. Until we know for sure that he's not present, I can't trust anyone—not even you."

Hassain looked decidedly sour, but it wasn't his place to have opinions about such things. His life had been full of unpleasantries as of late. He had been among the many in the midst of what the people were already calling the Sunrise Slaughter, when the ag'drurath had descended. He'd witnessed Tempus's shift from Zita's form into that of a horse as the monarchs barely escaped with their lives. He'd buried his sword into the gray flesh of the winged demon that looked nearly like a man. It had grabbed his blade with its bare hand, tar-black blood oozing as it pulled the weapon from its chest. It had pulled its nearly human lips back from the needles posing as teeth and hissed its murderous intent.

She knew from his account of the incident that it had been the single most terrifying moment of his life.

He said, "Last reports suggested that Suley was in a fishing village off the southeastern coast called Valor Mast."

Zita's brows met in the middle as she thought of the fishermen clinging to life in the coastal villages. Seafood was abundant and the temperature was cooler, but jagged red rock ran for miles from the sea to the sand. She didn't like picturing Suley there. It was impossible to build homes on the unforgiving stone—merely chisel and carve shelters into the cliffs themselves. Nothing grew. The only fresh water came from collecting rain. Tarkhany's southeastern coasts were the most goddess-forsaken places in her kingdom. At least in the capital, her people had water, gardens, shelter, and resources. Zita had petitioned the smatterings of desert populations to relocate to the capital, even visiting the cliffside towns and the nomadic clusters herself, but they'd resisted.

They had their reasons for not wanting to be around others.

She supposed this was why Suley had left. The village would be quiet. She'd always craved quiet.

"I'll send a few men to collect her," Hassain said.

"And?" Zita asked. "Have we learned anything more about the demons? What did the oracle say?"

"Our oracle knows nothing of their origin."

"Of course." Zita pinched her chin thoughtfully. She looked over Hassain's shoulder at the door, mind wandering out of this room where they so often had meetings of the minds. She let herself think of the star-studded sky, of the chilly breeze that rolled off the dunes at night, and of the burbling fountains. She focused on the good, the beautiful, the things she loved about her palace and her people. Her mind then wandered to the ruins in front of the palace. She saw the splintered platform, the tar stains of viscous blood that had proven unable to be cleaned, and the pyre of bodies that had been sent to be with the All Mother in the wake of the carnage. The oracle—Tarkhany's prophetess—needn't have been present for the Sunrise Slaughter to know it had been a tragedy the likes of which had not been seen in hundreds of years.

The oracle saw only the future.

"Her reports were...bleak."

Zita arched an expectant brow.

"These were the first roaches of an infestation," he said. "The prophetess sees demons filling the content, spilling out from a single, moving source. It's rare for her to see something with such clarity."

She considered this. "Inevitability," she said quietly. "An event as rare as it is bleak. So, there's no stopping the demons. And what of the summit with the neighboring kingdoms? Does she offer predictions on its outcome?"

"The oracle's visions were muddy regarding the meeting. You get everything you want yet leave with nothing. It will be flawless, and it will be chaos. You know when you speak of time..."

"Yes, yes." Zita knew groans were undignified, but oracles were exhausting. This was precisely why the prophetess remained mostly undisturbed. Speaking of the future was like unraveling knotted yarn. "What of the guests from Farehold? Have they recovered?"

"The men called Harland and Samael? Yes. Both are healthy. Only one ingested the toxin, and he's made a complete recovery. Shall I ready their provisions for their return crossing?"

She got to her feet. "No. I'd like to speak with them. I'm hoping they'll accompany me to Gwydir. I can leave them with their king at the meeting. It would be advantageous to have members of Farehold on our side before the summit. Perhaps they hold sway over Eero and his judgment."

"As you wish," he said.

"If our meeting is concluded, will you fetch the men from Farehold? Harland and...Samael, you said? That name doesn't sound local to their kingdom."

"I believe he's foreign, Your Majesty."

She considered the name. "A citizen of Raascot?"

"I assume so. His birthplace remains unconfirmed."

"Could he be swayed to our cause, if he's beholden to no kingdom?" Zita asked.

Hassain chewed on the question. "I don't get that sense from him. The man acts as if he's helpful to the kingdom because he's above the constraints of his homeland—not because he's looking for favor in subterfuge. He may be an asset to us simply because he can be persuaded by truth."

He bowed at the waist before departing. Zita exhaled slowly and sank into the chair, feeling the weight of the world collapse around her. She'd navigated her people through an exodus from their land. She'd kept Tarkhany alive. She'd rebuilt her empire. She'd done everything she was meant to, and yet the first time someone from Farehold had stepped foot on their soil in centuries, their people suffered.

Tempus would tell her that the All Mother was trying to teach her a lesson. He'd say that the omens had been painted on the wall: Farehold was the root of all problems.

But it wasn't Farehold who'd deceived the crowd, imitated her, attempted to lock her in her chambers, and poisoned their guests. Her now-banished husband had been little more than a self-fulfilling prophecy. He'd become the thing he hated. Perhaps that was why they'd been punished. Then again, perhaps looking for meaning where none existed was the most fruitless of all.

A light rap of knuckles on the door preceded the entry of two men. She straightened, leaning into the table to resume her poise.

"Harland," she said, pointing to the one with the obvious pink undertones of Farehold. "And Samael. Where do you hail from?"

"Aubade, Your Majesty," Samael said.

Sly, she thought. He'd undoubtedly understood the underlying question. Zita had received the pair upon their arrival but had had little incentive to get to know them while awaiting Berinth's execution. Ophir had been her only concern. Now she was left with the splintered remains in the princess's wake.

"You may leave us, Hassain," she said.

He hesitated, then closed the door behind him to offer them privacy.

The men offered respectful greetings before taking seats across from her.

Zita tapped her fingers on the table. She gave a coy smile, switching to the common tongue as she said, "It's perhaps a more eventful visit to Tarkhany than you might have expected, no?"

The man called Samael spoke first, greeting her in the official language of Tarkhany. She made no attempt to conceal her appreciation or surprise as he said, "It's not an event anyone would desire. Now we're every bit as invested in healing the land as you. Do you have a proposed path forward?"

"My, oh, my," she said. "And what, pray tell, prompted you to study our language?"

Samael smiled. "Time is long, and the world is big. It would be a shame to limit oneself to only one corner, don't you think?"

"I do," she said. She looked to Harland with a quizzical brow, but he merely shook his head apologetically. She returned to the common tongue. "It's no problem," she said. "I expect as much from someone from Farehold. You, however"—she looked at Samael—"are not from Farehold."

He propped his elbows on the table and leaned forward, saying, "I am not. Following a rather unprecedented encounter with King Eero, I have been living and serving in Aubade for some time."

"Then you call Raascot your true home?" Zita prompted.

"You may as well consider me a citizen of the Etal Isles," he replied. "For I'm beholden to no one by birthright. I think of myself as a citizen of everywhere and nowhere."

"A true expatriate," she murmured when it became clear she would get nothing more from him, as he was not her subject to command. "Now, on the topic of expatriates, our dear Princess Ophir has marked up the map rather spectacularly. Which brings me to why I've asked you to visit with me." She eyed the men carefully before saying, "I've called a summit between the kingdoms of Raascot, Farehold, and Tarkhany. We're to meet in Gwydir."

Harland spoke first this time, asking, "Why Gwydir?"

The corner of her mouth quirked upward. "Because the door presently standing in my courtyard leads directly to the forest just beyond the city. I've never seen anything like it. It took a few days for us to find someone who could speak to stone once we realized it had been obstructed from the far side, but once we sent men through, it only took a few hours to understand where they'd ended up. Raascot's wings do make it rather easy to put your thumb on geography, don't they?"

Samael confirmed. "Flight is the common gift among their people. Now, Tarkhany and Raascot have a direct line to one another? That's remarkable."

"It is indeed," she agreed. "The summit is to take place in one week. I'd like you to accompany me to the meeting, and then, of course, you're free to return with King Eero. You're guests of Tarkhany, so you may decline the offer and begin your crossing now should you wish to go directly to Aubade. It will be shorter to wait one week and walk through a door than to spend two weeks on the dunes, but it is up to you entirely."

The men nodded thoughtfully, but she didn't give them time to respond before she continued.

"My true question lies with the door itself. It's well known that your princess conjures flame. However, the morning of the execution, she was seen with a foreign woman that none of us had so much as seen in the palace. If she was able to step into my kingdom—my *home*—without anyone seeing her, then I can only assume this is her gift. Do either of you know this woman?"

Harland stiffened visibly. She leaned toward him to press the issue, but Samael drew her attention away from the fair-haired man.

"She's been Princess Ophir's companion for the better part of a year. You know of the tragedy that befell the kingdom, yes?"

Zita did. The blood of Caris's death had soaked the soils of the world.

"The companion, a Sulgrave fae called Dwyn, has an ability for water. She was paired with Ophir to spare us all from the night terrors and flames that were burning down the castle. It stands to reason that she steps through locations like a fold on a map. How else is one meant to cross the Frozen Straits?"

Zita looked from Samael's relaxed posture to Harland's still-rigid form. Her eyes narrowed slightly.

"Harland?" she asked.

He gave her the wide eyes of a sand mouse.

She tapped her fingers against the table once more before

asking, "Do you have any feelings on this companion? This...
Dwyn?"

"I don't like her, Your Majesty."

Zita allowed the pause between them to stretch like
cooled honey.

He released a long, slow breath before saying, "I've served
as Ophir's personal bodyguard for many years. I have a vested
interest in her safety, a predisposition for suspicion, and a
firsthand understanding of Ophir's preference for unsavory
characters. I think Ophir would be better off without an
unknown variable influencing her life, particularly as she's
meant to serve both Raascot and Farehold."

Zita chewed on this answer. She nodded with slow acceptance before eventually informing them that attendants would
oversee their needs throughout the next week as they made
plans for their summit. She thanked the men and walked
them out the door, parting ways so that they might return to
their rooms while she drifted into the courtyard to stare up at
the vast, diamond-studded sky.

✦   ✦   ✦   ✦

"Lying to queens, now?" Harland whispered after they'd
rounded a number of corners and returned to their rooms.

"You trust my judgment, don't you?" Samael said in
response, keeping his voice low, as most walls had ears.

Harland's lip twitched. Samael played an unfair hand, as
it was positively annoying to argue with someone whose gift
was perfect judgment. "I'd be a fool not to."

Samael shrugged. "Then don't worry about it. Queen
Zita would be no safer knowing the truth. It works against
Ophir's best interest if anyone knows she's a manifester."

Harland sucked a lungful of air. He'd tried, and failed, to
keep Ophir's gifts a secret. He should have known it would
be impossible to hide anything from Samael.

"It doesn't become you to keep things from me," Samael
replied. "We both know that I'll find out if it wasn't something

56

I knew already. Additionally, we both know she'd be hunted and killed. Or if she feels cornered, she may react in ways we can't predict. Given her breadth of power and the slaughter we saw the morning of the execution, that's not a risk I'm willing to take, are you? Besides, Ophir is far from the only threat. The moment Dwyn knows she's suspected, she becomes the single most dangerous person on the continent. Right now, the only people who know everything are you, me, and Tyr."

"I don't love that Tyr is included in that list," Harland grumbled.

"Don't let your affection blind you," Samael chided. "He clearly cares for Ophir's well-being—" Samael paused at Harland's reaction and pressed, "He does, Harland. If he didn't, he wouldn't have come to us. The man had no reason to risk exposing himself by divulging what he knew. If he were entirely self-serving, you and I would still be on the outside looking in. I can't speak to his other traits, but he cares for Ophir, and having a man on the inside is what will keep the princess alive. His ability to stay out of sight is astonishingly useful."

Harland hated everything.

He hated that sweat beaded on his lip even at night in the arid, desert climate. He hated the heavy scents of oranges and limes everywhere he went. He hated the white marble pillars, and the way that every corridor fell away to yet another open-air courtyard or garden. He hated the marmalade in the cookies. He hated that Tyr had affections for Ophir—and worse—that she clearly returned them. He hated knowing that Ophir was with Dwyn. He hated that she was marrying Ceneth. And most of all, he hated that Samael was right. Not only was there nothing he could do about it, but he was supposed to be grateful.

He'd be sure to find gratitude as soon as someone slipped through the stitches of events and took him back to the night he'd first helped Ophir with her bodice. He'd be grateful if he could spare Caris her fate and keep Ophir in Farehold as the happy, carefree princess with no obligations or responsibilities, save for getting drunk on the wall with him. He'd be grateful if the All Mother turned back the sands of time, and not a moment sooner.

SIX

✦   ✦   ✦   ✦

VALOR MAST, TARKHANY

THE MEN WERE NOT UNIQUE IN HATING THE CROSSING. Most would happily live their days within the capital and never set foot in the desert. Four days on horseback of sweat, misery, shimmering heat, and baking sand were spent in silence if only to conserve energy. When the first distant, silvery glint of the sea shimmered into view, one of them cried out with joy, but the oceanside was every bit as unforgiving. The men and horses alike were not seafaring, and the day's voyage to Valor Mast was, for most of them, a fate worse than death. Canteens refilled and foods replenished, they finished the last leg on horseback. Within hours, they'd crested the final hill to the coastal village that had been famously carved into the burned-red cliffs of Tarkhany's only inhabited island. They knew they were getting close when the empty skies gave way to the presence of large seabirds. They urged their horses over the final dune and their smiles quivered at what they saw.

"Sir?" asked one, voice shaking.

The lead waved a hand as he nudged his horse forward. They'd expected to see the ocean, the plummeting cliffs, and the telltale canvas tents perched above ledges for markets, exchanges, and the milling village folk to interact. One fallen tent shuddered against the sea breeze, its ripped canvas dancing in the wind as it tried to escape the tether that remained sandbagged to the stone. Beside the tent was the bloated top half of a man, flies buzzing around the entrails that had dehydrated against the burning stone. The lead realized he was seeing not seabirds but vultures.

The smell of baked, rotting flesh hit him on the next sea breeze.

He dismounted his horse on shaky legs. It took a moment for him to understand the arms, the bones, the long brown smears of dried blood, and the single foot, still in its shoe. The high, single note of dizziness joined the crashing of the waves and the throaty growls that had always seemed too mammalian to belong to the ugly, scavenging birds, but he knew enough of death to recognize their sounds. His men dismounted behind him. The sounds of their feet scraping against the rocks joined the ringing threat of unconsciousness.

The man approached the cliff on uneasy legs, knees wobbling. He hadn't thought it could get any worse.

He had been wrong.

The waves carried the bloated, bobbing forms of scores of villagers as the tide pushed their bodies lazily against the rocks, jostling the corpses together. The long hair of women mixed with the kelp. His eye caught on a shape no larger than a peanut from where he stood on the cliff's edge, staring at it until he realized that the still form of an infant rested on the wet sand below, never to wail against its mother's breast again.

He opened his mouth to cry out for any survivors but found his breath stolen on the wind.

His eyes dragged along the squares of windows and rectangles of doors that had been carved into the crimson stones, searching for any sign of life. Sun-baked smears of red-brown blood marked the cliff. A single body dangled out of an open doorway, arms moving gently in each strong gust from the sea.

"Sir?" the man asked again.

He nodded swiftly. He needed to get his wits together. If there were survivors, he had to know. He calmed himself before calling out a single word. "Hello?"

The men joined him on either side, all slack-jawed as they stared at the unspeakable carnage.

He jumped so suddenly he nearly tumbled off the cliff when he caught movement from the bottom of his eye. His breath caught in his throat as an enormous lump, as if he were trying to swallow a lemon, rind and all. He stared straight down with wide, startled eyes as a hand emerged from the cliff directly below him. A woman's head peered out slowly, then disappeared again. A few moments later, she wordlessly mounted the ladder that led from her cliffside home to the landing directly at his feet.

A fae woman stood before him, a full head and shoulders shorter. Her black, braided hair was nearly an arm's length longer than it had been a decade prior when she'd left the city. He wasn't sure if she remembered him, but he certainly remembered her.

She threw a big bag off her shoulder first, then hoisted the rest of her body onto the cliff. The woman rose to her feet as she looked at each of them intently.

"Yes, I remember you," she said, breaking the silence. The other men shifted nervously on horseback. "No, I have not done well. It was not remote enough. Thank you for wondering. Yes, my hair is longer. No, there are no survivors."

This was Suley. Her gold-brown face was dotted with jewels, chains, and piercings in a way that no conservative cliffside villager would have dared. Speaking around her was of no use.

"Is this my horse?" she asked, gesturing to one of the two mounts without a rider.

He opened his mouth to tell her that the horses needed water, but he didn't have the time to say a word before she responded that it hadn't rained, and they'd have to wait until they reached the port that would take them back to the mainland—nearly one day's ride.

"Ma'am, the—" one of his riders attempted to argue.

She looked at the men dismissively as she swung up onto the creature. It huffed beneath the weight of a new rider, but she seemed unbothered. She looked at him and answered his unfinished question. "The horses will make it because they don't have a choice. Valor Mast has no water. No provisions. There is nothing here for any of us. What happened here? Yes, excellent question, and one that I can answer, even if I do not understand. No. Yes, I am always like this. What can you do?" She looked at the leader, cocking her head to the side. She didn't wait for a response as she said, "Stone, is it? That may prove to be a useful ability if we reach the oasis and it's dry. Don't bother me until then."

The girl was so peculiar. He'd never gotten used to it. He tried again to ask what had happened. "And—"

"And the rest, I will tell only to the queen."

+ + + +

MIDNAH, TARKHANY

"Suley." Zita opened her arms wide.

The queen had given her the chance to rest, eat, and bathe from her travels before she forced the young fae woman into a hug. It had given the men a chance to describe the gruesome graveyard at the cliffside village to the queen in excruciating detail. By the time they met, night had fallen, its hushing effect quieting the palace as everyone tumbled into sleep.

"I'd hoped we'd reunite under better circumstances," Suley said.

Zita tightened her embrace. "I'm so sorry," she said, and she meant it. Her heart ached at the sight of the young fae before her. "I'm sorry for the horrors you endured. I'm sorry for the nightmare you survived. I'm sorry for forcing you back into the noise," she said, cupping the young woman's face in her hands.

Suley closed her eyes.

The fae was as lovely as Zita remembered. She brushed her fingertips against the complicated ink that ran from her temple to her cheekbone, covering an uneven scar. She was glad Suley had found something beautiful to decorate the pain.

"You need me to stay here at the palace in case Tempus returns in a different form?"

Zita nodded and didn't bother to ask how she knew. Suley always knew.

She arched a brow. "And to the summit? I suppose that makes sense. Who's more qualified, after all…?"

"I truly am sorry. Your gift—"

"My curse," she emphasized.

Zita's hands had remained cradling Suley's face. She ran a gentle finger along the horrible scar that Suley had covered with the black ink of a crescent moon tattoo. If Suley's mother hadn't been a healer, the girl would have succeeded in ending the noise. She'd been only nine when she'd tried to carve it out of her mind.

"I've already summoned a number of harpists, Suley. They're meant to play outside of your room around the hour. When one tires, another will take over."

Suley nodded slowly. "That might help with the worst of it, but you'll need to do me a favor."

"Anything," Zita agreed.

"The palace is too loud. I'll never be able to hear his voice unless you send the men away. Every male guard, attendant, noble, guest, eunuch, and courtesan will need to find somewhere else to stay while I reside in your walls. Can that be arranged?"

"Within the hour," Zita promised. Irrespective of the time or their state of sleep, she'd have every fae and male human shaken awake and escorted into housing elsewhere in the city. She clapped her hands, and a bright-eyed attendant rushed to her side. Zita issued her command, and the attendant set to work.

Suley relaxed visibly as the servant disappeared into action. The thin lines of her frown dissipated as she said, "Yes, I'll be okay. The travel was dreadful. No, the events were terrifying, and I'm shocked I survived them. You needn't worry about me. I survived in the city for years."

If Zita allowed herself to feel annoyed, Suley would hear the thought. She elected pity, instead.

Suley was a child by fae standards. She was scarcely in her third decade of life. She'd barely made it out of infancy with her life intact, let alone to adulthood. She'd moved to the arid wilds as soon as she was able, but the nomadic desert tribes had been every bit as miserable as the city. As far as Zita knew, Suley had survived at the cliffside village longer than anywhere else. Until—

"Shall we sit, or would you prefer to hear about the incident here?"

Zita's expression was one of guarded caution as she asked, "Are you sure you're ready to talk about it?"

Suley fished in her satchel for a small, leather-bound book. The book, scarcely larger than the hand that held it, was tied shut with a soft leather cord. Suley unraveled the binding and opened to the first page, turning the book toward Zita.

A jolt went through the queen.

Her eyebrows perked in surprise. "You recognize it?"

Zita's lips parted to speak.

"Here? Outside the palace? How many dead…oh my. Yes, that is a problem. I do suppose they stood more of a chance at escape than we did. They had alleys to dodge through, guards at the ready, shelter… Oh, of course you're wondering how I escaped. Did you encounter the winged, shadowed man—yes, you saw the one like a twisted fae as well. I heard its noise. Yes, they have noise. I spoke to it. I knew from its noise what it needed to hear, and it returned to its beast. Ag'drurath, you're calling the beast? Winged death? That's appropriate. Ag'imni? Fitting."

Zita's lips became a line.

Suley's face bunched. "I'm sorry, Zita. I mean, my queen. I'll be better at it."

"No, no, dear," Zita sighed, "I'm not agitated in the least. And for you: It's Zita. I know the gift is terribly frustrating for you. We'll keep the speaking to a minimum throughout the palace until the summit. Between that and the harpists—"

"How many will be at the summit? Oh, you don't know yet. Eero, Ceneth, Ophir—oh, you're bringing two men from the Farehold court? They'll also leave the palace grounds, correct? Good. I'm sure they'll find suitable accommodations. A door directly to Raascot? How fascinating. No, I've never encountered such a power. Into the forest?"

Suley went unnaturally still.

Zita pressed, "What is it, dear?"

Suley blinked rapidly before meeting Zita's eye. "Could I live in the Raasay Forest? Why didn't I think of it sooner? I've picked up a lot of the common tongue from the noise alone, even if I've never studied it formally. I would have lived on the dunes if it was sustainable. No, Zita, hear me. It doesn't have to be the forest. There are entire empty mountains without another human or fae in sight, and with fresh water, and—"

Suley caught her frown, searched her face, and nodded.

"Yes, of course," Suley agreed. "After the summit, we'll ask Ceneth. I'm sure he'd be willing to accommodate a single foreigner in the forest. Yes, I will be on my best behavior. No, I'll stay silent. No, I'll speak to no one but you. Yes. No. I understand. I won't. Don't worry. Please, stop worrying. I'll be fine. Yes. Of course. Yes, I am tired now. Thank you for meeting with me, but I'd prefer to lie down while the other voices are removed from the palace if I'm to listen for Tempus. Yes, I'll see you soon."

SEVEN

✦   ✦   ✦   ✦

GWYDIR, RAASCOT

O PHIR RAN A HAND ALONG THE BODICE OF HER GOWN. THE dresses in Gwydir hadn't been nearly as constricting or formal as those in Aubade, but this was a special occasion. She knew this dress had been tailored with Caris in mind. It was an off-white shade of blush with the tiniest flecks of starlight interwoven throughout the soft chiffon of the wide, flowing skirt. The dress hugged her torso and breasts, offering structure and support while keeping her upper chest and shoulders completely bare. The sleeves began in the same flowing chiffon material halfway down the shoulders and draped all the way to her wrists. It was the single most beautiful dress she'd ever seen in her life. If this was merely something intended for their banquet with Raascot's inner circle, she wondered idly what stunning piece of moving art they expected her to wear to the wedding.

One attendant had wrenched Dwyn from her side, forcing the siren to go on ahead to the party while the other servant fussed with Ophir's hair for twenty more minutes. In the end, her left side was swept back with a tight line of tiny, hand-painted cherry blossom pins, fastening her slicked hair just behind her arched ear. The rest of her gold-brown hair tumbled down her back and over her right shoulder in loose, shiny curls. Her lips had been lightly painted, her eyelids smudged with a shimmer, ending with a thin swipe of charcoal to line the outer corners.

When the servant finished, she escorted the princess to the hall.

"Good luck in there," the servant said.

The princess offered a skeptical look in return.

Ophir stepped into the banquet hall and gave the room an anxious scan. She was looking for Dwyn, but before her eyes found the siren, a bent elbow extended to her.

"You look beautiful," Ceneth said, if a bit woodenly.

Ophir's jaw clenched as she looked at him. It was true. She looked lovely. Dwyn had told her so. She'd even seen herself in the mirror and thought as much. Yet hearing it from Ceneth sounded worse than not hearing it at all.

She'd seen him scores of times on his visits to Aubade, and even once on an ambassador mission to Raascot. He was conventionally handsome, not only in the ways that fae were beautiful, but with a distinctly rugged edge to his jaw and remarkable flecks of amber in his eyes. Tonight, he wore a rich shade of navy blue, dressed to match the blue eyes of his would-be betrothed. Looking at him made her uncomfortable, if only because she had no good reason to dislike him. He wasn't unkind. He wasn't rude. He wasn't anything.

"You don't have to say things like that" came her quiet response.

She didn't think he could make it worse, but he did.

"You look a lot like Caris tonight," he said.

Ophir didn't know what to say. Perhaps she had more in common with Ceneth than she gave him credit for. They shared a single shattered heart over the princess who should have lived. It would have been a different event entirely if Caris had been the one slipping her fingers over his arm. She would have overseen decorating the banquet hall in colors that celebrated both of their kingdoms. She would have played the cheery role of hostess, greeting and hugging and laughing as she intermingled with her new subjects. Ceneth's face would have creased with smiles as he watched his wife-to-be. The music would have been bright and lively. The food would have overflowed.

Instead, a solemn harpist plucked her chords in the corner while civil chatter filled the room. The decorations were pretty but modest. Eyes fixed on the couple as they walked to the head of the table, arm in arm. Ceneth pulled out her chair and Ophir slid into the seat as he took his place beside her.

The moment she sat down, her eyes caught Dwyn's anxious stare. As a guest of the castle and personal friend of Ophir's, she'd been extended grace and sanctuary. She was clearly deeply uncomfortable as the men ogled her. She wrinkled her nose in distaste at the attention of strangers and busied herself with her drink. She was a vision in an icy shade of blue—a color just as fitting for a summer day as the sparkling winter snow. Ophir's mouth twitched into a smile as the siren locked eyes with her and mouthed a single plea: *help*.

Dwyn would have to fend for herself tonight.

"I'll make a toast," Ceneth said, "and then you should say a few words. This is our last dinner with just the citizens of Raascot before our foreign guests arrive. It doesn't have to be much. Keep it short, but the people would appreciate it."

Ophir swallowed. "I'm not sure if I'm comfortable…"

His brow creased, but he didn't argue with her. Instead, he looked over the rows of tables throughout the banquet hall and distracted himself with glances at civilians and nobility alike. "I'm going to make the rounds. Please consider it, will you?"

She wasn't sure if Ceneth truly needed to speak to other people or if her answer had been so wholly disappointing that he couldn't sit beside her a moment longer. Ophir twisted the cloth napkin in her lap until she felt lips brush against her ear. Keeping his voice low, Tyr whispered at her side.

"Just tell them you're grateful to be here and that you

look forward to a long and peaceful relationship between your kingdoms."

"But—"

"Shh, don't talk. They'll see your mouth moving as you speak to the air."

Ophir made a small, frustrated sound but kept her mouth shut.

Tyr kept his voice so low, it was practically imperceptible. Ophir leaned forward over the table, and he rested a hand against her back as he spoke. "I've done laps around the castle, and I've learned a little that might be worth knowing. Do you see the fae the king is with now? That's his primary advisor, Evander. From what I can tell, his skin is impenetrable. That means if you needed to kill him, you couldn't do it with flame or a hellhound."

"Vageth."

"I said: don't speak."

Ophir's fingers flexed as she fought the urge to make fists. Her eyes flitted around the room to see if anyone was eyeing her suspiciously, but no one seemed to be looking at the unwanted princess. She slipped her fingers around her knife to squeeze it for effect.

"The woman to Evander's left? Her name is Onain. They've brought her in for advice on at least two of their meetings. She seems to be a military liaison to the castle, though it's unclear if she's a native to Raascot. I haven't uncovered her abilities yet. The advisors have never said anything with much clarity, but they do take her word for things when she weighs in. She does not appear to be a threat to you and has offered no negativity about your upcoming marriage."

"Did he ask—"

"How many times am I going to have to tell you to stay silent, Princess?"

She wiggled her back in an attempt to shake his hand off, but he left the weight of his palm against her spine.

"I'm going to go listen in on their conversation. Ceneth's

right. Please, just say a few words. When the ambassadors show up tomorrow, you'll need Raascot on your side, at the very least. Keep it simple. You'll do more harm if you stay silent, and you don't need the critical eyes on you. And Ophir?"

She tilted her head expectantly.

His lips brushed against her temple. "You look breathtaking."

The moment the warmth of his hand left her back, she felt a crippling wave of abandonment. Ophir's chest squeezed with a terrible anxiety as she forgot how to breathe. She wasn't sure what brought it on, but between the unfamiliar faces, the new foods, the judgmental gazes, and the inability to have the comfort of her friends, she felt suffocatingly alone. A viselike grip twisted her lungs with cruel, unforgiving hands. Her breaths came out in shallower and shallower gasps until the people on either side began to cast worried glances.

The moment Dwyn saw her, she was on her feet.

Decorum be damned, Dwyn crossed the banquet hall and walked directly for the princess. Half of the heads in the banquet hall turned to watch her as she breezed past them, but they may as well have been invisible to her. She rounded the long table to stand in the empty spot that Tyr had vacated only moments prior.

"Are you okay?" Dwyn asked.

"No," Ophir answered, still unable to breathe.

Dwyn slipped her hand over Ophir's only to realize she was still tightly clenching the knife. Ophir released the utensil, and it clattered to the table with a dull thud. "Let me grab a chair," Dwyn said, excusing herself. She made idle chatter with a nearby attendant until a chair was fetched and squeezed into the place beside Ophir. It banged rather noisily against the floor and table as it slid into a spot that it most certainly did not fit.

It wasn't proper. It wasn't elegant. But Ophir needed her.

Court politics wouldn't get in the way of her readiness for emotional support.

Ophir caught Ceneth's creased forehead as he glanced up at the commotion. His look wasn't one of disapproval but of some resigned, sorrowful acceptance that his life was destined to be filled with deeply unfortunate absurdities. She broke eye contact first, hoping Raascot's king would resume whatever conversation he was having with the advisor Tyr had called Evander. She peeked through her curtain of hair to see Ceneth clasp the man on his shoulder as he continued to walk around the banquet hall and address others.

"Firi, talk to me," Dwyn said quietly. "You looked like you were having a panic attack."

"I am." Ophir struggled through the two simple words, tears threatening to spill over. "I can't breathe. I can't—"

Dwyn reached under the table and pinched her thigh with excruciating force. Stars exploded in Ophir's vision from what would surely be a magenta bruise in the morning.

"Fuck!" Ophir realized too late she was cursing aloud. Several heads turned as she made a half-assed attempt to twist it into a smile, forcing a laugh as if she'd just been told an obscene joke. As soon as the curious partygoers looked away, she narrowed her eyes, hissing, "What is wrong with you?"

"Are you angry?"

She bared her teeth. "Yes! Of course I'm angry!"

"But can you breathe?"

"I…" Ophir's tirade stopped short. She checked in with her body. The red tingle of anger had replaced the shallow, squishing anxiety that had consumed her only moments before. Its ruby glimmer ebbed as she examined her thoughts, her feelings, wiggling her fingers, testing her toes. She took a careful breath in, then released it. Ophir looked at Dwyn to protest, but her lips only moved noiselessly.

"You're welcome," Dwyn said, squeezing her hand.

Ophir was vaguely aware that people would have noticed their pairing even if they'd operated with perfect, stately behavior. Instead, Ophir had choked on air, yelped, and then promptly held hands with the strange Sulgrave friend. Ophir dared to glance at Ceneth, expecting a disappointed glare for sure this time. Instead, she had the odd sensation that he was both aware of her actions and pointedly ignoring them. It was worse, somehow.

"Thank you," she said at last.

Ceneth nodded to the guests before beginning his return to the table. She didn't release Dwyn until the moment she felt comforting, unseen fingertips slide down her back. The tension leached from her body as she leaned into the touch. Ceneth pulled out the seat beside her, then offered a hand. She took it, standing at his side.

The gentle tinkling of cutlery on stemware silenced the chattering in the dining room as conversations ebbed and faces turned in polite attention.

Tyr left his palm flatly against Ophir's back while Ceneth addressed the audience.

"Thank you for joining us," Ceneth began. His tone was bright and his words were warm, but the emptiness behind his eyes fooled no one who'd known pain. "Princess Ophir and I are so pleased to announce the joining of Farehold and Raascot. Your support of this union means the world to us."

Ceneth tilted his chin slightly, and Ophir understood the gesture.

He was asking her if she wanted to speak, rather than giving a command. It was subtle enough that, should she decline, she could merely sit. It was one of the many things that made their marriage sadder, somehow. She would have preferred that he be cruel. She could have hated him if he were boorish, or offensive, or cowardly. He was none of those things. They just didn't love each other.

She squeezed his hand gently, surprising them both as she spoke.

"Thank you for welcoming me to Gwydir," Ophir said. Her voice was a bit too soft for someone of noble upbringing, but then again, she'd never been one for royal proclamations. She'd preferred to get drunk on watchtowers with Harland while avoiding the obligations of a monarch. But those days had come and gone.

"I'd like to acknowledge something," she said.

Ceneth tensed beside her. The entire room sucked in a quiet, anxious breath.

"There's no integrity in pretending this is the future we'd planned. There'd be no honor in expecting you to see me as the queen on Raascot's throne." She looked at Ceneth, and he looked back at her with gentle concern. She returned her gaze to the people. "I loved my sister very much, and that's something Ceneth and I have in common. A love for Caris, a love for our countries, and a hope for unity between Farehold and Raascot. This is my toast. Not for warm wishes, or for marriage, but to a better, unified tomorrow."

Tyr flexed his fingers supportively against her back.

Ophir clutched her glass, and Ceneth was quick to follow.

"To tomorrow," she said.

"To unity," he concurred.

EIGHT

✦　　✦　　✦　　✦

Y OU WERE SENSATIONAL! YOUR SPEECH? IT WAS SO HONEST,
so simple. You've won them all." Dwyn preened,
giggling as she kicked her heels off. They'd scarcely gotten
through her bedroom door before the siren had begun
undressing. "Firi, help me with this, would you? The buttons
are at the worst spot. It's almost as if—"

"Almost as if servants are supposed to help you with it
before bedtime, rather than you stripping nude all hours of
the day?" Ophir finished the thought as her fingers began
to work on the buttons of Dwyn's pretty blue dress. After,
Ophir turned and offered her back without being asked,
knowing it was her turn to step out of her blush gown.
The servants knew enough by now to expect that the
women would not be clothed unless they were given proper
forewarning.

Dwyn needed very little encouragement to have her
hands on Ophir. Her fingers worked against the buttons as
she planted hot, light kisses on the soft place where Ophir's
neck met her shoulder.

"I wanted to get you out of this the moment I saw you
in it," Dwyn said.

Ophir smiled, back still to the siren. "Yes, but you say that regardless of what I'm wearing."

Dwyn's fingers stopped.

"What?"

Dwyn rounded her slowly, a mischievous smirk tugging her lips up at the corner. "I have a wonderful idea."

"Again, you say that regardless—"

"Yes, because all my ideas are good. Hush, Firi. Believe me, you'll like this."

Dwyn took her hand and led her to the enormous full-length mirror mounted beside the armoire. The wooden frame had been carved with elaborate twisting designs. Some looked like they could have been crows; others serpents or lions, but most were just the miscellaneous twists of the fantastical.

Dwyn stood behind her and said, "Look at yourself."

Ophir fidgeted. "Yes, I've seen myself. It's a very pretty dress."

"No," Dwyn corrected, "don't look at the dress, look at *yourself*. Look at those golden eyes of yours. Your irises are brighter and more royal than any crown they could put on your head. Look at the slope of your nose, Ophir. Look how it curves up ever so slightly at the end. Count your freckles. See how your teeth are sharp enough to tear out a man's throat. Look at your—"

Ophir tried to turn. "I don't want to—"

"I said: *look*," Dwyn insisted.

At first, Ophir looked only at the siren. She looked at Dwyn's coffee-dark eyes, the gilded undercurrent of her skin, her full, pink mouth, her cascading hair. She described Ophir's shoulders, the pink blush of her soft cheeks, the sharp line of her collarbones, the gentle curves of her breasts, the cinch of her waist. She relinquished control at last, ceding to the siren's instructions. Dwyn watched in the mirror as Ophir's eyes obediently traced every feature Dwyn listed. Dwyn urged them closer to the mirror, an arm's length from its glassy surface.

"Make me a promise?" Dwyn said.

"What?"

"For the next fifteen minutes, don't break eye contact with yourself."

Ophir blinked rapidly. Her heart rate spiked, cheeks flushing with heat. "What?" she demanded, spinning toward Dwyn.

"We'll restart the clock now, since you've already lost. Now, look yourself in the eye," Dwyn said as she slowly lowered to her knees.

"Dwyn, what are you—"

Dwyn disappeared beneath the blush chiffon of Ophir's skirt and stole the words from her mouth.

No teasing, no tantalizing, no foreplay.

Ophir suddenly understood why they'd needed to be closer to the mirror as she collapsed against the cool, silver surface. She braced herself with her forearms as her knees buckled, a moan escaping her lips. She leaned her forehead to rest against the mirror, but at the last second, she caught her reflection.

Holy fucking shit.

Ophir swallowed, gasping against the rhythmic pleasure of a warm, wet mouth working between her thighs as she locked on to the golden eyes looking back at her. She watched her pupils swell with telltale arousal as wave after wave of tantalizing ecstasy soaked her. She could see the way her lips parted, the teeth that flashed as she groaned, the tendons in her neck that went taut. Her fingers tensed against the cold mirror as if trying to dig into the solid surface. She gasped for air, drinking in the contrast of hot and cold. Ophir stifled a cry as two fingers slipped inside her, flexing gently as if beckoning her to climax.

Her eyes had closed again as they rolled into the back of her head. The moment she felt Dwyn's lips clamp around her clit and suck, they popped back open in shock. The breath left her lungs as she fixed eye contact to the mirror for the final moments before she knew she was going to come. She bit her lip to stifle her scream but couldn't stop the sound, absorbing the glistening of sweat on her skin, the blush of her cheeks, the glaze of her eyes as pleasure clouded her ability to think or see.

Like climbing a spiraling staircase, she was wound tight as she was carried up ten steps, then twenty, then another and another and another more, until there was only one left before she reached the top. She knew that the top of this staircase had no landing. Once she crested the final step—

Ophir broke, collapsing against the mirror as she choked on her cry. Her body tumbled from the top of the staircase through the dark, sickly-sweet void, into oblivion as pleasure coursed through her. She flexed and tightened as its final pulsations wracked her body. Dwyn waited until Ophir's legs, her stomach, the wet grip of her innermost self relaxed before she slowly slipped her fingers out. Ophir groaned at the sensitive contact as Dwyn freed herself from the chiffon and grinned up at her, lips shimmering, hair askew, skin dewy and flushed from the heat of being trapped beneath her skirt. She bit her lip to stop the wicked grin from spreading.

Ophir lowered herself to the ground, a final pulse still coursing through her as she joined Dwyn on her knees. She wrapped her fingers in Dwyn's hair and drank in the kiss, tasting sex and sunshine on her tongue.

"Did you look?" Dwyn asked, breaking the kiss.

She panted, unable to stop herself from smiling.

"And? Can you appreciate how fucking incredible you are?"

Ophir averted her eyes, but Dwyn grabbed her chin.

"Hey, you're the princess—soon to be queen. Nothing, *no one*, embarrasses you. Own who and what you are, Firi. You *are* power."

Ophir examined her face and saw the same look she'd seen before. She had seen it when Dwyn told her that she was a deer limping through the forest. She'd seen it on the cliff when Dwyn had struck her into conjuring a snake. And she saw it now.

"What is it you're trying to get me to become?" Ophir asked. Her question dropped to a barely audible register as she reflected on Caris's goals for unity, met with her inclinations to tear the world from its seams.

Dwyn smiled at her, running a gentle finger over her lips. She searched her eyes for a long time, studying, appraising, weighing, allowing a curious silence to fill the room until at last she said, "Everything."

NINE

✦　　✦　　✦　　✦

I T WAS HARD FOR TYR TO KNOW WHAT WAS USUAL AND WHAT
was unusual in a new kingdom. He'd mistakenly followed
a few people up and down the castle's corridors, certain that
they didn't belong in the innermost walls. He'd discovered,
instead, that Gwydir's culture of informality created both a
curious lack of security and an environment of implied trust.
Unfortunately for them, trust was easy to exploit for someone
hiding in the shadows.

Tyr spotted a curious person with a bright yellow scarf
wrapped tightly around their head. The individual wore a
flowing floral shawl—one that he would have described as a
kimono if they'd been in Sulgrave rather than Raascot. Tyr
would have merely marked the person as peculiar, had the
individual not been walking directly for the king's personal
bedchambers. With nothing to do and all the time to do it,
Tyr walked silently behind the stranger, barely slipping into
Ceneth's room before the door shut behind him.

One of these days, he'd surely get caught in the door and
give himself away. It hadn't happened in centuries of sleuth-
ing, so he was long overdue for a slipup.

Instead, he snuck along the far wall and eyed the setup

with heavy skepticism. Ceneth sat at an empty table, curtains drawn, with only the fireplace to light the room despite the happy midday sun. The one in the yellow scarf slid into the chair and immediately extended their hands.

Ceneth reached across the table with eagerness, but the person snatched their hands away.

"Every time we meet, you tell me she's begged you not to call on her again. You are my king, and I will answer when you summon me. We can meet every day for five centuries. However, I must ask: Are you sure violating your late bride's wishes is what you want?"

Tyr's pulse skipped. Were they truly summoning the dead? No, that couldn't be. Consorting with spirits was forbidden across the kingdoms, wasn't it?

Ceneth withdrew his hands, burying his head in his palms. "I can't do any of this without her. Maybe if I could just dream of her again..."

The person frowned. "Your Majesty, do you still dream?"

Ceneth nodded, though his head remained buried in his hands.

Their frown deepened. "King Ceneth... Have you considered that you were never dreaming of Caris?"

The king's face rearranged in a painted mask of confused displeasure.

The scarfed stranger pursed their lips. "Your Majesty, aside from your wings and perfect sight in the blackest of nights, what abilities have you demonstrated?"

He waved away the question. "I have the power to steer a nation and the ability to soar through the sky. The All Mother was perfectly generous with her hand."

"Of course, Your Majesty. However, I suspect you may have been...visiting Caris."

Ceneth leaned back in his seat. "Say your piece, Medium."

Tyr eyed the exchange from the space between things. It was true. The king of Raascot was summoning the dead.

"If you've never spoken to anyone about your dreams,"

the medium continued, "you'd have no reason to suspect them as anything but dreams. It's not uncommon for dream walkers to spend their lives without realizing they're predisposed to such a gift. It may be why you feel most connected with your beloved here near the bed. It would explain why you no longer dream of her."

Ceneth looked like he'd been slapped. "One doesn't simply discover powers at my age. It's not possible."

"With all due respect, Your Majesty, no fae would be expected to understand the well of their gifts unless forced into trials of demonstration, which simply aren't done."

He sighed. "Maybe they should be."

But Ceneth had lost his steam. His anger had waned before it had even had the chance to swell. He extended his hands again.

"Are you sure?"

"Please," said the king.

The word was so desperate. Tyr had heard that sound only in the voices of those lost to addiction in Aubade's alleys. He had never imagined such a broken word on the lips of Raascot's monarch.

Ceneth's fingers twitched, and the medium sighed. They slipped their hands into Ceneth's, held them for a moment, then frowned. The pair's faces were mirrors of displeasure. The medium tilted their head to the side, eyebrows bunching against their confusion. Finally, they sighed and released Ceneth's hands.

"What?" Ceneth demanded.

The medium shook their head. "There's something impure about the connection. Something isn't aligned. I won't be able to channel her."

Shit.

Tyr was certain his presence was to blame. If he could have slipped out of the room undetected, he would have done it. As it stood, he was grateful the medium had been unsuccessful. For all he knew, a ghost would have been able to see him in the space between things.

"Is it because of Ophir? I've seen Caris once since her sister arrived, I—"

The medium stood.

"Please don't go," Ceneth said sadly.

"Your Majesty, I have no control over the spirits. I'm a conduit. When the door is shut, it's shut. We cannot force it open, no matter how badly we want to."

"Just tell me." The king's voice was miserable. "Did Caris shut it? Is she unwilling to see me? Is this her?"

The medium made a pitying sound. "No," they said, "she has told you time and time again not to visit. If she could close the door, I believe she would have long ago. She has not, because she cannot. Something is amiss in your castle, Your Majesty. If you'd like, we can try again tomorrow."

Ceneth balled his hands into his fists, then relaxed them. He stood, rubbing his temple as if he were battling a blooming headache. He escorted the medium to the door and ushered them out with a curt nod. Tyr made a dash for the door, but it closed before he could slip out.

Shit, shit, shit.

He relaxed against the wall. This was a situation he'd been in plenty of times. Entering places you didn't belong often meant remaining in those places for longer than you intended. He wasn't sure whether he wanted to tell Ophir that a medium was in Ceneth's employ. He trusted her with information, but he didn't want her to risk carving open a wound that had taken so long to knit its scarred, jagged patches over her heart. Perhaps he'd add it to the list of secrets that would damn him to hell. So, there he stood, in the shadows, pondering the fate of his immortal soul and his relationship to Ophir. Instead of escaping to the kitchens or spying on the princess and her witch, he was left watching Raascot's king as the man paced in tight circles at the foot of his bed. He continued to rub his temple, adding pressure until it looked as though he might injure himself.

Ceneth stopped mid-stride. He sucked in a shaky breath

before sinking to the bed. And, much to Tyr's surprise, alone in the dark of his room with the curtains drawn, the King of Raascot wept.

TEN

✦   ✦   ✦   ✦

SILK SHEETS. AN ARM DRAPED OVER THE WARM, FEMININE shape of a lover. Slitted gray beams of morning light. Ophir's first thought was one of comfort. Her second was to remember that happiness was an illusion when the world was ending. Sleep was her only true reprieve. She couldn't figure out what had woken her until the rhythmic rapping started up again.

"Princess Ophir?" came a muffled call from beyond the door.

Dwyn groaned. "I thought they were going to leave you be. What is this waking up at dawn's first light bullshit?"

Ophir wiped her eyes. She often stirred awake in the gray light of morning just as Tyr slipped out of bed. He had not shared her room that night, and as a result, she'd slept much later than she'd intended. She cracked open the curtains only to see that it was not, in fact, dawn. Given the bright, cheery light, it was safe to guess that they'd already slept in until after the morning's tenth bell. She looked at Dwyn's mussy-haired shape where the fae remained half-buried in the sheets.

"I think it's about the summit," she said. "The guests are

set to begin arriving. I knew we couldn't avoid it for much longer."

Dwyn sat up. "Oh, good. Your parents like me."

Ophir frowned. "They *liked* you before you aided and abetted my criminal escapades."

Dwyn's lower lip jutted out. The knocking continued.

"Princess Ophir, I'm going to open the door now, okay?"

Ophir barely had time to shrug into her robe before a pair of attendants let themselves into the room. The woman sighed at Dwyn's indecent form. The attendants didn't care that Dwyn and Ophir were women. They didn't even care that they were sleeping together on the eve of Ophir's betrothal to the king. They did, however, seem to find it endlessly tiring that Dwyn couldn't be bothered to put on a stitch of clothing in anyone's presence unless coerced through threat of force.

The first woman drew a bath while the other shooed Dwyn out of the bed and began to fix the sheets. Dwyn crawled back onto the bed the moment the comforter had been tucked neatly into place. The attendant ignored her, picking out clothes for each of the girls.

"What time will the guests arrive?" Ophir asked.

"Everyone's here," the woman answered.

Her jaw dropped. "What?"

"The royal party from Farehold arrived yesterday, and Queen Zita and her retinue were at the bridge to the castle just as the sun rose. They've all been given a chance to recuperate from the road, but everyone is eager to meet. You'll be expected this afternoon."

"But it's only been a few days since the banquet…"

"It's been eight days, Your Highness."

Ophir gnawed her lip at that, marveling at how easy it was to lose track of time when nothing mattered and you didn't care about anything. Whenever she attempted to contemplate the motives that brought her to this place in earnest, she developed yet another thumping pain in her temples. At first, she'd written them off as inopportune headaches. Now, anytime a renewed migraine bloomed between her ears, caution brought her to stare at Dwyn, whether she intended to or not. She couldn't explain her wariness, but at this pace, she put nothing past the siren and her powers.

Ophir spent her time either in bed with Dwyn or making excuses for alone time in the late-autumn gardens so that Dwyn wouldn't be suspicious when she stole away with Tyr. He always caught her up on vital information regarding the castle. He often held her hand, or brushed hair away from her face. Sometimes he'd pin her against the dark, icy wall in a shadowy corner and hike her skirt up over her ass as he took her hips in his hands, waiting for the sweat of their entanglement to heat her. All things considered, her sex life had never been better.

"Dwyn is coming," Ophir said quickly to the attendant.

The woman made a tired face and said, "Yes, we've expected as much. You've really shoved your lover down the court's throat, you know. You could try a little decorum. We'll have lunch sent to your room, but someone will be back around three to fetch you. Please don't be indisposed."

The attendant said the final word with heavy implication.

Ophir was stunned to have been spoken to in such a way. Dwyn's hand flew to her mouth as she failed to stifle her laugh. The attendants left the room before Ophir had a chance to collect herself.

"Oh my goddess." Ophir blinked as the door shut.

"I would love to have that woman's gonads."

Ophir rolled her eyes as she approached the dress they'd laid out. "Dwyn, you have bigger balls than anyone I've ever met. You don't give two shits about anything."

Dwyn smiled as she peered at their clothing choices. "I am quite bold, aren't I? But you're wrong. I give at least one shit."

"Oh?"

Dwyn smiled at her sweetly, and Ophir flipped her a vulgar finger. Their means of flirtation had never been predisposed to gentleness.

86

After Ophir had bathed and dressed, it was time to eat. Much to her surprise, Evander, Ceneth's primary advisor, popped by her personal chambers while her lunch was being delivered. He offered a three-minute briefing on what was to be expected, bowed uncomfortably, and departed. His visit was so short, Dwyn had missed the entire thing simply for washing her face in the adjoining bathing room. After the food was digested, the plates were cleared, and the hours ticked by, the time had come.

They slipped from the room and began their trek down the hall.

"Is Ceneth escorting you in?" Dwyn asked. "Or do we get to enter together?"

Ophir shook her head. "He'll already be in the room. I'm expected to sit at the table halfway between Raascot and Farehold. I'm neither at my father's side nor at my fiancé's." She said the word bitterly. "He'll be accompanied by Evander and Onain. At least, so I've been told. I informed him that I was bringing you with me, and he didn't seem to take issue with it."

Warm daylight spilled through the windowed corridors and lit Dwyn's smile as they walked. "I'm liking him more every day."

Ophir shrugged. "I think he's resigned to your presence. We arrived as a unit. There isn't a monarch, past or present, who hasn't had the luxury of appointing advisors."

Dwyn's eyes twinkled with what was unmistakably pride as she said, "Look how far you've come, Firi. From a drowned ocean rat to the one uniting the kingdoms."

Ophir extended her hand and took Dwyn's with a sincere squeeze. "You did this, you know."

Dwyn scoffed. "I did, didn't I?"

Ophir rolled her eyes and tried to release her hand. "Oh my goddess, your humility is staggering. This was supposed to be a sweet moment!"

There was no further delaying it.

The summit would commence whether they were ready or not.

They dropped hands as the servant opened the door to allow Ophir and her guest to enter. They were the last to arrive.

Ceneth stood when she entered, and he didn't settle into his chair at the head of the table until she'd taken her seat. Normally, she'd think that it was an empty gesture fitting for the betrothed, but with Ceneth, she wasn't so sure. The man was kind, which pained her all the more.

The Raascot fae—winged and otherwise—copied their king's movements. They ceased their conversations and stood politely until their ruler returned to his high-backed chair.

The side farthest from the door had been allocated to Farehold. Ophir felt some small hurt that her father hadn't risen to greet her. He couldn't even be bothered to echo her husband-to-be's perfunctory manners. Harland was at King Eero's side, though he'd stopped speaking the moment she walked in, accompanied by Samael and a woman she didn't recognize.

Ophir wasn't sure whether she'd fully earned the vitriol in Harland's once-loving eyes, but chances were that, yes, she deserved all his hate and more. She wished he were still the man who wanted to share drinks with her on the wall. She wished he was her friend, her confidant, her ally. He'd lost the right to those titles the day he'd trapped her in her room, intent on shipping her off to marry Ceneth.

In the end, they'd both gambled and lost. She'd ended up engaged and in Gwydir, and he'd watched her slip between his fingers until she was no longer someone he recognized.

She waited until she was in her seat to dip her head in polite acknowledgment of the royal party from Tarkhany.

Gilded trays of fresh fruits and pitchers of hot tea, wine, and water separated her and the Queen of the Desert. Zita chatted with Ceneth's stiff-backed advisor—a woman Ophir knew to be Onain—close to the door. She broke conversation long enough to offer Ophir the greeting her father had neglected to.

"Princess Ophir." Zita gave a light bow, dipping her chin in a true, slow apology. "I want you to know that those responsible for the banquet have been dealt with swiftly and without mercy."

Ophir swallowed, unsure of how to respond. The smell of roses was as distant as the perfume of a dream upon waking. She saw the lavender of dawn, the dark flash of wings, the fluttering eyelashes as Dwyn wilted before her eyes. The events of that morning were a brand of chaos she'd tried to forget. Conflicting truths formed the early warnings of a pulsing headache before she tore her thoughts away.

Tyr must have been nearby and sensed her spike in blood pressure, for his hand began to move in slow, comforting circles against her back. He was always careful to keep his touches light and noiseless. She knew he'd spent centuries perfecting the craft of remaining undetected.

Unable to speak, she supplied a weak smile.

Zita gestured to the man at her side. "This is my advisor, Hassain. And serving as my second is my companion, Suley."

"Pleased to meet you." Hassain dipped his head.

Suley tilted her head, hundreds of long braids spilling to the side. The woman's mouth twitched as if it was a struggle to refrain from speaking. She eyed Ophir skeptically, brows arched as she studied the princess. Suley dragged her gaze slowly around Ophir, as if not looking at her but through her. She did not bow.

Zita had the timeless, unquestionable elegance of a monarch who'd reigned for one thousand years. While her black dress hadn't deviated too dramatically from the fashion of Tarkhany, she'd wrapped herself in a floor-length fur shawl in matching black to stave off Raascot's chill. She needed no adornments, no jewels, no bangles or crowns for the room to know of her sovereignty. She wore a gold band atop her head with royal beams radiating outward, resembling the dawn and its light. There were no gems, no embellishments, simply the gold bars that created a halo around her ethereal face.

Suley, on the other hand, wore the divisive fashion of someone who had either everything to prove or nothing to lose. The long braids hung to the middle of her back with two tight buns above each ear, both decorated with gold, revealing to the room that she was, in fact, fae. She wore sharp, elaborate kohl darkening the corners of her eyes. An interesting black tattoo emanated from Suley's temple, cresting just above her eyebrow and just shy of her cheekbone. Ophir spied three celestial bangles, one in each ear, and a third brilliant sunburst hooped through the center of her nose.

Ophir nearly gasped at the wave of scent that poured from Suley. Atop the fragrant spice was a sharp, almost painful scent that reminded her of kitchen herbs, but not quite. She couldn't quite place the scent, though it reminded her of healer's halls and hospital beds. She'd never been so overpowered by a single fae's personal perfume.

"Speak with me soon, will you?" Zita asked. "We have much to discuss."

Ophir didn't dare look at Dwyn.

She didn't know how much of the room's reaction was on Dwyn's shoulders. Did Zita wish to discuss how the siren had gotten behind her walls? Did King Eero refuse to greet her because Dwyn's arrival had preceded Ophir's departure? Running from Aubade and leaving a trail of carrion in her wake was hardly an action that would make a father proud.

She stole a glance at Harland.

Her former bodyguard hadn't stopped staring at her since she'd entered. He sat at her father's side, though King Eero still played the rather cold role of a dignitary and chose to remain neutral where his daughter was concerned.

A man spoke in her ear, too soft for Dwyn to overhear, almost as if it was little more than her innermost thoughts in a deeper voice.

"You know better than to respond aloud," Tyr said,

"but tap your finger once if you know the woman to Eero's right."

Ophir let her finger hover, then flattened her palm. She did not know who'd accompanied her father. She'd never seen the woman. Ophir frowned slightly as she looked between Harland and the strange ambassador, wondering why an unknown to the royal family would have been elevated to such important status on a mission.

"If you'd like me to find out—"

She tapped twice. No, she did not want Tyr to leave. Even with Dwyn at her side and Tyr so subtle that his voice was scarcely the volume of two autumnal leaves rubbing together as they brushed against the ground, she was terrified of being abandoned.

Ophir kept her gaze as casual as possible, touching the eyes of each ambassador as she scanned the room. She made a pointed effort not to land on any one set of eyes or let herself linger anywhere too long. Her gaze caught another woman's as they looked up at the same time.

Suley. The one who'd been introduced as Zita's escort. She'd lingered for far too long when shaking Ophir's hand, and now her eyes remained trained on her with too much intensity. The time had come and gone for her to politely avert her gaze, but the woman stared over the piles of fruit and bottles of vintage wine. She had not looked away from them.

Them.

Ophir's pulse quickened.

Suley couldn't see Tyr. Surely, Ophir was being paranoid.

But the tattooed fae who smelled of spice and healing herbs wasn't looking just at Ophir. As it had upon their introduction, Suley's lingering gaze slid throughout the space around her. Ophir's breath caught as Suley leaned to the left, pressing herself as close to Zita as possible. She whispered several inaudible sentences to Tarkhany's queen. Zita scanned the room as Suley spoke, sticking intently on Ophir. Zita's lips tugged up slightly at the corner.

No. They knew nothing.

Ophir convinced herself that she was just anxious. There was no way they were talking about her. There was no way they, or anyone, knew anything. The Tarkhany party couldn't see Tyr. No one could. It was impossible. And yet…

He'd seen it, too. Tyr's motionless silence spoke volumes.

Cool air filtered in to brush her cheek as Tyr slowly pulled his face away. The unseen hand left her back. Ophir watched as Suley's gaze moved with painstaking slowness from Ophir like rain from a window, wandering to the left with curious intensity. Ophir looked over her shoulder to see if there was anything worth regarding, but no. She was looking at the empty corner in the room. Ophir was willing to bet it was where Tyr had gone. Ophir didn't know how it was possible, but Suley knew he was here.

Her fear was cut short by a welcome distraction.

Ceneth got to his feet and all idle chatter quieted.

"Since we're all present," he began, "I'd like to welcome everyone to a long-overdue meeting of our three kingdoms." All eyes were trained on the stately king of Raascot. Ophir swallowed as she looked at him. Her husband-to-be. Blue-brown smudges beneath his eyes betrayed his stress and sleepless nights. He'd always been clean-shaven and bright-eyed when he'd visited Aubade. His face had melted into kind, easy smiles when he'd swept Caris up in his arms. He'd glowed while clasping hands with her father and had treated Ophir with a friendly, if not mildly annoyed, indifference. Now, if she wasn't mistaken, he'd lost some weight. His well-tailored suits no longer hugged his muscles. The evidence of stubble never fully left his face. He was still handsome, even for a fae, but he was not the man she'd once known.

"I'm happy to host this meeting," he went on, "but it is Queen Zita of Tarkhany who's requested the presence of our three sovereign kingdoms today. Your Highness, the floor is yours." He gestured to her and took his seat.

Zita tapped her fingers on the table with a look that

might have almost been boredom. Ophir's lips twitched against a smile. She'd gotten to know the woman in Tarkhany well enough to understand that her coy laughter, disinterested glances, and impatient sighs were all beautiful masks. They invited just enough curiosity to pique the interest of the listener and offered just enough calm to cause those around her to drop their guard. It had been a charming tactic that had worked flawlessly on Ophir, and it was one she suspected would work again now.

Zita did not stand. Instead, she said, "Today, I'd like us to share the states of our kingdoms and our hopes for future relations. Then, I request a three-day recess, after which we can reconvene and make plans for our respective futures."

Ophir scanned the room. Ceneth nodded appreciatively at one end of the table, and on the opposite end... She'd never seen this expression on her father's face. His eyes were tight with an unknown stress. She met Harland's eyes briefly, but she was the first to look away. Her eyes returned to Zita.

Ceneth straightened his shoulders. "Raascot shares in the loss of Princess Caris," he said quietly, "but the kingdom is doing well. Our numbers grow as the migration continues from Farehold, but we've been able to accommodate everyone. The following season will focus on our growing need for infrastructure, but that will take a back seat to acclimating Raascot to its new queen," he said.

Ophir's lips flattened into a line, but she said nothing.

Eero sighed. "With the loss of our firstborn and marriage of our second, Farehold will be without an heir to sit upon the throne in Aubade in the event of our passing. Darya and I have been discussing if we will attempt to fulfill the need for another heir, or if we'll begin to look into nobility who might fill the title when the time comes. Our people have enough to eat, and the economy is stable."

Zita looked to Ophir's side. "You, girl. You were at my palace, and yet we did not meet. I'm told your name is Dwyn?"

Dwyn looked delighted to be included in the conversation. "Indeed it is," she said.

"And you're from Sulgrave?"

"How did you guess?" Dwyn asked irreverently. In the interest of formality, perhaps only for Ophir's sake, she amended, "Yes, Your Highness, I am."

Though she didn't appear satisfied with Dwyn's decorum, Zita asked, "And Sulgrave is no longer ruled by an Imperator or Imperatress, correct? What is its status?"

Dwyn did not seem like a commoner at the table with kings and queens. She appeared born for the role as she said, "We did away with monarchs some time ago. We're composed of seven independently governed districts, each with an elected Comte. Sulgrave thrives."

"Then why," Zita asked, "would you leave?"

Dwyn looked at Ophir, then at the others. "Because I can."

Zita seemed to have more on her mind. Despite the congress of foreign rulers, she remained interested in the Sulgrave fae. She asked, "I'm told you have a gift for water, and it's been suggested that you're responsible for the door in my courtyard. Is your gift for travel how you were able to achieve what so many have tried and failed to do in crossing the Frozen Straits?"

Without missing a beat, Dwyn beamed. "That's right."

Ophir wasn't sure if she loved her or hated her. Dwyn deserved to be kicked under the table. Though she supposed that it was wise for one to take an easy lie when it was offered on a silver platter. Dwyn creating doors for travel would certainly tie up the loose ends of a number of questions.

Whether or not she was satisfied with Dwyn's dispatch, Zita didn't share. Instead, she turned lazily to Farehold's king. "Eero," she said, using his name with all the informality of childhood friends. "Tell me, how have your people been enjoying my land?"

The air left the room.

It was quiet enough to hear a single bead of sweat fall from the tense king's brow. Ophir didn't attempt to hide her surprise. She gaped at her father, looking between him and Zita while she silently demanded an explanation.

After a long, pregnant pause, Eero lowered his voice as he said, "You know I wasn't responsible for that."

It was as though Ophir's eardrums had shattered. Stars exploded in front of her eyes. She'd been hit with a wooden plank. Before she even knew she was speaking, she blurted out to the room, "What the hell is she talking about?"

Ophir shot a look to Ceneth. His face was also strained, but he did not appear nearly as shocked as Ophir. Beside her, Dwyn's eyebrows were raised in little more than quiet interest.

Ophir returned her prompting stare to her father.

"Well?" Zita asked lightly. "Are you going to tell your daughter, or should I?"

Eero motioned as if to bang his fist against the table. It appeared he possessed the strength to think better of it. "It was six hundred years ago, Your Highness, and—"

"Yes!" she called, smiling. "It's been merely half of my lifespan thus far. For six hundred years prior, and generations upon generations before that, Aubade belonged to Tarkhany!" She flashed her teeth brightly at the room. "In fact"—she turned her eyes to Ceneth—"if I'm not mistaken, your grandfather and my grandfather were coastal neighbors, were they not? My, what a fun game of trade we've all played. Tell me, Ceneth, do you enjoy the cold? Have your people been amenable to the migration from their ancestral lands into the mountains so Eero and his pale citizens might enjoy milder weather?"

"Zita—" Eero attempted.

"*Queen* Zita," she corrected. "And no, Eero, you did not hold the sword to my throat. That was your father. You did not force us to cross the desert and drive my human partner to his death under the sun; that was your father. But tell me,

Eero, in six hundred years, how have you made efforts to right these wrongs? Because from where I sit, not only are you still on a stolen throne, but you have two monarchs in lands that the goddess did not give them." She turned to Ophir. "Tell me, child, what do you know of melanin? Have you never questioned your colorless skin in the coastal heat, the year-round sun, the endless spring, while Raascot's people sit in the snow? Don't get me wrong, Princess Ophir; you can't be held responsible for what you did not know. But I'm curious, now that you do know, what obligation might you feel to make things right?"

Ophir's mouth dried. She looked between her father and Zita, then to Ceneth.

"I had no idea..." was all she could say.

Zita rolled her eyes. "Yes, dear, but now you do. You didn't know of our customs until you did, and you adapted. You didn't know of our food or our clothes or our palace until you did, and you adapted. And now you know of our history. How will you adapt?"

"Say, now—" Eero cut in.

Ophir looked to him, then to Harland. The baffled look on his face told her that Harland was just as surprised as she was. To his side, Samael's expression remained impassive.

"Oh, please." Zita brushed his interjection away with a flick of her wrist. "I'm not asking you to abandon Farehold. I'm not a monster." She narrowed her eyes slightly. "I don't expect to ever step foot in Aubade again. But we were overdue for a conversation, and frankly, my people are owed far more than an apology."

Ophir didn't realize she was shaking her head until the motion had unintentionally gained the room's attention.

Zita shot an irritated look. "What is it?"

Ophir's eyebrows remained bunched as she looked at Zita. Again, she spoke without thinking. The first thing that came to her lips was "After all this time, what shape could justice possibly take?"

Zita's face relaxed. She leaned back in her chair, coy smile returning.

"I was right to give you a chance. Justice," she repeated. "Seeing its need and understanding its impossibility. Maybe you are the princess this continent needs." She folded her hands in front of her before flashing a bright smile. "Tarkhany is doing beautifully, for the most part. Save, of course, for the winged serpent no smaller than a mountain. Has word of the demon slaughters reached Farehold or Raascot yet?"

Ceneth offered a strained motion of acknowledgment.

Zita looked to Harland and Samael. "And you? Did you tell your king?"

Harland nodded mutely.

Zita had complete control of the room.

"So, since we're all on the same page: A new beast is upon the land. A serpent the size of a legion of horses with four legs and black wings to match arrived at our palace, devoured our people, and wreaked havoc on our capital. It had a terrible companion of sorts—a demonic creature that was nearly a fae, but not quite. Our people are calling the large beast the ag'drurath—"

"Winged death," Samael translated for the room.

Zita made a small, satisfied sound before adding, "And its familiar, the ag'imni. Now, this is the state of Tarkhany."

Ophir could barely make sense of what had happened.

She'd known Zita to be friendly, to be controlled, to be diplomatic. The woman had seemed so amicable when she'd greeted her at the door. Instead, she'd come into the meeting with razor-sharp talons and shredded any hope of amicable relations. Ophir's very grip on the continent and its reality spun like a seedpod fluttering to the ground in late fall. It was chaotic, disorienting, and ushering in the sign of a new season.

The room sat in crackling silence.

Turmoil raged behind every pair of eyes in the room. Anguish, confusion, and fury flickered and burned in various stages on the faces of the respective monarchs of the continent. If energies could get up and flip tables, then every one of them would have been yelling, smashing goblets, and flinging any number of ungodly powers at the other. Instead, they let the taut quiet fester.

Finally, with the friendly ease of someone who'd merely come to chat, Zita said, "And this is why I proposed a three-day recess. Now, why don't we call our meeting adjourned for the day? Meet with your advisors, discuss your events, and in three days' time, let's come together again and see if we can't find a solution." Zita pushed back from the table. She stood, and Hassain and Suley joined her.

Eero and Ceneth stood at the opposite ends of the table in knee-jerk respect while Tarkhany's monarch left the room.

The second the door closed behind them, all eyes were on Eero.

Ophir had no trouble breaking the silence. She was horrified. "What the fuck, Father? Are you going to explain what she's talking about?"

"Ophir, it's not your burden to bear. It's not your responsibility—"

"Why don't you tell me and then let me decide if it is or isn't my responsibility?"

"Because!" he burst. "It wasn't my burden, either! We are not responsible for the sins of our forefathers!"

"Aren't we?" she seethed. "If our presents are all that matter, how can I be held responsible for the kingdom's future if I have no obligation to its past?"

Dwyn plucked at the piles of untouched fruit. She crunched loudly on an apple and spoke through a mouthful of food, saying, "Ophir's right. She shouldn't be responsible for either. I think this is a good time to let her out of the marriage."

Ophir stepped on Dwyn's foot. Dwyn grunted lightly but took her cue to be silent. Ophir often found her irreverence charming. This was not one of those times.

"Ophir, would you give Ceneth and I the room, please?" said Eero.

She shot to her feet, flame licking her palms as she planted them against the table. Her nostrils flared as she said, "Of course! Why would I need to be present for this or *any* conversation!" She turned on her heel, yanking Dwyn roughly to her feet. The siren made a sad, pouting noise as she dropped her apple. They stormed from the room and slammed the door behind them only to find Zita and Hassain waiting patiently outside the room.

"Princess Ophir." Zita smiled. "I was hoping you'd join me."

ELEVEN

✦   ✦   ✦   ✦

O PHIR PLUCKED THE APPLE FROM DWYN'S HAND. "I'LL SEE
you soon."

"Are you sure you don't..." Dwyn attempted to argue.
Her sentence drifted at Ophir's serious look.

Dwyn folded her arms across her chest as Ophir disappeared around the corner. She shrugged into the soft wool
shawl offered to her as Zita interlaced their elbows and led
her down the corridor and out the hall to what remained
of the late-season gardens. Ophir was glad she'd stolen the
apple, if only for something to do with her nervous energy.
She sank her teeth into the crisp flesh, but nerves made the
fruit taste like acid. Despite the intense display in the summit,
Zita seemed as unperturbed and graceful as ever, which only
heightened Ophir's tension.

The air should have been laced with ice, with the river,
with the brisk, impending scent of early winter. Instead, the
smell of oranges wafted gently from Zita. Hassain trailed
several paces behind them. Perhaps if Ophir hadn't known
that Tyr was nearby, she would have been afraid.

"So, what did you think of the meeting?" Zita asked
coolly.

Ophir sounded a bit like a whinnying horse as she exhaled with honest, thorough confusion.

"It's interesting, the secrets we keep, isn't it? Farehold sits on a throne of secrets. And then there's you. But you don't have any secrets, do you, Ophir?"

Ophir tripped mid-step. Her foot caught on empty air, too distracted by Zita's question to manage a flat, straight path through the garden. Did Zita know she could manifest? No. Impossible. Did she know Ophir had murdered? No, she was supportive of Ophir's path of vengeance. What could she possibly be referring to?

"Suley hears thoughts," Zita said, as if answering her stream of unspoken questions.

Ophir's blood chilled. She coughed on her bite of apple, nearly choking.

Doing her best not to panic, Ophir sifted through the memory of the meeting, wondering what treacherous thoughts had given her away.

"So, what better way to get the kings of the continent thinking their darkest thoughts than to agitate them at your summit?" Ophir said slowly, understanding Zita's performance in the room. Whatever Eero and Ceneth had thought in the wake of her words, Suley would surely report later.

"It's an unfortunate gift," Zita continued. "She hears them all at once. It's like always being in a loud crowd. She hates cities, hates my palace, hates this castle. She calls it the noise. Everything is noise. But do you know what's interesting about her noise?"

Ophir remained silent. Her secret was out. She was responsible for the ag'drurath. She'd created the ag'imni. She was the mother of monsters, the princess of demons, the reason for the blood and bodies that littered the streets of Tarkhany. Had she thought those things when Suley was around?

"You have an unseen presence," Zita said finally.

Ophir's muscles went rigid.

Tyr.

Suley had heard Tyr.

"Who knows of your hidden companion?" Zita asked.

Ophir shook her head mutely.

"Oh, don't play coy. Suley is never wrong. I trust her with my life. A male voice—his male thoughts—hovered beside you. She said as much to me before the meeting began. Is he with us now? As we walk?"

Ophir wasn't sure if she could speak even if she'd wanted to. Her tongue tied itself.

Zita stopped to appraise Ophir.

"Goddess, child, who will I tell? My very good friends in the castle? My close allies, Eero and Ceneth? Perhaps you were not in the same meeting just now, but I have not come to build bridges into the past—though I'd be lying if I claimed judgment had not been served to the parties in play. I do, however, think that you might operate outside of Farehold's customs. You're a contrarian, Princess Ophir. Now, respect me enough not to lie."

Zita held up a hand so that Hassain stopped several paces away. She flicked her wrist, and the man took multiple steps backward, creating enough space that Ophir could rest comfortably in the knowledge that he could not overhear their conversation. Ophir stood in the rapidly cooling evening as she met the expectant gaze of Tarkhany's queen.

Finally, Ophir asked the air, "Tyr?"

A resigned male sigh came from the space beside her. He squeezed her bicep, then dropped his hand. He'd heard everything, of course. He didn't bother with pretenses. After a moment, the empty space between them said, "I'd never been detected before today. I've also never met someone who could hear mind to mind."

Zita looked mildly impressed with herself as she asked the air, "And, Tyr, is it? Are you also from Farehold?"

"I'm from Sulgrave, Your Highness."

Zita made a curious face. "How interesting that you

haven't chosen to surround yourself with those who share your culture." She folded her fingers in front of her. The studious look on her face suggested that she did, in fact, find it interesting. "Dwyn and Tyr arrived together, I assume?"

And, because no other answer would possibly be satisfactory, Ophir simply said, "Yes."

"And," Zita continued, "does anyone else in the castle know about him?"

Ophir chewed her lip. "No. Not even Dwyn."

The queen's expression was one of true shock this time.

Ophir dropped her voice. "Dwyn believes Tyr was left behind in the massacre in Tarkhany. They had a…falling out. It was easier this way. Not many people have the luxury of being able to remain unseen if others don't want them around. I would prefer if you did not tell anyone."

"Ophir," Zita said firmly. "I've called a summit to discuss our endgames. I'll hear Ceneth and Eero, but they are men of our past. What is *your* desired outcome? What do you want? Why agree to this marriage if you're hell-bent on flying in the face of court customs—not that Dwyn isn't terribly amusing, but you must have the wisdom to understand you can't possibly keep her around you if you ascend to the throne. And to find you have another companion lurking in the open air… Well, what is your agenda?"

Ophir bit into the apple once more. Its flesh was acrid and ashy—not in the way that a poisoned drink tasted amiss, but with the unpleasant flavorlessness that came from uneasiness and distraction. She continued to chew, needing the time, craving the familiarity of a life before politics and plans. Ophir would have been better off snagging a goblet and a bottle of wine.

The idea of intention and a plan for the future was something her mother had discussed with her in childhood— always to their combined frustration. She wanted nothing. Not only did she not want the obligations of a monarch, but she was not even sure if she wanted to be a person. An agenda was beyond her wants or needs.

She made an uncomfortable face, lifting a hand to cup her quickly reddening ears. Maybe she could use the temperature as an excuse to escape the conversation. Ophir frowned as she weighed her answer.

"Truthfully," Ophir said quietly, "I never thought I needed one. Caris was the heir who mattered. She was groomed to rule. My task was simply to stay alive. I'd remain in Farehold doing goddess knows what until centuries from now when my parents were too old or tired to continue their reign. Hopefully, by then, I'd be sensible. Besides, I'd have a firm ally in the north with Caris ruling. That was the plan. After she died… My only plan has been to end the lives of those who took her."

"Vengeance and justice"—Zita tested the words—"are such slippery slopes, aren't they?"

"The difference is in the eye of the beholder," Ophir said.

"Do you know what I like about you?"

Ophir shook her head.

"I have waited for centuries for someone discontented with the status quo. And that's what you are, Ophir. How it reveals itself, I don't truly care. If you want to be a warrior for truth and make amends across the lands, then you have my blessing. If you want to be an agent of chaos and burn it all to the ground, my support goes unchanged. In fact, it may serve us all the more to break the wheel rather than patch a system built on the backs of oppression. Just, do me a favor?"

Ophir looked at the queen expectantly.

"Whatever you do…do *something*."

◆   ◆   ◆   ◆

Dwyn hated that Ophir had left her behind. She didn't know how to convince Ophir that she should be allowed to accompany her everywhere—from parties, to the bedroom, to important, clandestine political meetings—but there had to be a way. In the meantime, she didn't want to play nice with the advisors from Tarkhany. When her annoyed expression hadn't done enough to dissuade the fae called Suley from speaking with her, she spoke through her teeth, doing nothing to conceal her irritation.

"Look, it was nice to meet you, but I'm going to head back to my—"

Suley grabbed Dwyn's arm. Dwyn was hit with the scent of cloves and a sharp wave of eucalyptus—Dwyn hated the plant. She affiliated it with hospitals and sickbeds and death. The scent was overpowering, dripping from the girl to accompany her intensity. Though she spoke the common tongue, it was in a far more interesting accent than Zita's as she asked, "Can you take it from me?"

Dwyn recoiled. "Excuse me?"

"The noise," Suley pressed. "Can you take it?"

Dwyn tried to shake her arm loose, but Suley tightened her grip. She hated being touched. She didn't even like to be bothered, let alone grabbed by a stranger.

Suley looked over her shoulder and dragged Dwyn around the corner to a small alcove. "You can drain. You can steal powers. You can—"

Dwyn's irritation evaporated. It had been a long, long time since she'd felt true, paralyzing fear. The air left her lungs.

Suley's eyes widened, words skipping like stones over the surface of a pond as she asked, "She can't be. That can't be true. A manifester?"

Dwyn's heart skipped arrhythmically. Her head spun. This had to be a dream. If she ran to the room, she could crash into bed and wake up from this nightmare. She tried once again to pull away from Suley, to run down the corridor, but the erratic fae dug in her nails more deeply.

"You're considering killing me now, but the entire castle would know it's you. Yes, you'd be taken from Ophir's side. Oh, you don't think they could stand against you? You've taken on many, I see, I see. You don't know what I know, Dwyn. There's a neutralizer in Ceneth's party, did you know this? They render everyone worthless—little more than pretty humans. No, no, not Onain. No, you haven't met them. Yes, you'd be useless. You wouldn't be able to fight, or defend, or drain. No, I won't stop reading your mind. No—"

"Stop! Let me go!" Dwyn jerked, but Suley dug her nails in hard enough to draw tiny specks of blood.

"Take it away from me. Take the noise, and I'll tell you something that you need to know."

"What do I need to know?"

A slow smile spread across Suley's face. "Everyone is keeping things from you, Dwyn. Everyone in that room. Yes, even Ophir. But oh, goddess, it gets better than that. There's a rather delicious secret or two they're keeping from Ophir. Three in that room know something that neither you nor Ophir know. I will tell you the moment you take the noise from me."

Dwyn stopped trying to free herself. She studied the intensity in Suley's eyes, truly absorbed the details of the woman's face. The jewels, the piercings, the hair, the tattoo—they'd drawn attention away from a crueler detail. The crescent moon tattoo had been interesting from across the room, but now that she was up close, she saw the mangled scar tissue that the ink covered.

"Yes," Suley said, hearing the question clang through Dwyn's mind. "I did that to myself. I've wanted nothing more than to be rid of this power. It's why I seek out neutralizers everywhere I go. The quiet, the relief, the calm, even if it's for one night and a lousy fuck. I spent six years in the capital with a piece of shit simply because he had the ability. For six years, I slept in silence. I had dinners with no noise. I'll throw myself at Ceneth's neutralizer the moment we stop talking just for the chance at relief. If you can take it away—"

Dwyn had no snide remarks, nothing clever, nothing that would make this go away. Suley was right: killing her was

106

the only solution, and even that was a nonsolution, especially if her queen and fellow advisor truly knew something that could be held over Dwyn.

In a rare moment of honesty, she said, "I don't know if I can."

Suley's nod was fast and encouraging. "If anyone can, it's you. Yes, I've seen. Yes, I see. You've done it all, Dwyn. I don't care who you have to kill. Kill them all."

The words could have been comforting on someone else's tongue. In a way, this complete stranger understood her and didn't judge her. This was the first time she felt fully seen, and it was terrifying.

A rare burble of panicked tears threatened to choke her. "I don't even know what ability that is! Neutralizing is temporary! I've never heard of something like this. It's—"

"Make me mortal," Suley said, eyes wide.

Dwyn recoiled further. "I can't!"

"If anyone can," Suley emphasized, "it's you. If there's a solution, you can find it. I've seen what you've done. I know—"

Dwyn took a step back, moving out of the alcove and into the hall. "How can I even trust that you know anything? Why would I believe you? Clearly, you're desperate. And not that I blame you, but desperate times call for—"

"I'll tell you one now, a smaller truth now. Then once you believe me, you will take away the noise. Once you do, I'll tell you the bigger truth. Yes?"

Dwyn's entire face puckered in confusion.

"I hear you. I hear the problems. I hear your struggle. Agree to my terms, and I will tell you."

Dwyn squeezed her eyes tightly to clear her head, then leveled her gaze. "Fine," she said. "If you tell me something useful and honest, then I will do what I can to remove your ability. Once I do, you owe me your bigger truth. And if you lied, and there is no bigger truth—"

"Yes, you will murder me. I understand: you're very violent," she said dismissively.

"So?" Dwyn asked, voice dripping with impatience.

"Ophir was not alone in that meeting. A man was with her. Someone you know, I believe. Someone in the unseen space. Someone called Tyr."

PART II

Unravel

TWELVE

✦   ✦   ✦   ✦

O PHIR'S THROAT CONSTRICTED AS A HIGH, HORRIBLE SOUND sliced her courtyard meeting with the queen in half. She and Zita whipped their heads toward the castle following a bone-chilling scream. The bushes, the cloudless sky, the relaxing statues in the gardens fell away as her eyes fixed on the door that separated them from unknown horrors.

A thousand possibilities flashed through Ophir's mind. Her first thought was a childlike fear: intruders, strangers, invasion. Her second was far more likely: they were living through the Sunrise Slaughter of Midnah all over again, and her creations were to blame.

"Hassain!" Zita called for her man's readiness, but it was unnecessary.

The guard's hand had flown to the hilt of his sword the moment they'd heard the scream. He took off toward the noise.

Someone else might have frozen, or hidden, or run away. Not Ophir. She rushed from the garden with the queen quick on her heels. They scarcely exchanged glances as they hiked their skirts and rushed over the stones. The single screams became two, three, dozens of voices reacting in horror.

"Stay back, Your Majesty," Hassain urged.

Sedit? Ophir prayed her hound hadn't darted into the castle. She'd commanded him to stay away and would be horrified if her demonic beast had rushed in on the servants.

Hassain unsheathed his weapon and crouched, ready to strike, as he moved toward the impending danger.

Neither Ophir nor Zita, it seemed, was one to take advice. They hurried behind the man. Ophir was confident she could handle whatever nightmare gripped Castle Gwydir, first with flame, then with everything she possessed. It was challenging to run in skirts, but they rounded two corners and pushed past the door to the kitchen to see—

Shit.

Ophir skidded to a halt. Her heart dropped into her stomach.

A pot of stew bubbled happily over the crackling fire. Half-sliced bread remained on the counter. Piles of fruit and chocolates had been pushed to one side. A single bottle of wine was tipped over, the berry-dark liquid dripping from the butcher-block table onto the stone floor, as if everyone had been halted in the middle of suppertime duties.

Fuck, fuck, fuck.

The withered, papery husks of six servants littered the kitchen floor, mouths ajar in silent, frozen screams, eyes shriveled like grapes dried to raisins in the sun. Their linen clothes clung to their limp forms, now three times too big for the skeleton-stretched skins they wore. A plump, healthy human continued screaming, each sound as deranged as the one before it. A fae male rushed to her side and pressed his hands into her temple, soothing the unhinged onslaught of wails. She sniffled slightly as she sank to the floor, quietly clutching her knees to her chest.

Ophir knew only one culprit who left mummified husks in her wake.

Dwyn, what have you done?

The princess turned and pushed past the gathering crowd

of shocked servants, of agitated castle guards, and the jostling form of the king's advisor as she stumbled toward her room.

"Princess?" Evander asked, eyes wide at her harried expression. He reached out a hand to steady her.

"Help the servants," she said, pushing him to the side.

The man released her. "I'm sorry. You shouldn't have had to see such atrocities."

She faced away, hoping he thought she did so in mourning. Yes, of course, she should have been upset by seeing dead bodies. She was meant to be a delicate princess, untouched by senseless brutalities and the horrors of magic. She was upset, all right, but not for the reason she should be.

Fury was her guide as she felt her way back to her rooms. She hadn't spent much time out of them since arriving in Gwydir. She also hadn't left her room much in Tarkhany, or her one in Aubade after Caris's death, for that matter. Despite her insistence on introversion, she knew enough of the castle's layout to storm back to her chamber. She put as much distance between herself and the kitchen as she could before a low, firm voice halted her.

"Ophir, stop!"

She ran into a hard, invisible wall.

A male grunt mixed with her angry cry.

Tyr's voice was tense and hurried as he begged her to listen. "Think about what you might be running into. If Dwyn—"

"She won't hurt me." Ophir shoved past Tyr.

He grabbed her wrist so hard that she almost yanked her arm from its socket in her haste to get away. Tyr pressed, "You have to see what this means, Princess. Look at what she did. Maybe she won't harm you, but clearly, she'll hurt anyone else. This wasn't one murder. She killed *six*. She is ready with an arsenal of powers, Ophir. Whatever she knows—"

"What is there to know!" Ophir practically shrieked. She couldn't see his face, but she knew he'd flinch away from her refusal to lower her voice. "Dwyn knows you're here. That's why she did this. We heard it from Zita herself. I left Dwyn alone with Suley. What else could it possibly be? Those servants' lives are on our hands, Tyr. If we had just told her—"

"It is not normal, it is not *sane*, to hear someone you dislike is present and go on a murderous rampage. She is unwell, Ophir. She's dangerous. She—"

Ophir rammed her opposite hand against the empty air and connected with his chest. When he remained immobile, she shoved again. He was ten seconds away from becoming a gaping hole of singed clothes and blisters if he didn't get the fuck out of her way.

"What, Tyr? What else could be worth murdering six of Ceneth's attendants after several weeks of good behavior? She's stockpiling. She's fucking furious."

"This is my fault," he said quickly. "I'll come in with you."

"You're right. It is your fault. If we had just *told* her, this wouldn't be happening. You're the problem, and you will not be a part of the solution."

He squeezed her arm. "Yes, I will. She can't hurt me. Anything she does to me—"

"Your tattoo? Yes, I know. I understand enough about your fucking blood gang." Ophir shook off his touch. "But this isn't about your safety. She feels betrayed by *me*, and she deserves to hear it from me. I need to make this right between us."

Tyr made a surprised noise.

"What?" she bit.

"I just… I didn't think…"

Ophir narrowed her eyes. "Didn't think I cared about her? Why, because you and I sleep together? Don't be possessive. It's not a good look for you." This time, when she stormed past him angrily, he let her by.

She'd been poised to look like a villain in Dwyn's eyes after all the siren had done for her, and she resented Tyr for it more than she could say.

Ophir paused at the door to her room. Her fingers

hovered just above the handle, gathering her breath. After she rallied her courage, she pushed into the room to find... nothing. Dwyn wasn't on the bed. She wasn't in the bathing room. She wasn't at the window, or at the desk, or hiding in a shadow. She was nowhere to be found.

+   +   +   +

Tyr watched Ophir's posture change. She went from tense and ready for a fight to the sloped shoulders of disappointment. She'd wanted to find Dwyn. She turned from the room and headed back down the hall without another word.

Tyr knew better.

He slipped into her bedroom chambers before the door closed.

He'd barely rematerialized, still stepping out from the place between things when Dwyn descended on him.

Her dark hair billowed behind her like a goddess of the underworld. Despite the early evening, she was in a nightdress that scarcely graced the tops of her thighs—perhaps the closest piece of fabric in arm's reach before she'd torn off on her tirade. The stark black tattoo crawled from her knee up her thigh, disappearing beneath the silky slip of fabric.

She raised her hand just in time for him to react. Dwyn threw a ball of flame so large it filled the entire hall. Tyr barely jumped into the alcove to avoid its inferno before she was upon him. The fire glanced harmlessly off the stones and windowpanes, catching on the curtains and rugs until they were little more than smoldering ashes.

"Let me guess," he said, gasping as he stepped out of the alcove. "Tracking, true sight, and flame?"

"Great job, dog. Three down, three to go," she said through gritted teeth. Dwyn's dark eyes glinted with the wildness of a rabid animal.

"Dwyn, hang on." He lifted his hands as he stumbled to the side. Tyr had grown rusty. He'd relied so heavily on stealth that he wasn't prepared to face anyone in combat. Especially not someone who would reflect his injuries. He couldn't risk hurting her.

Fire sparked between the knuckles of her raised fist.

"They're going to put the castle on lockdown after your rampage. The summit is at stake. Ophir will surely be met with suspicion. If you—"

She lifted a handful of fire and flung it for him once more.

"Dwyn! I'm not the only one you're going to hurt if you keep this up!"

"I have a plan," she grunted. She flicked her hand at her side, but only a few sparks came from her fingertips. If her fire was wearing out, then perhaps her true sight was as well.

"The secret is out, Dwyn," he said, keeping her at a distance. "You learned this from Suley, right? I know. The fae hears thoughts. She informed Zita. She told everyone. But Dwyn!" He had to jump to stay out of range of her thrashing. He shouted to get her to listen, saying, "Ophir is not at fault for this. She wanted to tell you! I made her promise."

Dwyn gasped against another thrust fist.

"Ophir didn't do this," he said again, praying no one in the castle would hear.

"Explain!" She made another animal sound as she lunged for him, ready to tear out his throat.

Tyr flattened his back against the wall, waiting until she swung her fist. The moment he saw it descend, he dove out of the way, narrowing avoiding the strength she'd stolen. His eyes widened at her recklessness. If she'd broken his skull, she'd be dead. Could she truly be so angry that she'd sacrifice her own life for revenge? His hand slipped against the arched windowpane, and he skidded out of its radius. He couldn't risk the tinkering sound of shattered glass if he hoped to keep them concealed.

"Because!" Tyr gasped, barely dodging her fist again. He struggled to control his tone as he emphasized, "After you and I made our deal, I didn't think we'd be able to keep Ophir in the dark, and I didn't want her to have to see our glances.

I didn't want her to feel like we were hiding anything. She needs to know she can trust us, and that's easier for her to do if she does it individually."

Dwyn froze, fist still raised. Her chest rose and fell with angry huffs as she stared at him, muscles still flexed in impending rage. Her bare feet remained glued to the hall floor, lips peeled back in a permanent snarl, but she did not advance. Her anger visibly sizzled and smoked out as she considered his words. As her rage dissipated, it was almost as if he watched Dwyn shrink from the size of the mighty ag'drurath to her fae form, a full head and shoulders smaller once more.

"It seemed easier for neither of us to speak. I'm sorry, Dwyn. I spared us all from having to act."

Her dark eyes rose to meet his. A distant, mistrustful flame reignited as she frowned, saying, "Except, Ophir was acting. She knew you were here."

"All she knew was that I didn't want to be seen by anyone in the castle. She's innocent in this."

He continued to watch her face as it twitched, emotions ranging from acceptance, to confusion, to anger. He saw fury course through her in moment of realization as she used her forearm to pin Tyr to the wall. She stood on her toes to ram her arm into the tender space against his jugular as she snarled, "You're sleeping with her."

It wasn't a question.

"She genuinely cares for you," Tyr grunted against the pain in his neck, wondering how Dwyn wasn't also harming her own windpipe with the pressure. "Believe me, I wish she didn't. I wish she couldn't tolerate you. I wish she thought of you as a friend or a distraction, but she cares for you, and I hate it, Dwyn."

Dwyn coughed, words strangled as if muffled beneath a pillow as she responded. "Come on, you sop. You do not—"

It was the only confirmation he needed. This hurt her every bit as much as it hurt him. He nodded slowly against the pressure on his throat. "I do."

"You...you love her."

Her shoulders slumped. She eased her weight off his throat as she sank onto the flats of her feet. Her face continued to flash between conflicting emotions as she tore her eyes from him, staring into the depths of the blue-black stones of Castle Gwydir. She pushed away from him at long last, standing in the middle of the hall.

"What do we do?" she asked.

He knew her well enough to know that she wasn't asking him. She didn't give a shit what he thought. She merely talked to hear the sound of her own voice. She rolled the question over in her mind, testing its weight in her hands as she thought through the problems and their outcomes.

"We work together," he answered with pained reluctance.

If it weren't for the distant sounds of still-crying servants and the burble of evening, they may have been given over to the belief that they were alone in the world. They stared at one another for a long, long while.

"I won't share her," she said quietly.

He knew from her posture, her tone, her demeanor, that she understood.

"You don't have a choice."

THIRTEEN

✦ ✦ ✦ ✦

O PHIR TURNED FROM THE ROOM INTO THE HALL. SHE DIDN'T know where to start looking for the siren, as they'd spent nearly their entire stay in bed. An orange glow refracted off the sparkling labradorite of the castle, drawing her attention to her hands. They'd lit in her anger, causing the gemstone bricks to glitter. She struggled to calm herself, forcing the flame to evaporate from her fingertips. The reds and yellows disappeared, leaving her alone in the dark hall. She strained for any sign of the siren but could hear nothing beyond the commotion of the rightfully anxious servants in the kitchen.

"Goddess fucking dammit, Dwyn, where are you?"

"Princess!" Ophir turned to see an attendant jog up the corridor. "Your Highness—Majesty—um, what do we call you? Shit. Princess Ophir: Please return to your chambers until Raascot's military can secure the castle. We're concerned for your safety and we—whoa, hang on!"

Ophir jostled past the attendant without addressing them.

"Princess Ophir, I'm so sorry, I'm afraid I'm going to have to insist—"

Ophir rose to her full height before turning. "Then do it. Insist it."

The attendant's jaw opened a click.

Balls of flame encompassed Ophir's hands as she said, "Tell me that a servant can protect me better than I can. Can you reduce an enemy to ash in an instant?"

She extinguished her flame at the answering gulp. "Return to whoever issued your command and tell them I *insisted* upon defending myself. You are in no trouble. Go."

A moment later, she was left to contemplate just how much damage Dwyn's rampage had done. Not only were six innocent lives lost, but if all foreign ambassadors had been subject to the same attempted quarantine she'd just received, the whole endeavor had to be at risk.

"You ruined the attempt at a conclave, then disappeared? Where the fuck did you go?"

She asked herself what Dwyn would tell her to do if she were here, and suddenly, she had the answer. Dwyn would tell her to make something. She hadn't been particularly skillful at the art of creation, but so far, they'd all worked…more or less.

Ophir cupped her hands on top of one another and whispered into the small space between her thumbs, "Show me where I need to go."

She focused on a hummingbird, wanting something quick and lithe to guide her to her destination. She opened her hands and yelped at the strange, fluttering moth that emerged. The sound of its rapidly beating wings was little more than the high-pitched buzz of a hornet. Where she'd expected a beak, a mosquito-like straw with a sharp needlepoint glistened. It looked at her with a honeycomb of glistening eyes, beating its wings expectantly in the middle of the hall.

Ophir shuddered as she looked at it.

"Don't hurt anyone in the castle," she said. It darted in a contained space, up, down, left, right, too agitated to stay still.

"Well? What are you waiting for? Take me where I need to go!"

The moth darted down the hall so fast that it had rounded the corner before Ophir had even started moving.

"Slow down!" she panted.

The moth stopped in the middle of the hall once more. It darted from one corner of the corridor to the other in a dramatic display of discontent. Ophir flashed her annoyance at the moth before it darted down the hall again. This time, it stopped every twenty feet or so until Ophir jogged to catch up. When it reached the door to the garden, it began bopping against the wood as if it were a common insect hitting a fae light in the dead of night. Ophir opened the door for the moth, and it shot into the garden. She'd chased it through the bushes and around the benches, statue, and a fountain that had been drained for the season when she heard a yelp.

Ophir skidded around a bush to see a rather androgynous fae in the fur of an elaborate leopard hat cry out in fear. Her moth landed on the individual just in time for her to see it plunge its long, needlelike mouth into the person's jugular. They tore at their neck, swatting and scratching at the monstrosity while it sucked.

"Stop!" Ophir yelled at the moth. "Leave them alone!"

The stranger succeeded in grabbing the moth, yanking it from their neck in their panic.

The moth plopped to the ground, black goo oozing from its mangled form. The moment Ophir saw its white tendrils, she knew she needed to draw the stranger's attention away before they noticed. She rushed up to them with wide, fearful eyes.

"Holy shit!" she gasped, grabbing them as she spun them away from where the crumbled moth knitted itself together on the ground. Her only course around her demons was to play dumb, so she kept up the act as she said, "What the hell was that? Are you okay?"

Their palm had been pressed into their neck. They pulled it away to reveal a fresh crimson smudge of blood. They frowned at the princess. "I just need to get inside to get a bandage. Are you seeking asylum from the murders?"

She was glad for the excuse to keep moving. "No, no, I don't need safekeeping. In fact, I might be able to help keep you safe, if that's your fear. My name is Ophir."

"I know who you are, Princess. As does anyone who spies you. There aren't many of your color north of the border." After a pause, the stranger said, "Are you sure you're meant to be out of your chambers after a killing spree within these walls? A murderer is loose in Castle Gwydir."

Ophir worked to control her tone before saying, "I'm perfectly safe. But you? Why are you allowed to roam free when the grounds are on lockdown?"

"Not a very effective lockdown, is it?" they replied. "Not when each fae knows best for their gifts and their fate. Militant law is less effective in a kingdom where autonomy is respected."

Such a strange comment. Ophir hardly understood if it was a compliment or condemnation of Raascot's means of rule.

Ophir helped them to their room while they made idle, uncomfortable chatter. She offered a few more bewildered proclamations over the strange insect, a flimsy attempt to compliment Gwydir, and a disconnected ramble about the terrible events regarding the servants.

"Are you an attendant?" she asked.

"No," they said, "I'm the court-appointed medium." They released a long, slow exhale as they reached their door, dragging their eyes appraisingly up and down Ophir's form. They swept an arm into the open doorway and ushered Ophir toward a round table stationed in the middle of their room. "If I had to guess, I'd say that's why you've truly been brought to me. So tell me, Princess Ophir, would you like to see your sister?"

✦   ✦   ✦   ✦

The second hand of a clock ticked, ticked, ticked, until the seconds slowed.

Time bent. The clock sped up, then slowed down, then, if Ophir wasn't mistaken, began to tick backward. She opened her mouth to ask the medium what was happening, but the person in the yellow scarf had vanished.

Her need for dark hair and mint and to locate the siren's bloody wrath dissipated.

The moment the smell of cherry blossoms and petrichor washed through the room, her nerves, her sickness, her uncertainty and panic and chaos all faded away.

She blinked as two beautiful blue eyes stared back at her.

"Firi," Caris said quietly.

Ophir gasped on her sob, though no tears fell. She tightened her hold on the soft, angelic hands that gripped her own.

"Is it really you?" Ophir asked.

Caris frowned, golden brows meeting in the middle as she asked, "Who else would I be?"

Ophir's chest heaved as she swallowed her next sob. "Caris, are you okay? Are you safe? I'm so sorry. I'm so sorry about the party—" Her voice broke as the tears began to fall. They hit the table with the volume of rainwater, each salted splash shattering into a million smaller pieces. Ophir wanted to wipe her face but knew she couldn't break her connection. "I never should have brought you to the party. It's my fault. I'm so sorry—"

"I always was there," Caris said softly. "I will be there forever. I am always meant to be there. It is the only thing that could have happened. The only thing that will."

Ophir's toffee strands of hair swished around her shoulders as she shook.

"You are a beautiful bride," Caris said.

Ophir pulled a ragged breath through gritted teeth as she said, "I don't want to marry him. He's your fiancé. The two of you... That was real love. He's still so deeply in love with you."

"You always will," Caris said. "You already have. Your

wedding is at sunset…was at sunset…will be in Aubade, near the cliffs." Her lower lip quivered slightly as she looked to the side. "It's important. It's terrible. It's perfect. It's a nightmare. It needs to happen. It always has."

"Why are you talking like that? What are you saying?"

Caris tilted her head, golden curls tumbling softly over her shoulder. Ophir realized that Caris was in the same lovely pink dress that she'd worn on the night of the party. She scanned Ophir, then the ghost of a smile danced on her eyes as she said, "A marriage to Ceneth will have been your only path forward. Only one sister could wed Raascot's king. It will be the sister who needs it more. He was so beautiful. He is so kind. He will make a splendid husband to his bride."

Ophir could scarcely see Caris's blurry shape through the wall of tears that refused to clear from her vision. "He will never love me," she said. "We will never be good spouses to one another."

"No, no," Caris responded airily, "not to you—to his wife. Move forward, Firi. Take each step forward until you reach the woods. He is happy. Almost. I would miss him, if I could."

Her smile faltered. A sharp intake of air broke Ophir's sadness.

"The woods," Caris repeated. "You're alone. He's not there. The monsters. The demons—"

Caris's tug was sharp and sudden as if trying to break the connection.

Ophir clamped onto her sister's hands, unwilling to let go.

"I didn't mean to make them!" Ophir argued. Her voice hitched into begging as she said, "It was an accident, Caris. It's why they murdered you. The men at that party. They wanted your heart. It's about creation, Caris. It's about manifestation. The things I can do—the things you might have been able to do. These monsters—"

"Killed me?" Caris tasted the words.

Ophir struggled at the pain of seeing her once-brilliant sister utter nonsensical phrases, repeating back questions with words out of order. Memory had been Caris's beautiful, perfect power. She'd retained everything she'd learned with an ironclad mind. Caris, who never forgot a detail, now spoke with the calm, distant confusion of someone who had caught the edge of a conversation from across the room, half interested, half listening.

"You already know who killed me, don't you? She told you, didn't she? She said it—will say it?—confessed to you. And… You feel nothing. How strange. Yes, I see it. I see the bed. You lay there at sunrise in the Kingdom of Sand, the morning of the man's execution—the one you blamed. You will remain with her as she strokes your hair. You were relaxed, you are, you will be calm. You know she's responsible for my death. Yet, by some power, by some curse, she had you feel nothing. She steals your rage. She tells you what you feel, and so you shall. Is that her gift? Can you see her? The one with the hair as black as night, from a far-off land. She's so pretty, Ophir. This woman… She will be your fiercest lover, your greatest enemy. She… Is it love she feels? Yes, I think so. I felt your pain, yet… It is, and it isn't. It radiates, and yet the void… How curious…how peculiar…how logical. How frustrating."

The tumultuous storm within Ophir cooled. She was nearly expressionless as she said, "It was Berinth's hands that killed you. It's his dagger that cut into you, Caris. And I know he wasn't fully responsible. Yes, I know who killed you. And Berinth was to blame."

"So calm," Caris repeated. "The palace, the heat. Yet you feel nothing? You cared only for who killed me, and suddenly, you won't care at all."

"Because I know," Ophir said.

"Because you know," Caris repeated. "It will be so hot. It was lavender, wasn't it? The morning is warm. The beasts were so large, the wings are enormous, the fear, the blood, the death…and yet… You never meant to create death, Firi. I understand that. I see you. You felt death. Please, you must hear me: When you create, you will not birth life. The death you feel, the unmaking, it soaks through you, even now. You must know it as I do."

"Caris." Ophir repeated her sister's name uselessly. "I went to Tarkhany to avenge you."

"To Sulgrave," Caris responded.

"No." Ophir struggled against the futility of her conversation with the dead. "I went to Midnah. I went south. It's where Berinth was hiding. Everything went to hell, Caris. I fucked everything up. The dragon I created, it was so innocent. I made it for travel, simply to get across the desert. I made its rider to tame and control it. I tried my best. You have to believe me. I can't make anything good. You were meant to unite the kingdom, and here I am, destroying it."

Caris squeezed her fingers intensely. "Sulgrave," she repeated.

"I don't understand." Ophir's frustration bubbled over. "The way you talk, I can't tell if you're telling me of my past or my future. Do you mean Dwyn? Tyr? They're from Sulgrave. What about them?"

"You do understand. You understood."

Ophir pounded a fist against the table. "Speak plainly!"

Caris relaxed, if only a little. "You will be so calm when you were told. The pain will be taken, the sting was removed, the information from Sulgrave. What an oddity. So interesting. I would like to see Sulgrave, but you didn't. You aren't. Yet, you see them now? I'm…" Caris's voice drifted off as she looked to the wall. "Will Ceneth be here?"

Ophir's lashes fluttered. "No, Ceneth doesn't know I'm talking to you. Does Ceneth visit you? Is that why he appointed a medium?"

"His pain intoxicated him. He will be drunk on it. He is addicted to the wound. He hasn't stopped, and I…I see something now. He never stopped. Then his kingdom blossomed into wings and dreams, black flowers made of feathers and generations and sorrow. He becomes what he was. Who he is. I love him, you see?"

"Yes, I see. I understand," she said.

"I will always love you, Firi. You must remember what love is, and what it isn't."

"What do you mean?"

"Please," Caris said quietly. "There are some things love isn't, even when it insists it's so—what it will never be."

In one moment, Ophir was clenching her sister's hands. In the next, Farehold's firstborn, the hope of the continent, was gone once more.

The scent of fresh earth after a spring rain lingered in the room after Caris departed. Ophir choked on the sight of the medium in their iridescent snakeskin scarf where only moments prior, her lovely, perfect sister had been.

"What the fuck was that?" Ophir asked breathlessly. She blinked in disbelief at the androgynous face that stared back at her, handsome and beautiful all at once. Their large hands held hers just as Caris's soft fingers had slipped into her palms. There was no evidence that springtime had ever wafted through this room.

The medium's eyes were kind. "Is this your first time speaking with the dead?"

Ophir dipped her chin. The tears flowed in relentless rivers, no matter how many times she wiped her face.

"They don't see time as we do. Past, present, future, it's all interwoven to those who live in every moment but now. You either get the hang of it or you don't."

"So, what she said about—"

"Don't ask me of your visit," the medium interjected, "as I was not present. I am a conduit. I hear and see nothing of the conversations that occur between the living and the dead."

"She wasn't herself," Ophir said, barely more than a whisper.

The medium shrugged, but the gesture was not

sympathetic. "She wasn't the version of her that you remember. Her speech patterns might have changed, as has her existence on our timeline, but Caris is still Caris. She will continue to exist in the *then* and the *next*, but never the now."

Ophir searched the medium's eyes, asking, "How can that be? She spoke of my wedding to Ceneth. She saw it at sunset. She saw his kingdom, his future. The things she said… I can't make sense of any of it."

"Like I said," they responded, "the dead do not live in our time. Past, present, and future are a landscape with winding valleys and rolling hills. The dead appear to stand on one and jump to the next with each word. She exists still. She lives in our world. Caris and the ancestors before her belong to every moment but the one you and I share."

"But they live?"

The medium softened at last. "They live. In every moment but the present."

Ophir opened her mouth, but the medium shook their head to cut her inquiry short.

"You'll want answers, but I don't have them. I know only what I've said, and even that is merely from discussing conversations with clients, visitors, patrons, and yes, your king. He sees your sister often." The medium sighed. "Too often."

Ophir's prodding frown implored them to go on.

"It's not my place to defy my king, and never will I try. However, he is your betrothed. His attachment to his departed fiancé is bringing him to ruin. From what he's said, I believe he has the possibility for a bright and happy future. I believe his fate becomes clearer with each passing visit, for better or for worse. It stands to reason that there is no good future while he clings to her."

"She misses him?" Ophir asked.

"No." They shook their head. "She has blessed your wedding, from what I understand. She has blessed his future marriages in her conversations with him, and with you, it appears. She has begged him to let her go. Yet, she has no agency through the conduit. She comes when he calls to her. Whether because she wants to or because she must remains unknown. I do hope that His Majesty will heal. I will allow him access to his beloved every day, as it is my ability, and he is my king. However, I can say with confidence that our kingdom will not flourish if he holds on to her ghost. He loves her more than life. But death is not the present. The phantom of her memory will not fill the void left in her absence."

"He won't listen to me," Ophir said, voice low.

"Perhaps not," they responded. "But he may listen to Caris. And you spoke with her."

She continued to search the medium's eyes, asking, "What is it you want me to do?"

"I want you to save our king from himself."

FOURTEEN

✦   ✦   ✦   ✦

AN IRIDESCENT BLACK SMUDGE IN THE GARDENS WAS ALL
that remained of Ophir's bloodthirsty moth. She
wondered where it had gone, or what it would do now that
it was free. She thought despondently of the vageth she'd set
free, the serpents slithering along the coast, and the undead
horse that wandered somewhere on the outskirts of the
desert. She trudged through the halls, her mind flashing to
an enormous winged serpent and its twisted familiar before
she slammed the door on the memory, and with it, the door
to her bedchambers. Some part of her knew that there were
consequences to creation. Some part of her knew that the All
Mother would hold her accountable for the nightmares she'd
released into the world.

She held the knowledge close to her chest, squeezing it
into the space between her ribs as she tried to feel something
about the morbid information. But she did not. Perhaps the
part of her that was meant to care had died with Caris.

"Princess Ophir?" a muffled voice called from the hall.

She cracked open the door to see her usual attendant. She
was too tired for politeness, so she offered only an exhausted,
quizzical brow.

The woman had seen enough of Ophir's antics to avoid ever being nervous or overly polite in her presence again. There was an informality about the exchanges among attendants, guards, military, nobility, and everyone in between throughout the citizens of Raascot that Ophir would never understand. The servant rested her hands on her hips as she said, "King Eero has requested your presence for dinner. King Ceneth has granted the use of his dining room. His Majesty will not be in attendance—this meal is only for the citizens of Farehold. Shall I tell him you've accepted his invitation?"

It was the longest day of her life. She'd woken up naked beside Dwyn, then suffered through a summit, a clandestine meeting in the gardens with Zita, the discovery of six withered husks in the kitchens, and an encounter with her sister's ghost. She wanted to tell the woman that no, she didn't have it in her to suffer any further. Then again, perhaps it was better to compile all of the unpleasantness into a single unbearable day rather than draw it out.

"When is dinner?" Ophir asked.

"One hour, Princess. Would you like me to lay out fresh clothes?"

Ophir looked at the bed. "No. I'm going to lie down until dinner."

"In that case, I'll knock when it's time to head to the dining hall."

"You don't have to."

"Yes," the attendant said, "I do."

The woman departed without further argument.

The attendant had been right. Ophir had promptly fallen asleep in her clothes without bothering to crawl beneath the covers. If it hadn't been for the incessant knocking, she would have slept through dinner. The attendant let herself into the room after a minute of relentless pounding only to roll her eyes at the deep red lines of evidence that the creases in the decorative pillow had left on Ophir's cheek. The attendant had a brush in her hand and began smoothing out the stray hairs before Ophir was fully awake.

"And your companion is where?" asked the attendant.

Ophir yawned as she looked around. She remembered with a jolt of alarm why she'd gone looking for Dwyn in the first place. Her meeting with Caris had had a drugging effect, wiping her memory of the unpleasantness of the day as she focused only on the rip in her chest that her sister had left behind. The servant's hands stilled in their urgent tugging as she sensed Ophir's breathing change.

"Your Highness, are you okay?"

"I'm fine," Ophir lied. Dwyn knew. Dwyn had killed six servants. Dwyn knew about Tyr. Dwyn was furious, and she was loose in the castle. Dwyn was—here.

"Firi!" Dwyn said brightly from the door. She smiled sweetly at the servant. "May I have five minutes with the princess?"

"She is needed at dinner."

"It's only five minutes. I promise on the All Mother's honor. Step into the hall, count to three hundred, and let yourself back into the room. Then you can escort our fair princess to wherever it is that her royal obligations have taken her. Okay?"

The servant glared. She looked between Dwyn and Ophir before making a small, defeated noise. She closed the door behind her as she stepped into the hall.

"Dwyn, I—"

"I was angry, but it's over now. We're all on the same page," Dwyn said. "I definitely tried to kill Tyr. I may have overreacted."

Dwyn flattened her palms at Ophir's wide eyes.

"I was unsuccessful, obviously! We exchanged. I yelled. He explained why it was his stupid idea in the first place, and that you were not to blame. I was hurt, Firi, but I understand. I am sorry for killing... How many was it?"

"Six."

Dwyn bit her lip. "That's right. Sorry about that. I know they'll be your subjects soon."

"The castle is freaking out, Dwyn," Ophir hissed. "Everyone's on the fritz. I was nearly forced back to my chambers on lockdown for my own safety. I can't imagine what the other ambassadors are facing. I assume this dinner I'm about to attend will be surrounded by a dozen guards."

"A lot of guards?" Dwyn chewed on the consequences. "That can be difficult to get around, but I'm sure I can manage them."

"The answering guard is not the problem!"

"Oh, right. The security is a challenge, and I'm sure it's made the summit more difficult. But the problem is because..."

"They were innocent people," Ophir said through clenched teeth.

"Right."

"If I may." Tyr's deep voice sounded from near the door as he stepped into sight. Ophir's heart lurched. She resisted the urge to run to him. Though he'd been with her, she hadn't seen his strong arms, his broad chest, his sly face in weeks. "I'm sorry for putting you in the position to keep my secret, Firi. Dwyn understood that I thought it would be easier to hide my presence from Ceneth and the castle if I wasn't making both of you lie."

Dwyn hissed. "As if I can't keep a secret."

"Yes, but, we...fought it out," he said.

Ophir's eyes widened further.

"We're both fine," Dwyn said seriously. "And we can talk about it more, but clearly you have somewhere to be. Where are you going?"

She looked at her feet as she said, "My father has requested my presence. It's only Farehold's party."

Dwyn frowned. Without missing a beat, she said, "Tyr, go with her."

They blinked, startled, at Dwyn's request.

"I can do it," Dwyn said, "but if I step into the place between things and my borrowed ability runs dry in the middle of dinner, we might have a rather uncomfortable conversation ahead of us. You shouldn't go alone." She turned to Tyr and pursed her lips, tapping her fingers impatiently against where she'd folded her arms over her chest.

Tyr was quick to agree. "Yes, of course I'll come. Is that okay, Princess?"

Ophir made a face. "You have never *once* asked my permission before invading my privacy."

"You're exactly right," he agreed. "No reason to start now. And unless my ears betray me, your attendant is just about to hit two hundred and eighty-five seconds. Let's get going." He took a backward step into the place between things.

Dwyn closed the space between them and snatched Ophir's hands in her own. She didn't bother to look at where Tyr undoubtedly hovered. Dwyn gave her a squeeze just as the attendant opened the door. Ignoring the woman, Dwyn stared deeply into Ophir's eyes as she said, "I truly am sorry for how I erupted. I was hurt, and I have a propensity for being a tad…reactionary. I'll be here when you get back, but I just want you to know that it's okay. Nothing has changed between us."

She brushed Ophir's lips lightly with her own before stepping away.

Ophir blinked in surprise.

"Princess—" came the attendant's impatient voice.

Ophir walked wordlessly into the corridor and followed the woman to the dining room. She wasn't surprised to be the last one to arrive. Punctuality had never been her strong suit.

"I expected armed guards," she said. "Is no one concerned?"

"The attendants? They were just servants, Ophir," King Eero said by way of greeting.

Everyone at the table stood as she entered. She scanned

the room that she'd visited only a few times during her stay in Gwydir. The dining room was lined with floor-to-ceiling windows in beautiful glass arches with iron detailing on one wall, and the blue-black labradorite on its opposite walls. Her eyes went first to Harland, then to her father. She noted Samael on her father's opposite side, and the same unknown woman beside the place setting that had undoubtedly been made for Ophir.

"Come here, Ophir," said her father.

She approached him gingerly.

King Eero wrapped her into a hug. Despite the awkward angles of his uncomfortable arms, ones that had never been familiar with hugging his daughters, he said, "I'm truly sorry for everything. I'm especially sorry for how that meeting went."

She had nothing kind to say nor anything clever at the ready, so she remained silent.

She peered over the shoulder of the hug to see Harland waiting behind him.

Her father released her, and she took a step toward her chair. She wasn't sure if she was relieved or irritated that she'd been seated beside Harland. Last time they'd spoken, their words hadn't been pleasant. Their final morning in Tarkhany, she hadn't even been able to say goodbye as he'd sipped on the rose-scented poison. He'd been unconscious before she'd escaped through the door.

"I'm glad you're okay, Firi," he said quietly.

"Given the murders?" she asked as he pulled out her chair.

"That, and more," he said. Harland's hand hovered in the place just above her arm. It flexed as he stopped himself from touching her, falling limply to his side as he took his place in the chair beside her. A reluctant part of her belly ached at the absence of his once-familiar touch.

Samael offered a cordial two-fingered wave from across the table before she turned to the woman beside her.

"I'm sorry, have we met?" she asked, confused as to why

no one had introduced the stranger. The woman had sat next to the king at the first summit meeting as well, and Ophir was just as surprised now as she'd been then that someone so unfamiliar had been included.

"Sit, sit, dear," said the woman sweetly. She had the golden curls so coveted along the southern coast. Her face was pretty, even by fae standards. Her large jade eyes were as vibrant as newly budding leaves in spring. "I'm Cybele," she said in a calm purr, taking Ophir's hand and tugging her into the chair. "I've been a friend of the royal family for centuries. I'm so glad we finally get the chance to meet."

The woman continued to kindly pat Ophir's hand. Ophir's gaze darted in confusion to her father, who offered an apologetic shrug as he explained, "She's been an important advisor for the past three crowns, from my father and his father before him. There hasn't been much reason for the two of you to meet, as waters have been still in Aubade throughout your young life. Times are different now."

Ophir lowered her brows as she looked at the men at the table.

Harland didn't break eye contact with Eero throughout his speech. Samael was similarly interested in Eero's explanation, but with one arched brow.

Ophir reciprocated with an uncomfortable smile and pulled her hand away, realizing the woman was still stroking it idly. Eero led the table in rather unimportant chatter about their travels. The men gave a disconcertingly vague explanation as to how their journey from the desert to Raascot had gone. Eero answered with something dreary and long-winded. A number of servants emerged from the kitchen, though none of the faces were ones Ophir recognized. She considered how quickly the kitchen staff would have had to replace its missing workers to compensate for Dwyn's recklessness. They ladled a spiced potato dish, a fragrant cut of lamb, and an assortment of rice and vegetables onto their places. Chilled fruits were scattered on gold and silver platters throughout the table. Eero remained intentionally silent until the last of the servants had finished filling their respective goblets with water and wine. Once the door swung behind the final attendant of Raascot blood, his face became serious.

"It's time we discussed what happened at the meeting," he said.

Samael raised a warning finger. "I would caution you to consider, Your Majesty, that even in privacy, the walls have ears."

Ophir's face pinked. She knew that Samael had been gifted general wisdom, but she couldn't help but feel the tingle of eyes on the back of her neck from where Tyr doubtlessly leaned against the far wall.

Eero nodded his agreement. "I'm not here to say anything controversial. Quite the opposite. Ophir, I feel you're due an explanation."

She hadn't realized she was clenching her muscles until she relaxed into her chair. "Yes," she said, "I feel I am."

Eero cleared his throat. "I'm terribly sorry for the position you're in. I'm sorry that you're Raascot's bride, and that you're the target of Zita's—"

"May I stop you, Father?"

He paused, a frown on his face. No king was used to being interrupted. The golden-brown strands of his unkept brows bunched together as he turned to her with a quizzical expression.

"Neither of those things has anything to do with me. Queen Zita is angry because of an action committed before my lifetime, and the inaction pursuant since. I'm Raascot's bride because of an archaic law upheld by kings before my birth. So, before you commence your apologies, can we amend your language? Don't apologize as if you're a victim of circumstance. You're the king of Farehold. Your word is law. You could snap your fingers and dissolve the marriage. You could give the word and return Zita's lands. Please, tell me what happened. But tell it correctly."

Every mouth at the table dropped. She could feel Harland's eyes bulge, despite her refusal to look directly at him. Though he remained unseen, some part of her knew Tyr, too, gasped. Her eyes stayed on the crimson face of her father. His skin dipped into an unrecognizable shade of ruby. Whether rage or shame, who was to know. When he finally spoke, she had her answer.

"What do you know of kingdoms? You've spent your life drinking and whoring—"

Ophir's lips pulled upward in an eerie, pleased smile. Eero stopped himself before he said anything further. The men at her side tensed. Even Harland looked as if he was set to jump to her honor. Cybele clasped her hand as if to comfort her, but she jerked it away. Renewed annoyance flashed through her like static.

"I didn't mean that," Eero apologized.

"You did," she said, her smile now revealing her teeth. An amused calm settled over her. She leaned forward onto her elbows as she looked at her father. "Caris was the virgin, and I'm the whore, right? Because a woman cannot exist outside of dichotomies."

"Ophir—"

"Stop me when I'm wrong, Father. Caris was the monarch that would make the kingdoms proud, and I'm the disappointment that was best left to get drunk on the wall and avoid meetings, right? Caris was the golden child, and I'm the mistake."

"You're not a mistake, Ophir." Her father stumbled over his words.

She laughed brightly and shoveled a forkful of food into her mouth. She grinned as she chewed, smacking through her meal. "I know that more than you ever will, Father. You have no idea what I can do." She swallowed, licked her lips, then wiped her mouth with her cloth napkin. "Now, is there anything else you need from me? Or am I free to return to my drinking and whoring?"

She was surprised when Harland's hand settled on her forearm. She looked into his hazel eyes and felt a twinge of regret as memories coursed through her. She felt their laughs, their bottles of wine, the moments he'd pulled her from her night terrors, the love they'd made, the friendship they'd had all in one tense gaze. His eyebrows bunched with concern as he tightened his fingers gently around her forearm.

His sincerity didn't fit the evening's mood. His brown-green eyes leveled with hers as he said, "You are perfect exactly the way you are, Ophir. Don't leave the table. Please stay. Your father needs you more than you need him right now."

She'd been ready to stand up and leave. His words knocked her off-kilter, if only for a moment. Her eyes darted from Harland to Eero, expecting fury and betrayal on the king's face. Instead, Eero looked at his plate.

Her resolve fizzled. She glanced up at the ever-calm face of Samael, but he merely tilted an intrigued face, as if curious what she would do. Her shoulders slumped slightly.

She took in Harland's hopeful plea, Samael's impassive stare, and the stranger Cybele's undue cheer, hoping her father would look at her. He did not.

"Fine," she said quietly. Harland's hand remained on her until she spoke her single, reluctant word. Then it slipped from her forearm as she asked, "What do you need from me?"

Her father lifted his eyes at last. With gravity, he said, "We need this marriage more than ever. For six hundred years, Tarkhany has remained silent. Now, on the eve of your wedding, relations are taut. We need a firm ally in Raascot. I don't know if Ceneth would stand with us without the union."

She considered the truth of his words.

She knew in her bones that Ceneth's love for Caris was true. He would have brought her the head of every man, woman, and child from every corner of the continent if she'd asked—a gruesome, ridiculous thing to imagine, true as it may be. But with Caris dead? Would Ceneth feel any obligation to send aid to Farehold if Tarkhany invaded their land? She considered the possibilities. It occurred to her that even if Tarkhany had marched on Aubade with Caris as his bride, she may have asked him to stand down in favor of peace talks. No, there was certainly some veracity to Eero's fears. As it stood, Farehold could not count on Raascot as an ally in the event of war.

She opened her mouth to ask whether or not she should care, then snapped it shut.

"From what I know of Onain," Samael said calmly, "she'd advise against him meeting anyone in all-out war."

"Onain?" Ophir prodded. "The woman who advises Ceneth?"

"My twin sister," Samael shared, as casually as if he'd been speaking of the weather.

The entire table turned its attention to Samael. Pairs of eyes widened, postures stiffened, and breathing stilled as they regarded the quiet fae.

"Your sister is Ceneth's advisor?" Eero clarified with quiet urgency, face painted with both shock and displeasure.

Samael's face remained neutral as he said, "I think you can trust my judgment enough to believe me when I say that I share what's relevant and withhold that which would openly distract or be disruptive. As siblings, we were born with shared gifts. The blessing of preternatural discernment is not allowing blood to cloud decisions. I can tell you with some confidence that neither she nor I would advise any monarch to meet a kingdom in open war. And if I were her, I would advise Ceneth to stand down. Now, if Tarkhany is at his door, his hand may be forced."

Eero's eyes narrowed. With thinly veiled hostility, he asked, "Am I to be wary that your twin is advising a potential enemy in the kingdom you call home?"

"An enemy?" Ophir blanched. "I know you wouldn't have deemed him such in Caris's presence, and he's done nothing to gain your mistrust. In fact, he may be the only honorable man in this castle."

Eero's fist-banging, red-faced outrage was interrupted by his advisor.

Unperturbed as ever, Samael said, "It would be unwise to draw a correlation where one does not exist. Neither Onain nor I call this kingdom home. We've sworn separate fealties and duties to advise, not to sway with an agenda. Might I suggest we stick to facts and not project mistrust upon our allies?"

Ophir found the tie interesting, if irrelevant. She was fine leaving, but not with her father leading with his temper. The meeting wouldn't fall to distractions while she was present.

Intent to get them back on track, she asked, "Would you go to war with Tarkhany?"

"Absolutely not," Samael said. "Sometimes, however, war comes to us. It's wise to be prepared."

Cybele grabbed her hand again, squeezing it gently.

Ophir flinched at the unexpected contact. This time, she openly grimaced at the woman as she shook free of the unwanted contact.

"Oh, I'm sorry," Cybele apologized. "I'm prone to touch as my language of comfort, whether I realize it or not."

"Cybele came with a wedding present," Eero said. Perhaps the news of Samael and his sister was too much for the king to handle at one dinner. She kept her eyes on Samael for a moment, though he remained unbothered.

She scowled at her father in response, but he jutted his chin toward the woman who sat beside her, insisting upon the present.

Cybele procured two small boxes. She slipped her fingernail into the crack of one and popped it open to reveal the treasure within. She gazed upon the oval-cut ruby with glassy white diamonds set on a gold band.

"That one's yours, dear. Take a peek at Ceneth's."

Ophir opened the second box. The masculine band

was adorned with a sapphire, two black diamonds flanking it.

"I had them made with a manufacturer," Cybele said, voice sugar-sweet in an obnoxious attempt at being soothing. "They're excellent tools for connection between husband and wife. These rings help to strengthen bonds."

Ophir turned her skeptical frown to her father.

He said, "Your sister desired unity, correct? This ring will help you be more like her. After the wedding, your rings will help join your will. That being said, if you need an ally, he'll be compelled to oblige."

Ophir blanched at the gift. She shoved back from the table, head ringing. "You want me to not only marry this shattered man, but to—what—brainwash him?"

"Ophir, sit down," her father said. "This is a marvelous gift."

"This isn't how Caris wanted it," Ophir said. She took a step back. "You're bastardizing her dream."

Harland got to his feet, pleading with her. "Firi," he said, "it's not as bad as it sounds. This could protect the continent. You'd be the most powerful person in all the kingdoms."

She gawked at him as if he'd grown a third eye. "Are you trying to be reassuring? What's wrong with you? This isn't what I want." She shook her head so hard that it ached. "I want Caris back, and it's goddess-damned impossible. But if I can't have her, I can hurt those who did this to her. The rest? This chessboard? These wars of puppets and fools? Leave me out of it. I'm no pawn in your game."

"Firi," Harland urged. He reached for her again, but she smacked away his hand.

"Samael?" she asked of the man. "Are you truly an advisor if you believed this was a good idea?"

Samael looked calmly between her and the king before saying, "One might hope that wisdom would preclude suspicion, but such is not always the case. Acting in assumption of the worst-case scenario might become a self-fulfilling prophecy. I've shared my feelings with King Eero, and he knows my stance on any actions based in fear."

Her eyes narrowed at his riddle of a nonanswer, though she supposed he'd done as much to defy her father as he dared while remaining one of the king's most trusted men. He'd more or less said that it was a horrible idea, though in the most political way she could fathom. She glared at the still-smiling Cybele, then looked at Harland. He remained on his feet, hand outstretched, pain etched across his features.

"I'm finished," she said. Ophir headed toward the door.

"Ophir?" her father called.

She paused without turning, palm flat against the dining room's heavy door.

"You don't have to accept the terms, but please, for your kingdom and your people, don't tell anyone of this conversation."

She'd allowed him the kindness of a final word, and it had been more than he deserved. She did not look over her shoulder as the door slammed behind her.

FIFTEEN

✦   ✦   ✦   ✦

DWYN YANKED ON THE SMALL CURTAIN THAT OFFERED moderate privacy to the alcoves that dotted the corridors. Each was typically decorated with a fainting couch, a table, a vase with fresh-cut flowers, and some painting of a mountain range or noble or terrible battle.

"So?" Suley blinked.

"Your information was good." Dwyn glowered, hating every second of the meeting.

The rapidly fading light caught on the sparkle of Suley's golden jewelry. She nodded a bit too eagerly as she asked, "You found him, then? The unseen man?"

Bitterness rolled on the back of Dwyn's tongue at the question. She examined the tattooed fae. The woman had looked so mysterious, so alluring, so self-assured sitting next to Zita during the first summit meeting. Standing across from her now, Dwyn saw the cracks in the eucalyptus-scented façade. Her piercings, her tattoos, her dress all drew the eye away from the struggle within. Dwyn understood the impulse. She dressed the way she did—or didn't, for that matter—for the same reason. At least, she had for a long time. It was hard for friends or lovers to notice the internal struggles flickering behind her eyes when she was topless.

"This other secret you're sitting on...you swear it's better than your information about Tyr?"

Suley's eyes sparkled. "The fruit is riper and juicier at the top of the tree where it's been seasoned by the sun."

"Whatever the fuck that means."

"It means," Suley said, words thick with her musical accent, "that you can't begin to fathom what the leaves are hiding from your eyes. It means that if you succeed in giving me what I need, I'll give you more than you could have imagined."

Dwyn peered into the hall to ensure no one was coming up on either side, then back to Suley. She leaned in close as she said, "Look, I'll do it. The problem is, I need to understand what power I'm borrowing in order to create it. I don't even know what power would take away your noise—"

Suley raised a single finger.

"I can't make you mortal," Dwyn objected, whisper growing shrill. "At least," she amended, "I've never heard of such a thing. Every power I've borrowed is one I've seen or encountered before. I've lived a long life and have crossed many paths, but..."

"What?" Suley demanded. "I've witnessed your powers. You've drained, yes. You borrow. Yes. No. Don't bother with that! Why are you thinking of them? That won't be useful. No, we can't use that. Yes, I've thought of that. Wait, why them? Don't you need to train at the university? I don't understand."

Dwyn chewed on her lip, ignoring Suley's soliloquy as she said, "I think I may have a solution. You said Ceneth has a neutralizer?"

Suley sank into the alcove's chaise. She said, "Neutralizers are temporary. Military generals use them to level the battlefield so an opponent can't hide between fae powers alone. I've seen it echoed in your memories. Even if you borrowed the gift..."

"Yes, yes." Dwyn waved it away. She found Suley profoundly irritating. Then again, she found everyone irritating, save for Ophir. She said, "I can wield two powers, you see, but I can't use them at the same time. My thought is that if I borrow the ability to manufacture and collaborate with your neutralizer, we might be able to forge you something permanent. You do seem to like jewelry, after all. A cuff? A necklace? A collar?"

Suley considered this carefully. She asked, "Why wouldn't this have been suggested to me before? Tarkhany has manufacturers. Zita hasn't even thought such a thing around me. No one has."

Heavy with implication, Dwyn said, "Tarkhany has manufacturers, yes. But does it not also have need for someone who can speak mind to mind?"

Suley's braids moved so quickly that they created an obscuring blur as she shook her head. "Zita knows how much I hate this curse. She wouldn't—" But she was unable to finish her thoughts. She buried her head in her hands. "She wouldn't have been able to hide her thoughts from me. Don't say that about her. No, she wouldn't use me. Even if she wanted to, I would have overheard such ploys. Stop that. Don't think such things. She knows I'd rather die. I tried to die. I've lived with the nomadic tribes. I banished myself to a cliff. I've heard the noise of demons. No. Don't think that, Dwyn. Stop it! Why are you..."

But by the time she met Dwyn's steady face, she'd lost her fire.

Suley finally said, "You truly think the solution has been that easy? We can manufacture a neutralizing object? It would nullify my curse?"

The solution was like a balm, if only because it shut the fae up. Dwyn relaxed. "And you wouldn't even have to become mortal. You can keep that long, healthy life of yours—silently. Won't that be nice?"

Suley's eyes drifted, unfocused. Her face remained

pointed beyond the alcove, out the arched windows and into the fading light beyond the garden. Clouds emerged from the west, shutting out any hope of the reds or oranges of sundown. Various shades of white, silver, and gray faded into the distant black of Gwydir's stone buildings, its shops, its churches and trees, and the mountains that rimmed the city. After a long time, she nodded.

"Tell me what you need me to do."

+   +   +   +

Corridors. Lanterns. Bedchamber. Dwyn.

"Firi! How was—"

Ophir slammed the door so hard that the framed painting of the violet Raasay mountain range rattled against the stones. She didn't bother to meet Dwyn's smile. Tyr stifled a noise as if his fingers had nearly gotten jammed in her haste to put as much space between herself and the hallway as possible. He stepped into sight the moment the door latched. Dwyn's eyes widened as her concern darted between the two of them. She gripped uselessly for Ophir's hand, but the princess shook her away.

Dwyn barely jumped out of her way in time to avoid the impact of shoulder against shoulder. She blinked. "What the hell happened?"

He held out his hand toward Ophir. "Our princess has become less tolerant of disrespect."

Dwyn's expression changed in an instant. "There's our girl."

Tyr's outstretched hand became cautious. "You weren't there, Dwyn. The things they were asking of her..."

Dwyn's hair whipped around her face and shoulders in thin black lines with the speed of her turned head. She implored Ophir to speak, but the princess sank onto the bed and occupied herself with chucking her shoes across the room.

"She was presented with bonding rings," Tyr said.

"Cybele—the woman Eero brought with him—had wedding rings to strengthen their union. Her father wants to secure Farehold's allyship with Raascot, should Tarkhany march in open war against Farehold. As it stands…"

Dwyn tapped her chin. "They don't know if Ceneth would go to war for a bride he doesn't appreciate like he should."

"He wouldn't go to war for Caris," Ophir grumbled as she flailed against her buttons, "because Caris would never have condoned war. It's part of what united them. Fucking humanitarians."

Dwyn took a few careful steps toward Ophir and her attempts to disrobe. "Let me help you with your dress."

"I've got it!" Ophir snapped. She yanked in opposite directions until the buttons strained and popped against their thread loops. Two broke free from the dress and clattered to the stones. With compounded fury, Ophir snarled as she ripped into her dress. She tore at the fabric, thrashing and kicking until the expensive gown was left in ruined, pretty tatters at her feet. She tugged the sheet up over her head as she turned toward the dimming gray of the window.

Dwyn shook with inaction. She gingerly raised her fingertips as if she was desperate to be helpful. "But can I…"

"Shut the goddess-damned curtain."

"Sure thing," Dwyn said quietly. She slipped the tassel free from its iron loop and allowed the thick fabric to block out what remained of the waning evening light. Dwyn shot confused brows up to Tyr before returning her frown to Ophir. She slid onto the bed but remain seated.

Dwyn dared to ask, "They want you to wear a bonding ring to Ceneth? Is there more?"

Ophir twisted away from Dwyn, facing where Tyr leaned against the door. Tyr's frame offered little reprieve. She grunted as she threw the comforter over her frame and stormed off to the bathing room, slamming the door behind her.

Light from the bathing chambers filled the room, then disappeared with Ophir's open and shut door. Tyr remained in the bedchamber, dreading being left alone with Dwyn.

"What happened in there?" Dwyn demanded, voice barely a hiss above the sound of running water.

"She had no patience for their bullshit." He returned the whisper. "Eero wanted her to be a pawn, then a victim. She entertained none of it."

"Shit."

Tyr nearly flinched at her reaction, asking, "What?"

"I just resent that you were there and not me."

"Stolen power will only get you so far."

Dwyn bunched herself in a corner, tapping her fingers against her bicep as she weighed her options. "There have to be other things we haven't considered. I've been thinking about how to make certain abilities more permanent—"

"What abilities?"

"None of your business," she hissed. She paused and listened for the sound of running water. She nodded to herself, content that Ophir was fully distracted before she continued. "I either need to find a manufacturer or become one."

"Or," Tyr said dryly, "you could make good on your promise and teach me."

Dwyn arched a manicured brow. "Say that again?"

"We had a deal."

Dwyn raked her eyes over him slowly. She appraised him from head to toe before saying, "Are you sure you're ready to get started? The high and mighty Tyr thinks he can stain his hands? Once you start, there's no going back."

Tyr narrowed his eyes. "There's more blood on my hands than you realize."

Dwyn looked off to the side, unimpressed. "There's a huge difference between what you do and what I do."

"Are you going back on your deal?" he asked.

The sound of water stopped. Dwyn took a step closer,

lowering her voice as she said, "I'll honor the agreement. You've held up your end of the bargain…mostly."

"Mostly?"

Dwyn made a disgusted face. "As if you didn't conceal yourself and lie to me—as if you didn't force *Ophir* to lie for you." She sucked on her teeth before raising her eyes to meet him. "Did you say the woman's name was Cybele?"

His mouth twisted to the side at the sudden change of subject. "Yes," he said. "Why?"

She sank to the bed, leaning her head against one of its tall, ornate posts as she looked into the middle distance. The frown leached from her face into her posture. Her skin, normally smattered with gold, faded into a ghostly shade of pale gray.

His eyes flashed to the closed bathing room door, then back to the siren. "Tell me."

Her eyes darkened. They seemed heavier, somehow. An eerie vacancy rang through her voice as she quietly repeated, "Cybele? You're sure that's the woman's name?"

"Yes. Why? What do you know?"

Dwyn's expression was unreadable. "And she sat beside Ophir? The woman touched her? She touched Ophir?"

He stepped until there was little more than an arm's length between them. He blinked down at where she remained sunken into the mattress, confusion thick in his tone as he repeated his question. "Yes, she grabbed her hand throughout the dinner. What is it?"

She shook her head before saying, "I need to ask you a favor, and I need you to believe me when I say it has nothing to do with jealousy. This is important, Tyr."

"What?"

She looked at the door as if watching the princess behind its wooden barrier, undoubtedly scrubbing herself with soap and sponges and rags until she was clean of the exhausting day. Dwyn continued to stare, lost in thought for a long moment before she responded. She didn't lift her eyes as she said, "Tyr, whatever you do, you can't sleep with Firi."

"Dwyn—"

"Promise me—no, Tyr. Don't promise me. Promise Ophir. Whatever you do. It can't happen again."

+   +   +   +

Ophir tightened her hold on her towel. Damp tendrils soaked the cloth as she looked suspiciously from Dwyn to Tyr. "Why aren't you two fighting?"

Dwyn smirked, while Tyr said, "Excuse me?"

Ophir leaned into the door frame. "There is no circumstance where I see the two of you being civil, and now you're both just sitting here? What happened while I was in the bath?"

Dwyn cast a pointed brow toward Tyr.

He glared back before saying, "Convincing Dwyn that you were not to blame for my secrecy included the caveat that I would stop making our issues *your* problem."

Ophir looked skeptically at Dwyn.

Dwyn, still reclining on the bed, merely shrugged.

"You're not going to fight because it's not good for me? Where the hell was that mentality before?"

Dwyn lowered her eyes to her nails, pressing on her cuticles as she inspected each finger. "Ask your dog."

Tyr blew out a loud breath. "We're…trying. Some of us harder than others."

Ophir tilted her head against the doorway, gentle droplets of clean water splashing from her hair to the floor below. She said, "I was thinking about you while I was in the bath."

It was met with equal parts delight from Tyr and disdain from Dwyn.

"Not like that," Ophir said, exhaustion heavy. "If word is spreading of your presence, then we need to stage an arrival. You're going to have to show up at the castle's front door. You were last spotted in Tarkhany, so you can come in through

151

the forest. Zita and her retinue must have used the door. I created a boulder to block it, but I've learned a very important lesson on the difference between dissuasion and destruction. I think you need to make your entrance no later than tomorrow's breakfast."

Dwyn flopped backward onto the bed. She stared at the ceiling as she said, "Without the door, we'd just be sitting in anticipation for another month of travel before we had this war of kings and queens. At least this way we could get the meeting over with. Everything's out in the open."

"I guess..." Ophir said uncertainly.

Dwyn sat up. "You could end the wars before they begin, you know."

She frowned from where she leaned. Tyr had also grown strangely still, staring at Dwyn rather than Ophir.

Dwyn leaned forward conspiratorially. "I just mean, you're more powerful than they realize. You're more powerful than *you* realize."

Ophir shuffled uncomfortably from the bathing room frame to the armoire. She fished for a nightdress, a robe, and a pair of warm socks. Despite the fires and the castle's enchantments, the early signs of winter brought chill into the very air. She ignored Dwyn entirely as she disappeared into the bathing room to change. By the time Dwyn reemerged, she had an announcement.

"So, Tyr, are you ready to make your debut?"

SIXTEEN

+   +   +   +

DWYN HAD SCARCELY OPENED THE BEDROOM DOOR BEFORE regretting it. A wave of eucalyptus and the clang of bracelets preceded yet another assault of annoyances.

"Hi! Good morning! I just wanted to follow up on the noise, and what you were thinking? Perhaps we could strategize about the neutralizer?" Suley fidgeted against the wall just beyond the door to the room that Dwyn and Ophir shared. "I overheard something at the meeting. Something with—"

"Why are you here?" Dwyn quickly raked her fingers through her hair, smoothing out the pieces that had tangled in the night.

"I told you, I heard something…"

"No." Dwyn clicked her tongue. "Here. Now. Why are you outside my door first thing in the morning? I just need tea and to crawl back into bed."

"I waited until I heard you say you wanted tea. I made sure the princess was asleep so she wouldn't overhear."

"You spied on my mind," Dwyn clarified. "The servants weren't answering."

"I know," Suley agreed. "I intercepted them."

Dwyn wanted to hit the fae for interrupting any semblance

of morning peace. All of the bangles, beauty, and tattoos of the world be damned, she had no interest in breaking bread with the obnoxious.

Suley crossed her arms as she ticked through Dwyn's thoughts. "No, we've already been over this. You can't kill me. Draining won't work, as we discussed. You'd be discovered in under three hours, Dwyn. Yes, you got away with it before because you targeted marginalized servants. You're no fool. You know Zita would raise hell to find me. No, you can't slap me, either. You're the only one in the castle with such suspicion over their head; all eyes would be on you. Honestly, it's a shock they're not already targeting you after your murdering spree. Stop that, you know it's not wise. Dwyn, you're more intelligent than that. Good, that's better, but it still won't work. Oh, I'm not impressed, you'd never get away with that. What? Excuse me! That's very foul language."

Dwyn mirrored her folded arms.

"Ah, I see." Suley eyed her speculatively. "When I was silent, you were able to imagine me as cool, strong, and collected. Excellent. My armor works miracles. Your disappointment regarding my character is not my problem."

Dwyn chuckled lightly. "Fair enough. Is there a—"

"Yes," Suley clipped.

"I have—"

"Rules. Your first rule is that if you're going to help me, you need to be able to…finish your sentences. Ah, yes. I see. You have to realize I can't help what I hear. You expect me to hear it twice? First from the noise, and then from your mouth?"

Dwyn started down the hall, not waiting for Suley. By the time she caught up, Dwyn had already begun speaking. "Listen to me twice, three times, ten times. Listen until I've said it with my lips. Not only is it polite, it's my condition. The fact remains: you need me more than I need you."

"But you don't know what I know."

"That's right," Dwyn said, "I don't. And I don't care what

you know. Your information was excellent, and it was true. That being said, my life with Ophir, my plan, my path would have remained unchanged whether or not I knew. It will remain that way until I know what you will have to say, and it will continue even after you've spoken your piece. You, on the other hand, are clearly insane. So, either we do it my way, or we don't do it at all."

Suley's voice lost its nervous edge. Her spine straightened. She extended an arm to stop Dwyn. With excruciating coldness, she said, "I'd like to bring myself to regret giving you a piece of my hope, but regret is a useless emotion. I am disappointed in your ignorance, but you're right. That is my problem. And no, Dwyn, things will not continue for you if you don't learn what I know. Your journey may come to an end very, very soon."

Suley turned without waiting for a response, leaving Dwyn's eyes wide, her mouth parted in a silent protest as the *click-clack* of her shoes faded.

It took thirty minutes, two minor tantrums, an endless stream of panicked justifications, and tracking down two cups of breakfast tea before Dwyn was ready to apologize. She carried the second glass of tea laced with a shot of hot brandy in her hand as a servant led her to a new wing of the castle.

Tarkhany's royal party was staying on the third floor, their view of Gwydir unobstructed by low-lying walls and buildings. Dwyn paused in surprise as she stilled near a window. She hadn't realized how large the city was. It was rather charming in the pink morning light. While it was nothing compared to Sulgrave's sprawling territories, it wasn't nearly the cobblestoned town she'd imagined. The evidence of shops, churches, towers, cathedrals, restaurants, taverns, and homes rolled over hills and between trees, all against the backdrop of Raascot's snowcapped mountains. A tiny, nostalgic clutch in her belly reminded her of the sheer peaks she'd left behind when she'd crossed the Straits. She didn't miss Sulgrave. She didn't miss the family who'd never appreciated her, the peers that had scorned her, or the wanted posters and constabulary who knew her name. She did miss the food, though, and no matter how far she ventured or how many years passed, she always missed the mountains.

"Lady Dwyn?"

Dwyn realized she'd lost precious moments staring out the window. An uncomfortable embarrassment rushed through her, terrified that someone might see her as anything other than an ethereal, unapproachable fixture at the princess's hip. She couldn't risk word spreading that she had any traits beyond *reclusive* and *anomalous*. She snapped back to attention, gesturing for the servant to continue.

The attendant passed several doors before arriving at one in the furthest corner, opening the door without knocking. Surprise raked Dwyn until she realized the servant had led her into an antechamber with little but a window and a lutist. A tired-looking man in a pile of pillows rested in the corner, refusing to let his fingers still even as he looked up to greet them. His eyes held a world-weary heaviness that he didn't dare open his mouth to express. He looked away, returning unfocused eyes to a distant nowhere as he plucked the melancholy chords of a solemn song.

The servant paused before the second door. She lifted her hand to knock, but the door opened before her knuckles made contact with the wood. The servant adjusted her weight, her pattern clearly disrupted. "Lady Suley," she said, "Lady Dwyn is here to see you."

"We are many things," said Suley, "but neither of us is a lady."

The attendant dipped her head with a confused acknowledgment before excusing herself. Suley looked at Dwyn with neither forgiveness nor amusement. She stared at the siren for a long while before extending the gesture that would allow Dwyn to enter her room.

The moment Dwyn's feet crossed the threshold, she jolted as if stepping into the static charge of wool socks rubbed against coarse fibers. The entire room hummed with noise. Near the window, six birdcages were stacked, one on top of the other. Each bird chirped in musical chatter to the others, engaged in conversation with their unseen partners. A three-tiered fountain that should have only existed in the courtyard burbled noisily from the corner of her room, disappearing through an unseen enchantment as the water was funneled from its base to its musical top. Dwyn wondered what feats of strength and power it had required to get such an object onto the third floor of the castle. Even with her powers for water, she wasn't sure if she could keep something recycling with such consistency. She leaned in close to look at the runes etched into the fountain.

"Impressed?" Suley asked, voice cold.

Dwyn turned slowly, understanding the chill in the room. She deserved every drop of vitriol she received. She surveyed Suley once more, taking in a new meaning behind her appearance. She'd absorbed the initial wave of jewelry, tattoos, and hair. She'd seen an exterior meant to shock and distract. Speaking with Suley had revealed the weaponization of her appearance, protecting her from the pain, the roar, and the incessant misery within. As she eyed her now, Dwyn became aware of a third layer. She saw a woman in pain, a woman clever enough to distract, and also someone who had not only found ways to survive, but who'd done so in spite of that which plagued her. The frost of Suley's words, the ice in her posture told Dwyn that if she were to be struck by lightning and die in the room, Suley would not mourn her lost chance at an opportunity to live without noise. She'd just been excited at the prospect of a quiet life, and Dwyn had found her enthusiasm annoying.

"I'm sorry."

"You should be," Suley said. Her gaze was as cold as the Frozen Straits Dwyn had left behind.

"Not for what I said," Dwyn amended, "but for misjudging you. I'm sorry for my assumptions. I invalidated your excitement. I can't imagine how painful your existence must be. If I lived with constant overstimulation, I would also seek relief. I seek far more for arguably less substantial rationale."

Suley held Dwyn's eyes for a moment. The birds chirped, the fountain burbled, the tired lutist in the antechamber strummed as they stared at one another. At long last, Suley said, "Do you have a solution?"

Dwyn sucked in a breath. "I might. May I sit?"

She perched on the edge of the chair without waiting for an answer. Suley remained standing. She joined the birds, opening a cage and offering her finger until a small, rose-colored songbird hopped onto her outstretched hand. She cooed at the bird, and the bird tilted its head back and forth, the bright red feathers around its eyes exacerbating its curiosity as it eyed her. It chirped in return, both woman and bird ignoring Dwyn wholly.

"Have you met the neutralizer?" Dwyn asked.

"I have," Suley said.

"And? Will he be amenable to our cause?"

"She," Suley corrected, "is both comforting and disappointing in how easy she's been to manipulate. I am lovely, am I not? She's invited me to her room for drinks tonight, as I expected she might. Do you know the worth of an evening without noise?"

Dwyn shook her head.

"No, because there is no price. There are no silvers or crowns equal to a silent night."

Dwyn didn't bother to argue. Instead, she asked, "I know you prioritize your quiet night, but perhaps you could try to make an ally? Stay friendly long enough for me to borrow her gift for manufacturing. I assume you'll have her won over by the morning. This time tomorrow, I could have something made for you. I can't guarantee its effectiveness, but I'll try. Bring your neutralizer to meet me and we'll make our first attempt."

"Good," Suley said, still looking at the bird. It hopped

up and down the length of her finger, cocking its head from side to side as contemplated its shot at freedom. Rather than attempt to take flight, the bird was content to be returned to its cage.

Dwyn stood, face ripe with discomfort. She wasn't used to being so wholly ignored, but she'd said what she'd come to say. She rested her palm on the cool iron of the doorknob before she heard the voice behind her.

"On the topic of manufacturing?"

Dwyn paused, hand on the door. The music beyond stretched between them, bars spanning into a full verse as the musician plucked his tired notes.

"On good faith, I'll offer you a piece of knowledge that you do not deserve and that you have not earned. But I appreciate your apology, and for that, there's something I'll share with you. The woman, Cybele? Do you know of her?"

Dwyn's fingers tightened on the handle. Her heart kicked against her ribs. She turned, looking over her shoulder. "I do," she said.

"Then you know her gift?"

"I do."

Suley considered this. "The bands she offers Ophir do not strengthen bonds, as they claim. These rings *fuse* bonds." Suley closed the door to the birdcage and met Dwyn's eyes for a meaningful moment. "Do you understand the implication?"

"...I do."

"Tomorrow is the last full day before the recess has ended and the summit resumes," Suley said, voice free of feeling.

Dwyn's insides froze, down to her toes. She turned back to the door. Without looking at Suley, she said, "I'll meet you tomorrow. We'll put an end to your noise."

+   +   +   +

Ophir nearly swallowed her tongue in her surprise. She'd expected Dwyn had returned with tea and run out of hands, rendering her unable to open the door. She'd expected the knock to have come from impatient kicking, not from a well-dressed guard. She was glad she'd tucked herself into tall socks and a nightdress meant for sleep. Opening the door in her towel—or worse, following Dwyn's insistence on nudity when in the bedroom—would not have improved conditions.

She stood at the door, eyes wide, staring at Harland.

"Can I come in?" he asked.

Ophir looked over her shoulder at the room that had become her entire world. Her four-post bed, her writing desk, her mirror and armoire, her bathing room, and the heavy curtains that blocked the light of the garden. If it weren't for the servants' insistence on getting her up and out of bed, the sheets would be a rumpled mess, her clothes would be on the floor, and empty bottles of water and wine would be strewn about the chamber. Instead, she looked at a profoundly clean, empty room. Dwyn had left on some unknown mission, though given the empty teacups, she assumed it was for a fresh pitcher. Tyr had set out to announce himself to the castle as a new arrival. This might be the only opportunity for true privacy with Harland. But did she want it?

He didn't push. His hazel eyes, green dotted with flecks of brown and gold, turned down with an intimacy that she knew all too well. The dark stones of Gwydir cast a dramatic backdrop against his gold-brown hair, creating a stark outline for the fair fae in her doorway. Nervous tension kept his shoulders back, his muscles rigid. It told her that Harland had no idea whether she'd let him in or burn him with a ball of flame. Despite his concerns, he faced her, prepared for the consequences.

Ophir released a breath. A sadness washed over her. He had been her friend. Her ally. Her confidant, drinking buddy, and lover. Now he faced her like a man quite literally prepared to burn.

She pushed the door open, stepping away and gesturing for Harland to enter. He looked uncertainly about the space.

"He's not here, if that's what you're wondering."

Harland looked at her.

"I know that you two know of each other's existence—you know, beyond Henares. Tyr's introducing himself to the court at present. It was time for him to make friends in the castle."

Harland's lips parted in a question, but he closed them again. Clearly, he'd come with something else on his mind and now was not the time to be sidetracked. His eyes raked over her with aching slowness. It wasn't the lust she'd seen gleam from time to time, nor the jolly friendship, the coy banter, or even the cat and mouse of ward-and-charge. He looked at her with nothing but pain.

"I failed you," he said.

She looked away. They hadn't been alone like this in a long, long time. For years, Harland had been the only person who'd rivaled Caris for her attention. She'd had friends, and parties, and social circles before the incident. She'd enjoyed alcohol, dancing, and lovers before the sharp end of a dagger had sliced through an abdomen and ended life as she had known it.

"I've failed you in so many ways, Firi. But the thing I regret most?"

Ophir looked at him with weary eyes. "Letting me out of my room the night of Berinth's party?"

Harland sank noiselessly against the stones, echoing the motion he'd done on the wall in Aubade so many times. He'd never been one for the bench, or the chair, or the bed. A stone at his back and a smile on his face was how she knew him best. The only thing missing now was the joy. His arms rested on his knees, eyes fixed on an unseen memory as he said, "The night I came into your room and you were covered in sand and bandages and blood. You had manifested that night, Firi. And I... I regret what I said to you when you were in pain. I...the things I said..."

"You were in pain, too," she responded. Ophir resisted the familiar, unhealed impulse to sit beside him. Muscle memory longed for her to slide into the comfortable place near his heat, to breathe in his familiar scent, to feel safe in his company. A part of her realized that she could. They could just be Ophir and Harland again.

She leaned against the intersecting wall only three arm's lengths from where Harland sat. Ophir lowered herself slowly until she hugged her knees, eye level with the man who'd stood beside her longer than any other. Aside from Caris, he'd been the most consistent fixture in her life. Until he wasn't.

"I miss you," Harland said.

The words were a jagged thorn puncturing her heart. She slowly bled into her chest as she stared at him. She could make the pain go away for them both. She could end his suffering. She could make herself feel better. She could crawl into his arms, rest her head against his chest, promise a life free from chaos, dedicate herself to calm, to rationality, to a world without monsters or flame or turmoil. But her words would be lies.

"I could move to Gwydir," he said quietly. "I'd serve as your escort wherever you went, Firi. I'd respect any relationship you do or don't want to have, friend or guard... I just want to be with you, whatever shape it takes. I'd rather be here as a silent sentry than not be in your life."

"Harland..." She squeezed her knees to her chest.

"Things are different," he agreed, keeping his voice low. "Everything is different. I know. I'm not asking for you and I to shoot the shit on the wall like we once did. I'm not asking for us to watch the sun go down over the western sea. I'm not asking for..." His words caught, the russets, emeralds, and golds of his eyes snagging on her as he stopped himself from whatever memory threatened him. She knew precisely what tempted him. She could almost feel the calluses of his hands brush against the skin of her hips, his kisses on her throat, the tug of his fist against her roots as his fingers balled in her hair. Their sex had been spectacular—and it had been a mistake.

She wondered how much of its pleasure had stemmed from how profoundly inappropriate it had been. Would he have felt as wonderful, would she have felt as full, would she have seen the All Mother in the same explosion of tantalizing stars, if it had been a casual affair? They'd never let it happen again, so perhaps she'd never know.

Ophir extended a hand, wrapping her delicate fingers around the broad hand that had remained tucked against his knee. "I understand," she said, voice scarcely above a whisper. "I know you miss her, but the girl you cared for doesn't exist anymore. And I want you to be happy, Harland. I do grieve those moments. I grieve Caris. I grieve the days before I knew tragedy. I grieve a lot of things. But they're a part of the path that forged me. Would I take her back? Absolutely. Every moment of every day, I would take her back, but it's a bell, Harland. It's a bell that can't be unrung."

His gold-brown brows furrowed. He asked, "Do you ever get sad? Over...this?"

She matched his frown, her face crestfallen as she held his gaze. "It does make me sad," she said. "It hurts to see the ones I loved mourning the pieces of me I left behind."

SEVENTEEN

✦   ✦   ✦   ✦

NTERESTING." ZITA SMILED.

Suley followed her queen's gaze through the arched window into the castle's front gardens. Zita had caught Suley riffling through the kitchen's liquor cabinets, hoping for a way to quiet the noise. Her meeting with Dwyn had only exacerbated her state of relentless agitation. Zita had wrapped her fingers around a bottle of brandy and led them to a room off the primary dining area. She'd tipped a shot of dark, sweet liquor into each of their hot teacups. It was never too early in the day for a drink. The northern wind had picked up, rendering the evenings too cold for time outside. Besides, as Suley had pointed out, it was just as noisy in the garden as it was indoors.

Suley caught what Zita had spied between the iron lattice of the windowpanes. Past the half-naked branches, beyond the dark stone buildings, and just over the black, idle river that separated the castle from the city, a man approached on foot. No one accompanied him. While the streets were more or less vacant in the chill, she'd spent enough time in Raascot to spot the coppers and bronzes of its people. The face approaching did not quite have the colorless skin of Farehold, the rich tones of Tarkhany, nor the light browns of Raascot.

"Is that him?"

"You tell me," Zita responded.

"You haven't seen him either?"

Zita tilted her head. "I'm told there was a Sulgrave man spotted at the Sunrise Slaughter, but as you'll recall, it was not I who was present." Zita's eyes narrowed. Suley heard the onslaught of noise as the queen saw flashes of Tempus in the orange, black, and white gown moments before the winged serpent had appeared to forever change the world.

Suley leaned her forehead against the cool glass. "He's handsome," she said idly.

Zita took a slow sip of the hot tea, enjoying the burn of the liquor and the warmth of the aromatic leaves. Her gaze raked over the man in the distance before returning to the wine. She blew out a puff of air before saying, "He has a stronger build than I would have expected. Most fae men are lithe for agility."

Suley's lower lip lifted, pouting slightly as she continued to watch him through the window. Two Raascot centurions had exited the front gates of Castle Gwydir to meet him. She watched the exchange, not caring what was spoken. She watched the Raascot fae, one winged and one without the black, crow-like feathers, as they intercepted the man. "You'd think someone who could step into the place between things would care more about being silent than having strength. I can't fathom his incentive for all those muscles."

Zita said, "Perhaps someone who relies on their silence for survival knows a thing or two about what it means to feel powerless."

"It's odd, isn't it?"

Zita raised a brow.

"A princess of Farehold has abandoned her countrymen. Is it odd that she's surrounded herself with people who aren't her own? Do you think she's defected to Sulgrave?"

"You know her thoughts," Zita said. "You tell me."

Suley had nothing to say. She couldn't speak to the

princess's thoughts, or rationale, or of the company she kept. She asked, "What tale will they spin? On his arrival, that is?"

Zita lifted a shoulder. "Does it matter? I told the princess that you and I knew—no one else. To all the world, this man—one briefly spied at best—was left amid the calamity in Midnah. She decided of her own accord that it was best for him to step into the light. I'm curious to see how the castle will react to another foreign guest. It has its share of dignitaries from the continent's corners as it is. When it comes to Ophir, I don't know what to make of her, but... I like her."

Suley shifted her face slightly. She looked at her queen, resting her cheek against the chilled glass. She frowned. "I've heard the noise about Ophir and her sister. Everyone says the wrong princess died."

Zita reclined against the wall and drained her glass— thirty silver crowns of burgundy liquid vanquished in three swallows. She made a satisfied noise before reaching for the glass once more, refilling hers nearly to the brim.

"*Everyone*"—her voice rested heavily on the word— "allowed the world to turn precisely as-is for six centuries. Perhaps *everyone* does not have an opinion worth valuing."

+ + + +

"Dwyn. What a pleasant surprise to see you out of your room before lunchtime," Evander said tightly. She drifted up to four men: three of Raascot lineage and one all-too-familiar Sulgrave face.

Dwyn flashed her sweetest smile. "I'm so glad you think so."

Evander did an impressive job of maintaining a neutral expression, though his eyes betrayed his displeasure. His posture remained rigid as he stood in the foyer between two of Raascot's centurions and the man he perceived to be a new, unfamiliar addition to the castle. He kept his hands clasped behind his back, ever the courtly advisor.

"I presume you two know each other?"

166

Dwyn kept her expression soft. "You presume correctly."

She looked between Evander, the centurions, and Tyr, who was subpar at controlling his impatience. He did his best to express stately sincerity, and his best fell short. Dwyn recalled a poignant encounter where Harland had accused her of needing acting lessons. She had half a mind to whistle for the guard now to have him weigh in on Tyr's disappointing performance on the landing.

"We traveled together from Sulgrave," Tyr said, delivery flat. "After the slaughter, I was surprised to find my companions had left. I'm grateful there was a direct link between Tarkhany and Raascot."

Evander looked over Tyr's shoulder, as if to peer through the trees and perceive the door that stood in the forest. He frowned. "What's to keep everyone in Tarkhany from coming through the door?"

Dwyn scoffed, drawing their attention to her irreverent expression. "The climate, of course. We're already freezing, and it isn't even true winter. Do you think anyone from Tarkhany is going to want to step into the snow? In their fair-weather fashion? Prop another rock against the door during the temperate months if it gives you peace of mind."

"You're quite a bit farther north than us, are you not?" Evander asked.

"And far more powerful," she said. "We mastered the climate long ago."

He looked to Tyr for clarification, but Tyr did not contradict her.

The skeptical gaze hit her from two sides. Tyr seemed unsure as to why she was helping him. Evander maintained his walls of distrust. Fair enough, she thought. Evander was right to be wary.

Dwyn shrugged. "I was just headed out to see the city. Tyr, would you like to take a walk?"

Evander said, "Our guest has just arrived. There are

meetings to be had, things to be discussed, and I'm sure he'll want to settle in."

"He'll be free for all of those meetings when we return," Dwyn dismissed.

"I'll send a guard with you."

"That's quite all right," Dwyn said. "We're merely sight-seeing. I suspect we'll walk along the river and be back within the hour. I don't know if you know this about Sulgrave, but our city is beautiful. The mountains are to die for. I have no idea how Gwydir could possibly compare. I'm just curious what Tyr will think! I'd love to wander Gwydir so that he and I can judge your capital in private."

Evander blinked.

Dwyn looped her elbow through Tyr's arm and marched him beyond the castle doors. She regretted not grabbing a cloak, but it was nothing she couldn't solve within a moment. The early evidence of winter came in the form of a few stray snowflakes. A biting chill whipped her dress to the side, lashing her hair against her face. Despite herself, she huddled into Tyr's shape, hoping he'd block the winter wind. She waited until their feet hit the bridge over the dark, slow-moving river before she allowed them to speak.

"What are you doing?" he asked. He kept his voice to a whisper despite their distance from the castle.

Dwyn scanned the smattering of faces that rushed in from the streets to escape the chill. Inclement weather aside, it was still a city. She huffed. "We made a deal," she said. "And I'm here to make good on my end. Pick a civilian. It's time to teach you how to drain."

EIGHTEEN

✦   ✦   ✦   ✦

A MOURNING DOVE COOED GENTLY BEYOND OPHIR'S window. Her eyes remained closed, hand reaching to pull herself closer to Dwyn. She wanted to tuck their curves together until they melted back into the sweetest part of sleep—the moments after waking up when one realized that no responsibility in the world was more important than rest. Her fingers met empty air.

Ophir's lips puckered, her forehead creased, and her eyebrows bunched long before she allowed her lashes to flutter open. She saw only the nearly imperceptible shades of black, gray, and pewter as shadows and gloom intersected. The sheets were rumpled and turned down as if Dwyn had slipped silently from the bed in the night. She sat up, listening to the mourning dove's gentle cooing. She frowned at the world that existed beyond the drawn curtains. It seemed too cold for doves, though perhaps she didn't know much of where the little birds came and went. It wasn't even winter, and she was already colder in Gwydir than she'd ever been in decades of life in Aubade. Ophir rolled over in bed, turning to the empty space where she'd hoped Tyr's indentation might be.

No. Now that they knew of his presence, they'd set him up with his own room. Tyr could have still stepped into the space between things and slept beside her, yet he'd kept his distance since his formal arrival. Though that had happened intermittently throughout their time in Gwydir, she'd usually assumed he'd gotten stuck in another room while in the place between things, and she'd left him to live his unseen missions in peace. He was good at what he did, and she knew he'd be back. Now that he was in his corporeal form, would he be with her as often?

Ophir rubbed her arms, though she wasn't truly cold. The castle had been etched with engravings to capture and circulate the heat from the fireplaces that warmed their rooms even when the logs weren't burning. This cold was of an existential nature. Her chest squeezed as she thought of how Harland had sat on the floor and told he'd move to Gwydir, he'd be there for her, that he just wanted to be in her life. She could have accepted his offer. She could have awoken with the knowledge that he was probably outside her door as her ever-present centurion. She could have called out to him, certain he'd enter.

Knowing she'd been right to turn him away didn't make it any less painful.

Ophir slid out from between the sheets and pulled back the curtains. The sky was still a gentle shade of mauve, which was a color she never got to see when Dwyn was in her bed. She would have been well on her way to three more hours of sleep if she hadn't awoken to loneliness. Instead, she pressed her fingers against the glass to feel the late-autumn chill, watching the last of the leaves as they broke free from their prisons and whipped to the gray-brown grass. A few orange and red leaves landed in the large, dark river that separated the castle from the city beyond. She watched the specks of color disappear as the river snaked around a corner, content to journey from the snowmelt of the northern mountains until it emptied itself in the western sea. She idly wondered how many logs, leaves, stones, and trinkets from Raascot she'd seen washed up on the shores of Aubade's cliffs.

She kept the curtains open as she dressed. It was the last day of their recess before the summit would resume, and no one expected her. There would be no servants to help her interlace a bodice or attendants to pin and braid her hair. Instead, she selected a simple shift with a fur shawl for the winter chill. She bundled up for comfort over fashion, but she couldn't help but feel like a true northerner as she spied herself in the mirror. There was something wild and fierce about the fur and the way the cold light caught on her hair. She stared into the mirror, her thoughts drifting to what Zita had implied regarding her ancestors. Perhaps they had been meant for the arctic chill of the mountains. Maybe the intricately carved pillars, the northern pay of long-forgotten trade routes that had fallen to disuse, and the blue-black stones and snow had all belonged to distant pieces of her heritage. Perhaps she'd never know.

Ophir wasn't sure what to do with herself. She paced her room for a few minutes, brushed her hair, braided it, tore the braid out, and braided it once more. She moved restlessly about the room until she decided she'd lose her mind if she stayed within its walls while both Dwyn and Tyr were unaccounted for. She wasn't sure why she moved so quietly. She was meant to be Raascot's queen. She shouldn't have felt the need to ease the door closed so no one heard the latch click behind her. She shouldn't have tiptoed down the runners that lined the corridors. She shouldn't have held her breath around every corner. Some part of her knew that she'd never be comfortable here, irrespective of the circumstances. Whether she was here as a guest or had ruled as queen for fifty years, Castle Gwydir was not her home. Nor was Castle Aubade. Nor the Tarkhany Palace.

She squeezed her lids shut, willing moisture to soothe her dry eyes and hoping it might smooth out the wrinkles in her nerves. She wasn't sure where she was going, but her feet carried her forward, out of the castle and into the garden. She caught the remnants of a discolored smudge on the court-yard stones before she understood where her feet were taking her. She'd only been to their room once before, but it was a straight shot from the garden. Ophir followed the urge until she'd reached the medium's door.

She lifted her knuckles to knock but paused at the disruption of a gravelly voice that wafted through the door. Her breath caught in her throat when a feminine voice brighter than spring blossoms answered in soothing, windswept tones.

"The darkness is clearer every day."

Caris. Caris was speaking.

Ophir was going to be sick. She felt like emptying the previous night's dinner onto the carpet. She forgot how to breathe. Her eyes dried out once more, not from the cold, arid temperature but from utter shock. Her sister was in there. Her sister was...

She had seen Caris in this medium's room as well.

Caris was dead.

As if in answer, Ceneth said, "I'm doing everything you told me to do. You want me to marry your sister? I'm marrying her. You see a future of wings and dreams, and that just sounds like sadness and memories, Caris. You keep asking me to do this without you, and I can't. Have I made it darker by visiting you? Is this my fault?"

Ophir rested her cheek gently against the cool wood of the door as she listened on bated breath for her sister's response.

"I will tell you then what I told you once, twice, always. I said not to visit me."

"I can't let you go," he said, voice scarcely loud enough to seep between the fibers of the wood.

"I've known," she said, her answer just as quiet.

Ophir strained, fingers digging into the wood as she fought the urge to burst through the door.

"Everything has fallen apart, Caris. Not only is the

172

continent falling to pieces between Raascot and Farehold, but Tarkhany is now in play. Queen Zita has shown cards I didn't even realize might be on the table. Does she mean to go to war for ancestral lands? My forefathers were wronged by Eero's forefathers a millennia before they stole the seat at Castle Aubade. Zita was a fool for trusting them after seeing what they'd done to my people."

"You are not from the mountains, but here you thrive. You have retaken your homelands, though you are not alive to see the southern throne."

Ceneth's growl betrayed his frustration. "What does that *mean*? Do I go to war? Are you telling me that I win the war trying to retake Farehold but die in the battle?"

Ophir held her breath. She couldn't believe what she was hearing. Was Ceneth truly planning open war with her father?

Sorrow dripped like dewdrops as Caris replied, "This is not a war of swords and champions. It's one of dreams and—"

"Wings. So I've heard." After a pregnant pause, he said, "Tarkhany's involvement is not something I considered. It's not something I prepared for. Yet, she brings up the past and future with so much implication… We've barely evacuated our people from Farehold. I can't imagine standing against our lost land now. What does she want from me? What's the right move?"

"I was not your advisor," Caris said.

"You mean, you're not my advisor."

"I won't be, I am not, though perhaps, in a different life, in a life where I was beside you…"

"You are beside me," he said.

"No. There was no future where I sat beside you now, while you face my father, the Queen of Tarkhany, your bride, the darkness. Can you see the tapestry? It's murky. I see the tangled spool. In some places, it's neatly wrapped, and when I tug, I see where it leads. And then it catches, Ceneth. It snags. My eyes followed the loop. I saw the snarl. I will only see the knot. Will you understand?"

"What does this have to do with Ophir? Our wedding—I don't want it. I have no desire to marry your sister. I don't want anyone other than you. You know I'll be kind to her," he promised. "You know I'll be fair and just and treat her as though she were my sister. But I can't imagine how my life and hers intersect, Caris. Please, tell me. Please, tell me what to do. What does she have to do with any of this?"

Ophir's heart thundered.

Silence stretched between the three of them. Within the room, all was quiet. In the hall, nothing stirred. Ophir did not dare to breathe, lest anyone catch her presence. She pressed her ear against the wood even harder, hoping against all hopes that she wouldn't miss her sister's words.

"Ophir is the end of the world. She is its beginning."

NINETEEN

✦   ✦   ✦   ✦

D WYN'S BLINK WAS SLOW AND HEAVY. ONE EYELID AT A time, she forced herself to remain interested in those before her.

"Galena?" She repeated the name, a frown on her lips. She examined the Raascot woman, from the glossy sheet of black hair to the enormous dark eyes that faded into a golden gradient near her pupils. Perhaps Dwyn should feel more in common with Suley. They were both terribly foreign in a country that had no familiarity with their presence.

She couldn't bring herself to conjure sympathy.

Galena made a face. "And what kind of a name is Dwyn?"

Dwyn narrowed her eyes. "A lovely one, thank you very much."

"As is mine."

Suley clapped her hands together to draw their attention. Six cages of birds continued to chirp. Water babbled. A new lutist—a human in his late teens—plucked chords with musical enthusiasm beyond her doorway. "Galena is my friend," Suley clarified. "And Dwyn is a...manufacturer."

Dwyn's hand twitched against the urge to smack the fae. She'd confidently announced to all the castle that she manipulated water, and she had been thrilled to receive credit for the power to travel across the map. She hoped Galena hadn't heard of the aforementioned gifts, or the castle was going to get suspicious.

Suley turned away from the small writing desk in her room. She'd lined a number of raw materials—namely minerals, from iron and silver to gold and bronze—ready to be manipulated with a fae with the power to manufacture.

Dwyn sank her weight into her hip. "So, are we going to make Suley a pendant or not?"

Suley took a step to put herself between them. "I'd like it to be something that goes on my upper arm. Something that can't be removed unless they're willing to kill me altogether. Make it gold."

Galena, a striking fae with the glossy wings that adorned those of Raascot lineage, frowned. She tucked her wings behind her before moving to the bed. She sank onto its ledge as she examined Suley, saying, "I understand you not wanting it to be a necklace or earring or anything that could be easily torn free, but I'd challenge you to reconsider. If it's a ring, even if your enemies find you, the worst they can do is take your finger. If it's a cuff for your bicep..."

"I met a priestess with a ward on her bicep," Suley responded. "It's quite common among the holy. I think it would add an extra element of mystery, don't you?"

Dwyn and Galena swapped skeptical expressions.

"How long did you study?" Galena asked.

Dwyn looked to Suley before she realized that the question was being asked of her. "Oh, I'm a natural. I haven't trained."

Galena's dark hair danced around her shoulders as she shook her head. "Manufacturing isn't enough as an innate ability. Those who do it with lasting effects train under the master manufacturer at the continent's university. If I'm able to make something that neutralizes..."

"I can also speak to metal," Dwyn said.

176

It was the neutralizer's turn to blink. "Oh. That's...lucky."

Suley looked to her sharply, then looked away.

Dwyn had borrowed more than one life in preparation. Tyr had not been thrilled, nor had he been a quick study as they'd practiced. She didn't have the patience for his soft heart. A killer was a killer whether or not they felt bad about their actions. The pitying apology he'd offered to his targets before taking them down had changed neither their fates nor their eternal resting places. Still, he preferred to cling to his moral superiority as he honed his craft, and Dwyn had taken more than she'd needed. Manufacturing was a given. Speaking to metal was essential. But she knew she'd need to shield herself from Galena's neutralizing ability if she hoped to craft while withstanding the fae's abilities. She was also quite certain she'd need to heal if she was rapidly burning through one power after the other. Seven corpses later, she didn't know how long her stolen lives would last, but she was ready.

She had a ticking clock over her borrowed abilities and a need to know whatever secrets Suley thought were worth such a trade. Should Dwyn fail the first time, she needed to be sure she could make more than one attempt at manufacturing. She'd also prepared for the need to fuse metal, in case basic manufacturing didn't come with such nuance. She was ready.

"I've never worked with a manufacturer," Galena said.

With the flick of her wrist, Dwyn motioned for the raw materials to collect beneath them. Suley moved quickly as she relocated the precious metals.

"I've got it," Dwyn lied. "Just focus your intention."

Dwyn had seen manufacturing exactly three times in her life. The first had been before the age of seven in the company of her parents, years before they'd informed her that she was too chaotic and unlovable to live with them. The second had been in her third decade of life. She'd smiled as a manufacturer had worked with a fae to create a luck charm. The fae woman, imbued with fortune, had bowed and begun the auction for the sacred object at more than Dwyn's life was worth. The third had taken place in Aubade only a few months after her arrival in the southern kingdom. She'd watched a manufacturer and a fae with the desired ability cup their hands together as they brought their vision into the world.

"Are you ready?" Galena asked.

Dwyn let her hands bloom like a flower, palms open and ready.

Galena made no attempt to conceal her disbelief as she joined hands with the siren.

"Picture what you want," Dwyn said, closing her eyes. "Just... See your power flowing into Suley's cuff."

"And if it doesn't work?" Galena asked.

"It will," Dwyn said, eyes closed.

It wasn't the seamless magical event Dwyn might have imagined. She didn't peel back her hands to reveal a flawless cuff. Regardless, despite a number of misshapen bangles, a collection of grunts, three agitated noises from Galena, and a high-pitched whine from Suley, Dwyn convinced them to try and try again. The morning light that streamed through the window disappeared behind the gray, overcast clouds of a bubbling sky. Their frustrated noises were lost against the chirping birds and distant lutist.

Dwyn groaned. She dropped her hands from Galena's and bared her teeth as she looked toward the music floating through the door. "Maybe I need to speak to the lutist."

"No," Suley said quickly.

Galena's lips twisted into a frown. "If the music is disturbing her..."

"It's not," Suley said curtly. She glared at Dwyn, and Dwyn returned the fire.

Truthfully, she knew she wasn't in need of a new power source. Her metals were still bending. Objects were crafting. Her cup had not emptied. That said, she didn't appreciate Suley cutting off her possibilities.

Dwyn wasn't sure how much time she'd lost to the sun's slow passage across the sky. She didn't care how many disappointed faces Suley made or how many irritated noises came from Galena. She'd done her due diligence before arriving in Suley's room. Her actions would undoubtedly be a series of mysterious tragedies mourned by families and communities for years to come, but that was the price of art. The leader of the Blood Pact had once told the members of her gang that they couldn't make omelets without breaking a few eggs, though she hardly believed he'd invented the saying. Despite leaving Sulgrave's blood gang and everyone within it, she'd retained his irreverent saying.

Sometimes eggs had to crack.

Despite the sun's disappearance behind the clouds, the bright, shadowless day told her she'd nearly surpassed the noon bell. She grabbed Galena's hands a bit too roughly, intentionally ignoring Suley's silent disappointment from across the room as she squeezed Galena's fingers a final time. When she pulled her hands away, two halves of an antiqued-yellow cuff rested in them.

A slow, proud smile spread across her mouth as she turned her face toward Suley.

Suley heard the proud exclamation in her mind long before anything was spoken. She snatched the halves from Dwyn's hands and banged them uselessly together around her bicep.

"Hold still," Dwyn murmured, calling on the ability to speak to metal. She fused the cuff together before meeting Suley's stare.

Suley's braids swished from side to side as she looked at them doubtfully. "Galena, can you leave? So I know if the device working, that is, or if it's only quiet in your presence?"

Galena headed to the door. "How far do you need me to go?"

Suley shifted her weight impatiently. "I'll call on you tomorrow, I promise. Would you give me some time?"

Clearly unhappy with the outcome of the morning's taxing events, Galena departed.

Dwyn and Suley waited in silence for a long, long time. Suley ran to the door and demanded that the lutist cease his playing.

"I've heard it said that you speak to water?" she asked, voice hushed.

Dwyn flicked her wrist and paused the fountain without further prompting.

The birds continued chirping, but Suley's eyes showed something else entirely. They widened with each moment that passed, eyebrows lifting, fingers clenching the cool, gilded metal of her cuff. The birds continued to sing to one another, unbothered. Gray light refracted off of Suley's shocked profile, glinting off of the slope of her nose, the curve of her cheek, the bright gleam in her eyes.

"It's so quiet," she said at long last.

"And?" Dwyn prompted. "Prove to me that I shouldn't kill you right now. What information do you have that was worth such a gift?"

"And," Suley said, "everyone at the summit—save for Ceneth and his advisors—knows that you murdered Caris."

TWENTY

✦ ✦ ✦ ✦

SEEING TYR'S FACE AFTER ALL THIS TIME WAS LIKE WELCOMing him back from the dead.

"Goddess be damned, thank you, *thank you*," Ophir prayed and cursed as she hurried. The flood of emotion that washed over her felt as if the Raasay River had burst through its lazy banks surrounding Castle Gwydir and cooled the tension in the corridor. She rounded the corner to see Tyr emerging from the room he'd been assigned.

Still half a hall away, she beamed at Tyr, walk becoming a run as she closed the distance between them. Her gratitude swelled as he opened his arms, enveloping her in his fully corporeal form. Not only could she smell the campfire smoke, cedar, and leather, not only could she feel the skin, the arms, the cloth, but she could see the chest that she buried her face into, the hands that tucked themselves against her lower back, the mouth that buried itself in her hair.

"You were a ghost," Ophir hiccupped into his shoulder, doing her best not to cry. "I can't believe I have you back."

"I never left your side," Tyr said quietly.

"It's not the same." She tucked herself in more tightly, forcing her body against his as if wanting to crawl into his skin. No grip was tight enough; no grasp was secure enough. She wanted to vanish, her skin, her clothes, her hair, her breath becoming one with him. It had only taken a minute in his presence for her want him to consume her.

"Come, let's go," he said into her hair. "Back to your room?"

She smiled. "It's been a long time since I've been able to look at you while—"

The corner of his mouth tugged up in a crooked grin, but there was an emptiness behind his eyes. He loosened his hold as he said, "Ophir, I want to be around you for more than that."

She pulled away. "I can count on one hand the number of times you've called me Ophir."

His attempt at a smile was little more than a flickering candle in the wind as he repeated, "Come on, Princess. Let's go back to your room."

"And get you out of those clothes? After all, you must have traveled across the continent to get here. Let's get you into the bath." She waited for him to take the bait and laugh at their ruse.

He offered a half-hearted smirk in return. "Believe me when I tell you there's nothing I'd like more, Princess."

"Tell me what you would do to me," she said, stepping closer to him. He looked over his shoulder, but she looked only into his eyes. "Tell me," she repeated.

Tyr had begun to lead her down the hall but pushed out a breath of air as he stopped to examine her. "You want to hear what I want to do to you?" he asked.

"Deeply."

He held her unwavering gaze. After a pulse, he said, "Don't look behind you; just picture the hard wall of stone. Keep looking at me."

She blinked once as she refused to break his stare.

"Four steps backward. Your back would hit the wall so hard you'd see stars. First, you'd arch your head against the wall. You'd give me full access to your throat, your mouth, your breasts. Picture how your eyes would close, your lips would part."

"Tyr..."

"Hush, Princess." He ran his fingers through her hair. She felt a rush of wetness between her legs as he looked down at her. Her chest heated, cheeks flushing as he said, "It would take me three seconds to get the flimsy cotton of that dress up over your hips. I'd help you up just enough for you to wrap your legs around my waist. Are you wearing anything under it?"

"I—"

"I'll take that as a no," he said, voice barely more than a low growl. "Don't think I can't smell how wet you are."

She swallowed.

"You'd breathe out as I breathe in. You'd open up for every inch of me. Can you feel it?"

Ophir's feet remained planted in the middle of the hall, utterly frozen. She didn't want to imagine it. She wanted him to be forcing her against the blue-black corridor. She wanted his fingers gripping her hips, his mouth claiming her. She didn't understand the game, but fuck, if it wasn't tearing her to shreds. Her vivid imagination carried her forward as he spoke.

"Nod, if you can."

She struggled to breathe but managed the motion.

"That fur of yours would fall to the floor."

Ophir looked in both directions down the corridor.

"Don't look there. Look at me," he said assuredly. "I'll let you know when you can look away."

Heat consumed her. She'd spent her life commanding flame, yet it licked at all of the intimate cracks and parts of her, causing her toes to curl, her breath to catch, her breasts to peak against the delicate material of the dress. She resisted the flinching urge to check over her shoulder once more, eyes only on Tyr.

"You let your body go limp while I hold you, Princess," he murmured. "Trust me to catch you. You know I have you. You know you won't fall as long as you're with me."

She understood he meant more than tumbling to the ground.

"Tyr, let's go," she urged.

"I'm not done."

"Then fuck me," she begged.

He swept her backward in a single motion until she was pressed against the stones. She melted like butter over fresh bread, soaking into him. Her mouth absorbed each movement, the arch and caress of his tongue, the press of his lips, the grip of his hand as it cupped the side of her face, then half of her throat. She thought only of him. Of his mouth. Of his flavor. Of the fullness of him. Of how her heart expanded and squeezed at every touch.

"Princess?"

She looked up at him, eyes wide, desperate.

"You believe me when I tell you that I want you more than anything in this world."

It wasn't a question.

She nodded, shifting her head so her toffee-colored hair tumbled off her shoulder, baring her throat to his mouth. He dragged kisses down her neck, soaking whatever remained of the space between her legs. A distracting droplet of water dripped from her inner thigh. His thumb brushed over the soft curve of her breast. Given the abandoned fur, there was little more than a thread of hopes and prayers between his finger and the sensitive peak.

"And," he said, eyes glazed, "you believe that what I feel for you is so much deeper than sex?"

She looked up at him, hazy with hunger.

"What if I only want sex from you?" she asked.

His lips quirked up in a half smile. "I wouldn't blame you," he said. "I'm fantastic in bed."

She meant to grab his balls with anger, but his face

flinched in a way that told her the graze of her touch had an entirely different effect.

"Tomorrow is the meeting," he said. "It's the last day of the summit."

"I don't want to talk about the meeting right now."

"I know," he agreed, "but there are things you don't know. Things you deserve to know before you go into that room. Given the secrecy, my gifts for espionage, and Dwyn's overall ability to be a demonic terror, I have no idea who knows what. But I know one thing for certain: You're at a disadvantage. Can we go to your room and talk about it?"

"What disadvantage?" she asked, brows furrowing.

"Let's go to your room," he tried again. She could see his frustration, but she couldn't let this be another thing shoved to the wayside to protect whatever delicate royal sensibilities people projected onto her.

"What disadvantage?" she pressed.

His nostrils flared as he forced himself into a state of calm. "There's one I only learned about yesterday. The others…"

"What disadvantages!" she demanded, pluralizing the word as she pushed out from underneath him. The heat of anger replaced the desire that had consumed her mere moments before.

Tyr's face fell into a concentrated frown, from the knit of his brows to the sadness in his eyes. His hand remained propped against the wall even though the princess had escaped from beneath him. His gaze traced her as she put just enough distance between them to size him up.

"Tyr," she emphasized.

"That woman at your meeting," he said. "The woman called Cybele?"

"What about her?"

Tyr closed his eyes. He rested his head against the cool stones, taking a moment to himself before he spoke again. "We can't sleep together again. And you have her to thank."

Ophir pushed away fully. She took several steps backward. "What are you saying?"

It took Tyr a while to turn his body. He moved with uncomfortable slowness, each movement pained. His eyes remained closed as his head smacked the midnight stones behind him.

"Tell me!"

When he was able to meet her anxious stare, it was with a well of bottomless sadness. "The woman your father brought with him to the summit? What do you know of her gift?"

Ophir's jaw cut sharply to the side in a single confused gesture.

"Cybele's gift is fertility, Ophir."

Her lips parted.

"Princess—"

"No," she said, taking a step back.

"I didn't do this, Firi. I didn't—"

"My father?" she asked, voice a ghost of horror. She was scarcely able to squeeze the words past her roiling disgust. Her lips curled up in anguish as she looked at him. "He doesn't just want me to marry Ceneth, he wants to use magic to trick me into bearing heirs? Is that it? He thinks he can… *My father* thinks it's appropriate…my *father*?!"

Ophir scratched at her arms as if trying to scrape a thick film of algae from the surface of a pond. Angry red lines followed the marks of her nails.

"There's more," Tyr said.

Ophir ceased her frantic scratching, mouth ajar, eyes wide, frozen in the midst of panic as she looked up at him.

"Yesterday, I took a chance and followed Dwyn. It turned out she was meeting Suley. I know she can hear thoughts, but… She wasn't Dwyn's friend. There's more to Cybele's power than fertility."

Ophir's world spun. "It wouldn't matter. I won't sleep with Ceneth. Is that what you're afraid of, Tyr? Fuck me. Give me a Sulgrave baby. Let's show Farehold and Raascot exactly how willing I am to do my duty to unify the continent."

He huffed impatiently. "Will you let me finish?"

"What!"

He dragged his fingers slowly through his dark hair. "The rings intended for your wedding? The ones your father is presenting as gifts?"

Ophir rolled her eyes at the memory of the bands with bitter irritation. "They're meant to strengthen bonds, yes. He wants Ceneth as an ally, should war befall him. There's no honor in the rings."

"It's not just that." Tyr said each word carefully. "The rings would fuse the two of you together."

A long silence echoed between them like a hollow word ringing through a cavern.

"What are you saying?"

"I'm saying"—he scrunched his face—"it wouldn't just strengthen your bond. That wouldn't be enough to ensure Farehold against a war party from Tarkhany. They're looking for absolute devotion. They're looking for certainty. What one wants, the other wants. When one dies, the other dies. They want an heir, yes, but it's more than that. Farehold needs to know that your minds will become one in the same."

"I don't understand," she said.

"His will would fade into yours. But it's more than that."

She gaped at him with horror, asking, "It's more than what?"

"Clearly, your father knows neither of you want this union. Maybe Eero sees the gift as a kindness. Perhaps he thinks stripping Ceneth's true free will would help to soften your path. Farehold means to make you...one. There will be no way to know where Ceneth ends and where Ophir begins. If Eero knows that you and Ceneth are both reluctant to take the union, between the fusion and the fertility, you'll be so intertwined, you won't have a choice."

"I won't sleep with him," Ophir snarled.

"It's not just Cybele and her gift. With the manufactured objects Eero brought... All you have to do is marry him. With those rings on your fingers, you'll both disappear."

✦ ✦ ✦ ✦

"Talk to me!" Dwyn demanded. She'd pushed her way into Suley's room once more, anger boiling over as if she was little more than a neglected teakettle left to scream.

Suley's lips quirked up serenely. She reminded Dwyn of those lost to the addiction of the poppy haze as her eyelids drooped. "It's so quiet."

"We had a deal, Suley!" Dwyn's voice cut through the cold stones of the third-floor bedroom, echoing off the corners and filling the space like thunder and lightning all at once.

Suley's smile was slow, her eyes glazed and distant. "And I told you everything. Everyone in that room—"

"It's not possible." Enraged, Dwyn spun toward the table. She battled against the urge to flip it on its side. Her fingers dug into the wooden surface. Tiny splinters threatened to shove their spear-like shapes beneath her nails.

She grunted as she shoved off from the table. "What can they possibly know?"

"Tyr told them," Suley said simply.

"Impossible. He's just arrived, as far as they're concerned. When could he have possibly told them?"

Suley wandered to the window, leaning toward the birds that had rested beneath it. She picked up a single cage and carried it from her bedchamber. She smiled at the lutist, asking the musician to begin the process of carrying the birds from her room. The scent of cloves and eucalyptus seemed to lessen ever so slightly, as if her first breath of calm air in decades had allowed the perfume to dissipate. She informed him that once he was finished, she would ensure he was compensated for whatever the expected duration of his stay might have been. The young man hurried off, rose-colored bird in hand while it chirped maddeningly at the brethren it left behind.

Dwyn looked down at her hand, fingers twitching at the urge to drain Suley simply for fucking up her entire goddess-damned life.

"I can only hear what they've thought near me," Suley said. "I have no idea when, or why, or the context. I heard a voice echo through the heads of Samael and Harland. Harland told Eero. I, of course, told Zita. I expect she told Hassain, though I don't spend much time with the man. We all know who you are, and what you've done. They know you are Berinth, and Berinth is you. Are you wondering why King Eero doesn't fear you? Why he hasn't tried to eliminate you? Yes, I assume that's where your thoughts would spiral at this stage. He knows you're less of a threat if you're unaware."

Dwyn stumbled backward toward the door.

"Don't be dramatic," Suley said as she hoisted another birdcage from the wall and carried it toward the corridor. "I believe they've known since Tarkhany, yet nothing has happened. Besides, they believe the problem will resolve itself as soon as Ophir and Ceneth are fused. Their bond will nullify your influence. Clearly, no one plans to tell Ophir."

"Ophir isn't my problem."

Suley paused with the third cage in her hand. She quirked her head for a moment, straining her ears. She smiled. "Ah, that's nice. I listened, and nothing came. I will admit, I'm curious as to why you don't worry about the princess, but then again, I don't care. You gave me what I asked, and I've given you your weight in diamonds when it comes to infor-mation. It's not my business. Care for her as you will."

"There has to be something you aren't telling me," Dwyn insisted.

Suley considered this, fourth cage now in her hands. Her lip puckered as she nodded.

Dwyn gripped her shoulders, fingers digging into the bare upper arms just above where the cuff cut into one bicep.

Once again, she was surprised by the subtlety of the cloves and eucalyptus that were barely more than the memory of a perfume on the fae.

She pushed past the thought, glaring. "Tell me what you know, Suley. You don't have to read my mind to understand that perhaps, yes, it would be detrimental to kill you. Maybe people would put the pieces together. But maybe you've seen enough of my mind to know that I don't give a single fuck about you, your life, this castle, or its people. Take that risk, Suley. Look into my eyes and gamble with your newfound silence."

True concern wandered onto her face. Her brows met in the middle as she surveyed Dwyn. Yes, now she had something to lose. She shrank slightly against the increasing tension of Dwyn's fingers.

"Tell me."

Suley flinched in agitation. She didn't seem bothered by the pinching, the nails, the anger, or by Dwyn herself. She was deeply irritated by Dwyn's interference with her day of peace.

"Will you let me enjoy my evening?" Suley asked, voice ripe with displeasure.

Dwyn stumbled backward toward the cold glass window filtering gray, overcast daylight into their room. She lifted her fingers, flicking them ominously. "You don't need to read my thoughts to know where I'm going with this."

"Make your threats, siren."

Dwyn's eyes widened.

"That's what she calls you, right? That's what she thinks you are, despite learning of blood magic and the Reds? It's a lovely cover. What an organic way to hide who you are and what you do. A siren. A woman of the water, too beautiful for wayward sailors to help themselves. Such pretty lore for someone who borrows against lives to drain. Does she know sirens are a myth? No, I don't suppose she does. I would have heard if the princess understood that what you do can be learned."

"Are you just going to taunt me?"

"Are *you*?" Suley challenged. "Clearly I know something more you need. That was my curse, wasn't it? That's why everyone needed me to wallow in the noise? Nothing can be hidden from me." She exhaled heavily, setting the cage in her hands on the floor in front of her. "If I tell you, you'll leave? You won't bother me again?"

"I swear it."

"I don't just mean now, I mean—"

"I'll never harm you," Dwyn promised. "Not now, not ever."

Suley eyed her for a moment. She bent and picked up the birdcage, turning her back on Dwyn. She cooed to the blush-colored bird, speaking to it in a nonsensical language of soothing chirps while it eyed her curiously from within its gilded cage. Eventually, she said, "Tyr's voice was the one echoing through their memories. He told the two men accompanying King Eero. I don't know when or where or why, but he told them who you are and what you do. He told them what you did to Caris, and how you did it."

Dwyn may as well have been made of paper. She felt so thin, so frail, so chilled against the nonexistent wind as little more than cold blood pumped through her.

"I only know this because Harland couldn't stop thinking about you during the meeting. He hates you. He knows you're Caris's murderer. He knows precisely how you brainwashed a lordling, named him Berinth, and set up the beautiful, opulent trap that Ophir would be unable to resist. She's the weak-willed princess, after all. She was the one you could bend, if only she had a wound you could exploit. So, you created that wound by killing her sister, then arrived to make it all better. Harland knows. He blames you for everything, and rightly so. As such, he knows that once you're informed, you'll be the single most dangerous person on the continent. It's why no one has told Ophir. They think she's safer in the dark. So." Suley paused, having succeeded in removing the last of the birdcages. "Were they right? Was she safer before you knew?"

Dwyn's lip curled in disgusted snarl before her expression leveled out. Finally, she said, "Ophir knows. I used the last of my stolen powers and told her the morning of Berinth's execution that I was responsible for his puppetry, for Caris, for everything, so the reveal couldn't be used to turn her against me. She knows."

Suley made a face of mild disinterest. Dwyn wasn't sure if woman didn't understand or simply didn't care. She waited with gritted teeth until Zita's advisor spoke again.

"And now, it appears, so does everyone."

TWENTY-ONE

+ + + +

FOR FUCK'S SAKE. HARLAND JOGGED DOWN THE ORNATE runner in the corridor to catch up to his king. Samael trailed half a corridor behind, not bothering to run. Harland's temper curled up his spine like a snake weaving itself around a staff. He needed his king to take him seriously, but the man was impossible. Ophir was the best of them, even if Eero refused to see it.

"Your Majesty." Harland's voice came out tight with stress. The lack of concern in Eero's eyes only heightened his stress. "Something is wrong. Ophir declined our invitation to meet—"

"Ophir is temperamental," Eero said. "She always has been."

Harland's lips pursed. He looked over his shoulder at Samael, who eyed him with cool evaluation. He pushed, "It's not just that. We've tried to make contact with Raascot, with Tarkhany, even with her Sulgrave companions—"

"Cybele has it covered," Eero responded. The light caught against his golden eyes—as gold as the crown upon his head, as gilded as the royal irises that beamed from Ophir every time she looked at him. He'd only looked into her crown-gold eyes once in weeks, though he knew he was to blame for the shift.

Eero moved swiftly through the halls as he led them toward the meeting. Their time for recess had come and gone. Three days had passed, and only one thing remained. Three kingdoms hinged on a final decision.

"Sir, with respect, your fertilization fae does not have it under control."

"Don't question me, Harland. My family has used her for generations. A baby can fix any doomed marriage."

Harland felt like choking. He hated Cybele, from her tightly curled hair and her generous frame to her false smile and unconscionable power. He hated his king for bringing her. He hated the man's harmful, backward thoughts on the issue—though, given what he'd learned from Zita at the summit, perhaps Eero was more corrupt than he'd dared to imagine. The only blessing the All Mother had granted was in allowing the useless woman to sit in her rooms during the final summit. She'd played her role. She'd cursed Ophir. If they had her way and Ophir used the wedding rings...

Harland shook it from his mind, focusing on his king. "Dwyn poses a far greater threat than—"

"Once my insolent child has that ring on her finger, Dwyn's hovering influence will all but vanish. She will be checked by Ceneth's calm temperament, and he will be beholden to his bride's kingdom. It's a perfect solution."

Harland reminded himself that it was a crime to tell his king that any of Ophir's insolence was clearly inherited. He itched for Samael to arrive and use his coolheaded privilege to hold Eero accountable. In the meantime, Harland emphasized, "I'm telling you: something is wrong."

Samael caught up with them at last. Blue, evening light lit the level-headed advisor as he fell into step with them.

The king disregarded Harland entirely. He looked instead to the even-keeled Samael. "Settle an argument: Is something wrong, or is everything going according to plan?"

Samael didn't avert his gaze as he said, "That's a subjective question with an equally subjective answer."

Eero's eyebrows lowered. "Is something wrong for my reign as king and my power in Farehold?"

Samael looked up and to the side. "Probably."

Eero's mouth dropped open. "Why didn't you say anything?"

Samael didn't have to shrug. The relaxing of his face did it for him. He looked between Harland and Eero before saying, "It wasn't necessary, Your Highness. You've made it clear you're not receiving external advice at this time. You're on the path you wish to be on."

Eero was aghast. "You know I'd hear anything you had to say, Samael. It is your goddess-granted gift. Now, tell me: What do you say about this meeting?"

Harland gaped at his peer, unsure as to how Samael maintained such calm neutrality regardless of who cried out. He never seemed perturbed. Perhaps his gift for discernment comforted him, reassuring him that either the one screaming was wrong or that there was no use in worrying.

Samael merely looked at the king before saying, "Things are not stacked in your favor, Your Majesty."

"That's impossible," Eero insisted. "I brought Cybele and the gifts for the wedding for exactly this purpose! Perhaps I didn't go into the summit with cards, but by the goddess, I'll leave with them! Ophir will be forced to fall into line as soon as she's wed. We have it covered. We've thought of every conceivable outcome and acted to preempt it."

"If you say so," Samael said, his tone making it clear he had no dog in the fight.

"The problem is Dwyn, isn't it?" Harland needled.

Samael chewed on the question. "No. That said: she is a problem, and one that has not been solved, despite our king's insistence that his ruse is foolproof."

"Because it is!" Eero stamped his foot. "A foreign witch

arrived to influence my daughter? I will simply free her from the ability to be influenced!"

Samael leveled his gaze. "Powerful men who refuse to seek outside counsel must know what's best. Perhaps their wealth will buy their desired outcome. Or maybe it won't. I suppose we'll see."

"You're at my side to advise me," Eero snarled.

"What advice would you take, when it contradicts your desires? I suppose it's too late for your sycophants to be present at the meeting."

The king jutted a threatening finger toward Samael's throat. "Be careful if you wish to keep your head."

"As is your right, Your Majesty." Samael was unperturbed, to the king's speechless displeasure.

Eero turned on his heel as he stormed into the room. Samael's face remained impassive in the face of the king's agitation, but Harland knew this was why Samael hadn't said more.

Regardless of what Eero said or did from this moment on, the die was cast.

+   +   +   +

"I don't have to remain visible. I'll come unseen," Tyr said. He appeared to be trying to look relaxed against the wall, but everything from the flex of his shoulders to the tick in his jaw revealed his agitation.

"Don't bother," Ophir grumbled. They were less than ten minutes away from their final summit, and she was a restless sea before the storm.

He eyed her with extreme suspicion as she tossed gown after gown onto the bed. Her fingers wrapped around a thigh-length sweater and a fur-lined pair of leather leggings. He understood the warmth they served, but he couldn't comprehend Ophir's fashion choices. He knew, however, the message she intended to send by forgoing pretty dresses in favor of the only pair of pants in her armoire. She snatched a suitable pair of shoes. They were not the delicate shoes for princesses, not the heels for lovely evenings, not the flats for calm walks through the gardens, but warm, sturdy boots. She slipped into them without saying a word.

She'd silently seethed since their revelation. Whatever she was planning, he wished she'd trust him enough to let him in.

"Ophir, if this is about Cybele, we should talk."

She stopped amid her tirade, eyes flashing. She spun on him as she said, "Cybele is a symptom, not the disease. Eero is the sickness."

He'd never heard her refer to King Eero by his name. He wasn't sure that he had the balls to call his parents anything other than Mother or Father. He knew enough to tell that now was not the time to comfort her. She didn't need his head. She wasn't interested in idle chatter or the mind-numbing games of marionettes and their puppets. She needed his heart. She was intelligent enough to understand the way of the world, and she required only his validation. He could share her fury, or he could leave.

"Do you know what you're going to do in there?"

She finished tugging the sweater over her head. Locks of gold-brown hair sprang loose against the sweater's neck, now coiling around her face. She glared at him. "Yes. Either he'll admit his crimes to me or—"

"And if he does?" Tyr interrupted. "If he admits to everything? If he confesses? Will you forgive him?"

Her mouth bunched as if catching the forthcoming words like a net. She froze in place, fingers still deep in the thick sweater as she clenched them at his question.

"And what if the opposite? If he denies everything? I'm not going to tell you what to do, Princess, but for the love of the goddess, please tell me. What's your plan?"

"They've bet their kingdoms on underestimating me," she said, voice low. "My plan is to call their bluff."

✦　　✦　　✦　　✦

"You seem different." Zita's energy shifted as she surveyed her friend and advisor. A chill that had nothing to do with the weather descended upon her. She scanned Suley from top to bottom, eyes taking in the younger woman's hair, her jewels, her clothes. Everything was the same, yet... Her posture, the way her forehead had relaxed, and the gentle upward tilt to the corner of her lips suggested that something was off. "Suley, what's happened with you?"

Suley gave an aloof smile. "Do you recall me asking to live in the Raasay Forest?"

Zita offered a slow, careful tilt of her chin.

"I was on to something. I knew Raascot would be good for my health."

Zita wasn't sure how to explain it, but she felt her entire body frown, from the knit of her brows and the bunch of her lips to the tension in her shoulders. Hassain paused at their side, a distant worry creasing his forehead. She barely spared him a glance as she examined the young woman again.

Zita tried to stop Suley before the meeting room, throwing out her arm. "Suley, what do you know?"

"Everything, as always."

"Do you know anything that might change the outcome of this meeting?"

"Yes."

Zita's fingers flexed at her side. She caught Hassain's flashed expression from her peripherals as she focused her attention on Suley once more. In the distance, footsteps approached. They had fewer than thirty seconds before they'd be expected within the summit.

"And? Are you going to tell me what it is you know?"

Suley stared at her queen with unflinching neutrality.

"Suley! Does anyone else know what you know?"

"My friend, my queen," Suley said quietly. "I'm not worried, because I'm here with you. Your first gift is that of shielding, is it not? Even your second gift... Well, today we

198

won't need that. Someone else will do it for us. If I were you, I would ready myself for chaos."

✦   ✦   ✦   ✦

"Ceneth, listen!"

The King of Raascot paused in the hall. He glared at Evander, gaze bouncing off the corridor's stones as he searched for his other advisor. The distant sounds of voices bubbled from around the corner. Aside from the rugs, curtains, and windows, the hall was empty. "What? Where is Onain?"

"She met your medium." Evander grimaced.

Ceneth glared. "She had no right meeting with the medium behind my back."

"She has every right, Your Majesty. You trust her for her judgment," Evander argued. "She would never do anything if she didn't think it was in the kingdom's best interest. And—"

"The medium doesn't know anything Caris says," Ceneth cut in curtly. "They've told me time in and time out that they're little more than a conduit. They aren't privy to our conversations. I don't know why Onain would speak to them without my consent."

"The medium went to her, Your Majesty. They said that every time you met with Caris, your late beloved has reiterated that the darkness drew nearer. The only thing that grew sharper was blackness. Those were your words, according to the medium. Their concern is with the fate of the kingdom."

"Are you trying to tell me Caris's wishes?" Ceneth bit, no kindness in his voice.

"Please, Your Majesty." Evander's pleas were reverent but desperate. He positioned his body in the middle of the hall. "What if this was the storm Caris foretold? What if the closer we drew to the meeting, the more certainty she saw surrounding its outcome? When Onain met with the medium, she came to the conclusion that there would be no peaceable resolution. She called for the meeting's cancellation."

"I will not cancel it."

Evander clasped his hands tightly behind his back. "Six of your servants were murdered in broad daylight, Your Majesty. Your castle walls have been invaded. The lockdown has been ignored. The ambassadors and visitors have disregarded every precaution, each insisting they're uniquely prepared to fight off a murderer. The killer roams free. Onain understands this, and it brought her deep regret. She wishes you would reconsider, but she knows you will not."

"And so she stays back? Then Onain is a coward and not fit to be my advisor."

Evander lifted his hands as if to push back against his king's chest. He stopped just short of making contact, saying, "You trust her for a reason, Your Highness. If you were guaranteed to lose a battle, would you be a coward for refusing to fight? It sounds like wisdom."

"Evander, this is the most times you've used my royal titles in more than a decade. Speak plainly."

"This summit will go poorly, Your Maj—Ceneth."

"And?" Ceneth looked around. "The meeting is in five minutes. What would you have me do? You're my advisor and my guard, Evander. Am I not safe in your company?"

"In Onain's absence? I'd have you call Galena. You trust her gifts to neutralize those who might harm you, do you not?"

Ceneth frowned. "She's not an advisor. Would I summon her and offend the monarchs from two of Gyrradin's corners?"

"They don't know of her powers," he said. "They have no reason to believe her presence will be any different than having Onain beside you. They don't know our customs, our people, our ways. To all outside eyes, Galena is another court advisor."

"But with the woman there, I'd be calling a summit of humans," Ceneth argued. "The monarchs, their escorts, the—"

"No one would use their abilities within a summit unless they meant harm. There is no need for magic at a meeting of the minds. It's wise to have her at your side, Your Majesty... Ceneth."

The king frowned. "Your skin won't be impenetrable if she's present," Ceneth cautioned.

"I know. But it's the right call." Evander remained firm.

"Has Onain given her divine discernment on the wisdom of having a neutralizer present?"

Evander's struggle to conceal his frustration was not subtle. He said, "Onain's only position is that the meeting should be canceled. As I see it will not, please take my advice in her stead, and summon Galena."

"Fine," Ceneth conceded. "Call for her to attend. And do it quickly."

TWENTY-TWO

✦   ✦   ✦   ✦

THE BATTLE OF WILLS WAS OBNOXIOUS, BUT OPHIR HAD nothing but time. To her right, Dwyn seemed agitated, which was unusual. She cast a sidelong glance at the siren, but Dwyn wouldn't meet her eyes. Dwyn's hummingbird gaze flitted from Zita to Harland to Eero and everyone in between as if they were little more than flowers in her pursuit of nectar. Under any other circumstances, Ophir would have asked what was wrong. On her left, Tyr's tension was separate but equal. She wanted to find relief in his visible presence, but this constricting strain didn't allow for small pleasures. Rather than glance amid the surrounding kingdoms' ambassadors, Tyr's jaw was set, teeth gritted against nothing in particular.

Ophir leaned forward and looked expectantly to the end of the table at her husband-to-be. Evander sat stoically on one side, and on the other sat a rather pretty winged woman Ophir had never seen. Between her father and her fiancé, she absently wondered how many men in her life would show up at important meetings with unfamiliar women before it became a problematic pattern.

Ceneth met her eyes for a moment. There was no hostility in his face as he regarded her, nor was there kindness. He was a true neutral. The king of Raascot exhaled and stood. His well-tailored clothes hug a bit too loosely on his frame. It was not the first time she'd noticed his weight loss. In a sick way, it was something she liked about him. Their shared grief held a purity that no one else could truly understand. She watched the way the collar of the shirt gaped slightly against what had been the thick column of his neck, the cuffs around his wrists showing slightly too much space around his once-broad forearms as he spoke.

"I'm honored that the rulers of Farehold and Tarkhany have graced my castle with their presence. It's with a heavy heart that I draw our summit to its final day. Our three mighty kingdoms deserve a joyous union, but we must live within the world and its realities. Queen Zita, would you like the floor?"

Ceneth didn't wait for an answer as he sank back into his chair. He remained on the far end of the table, Eero taking its opposite end, as he had before. Ophir sat nearest to the door, while the party from Tarkhany remained backlit against a row of arched windows. Perhaps under mundane circumstances, Ophir would have been grateful for the distraction to look out the window at the dark river beyond, picking apart the violet mountains, counting the stones on the distant cathedrals. These were not mundane circumstances.

The Queen of Tarkhany had once again blended the fashions of the desert with the warmth required of the north. Though her pale gown suggested she might have awoken in her desert palace, the snow-creature fur that ran down her arms worked overtime to bundle her against the climate.

Zita looked at Ceneth curiously before leaning in her chair toward King Eero. She remained seated as she said, "I don't think I need the floor. Not only has Tarkhany done nothing wrong, but it shielded your daughter, Eero, and apparently kept the secret of the blood on your hands. I believe it's your turn to state your case."

Rather than meet her eyes, Eero stared into the middle of the table as if looking into the core of the earth. The room held its collective breath while everyone waited for Eero to speak. Eventually, the King of Farehold said, "After days of deliberation, Farehold has come to the conclusion that Tarkhany's request for accountability has long since passed any acceptable statute of limitations. Your quarrel was with my father, Queen Zita. It has nothing to do with me, and certainly nothing to do with my daughter or her heirs."

Tension thrummed through the table.

"Disappointing but not surprising," was all Zita said. After a beat, she said, "Perhaps the past is the past, but what of the present?"

"What of it?" Eero's throat bobbed.

"Before we make plans for our future, I'd like a promise today, sealed in magic. I move for Tarkhany's cities to be expunged from your maps."

His brow furrowed.

"Speak to your future, Eero. How can I know that the past will not repeat itself, unless it is not an option? I move for one thousand years of silence. Tarkhany may come and go from your lands, but you are not to cross into the desert."

"That's absurd! That's—"

"Please, King Eero," Ceneth said through his teeth. "Is it ridiculous for her to request that her homelands not be stolen a second time? After all, the north has yet to forget that these snowcapped mountains were not our ancestral lands. Your people have a habit of…migrating."

"That's one offense too many," Eero seethed.

Ignoring him, Ceneth said to Zita, "Raascot will honor this request. We will sign a treaty and have your cities vanish from all papers and documents, and we will vow not to cross into your lands for one thousand years. Though let it be known, if you choose to cross of your own volition, you will always be welcome in the north."

"I did not ask it of Raascot," she said.

"And yet, you have it."

The room's silence had a soupy, drowning quality. Each

breath was a struggle as monarchs and advisors sipped on spoonfuls of tension. Zita eyed the crowned men for a quiet while before turning to address Ophir.

"And you, Princess? How have you spent your three days of recess?" The queen watched her carefully.

The faces beside Ophir contorted with terse attention. Their heightened emotions stirred the already-simmering cauldron within her. Tyr's silent plea seemed to will her not to lash out, while Dwyn emanated a different nameless energy entirely. Neither breathed as they silently regarded her. Raascot, Farehold, and Tarkhany's attention remain trained on her as she held the floor.

"If you'll allow me a detour, Queen Zita," she said, waiting for Zita's nod before she continued. Ophir sucked on her teeth, allowing her anger to take root and grow into a magnificent, thorned weed before she spoke. "Raascot has shown me protection and kindness. Though it was meant to be Caris's kingdom through marriage, I'm grateful for my friends here. I have no reason to mistrust anyone in Gwydir." She nodded at Ceneth. His face tensed with uncertainty at the edge that crept into her voice, but he cautiously returned the gesture. She looked back to Zita, saying, "You not only sheltered me but aided in the pursuit of my enemies and my avenue for justice. No one holds you to blame for the actions of... What was the shapeshifter's name?"

Zita remained silent.

Ophir shrugged lightly before turning to her father. "I suppose he's unimportant. Alas, now it's time to address Farehold. Father?"

Eero stiffened visibly at the extreme rigidity with which she addressed him. Harland's eyes flared in a plea, but she held no space in her heart for his silent prayers. To his side, Samael leaned back in his chair, folding his hands in his lap as he observed.

"Farehold," she said to the room, "married me off to Raascot as if Caris and I were interchangeable. When I was not amenable and I fled, I was pursued." Ophir paused for effect, scanning the intense faces around the room before continuing. "Farehold did not trust our bond. Did you know this? In fact, the king sitting upon the throne in Aubade was so distrustful of our treaty, he made other arrangements to ensure his will is done." She looked at Ceneth, studying his face as she asked, "The woman he brought: Were you aware that her gift is one of fertility? Did you know that she's forced my womb to prepare for your child?"

Ceneth's jaw dropped.

Eero rumbled with a threatening growl, "It would be wise to cease speaking, Ophir."

The room bristled as if they were little more than a pack of dogs, teeth bared in their hostile standstill.

"No, I don't think it would. Should we consummate our union, Ceneth? Good King Eero can't risk missing his opportunity to have an heir sit upon both of our thrones. Yet, that wasn't enough, was it, Father?"

Evander and the nameless woman at Ceneth's side looked like they might back away from the table. The blatant evidence of revulsion rippled through their expressions like a stomach flu.

Ophir tore her gaze from Ceneth, looking to her father as she said, "Shall I tell Ceneth about your wedding present?"

Eero's voice rang with firm anger as he growled his daughter's name, chewing the syllables as if a hound snarling into a steak.

"Stop it, Ophir!" her father demanded.

Harland's plea rang out at the same time, her name little more than a desperate whisper on his lips.

"That's right." She looked to Ceneth's still-shocked face, then back to her father's. "The rings you offered as our wedding gift would not only bond us, but fuse us, so that we could not defy one another. You meant to make Ceneth a puppet. You mean to raise his armies against Tarkhany should they march. You meant to melt my mind—"

"Ophir!" Eero slammed his fist against the table. He was on his feet in one swift motion. His metallic eyes burned.

She was on her toes not a moment later. The fire within her burned beyond his. "You meant to meld us, *Eero*! What am I to you? Not only am I not your child; I'm not even a person. I have no autonomy. I'm a pawn in the game of kingdoms and castles. Isn't that right?"

He snapped, "Don't speak of what you do not know."

"What don't I know?" she snarled in return. "What have I left out, Father?"

No one else existed. The room faded into black and white dots of distant clouds and static as father and daughter matched each other step for step.

His voice boomed with decades of fury as he boomed. "You know nothing of running a kingdom. You know nothing of adulthood! You can barely stay alive! Would we have let a stranger into your bed if you hadn't nearly burned down the castle every night?"

She slammed a fire-laden palm against the table, embers gnawing at the wood as she yelled, "*You* know nothing of who I am or what I can do." Flame ate through its surface until the furniture bore the evidence of her cinders, but she didn't bother to look at the five fingers that marked her rage.

"How can she—" Evander tripped over his words.

Ceneth gasped at the fire at her fingertips.

The woman beside him shot him terrified glances. "Your Majesty, I don't know—"

She had no time for their squabbles. Their arguments were noise as she focused on her father.

"I know nothing of who you are?" Eero asked incredulously, voice mocking. Flecks of spit hit the table as he yelled, voice red with anger. "Tell me, Ophir. Tell me what you are. Tell me something your mother and I haven't known since the day you were born. Caris was meant to usher in an age of peace! What can you do except burn things to the ground?"

The world around her froze with a high, sharp ring.

Anger engulfed her, hotter than any flame. She guessed from the flash of muscle and flesh that her friends saw their fates before she grasped what she was doing.

Dwyn and Tyr were on their feet in an instant. From across the room, Harland leaped up as if to cross the table. She beheld them all as if they swam to her through the deepest trenches of the ocean, every labored movement happening bit by bit. All three lunged for her as if to soothe her, but it was too late.

With a banshee scream of decades of betrayal, of pain and hatred, Ophir thrust her hands to the side. She shrieked her bloodcurdling rage, ears ringing with anguish. The high-pitched humming of agony and fury drowned out the shouting of Dwyn, Tyr, and Harland as time slowed, the clock ticking so that every second became a minute. She saw their faces. She saw their fear. She saw the disappointment that soaked her father like a child's soiled pants. She saw the confusion on Ceneth's face. She even caught something akin to pride on Zita's bemused expression as her fingers, bent into claws, rose at her sides.

Perhaps they knew her better than she knew herself.

Ophir hadn't gone in with intent. She hadn't thrown out her hands with a plan. She knew only two things. The first was that rage was the only emotion that mattered. The second was that King Eero of Farehold would live to rue the day he'd spoken so glibly of her.

The spray of debris and pebbles hit her before she was conscious of the noise.

Decay hit her in conjunction with the arctic wind that poured in from all sides. Light, dust, screaming, and horror erupted through the cocoon of her violence. Feathers and flesh, the whites of eyes, the cries of panic and pain flooded her.

The room exploded around her, each stone bursting into ten thousand smaller stones. A shriek like rust, nails, and ice joined the raw, aching scream that tore from her throat. She didn't have to turn to see the enormous shadow that towered over the wreckage of the room. Membranous wings attached to a monster the size of the mountain ripped through the very stitches that held the castle together. She was spared from the rubble by the same wingspan that tore everything around it to the ground. The outermost wall to the castle crumbled, more early-winter chill spilling in like cold cream filling a teacup. The cold joined the dust, the rocks, the sound of coughing, the limbs that lifted to shield themselves from the pain.

"Firi!" Dwyn cried from her side. The siren's high, panicked voice was coming from the blackened bottom of the sea, shouting at her from deep underwater. Her sounds barely reached Ophir's ears.

Ophir didn't bother to look at her. Wrath was the only thing she knew as she cried out again. The spray of pebbles and chalk dusted her as the shape planted its mighty feet on either side. With two thunderous steps, the quadrupedal creature's front legs framed her silhouette. Her winged serpent arched its neck into the sky, bellowing the sounds of glass shards and hellfire.

The night-dark dragon drank in the sky as it shook off the remnants of the destroyed room around it. She looked up at her beast with fury and pride as it screeched once more.

Coated in a thick white powder of dust and debris, her father scrambled backward on bloodied palms. He tried to cry out against the dragon that had enveloped the wing of the castle but choked on the cloud of wreckage.

"Kill him," Ophir said with cool command. The winged beast poised to strike. Her lip twitched with the ghost of a smirk. In the midst of its arc, she shouted a single word. "Halt."

The corner of her mouth flickered up while her eyes remained cool.

The ag'drurath paused inches from Eero's whimpering form. Thick, iridescent fluid dripped from its thousands of needlelike teeth. It twitched anxiously as it stared at the king.

Hunger reflected in its eyes, mirroring the bloodlust she was certain shone in hers.

She maintained a vague awareness of yelling from all sides. Someone was shouting for a healer. The wailing of the wounded rose from across the table. Tyr tugged at her arm, but she didn't bother to look his way as she commanded her dragon.

"Pick him up by his collar," she said. She flicked a finger lazily from her creation to her father, though she was quite certain the gesture was unnecessary.

The ag'drurath leaned forward, sulfur and carrion filling the space as the stench of its rotten meat suffocated the piles of powder and stones. Icy, whipping wind joined the blood and cries of the wounded, but Ophir heard none of it. Her eyes remained focused on the careful way the ag'drurath's teeth snagged on Eero's collar, lifting him off his feet until he sputtered, purple with his need for air.

"Now set him down," she said.

The dragon complied. It opened its maw and released its royal prey. Eero crumpled to the ground with a fleshy thump as his shoulder took the brunt of his fall. Her gaze remained on her beast.

"Now go," she said, voice cold. Each word was laced with bitter intentionality as she added, "And please, don't hunt within the city. Fly to Farehold. Torment the citizens of Aubade for all I care."

Her hair kicked up against the force of the dragon's mighty wings as it beat once, twice, then again and again as it battled the pull of the earth to take flight. She closed her eyes against the fine mist of grit and sand from the stones and mortar of its destruction. The distant screams of the citizens beyond mingled with the pained cries in the room, soaking her with an unpleasant white noise. The shrieks of civilians tumbled over one another like a babbling brook as the world saw her dragon. She was unwilling to feel so much as a breeze until her eyes reopened to see its reptilian shape dotting the horizon. Her father gaped at her, as speechless and bug-eyed as a trout left on shore to die.

She barely had time to admire her demon child as it cast a spectacular shape in the sky before someone was grabbing for her attention.

Ophir swatted away the hand. "You think you're powerful, Father? You pass laws? You steal land? This—this is power. I hold life and death in my palm at a whim. Do you understand?"

"Firi," Dwyn begged, tugging at her sweater. Ophir blinked at the siren, surprised at the panic in Dwyn's voice. "Your father is not the only one present! You have to do something! You can help them."

"Help who?" Ophir said, still watching the dragon as it took to the south. "It won't hunt here."

"People are dying, Ophir. People *you* care about. I can't use my powers. I can't..."

The unfamiliar whites of Dwyn's frantic eyes shook her awake. Until now, she'd witnessed only her father's face as her dragon had shown her exactly what she could do. For those glorious minutes, no one else in Gwydir had existed. Blinking back into reality, she realized Dwyn was the only one who remained at her side. Tyr had run to the others. He was urgently shoveling rubble away from Ceneth while the strange woman grunted against the stones that had buried Evander. A distant part of her became aware of the sticky vermillion pool that gathered around Raascot's advisor. A pulp-like gore had smeared itself onto several of the cracked rocks. She tried to care, but she was too detached to comprehend the ruby-red liquid and its implications.

The adrenaline of her fury seeped from her. Her crimson rage faded into the pale blue of panic as she looked at the fallen men.

"Firi! Make something!" Dwyn begged, waving a hand to the stones that crushed the monarchs around them. The dust cleared enough for her to see the large boulder that pinned

Zita's leg to the ground, her head unmoving as it rested on the table.

Ophir shook her head blankly.

"Firi!" Dwyn shook her. "You can do it! You can make anything! All you have to do is think it! Make someone to help!"

She knew Dwyn was right. All Ophir had to do was imagine her intentions, and she could create something. She gaped at Ceneth's unconscious form beneath the stones. She could scarcely see the crying woman beside Evander. She'd done this. She'd hurt them.

"Firi!"

"I..."

"Do something!"

Fine. She could make something to dig. She could make something strong and capable and with hands that could fling the castle's stones from everyone around her. Ophir did her best to picture a helper, a worker, a fae who might possess the scooping hands and wide palms to free one from rock, but she saw only death. She tried to look at Dwyn and Tyr, but she knew that dead bodies remained pinned within the rubble. Her heart struggled with the pain of funerals, of loss, of Caris, of blood, of murder. She tried to tear her mind from the horrible night that had shattered her world, but trauma coursed through her as she summoned her manifestation.

She flexed her fingers and cried out in surprise at what she'd created. Even Dwyn stumbled behind her in reaction to the abomination that slouched before them in tattered, black rags. Its skeletal mouth hung loosely on its jaw. Its large eyes looked at them without comprehension. Enormous hands with palms too big for a humanoid creature hung limply at the end of its bent elbows.

She grimaced at her disgusting, broken, fucked-up manifestation. She hated it even more than her other creations. This was the best thing she could make, and it was an unholy nightmare.

"Help them," Ophir croaked.

Tyr didn't step away from the stones until the monstrosity approached him. Though he knew it was Ophir's creation and tethered to her will, the terror was plain on his face. The ghoulish monster freed Ceneth and his advisor from the enormous boulders with a few strong swipes. Acidic liquid dripped from its mouth as it cocked a too-human face toward her.

She blinked at it. She'd done this. She'd killed and maimed and destroyed. She'd set a dragon into the world without the aid of a sentient rider to tame it. She'd horrified her closest friends and confidants. And this was how she'd fixed it. Through another abomination.

The freakish beast looked at her with unintelligent eyes, and she knew that she'd made something that would never know love, or peace, or life. She created only death, thirst, and destruction. Ophir swallowed as it tilted its head again, head rolling like that of an insect.

"You can go," she said breathlessly.

The creature shrieked at her once, its noise the hellish sounds of rusted nails in tin cans, before turning toward the broken opening in the castle wall. It took off into the cobblestones and alleys of the city faster than man or fae. The monster glided into the woods as if it possessed not feet but traveled with the speed of mist and smoke.

The atrocity had shaken her to a waking state. She was too stunned by what she'd done to absorb the regret that clawed to enter the protective shield she'd formed around herself. She finally turned to appreciate the shock on her father's face. Eero remained on his back, propped up only on his hands from where he'd scrambled backward after the ag'drurath had released him. He looked at his daughter as if he'd never seen her before in his life. Nothing but stunned fear and repulsion painted his face.

The shock that had leached into her upon seeing Ceneth and Evander evaporated. She'd done all she could do. Zita and her party were fine. Tyr and Dwyn were helping. A new sensation filled her. It was not rage, or hate, or vitriol. Her fire died, giving way to the ruby smolder of whatever remained long after the hearth had been forgotten. She was not the campfire that warmed hunters; she was the kiln that forged the world. With a chilling calm, she knew with some certainty she was the most powerful being on the continent.

"What have you done?" Eero said, question ripe with his horror.

His words stirred the coal within her. Ophir took a few careful steps over the splintered table, picking her footing between the fallen stones and the shards of rocks and chairs that littered the space. She resisted the urge to brace herself against the cold as she stood over her father's fallen figure. She glared at him, all respect, love, and familiarity lost to the repulsion of her anger.

"I do more than burn things to the ground," she said. "I salt the earth when I'm done."

TWENTY-THREE

+ + + +

T HE DUST HAD SETTLED, BUT THE RUBBLE REMAINED.
The tide of chaos refused to ebb.

Harland's forehead remained creased in worry. He closed
his eyes as he began, "The healers say—"

"This isn't about the healers," Samael said calmly. In
the days following the destruction of Castle Gwydir, it had
taken every man, woman, and volunteer to piece together
the castle wing from its rubble. It was three days into efforts
to repair and recover before Hassain had fully healed and
it was revealed that he could speak to stone. Zita had
consented to his volunteering for Gwydir in spite of the
Farehold presence. The party from Farehold inquired as to
whether or not they should pay their respects at Evander's
funeral, but they were asked to remain in their chambers for
their day. Grieving his memory was for his people and his
family, they'd said.

"Did you know this would happen?" Eero asked Samael.
"Is this what you were speaking about so opaquely? Is this
why your sister was not in attendance?"

Samael showed no capacity for worry. He said, "I told
you that things wouldn't turn out in your favor. They have

not. I believe that means both my advice and predictions continue to be sound."

Eero and Harland looked at Samael with a mixture of panic and frustration. The three men, still bandaged and healing while the tonics worked through their system, sat around a low-lying table in the wing of the castle that had been allotted to them.

"But the oracle—" Eero countered.

Samael waved a hand. "May I, King Eero?"

Eero's expression crumpled. "You may."

A rare hesitance crept into Samael's voice. "You may not like what I'm about to say."

"Speak your piece. We are in this position because of my hubris. Ignoring your wisdom was my great mistake."

Samael met the king's repentant gaze as he said, "I'm calling in our life debt."

Eero's lips parted. The air escaped the room as the king focused on his advisor.

"Now? When I need you most?"

Samael was unmoved. "I believe this is my purpose. Not only can Ophir manifest, but we've seen how her manifestation leads to destruction in Tarkhany and Gwydir—and those were just two events for which I've been present. She sent her dragon south to Aubade, which means your people will face her wrath in the days to come."

Eero's voice was numb. "Tell me what to do."

"I cannot better the continent while serving you, Your Majesty. There is neither wisdom nor honor in allowing this to go unchecked. If I have a purpose in this life, I know it now. Judgment has led me to this calling. You can't be responsible for checking your daughter. She is your blood, and it wouldn't be right to call upon you to do what it takes. Ceneth can't be responsible for stopping his bride. Tarkhany has a laundry list of reasons to hold a vendetta against Farehold. The nightmare that's befallen the continent cannot be contained by any one of the kingdoms."

Eero mumbled something about not understanding, but Harland fell to a single knee.

"Don't make a scene, Harland," Samael said.

Harland whipped out a dagger and locked eyes with Samael. "Swear something to me."

Samael pursed his lips. He urged Harland to stand, but the man refused.

"*Swear* it!"

"What?" Samael bared his teeth, revealing his fangs for the first time. He was rarely one to be caught off guard. They'd never seen him openly angry before this moment. Harland, on his knees, eyes wild with desperation, seemed to be his tipping point. Behind him, Eero remained in shocked silence.

"Make an oath with me. Make it now."

"Stand, Harland." Samael glared, temper showing beneath his façade of calm. "You're making a spectacle of yourself. I'm doing what must be done."

Harland pressed the dagger into the meat of his hand. Blood trickled down his wrist. "Make an oath with me, Samael. Make it before our king releases you. Don't hurt Ophir."

Samael inhaled sharply through his nose. "Harland—"

"Swear it," Harland begged again. "You're right, Samael. Your gift has brought you here because this cannot go unchecked. Kill her monsters. Do what three of the continent's kingdoms cannot. Undo the blight she's bringing upon the land. Don't allow her to destroy the world. Protect the citizens. Monitor the magical imbalance. I honor it all, Samael. I concede to every bit of it. Do what you must, but don't hurt her."

Samael pursed his lips. "But—"

"Do what you must!" Harland repeated, hazel eyes alight with an inferno as if he'd borrowed Ophir's gift for flame. "But don't hurt her."

Eero looked between the men, then to his feet. "I second Harland. I have no more heirs, and it appears I never

217

may. Make this vow, and I will release you. Do not hunt my child."

Samael looked up with something akin to disappointment. It was not Ophir's father who argued on behalf of her life. The king stared mutely at the exchange happening before him. If it weren't for the crackling fire within the hearth catching against Eero's eyes, there would have been no evidence that the king was alive at all.

"What do you propose?" Eero asked quietly. "And what does it have to do with my life debt?"

It had been three days since an entire wing of the castle had been laid to waste by Ophir and her dragon. For nearly as long, Samael had remained a silent sentinel. He'd never been exceptionally conversational, but this particular brand of silence suggested that other workings had gone on behind his eyes. Now, on the end of the third day, he announced his plan.

"Your Majesty, I cannot act without bias in pursuing your daughter's creations while I serve beneath you. I cannot remain a servant of Farehold."

Eero's brows knit. He asked, "Do you seek to return to Raascot?"

Samael's frown deepened. "Raascot is not home. Neither for myself nor Onain. We're here to serve the realm. I've spoken with my sister, who has served an advisory role in Gwydir longer than I have in Aubade. The world changed with the flick of Ophir's wrist, Your Majesty. We agree, this is not a job that can be done with bias to kings or masters."

"Say what it is you intend to say."

Samael straightened his shoulders. "I'd request a reprieve from kingdoms and alliances. I will serve neither Farehold nor Raascot—no agenda, save for the well-being of the continent." He turned to Harland. "We know of at least two of her dragons and at least two humanoid demons. Has she made anything else, to your knowledge?"

Harland closed his eyes. He didn't look at his king before

nodding in honesty. Yes, she had. No, Eero would be neither thrilled nor impressed that Harland had hidden such an integral piece of information from him.

"Do you have any idea as to her rate of creation?"

Harland shook his head sadly. "She began manifesting before she ran."

"Manifesting," Eero repeated quietly from his chair.

"And the dagger?" Samael arched a brow.

Harland pulled the dagger out of his palm. Scarlet droplets ran down his arm, soaking into the cuff of his sleeve as he extended his hand to Samael. "Serve no king. Do what you must, you altruistic bastard. But don't hurt her. Do this and I'll spend every day until the end of my days ensuring that you're able to perform your calling."

He extended the dagger to Samael.

"Truly? You would call for us to exchange blood?" Samael looked to Eero.

Eero said, "Take this vow, and I release you."

Harland ignored their king entirely. He pushed out a rush of air through his nose before saying, "There are few moments in life that require a certain solemnity. This is one of them."

Samael looked between the blade, his kneeling friend, and the man who'd been his king. If the All Mother had put him on the earth for one reason, it was this. He knew in his marrow that no one else would extinguish the blight on the land unless he rose to the occasion. Wisdom told him this was the best deal he would be offered to fulfill his calling.

Samael accepted the dagger. His gaze remained on Harland's as pain shot through him. Hot rivers flowed from his hand, wrapping around his wrist and dripping onto the ground at his feet. He allowed the blade to eat into his flesh, slicing into the meat of his palm before he clasped hands with Harland. Their blood mixed as they sealed their promise.

"As long as you don't hurt her." Harland flexed his fingers, pulling Samael in closer.

"I'll do what must be done."

+   +   +   +

"Your Highness!" Harland cried after the northern king at the gates of Castle Gwydir. He'd scarcely caught the disappearing silhouette of Ceneth's form as the winged king of Raascot slipped behind the front gates. "King Ceneth!"

Ceneth paused in the last dark-gray lights of dusk. He made a show of attempting to conceal his displeasure at Harland's arrival, but his best was not enough. He snarled at the guard.

"I'm busy, Harland." Ceneth looked back at the woman who'd been at the meeting. Their voices stayed low as she helped him cinch his weapon's belt. This was something that an attendant should be doing, not someone the king considered an advisor.

"She shouldn't have been able to do that," the one called Galena was saying quietly. Harland had heard her say a variation of this lament for three days as she remained in her shell-shocked state. Every thought that passed her lips had been filtered through mourning and self-flagellation. Thanks to Galena's presence, Zita had been unable to call her shield. Evander's skin had been little more than flesh. They'd heard it from her mouth and seen it on her face: she'd never be able to forgive herself for the mortality she'd brought into the room.

Ceneth looked to the neutralizer. "No one should be able to do what was done in that room. It's manifestation."

Galena shook her head. "She shouldn't have been able to do anything. Why would everyone else's abilities be rendered useless, save for hers?"

"Because," Ceneth said, grunting absently as he continued to work on his hardened armor and the weapons at his side. He didn't look at them as he said, "Manifestation is not magic."

"Sir?"

"It's godhood."

"Is…" Galena struggled to keep up. "Is this the explanation for the six dead bodies within our walls? Another creature of hers?"

Ceneth's noise was unintelligible, yet unmistakably translated as: *How the hell am I supposed to know how far this bullshit extends?*

The king's eyes flashed back to the guard. There was no kindness in his question as he asked, "What is it, Harland? Why are you here? Hasn't Farehold done enough?"

Harland eyed Ceneth, from the fighting leathers and the weapons to the hat, gloves, and winter boots. "You look like you're going to battle."

"Very perceptive."

Harland's words came out breathlessly. "Samael is asking to defect. His sister, Onain—"

"I know who his sister is."

Harland bit down his reaction. He didn't have time to luxuriate in surprise. Onain had clearly deemed that more relevant within the walls of Gwydir than Samael had amid Farehold's party. "Has she spoken to you?"

Ceneth glared. "Yes."

"And?" Harland prompted.

"And they're right—that's their gift, isn't it? It's hard to argue with someone whose goddess-granted ability is unimpeachable correctness."

"Is she defecting with him?" Harland asked, shock coating his voice.

"She is."

His eyes widened. "They're positioning themselves against Ophir."

"They're positioning themselves against *evil*," Ceneth snapped.

"But—"

Ceneth stepped away from Galena. She dipped her chin, tucking her wings behind her in cordial submission. Harland knew nothing of the woman, but he understood everything of guilt. He had a feeling she'd spend her days trying to absolve the events of the summit.

"There's a pair of mountains on our southern border that have remained unpopulated. The territory has been under dispute for some time. If Eero is amenable, I'm happy to concede it to their efforts. Zita has already agreed to their use of her man and his ability to speak to stone. It's as good as done. Now, if you'll excuse me, now is not the time. I have business to attend to."

"Wait!" Harland reeled in surprise. Ceneth had treated the request for a neutral territory as if it were nothing. He'd reacted to the concept of Samael's demon-hunting league like it was little more than a fanciful idea. "I made Samael swear not to hurt Ophir. I was going to ask Onain to do the same, if they are to work together..." Harland observed the man's holstered weapons for the first time. He caught not only the daggers strapped to each forearm but the sword belted to his hip. "But perhaps there will be nothing to fight if you're off to harm her. King Ceneth, please—"

Ceneth turned without speaking. He began walking toward the river. Harland jogged to keep up, voice hitching into desperation as he asked, "If you aren't going to hurt her, then where are you going?"

Ceneth's eyebrows arranged themselves in a hard, stoic line. He bent his knees to launch into the sky as he muttered, "To find my fucking fiancée."

PART III

Tattered Fate on the Loom

TWENTY-FOUR

+ + + +

R AASAY FOREST WAS A MISERABLE BLUR OF EVERGREEN TREES
and jagged stones. Ophir had flung rock after trunk as
she'd thrust her rage into her creations.

"Firi…" Dwyn was rarely so hesitant. The sound almost
belayed Ophir's focus. Almost.

Ophir's fingernails bit the heel of her hand, eating into her
tender flesh as she clamped her fist down against the words. She
turned her face away from Dwyn, rejecting her name on the
siren's lips. A log popped and kicked up ashes as it collapsed,
sending specks and cinders into the air. Ophir flinched at the
sound, watching the gray and white tendrils pour into the
sitting room just like the stones and debris of Castle Gwydir.

"Unless you're going to say something helpful," Ophir
began, "keep it to yourself."

She caught the way Tyr's mouth turned down in
disapproval.

"What? Are you on her side now?" Ophir asked.

A muscle feathered in his jaw as he held her gaze. He
was a pillar of firm, patient strength. Her face heated as she
challenged him to look away. After a stretch of silence, he said
simply, "Yes."

She blinked as if he'd sprayed water in her face. She heard a small noise from Dwyn on the other side of the room.

"Then it's true," Ophir said. "We died, and this is hell."

His nostrils flared slightly as he pushed out an irritated breath. "I don't have to like her to know she's right, Princess."

"She's not right!"

Tyr remained firm. "She is."

Ophir called out for her hound, searching for the only thing in this world who would take her side.

Sedit leaped onto the settee from the cottage floor and nuzzled into her. She stroked her fingers lightly along his scalp and ran them down the protruding knobs of his spine as she would with any dog. He relaxed, his many eyes growing heavy as his breathing slowed. She smiled sadly at her beast. He was the best thing she'd ever made.

He'd been waiting on the edge of the forest, sitting still as a cloaked sentinel in the pine shadows just beyond Gwydir. They were nearly on top of him before he'd stepped tentatively into their path. Dwyn had gasped as the gloom came to life in the shape of one of Ophir's first intentional acts of manifestation, but Ophir had melted into a puddle of relief and joy. Her stony façade had fallen away in that moment as tears broke through. Sedit had crashed into her with the exuberance of a child, and as she'd thrown her arms around him, she had wept. The tension, the remorse, the panic, the uncertainty had drained from her as the dam had broken over the hellhound.

"We need to get Sedit someplace comfortable to sleep tonight," Ophir had said.

Tyr had attempted reasoning with her. "He's been alone in the woods—"

"Don't remind me what a terrible mother I've been."

Tyr had dropped the issue. He'd made no secret as to his disdain for her abominations, animal lover though he was.

"You can make something, Firi," Dwyn had said quietly.

Dwyn's energy had hung over them like an impending

storm. Her spirits had reflected the thick gray clouds that clotted the sky as they rumbled in with their threats of ice and water. The fiery, irreverent, beautiful siren was never subdued. In their time together, she'd never known Dwyn's shoulders to slump, her words to falter, or her eyes to look at the ground before her. Dwyn's transformation into a damp, near-silent traveling companion was every bit as terrifying as the ag'drurath Ophir had unleashed on the castle. Ophir had nurtured her feelings of suspicion and rejection toward Dwyn until a small, spiteful fire burned steadily within her.

She may have resented the fact that it had been Dwyn's suggestion, but she'd agreed. She had the ability to make them some place to stay. Ophir had focused her resolve and tried to picture a home. She'd attempted to see wood and windows and cornerstones, but her mind had flashed to tombs and blood and anguish. She was a monarch. Between her life in Castle Aubade, her time in the Tarkhany Palace, and her new residency in Gwydir, nearly every moment had been spent in luxury. She'd realized the only true homes she'd entered had been with the intention to kill or be killed. From the tragedy in Lord Berinth's manor and the farmer slaughtered in the woods to the merchant she'd killed outside of Henares, she'd never walked in or out of a house without the loss of life.

The house that had burst forth was built on a foundation of cracks. Death had rippled through the soil before the logs piled one on top of the other. Windows had tilted, the door had darkened, and the roof had slumped as if carrying the weight of terrible secrets. The three had quietly frowned, but now, as the weather of the Raasay Forest soured and the evening grew cold, they didn't have much room to argue.

Dwyn and Tyr exchanged looks. Their attempts to keep their disappointment discreet did not evade Ophir.

"You want something better? Make it yourself."

"It's not that, Firi," Dwyn said, speaking for them both. Still, her soul hung heavy, as if someone had snatched her spirit and left only her body behind. "The settee is nice, but maybe we could try beds? Blankets?"

Ophir grumbled like a scolded child. She knew they were not at fault for her unresolved issues of inadequacy. They'd been more or less supportive throughout her journey, from her royal life in Aubade, to her first taste of blood in Henares, to the baking sands of Tarkhany, to the cold, dense forests beyond the royal city of Gwydir as she'd fled. The more she put them through, the more she resented herself.

She thought of soft, rabbit-fur blankets, of cashmere scarves, of goose-down pillows as she closed her eyes. She opened them to a mysterious pile of sooty cloth that seemed to be part gauze, part cobweb. She winced in frustration as she turned away from the evidence of her failure. She felt the sting of silence when Dwyn said nothing. Ophir hadn't realized how heavily she'd relied on Dwyn's external affirmation until the moment it no longer came.

They were a party of secrets and silence, no one speaking as they fetched what they could from the fabric on the floor and took to their corners of the structure.

Rain froze into icy pellets before it pummeled into the ramshackle cabin. She could see her breath crystallize in the fading light but was too hurt to attempt a fireplace or hearth, certain it would result in her shelter going up in the smoke and flames of her failure. Ophir closed her eyes in the cold, dark room and hugged her knees to her chest. She leaned her head against the wall as the sound of gravel over tin filled the space until there was no room left for her thoughts. She didn't fight Tyr as his arm settled around her, scooping her to him. She didn't fight as he brushed the hair away from her face, looking at her with sad, kind patience, and planted a soft kiss on the crown of her head. She didn't fight Dwyn as the siren perched silently in a corner. She could no more change their emotions than end the sleet that coated their shack.

Somewhere between the steady pounding of the late-season storm and the rise and fall of Tyr's warm chest, she fell asleep. When the storm ceased, the absence of noise stirred her from a tumultuous dream of wings and fangs and pretty sisters who deserved so much better than they got. She peered into the scarcely discernible shades of black and gray for evidence of the moon, or dawn, or stars, but found nothing. The only break in the sooty darkness belonged to the pale slivers of flesh that Dwyn had left exposed to the air.

Maybe it was her newly awakened state that kept her from feeling the heaviness and pain of the day, but concern seeped into her as she blinked at Dwyn's limp form.

Ophir slipped away from Tyr's arm. He remained sound asleep as she shifted to her knees and crept to Dwyn. Worry ticked up within her as she closed the small, blackened space. She gasped when her fingers brushed skin so cold it might have belonged to a corpse. Dwyn jolted beneath the touch, teeth chattering as she looked up. Dwyn's face was moon pale against the night.

"Have you slept?" Ophir whispered.

Dwyn tucked herself in tighter as she shuddered.

Ophir clicked her tongue for Sedit, sandwiching Dwyn between herself and her hound as she conjured a ball of flame. Ophir's mouth parted in surprise as the fire illuminated blue lips and chalky cheeks. Sedit relaxed happily into Dwyn, and she accepted the blood, skin, and pressure of the beating heart beside her as she cuddled into the vageth.

"Dwyn," Ophir breathed. She shook her head in disbelief until she felt her loose hair tickle her neck and shoulders. The light sensation stirred her to her question. "Why would you stay over here alone? Are you that mad at me about the ag'drurath that you'd let yourself freeze to death rather than sit beside me?"

Dwyn trembled against the cold as she lifted her hands to Ophir's flame. Though her clenched jaw made it difficult for her to spit out the words, at long last, she said, "I'm not mad about the ag'drurath. I'm not mad at all."

"Then what?" Ophir looked at her. She studied the slope

of Dwyn's nose, her large, dark eyes, the downturn of her mouth in the light of the flame she held in her hands. "You've never created space from me like this. You've never..."

But Dwyn didn't meet her eyes.

"Is it the castle? Evander's death?"

Dwyn scoffed softly before saying, "No, Firi. You know I'd support anyone whose life you wished to end. If you killed for sport, I'd be your favorite spectator."

"That's fucked up," Ophir said, attempting levity. The moment passed, and nothing eased between them. Her face prickled with confusion. She flexed her fingers, urging her flame to burn brighter as it melted the tension from Dwyn's frozen muscles. "Then what?"

"You have to pick one, Ophir."

"What?"

Dwyn looked at her then. She offered the stern, unflinching gaze she'd once given on the cliffs of Aubade when Ophir had lost herself to nightmares and sorrow. She held Ophir's questioning gaze as she said, "You wanted to leave Farehold, and we ran. We took down Tarkhany. Raascot was ours. I've abandoned Sulgrave, so we can tick that one off the list. The four corners of the known world have been in your hands. There's nowhere left to run, Firi. There's nowhere to turn."

"We'll find another house," Ophir said.

"A house?" Dwyn repeated.

Ophir shuffled uncomfortably. She allowed her flame to swell, matching her intensity. It illuminated every corner in the humble shelter, filling the space with a cooking heat until she was certain any residual chill had thawed from Dwyn's body. "A real one," she promised. "Not one I manifested. We'll get the next one we find. We'll have proper beds and a nice fire, and I'm sure they'll have a kitchen full of food. There'll probably be some unsuspecting farmer you can murder. You love murder."

Once again, the attempt at humor fell on unreceptive ears.

Dwyn's spirit remained damp. She was no longer the teasing, goading person Ophir knew and loved. She closed her eyes, her fresh rosemary scent mingling with the flame as if she were a comforting spice in a homey kitchen rather than on the floor of a cold, empty shack. "And then what, Ophir? We live in the woods? We stay in Raasay Forest? Tyr chops logs and Sedit kills game and we learn to sew?"

Ophir chewed on her lip. "There's always the Etal Isles. We could be the first from the continent to make it there. What do you say?"

Dwyn smiled, but it didn't reach her eyes. She lowered her thick, dark lashes as she gazed into the flame that hovered above Ophir's palm. "If I thought you meant that, Firi, I'd be thrilled. You know I'd support you. We could walk across the continent, and I'd be with you every step of the way. But we both know we aren't going to the Etal Isles."

Ophir's voice dropped to little more than a whisper. "What would you have me do?"

The windless silence following the storm was oppressive. Nothing interrupted the painful heartbeats as seconds stretched into an eternity. Finally, Dwyn said, "We have to go back."

Ophir felt like she'd been slapped. "Back to Gwydir? To where my father and his rings and his fertility—"

"Eero will return to Aubade, and Ceneth isn't your enemy."

Ophir let her fire wink out. Sooty darkness engulfed them. Her eyes stung with an iridescent shimmer from where the flame had been only a second before. "You really want me to marry him, don't you."

She didn't pause for long before saying, "I do."

"How could you?" Ophir asked, betrayal leaching into her question. "From the moment I met you, you've told me to seize my independence. You've joked about letting me out of the marriage so many times. And now, what? Suddenly you want me to fall into line and become a good bride?"

"No, Firi. A marriage to him keeps you safe from Farehold's manipulation. It secures your allies in Raascot. It may even cement an allegiance with Tarkhany. Eero is a bastard. He deserves whatever fate befalls him. Send a hundred years of beasts his way. But Zita likes you. Ceneth tolerates you, at the very least, and would protect you, even just to honor your sister's memory. Returning gives you shelter, a castle, a title, and a kingdom. Go back to him. Though you may want to use different rings at your wedding."

Ophir scoffed into the darkness. "What does it matter to you if I have a kingdom?"

She felt Dwyn's now-warm fingers as they gripped her arms in a plea. "We'll make it right."

"I destroyed the castle. I created a dragon. I killed a man—"

"You'll be their queen! And you're a manifester, Ophir. You're a goddess. You're *the* goddess for all I care. They will revere you as such. We'll make gold statues in your likeness if that would make you happy. We will all worship at your gilded feet. And if they don't, they'll live in fear of you, which is just as good."

"Is this supposed to make me feel better?"

Dwyn's silhouette cast a long shadow as she turned to face the wall. "Feel whatever you want to feel. That's your right." A stretch of silence broken only by Sedit's breathing pulsed between them. At long last, Dwyn was ready to meet Ophir's prompting gaze once more. "But you are Ophir, Princess of Farehold, Creator of Flame, motherfucking *manifester*. You do not run."

Ophir stood from the wall, not bothering to slow as Dwyn caught herself against the sudden movement. She stared down at where Dwyn sat on the floor before saying, "You're right. No one tells me what to do. Including you."

+   +   +   +

Their fight in the dark of a crumbling building of cracks and nightmares had been three days prior.

Dwyn remained quiet as they awoke and continued their walk through the pine forest. She said little as they picked their way over the rocks and mountains. She didn't celebrate when they found a proper cabin. She didn't say a thing as Ophir caught the owner's attention with a wave and a smile, her gold-brown hair and pointed fae ears drawing a curious stare from the hermit. Dwyn didn't even take joy in draining the unsuspecting human who'd built a quiet life for himself in the countryside. Tyr disposed of the body in a shallow grave between the trees while Dwyn, Ophir, and Sedit made themselves at home.

The home had been rough-hewn from the forest around it. Each tree, a Raasay log, wept with coniferous sap that acted as amber glue, connecting the stacked logs. The four humble walls of the cabin were decorated for a man who lived alone. A hand-sanded table had been pushed against one wall, and a fireplace lined with carefully stacked and balanced stones had been built directly into the wall at the cabin's center. The hermit's bed had rested on the floor beside the fire so it might warm him through the night.

Ophir wasn't sure if she should feel sad that they'd taken the life of a lonely man or glad that it had been someone with no family so he wouldn't be mourned. As her thoughts flitted to Caris, she settled on the latter. Ophir slipped out of mud- and sweat-slicked clothes and stood in her shift as she attempted to create something soft and lovely. The resulting black dress belonged with her pile of cobwebs, not with fabric worn by humans or fae, but at least it was clean. Dwyn didn't even react as she stepped out of her shift and tied the dark, draping gown around her figure.

She and Sedit sat on the late homesteader's bed as Dwyn pulled together a few things from the kitchen and began a proper dinner.

"Has Ophir tried manifesting food?" Tyr asked. He dipped his hands into a shallow basin of clean water that the human must have recently gathered. The dirt and evidence of his gravedigging were washed away with a bar of homemade soap.

Ophir made a face, and they both looked expectantly at Dwyn for her retort.

Tyr was the first to speak up. "No witty comeback? Nothing about how she'd probably poison us with anything she made? Or how she should give it a shot and I should try it, or..."

But Dwyn didn't take the bait. She didn't look at either of them while she cut into the root vegetables the woodsman had in his kitchen and tossed them into the pot that hung over the hearth.

"You've been quiet for almost two full days, Dwyn," Tyr said.

Ophir scratched Sedit lovingly as she said, "We spoke."

Tyr looked between them, but Dwyn continued with her task. "And? Is anyone going to fill me in?"

Ophir absently hoped that Dwyn might cook for all of them, but she didn't hold her breath for such an outcome.

She met the look of concern on his face with the defeat on her own and said, "It's nothing worth repeating."

✦   ✦   ✦   ✦

On their sixth day, Dwyn and Tyr were in agreement.

"Firi..."

"Stop!" Ophir barked. She missed when they were at one another's throats.

She bristled at Tyr's heavy breath, knowing that whatever he said, he was not about to be on her side.

"You aren't going to live in the woods, Ophir."

"How the fuck would you know?" she spat. Sedit matched her energy, lips pulling back from his thin, venomous fangs as a low grumble escaped his belly. She was warmed by the solidarity her loyal creature offered.

"Well?" Tyr asked, looking around. "Is this it? Is this your dream life, Ophir? You want to be a frontier woman and live in the woods and drink water from a bucket and catch your own game? You, the princess I watched laugh and party and revel in life's many joys—"

"What's wrong with partying?"

"Nothing!" He clipped out the word, temper flaring. "That's my point! You were happy! You were yourself! Now, you're not running toward anything. You're only running away."

Ophir blinked in surprise. She looked up at Dwyn and couldn't determine whether she regretted doing so. Dwyn was looking at him with equal surprise. Her lips were parted slightly in silent agreement, eyes wide as she regarded Tyr.

"For fuck's sake, you two. Are you happy? You finally agree. Dwyn and Tyr against Ophir. How's it feel?"

Tyr lowered his brows in near-paternal disappointment. "Listen, Princess—"

"Listen, *nothing*," she said. "Your opinions don't matter. Agree with me. Disagree. I don't care. You can't make me do anything. You can't make me go anywhere. Try. I dare you." Ophir flung her hands out and flexed her fingers with her threat.

Tyr squared up for the fight. "Do it."

She lifted one brow.

"Do it," he repeated. He planted one foot in front of the other and pointed to the ground as he underscored the seriousness of his stance. "Call a dragon. Create a serpent. Summon an army of salamander hounds."

"Vageths," Dwyn said quietly from the corner, then looked away as if regretting speaking at all.

Ophir's temper flared. "What, you don't think I will?"

He laughed. The sound was the cold, loveless noise of coal tumbling into a firepit. "That's the thing, Princess. I *do* think you will. I think you're shortsighted enough that you will destroy your shelter, your friends, everyone you care about just to prove a point. I think your pride is stronger than your love, logic, or loyalty."

"Fuck you," she seethed.

"You have," he bit right back, "and goddess be damned, you enjoyed it."

She turned away in disgust, hands falling to her sides. Her flame scalded her from within as her face burned with anger. Sedit barked once in furious solidarity.

Tyr took a step closer. "Go back to Gwydir, and I'll go with you. Stay here, run, choose to let everyone around you win, to let the kingdoms and rulers and outside forces define who you are and where you get to be, and effectively and tell Dwyn and I that we don't matter. Stay here and send us away."

She whipped her head up again to judge the seriousness in his voice. He'd narrowed his eyes, stare unwavering. "Why do you want to return?" she asked. "You've never wanted power or riches or titles or—"

"For fuck's sake, Princess. I care about you. I've watched you jump from sea caves into the ocean. I've seen you engulfed in flame. I've watched you seek vengeance. I've seen you create. And now what are you? *You*! Creator of demons and dragons and unspeakably ugly hounds—"

"Hey..."

"You are hiding in a cabin because your father was terrible? You want to sleep on a hay mattress and eat rabbits because your dad's a miserable bastard?" He looked at the woman in the corner of the room. "Dwyn, how's your relationship with your parents?"

Dwyn abandoned her task, setting down her knife on the chopping block as she said, "It's terrible, thanks for asking. I hate the monsters."

"Exactly!" Tyr spun back to her. His voice filled the cabin as he boomed, "Do you think you're the first person who's been wronged by someone who was supposed to look out for her? You're right, Ophir: Your mother and father should have had your back. They should have loved you, and supported you, and not married you off to a faraway kingdom or manipulated you or brought a horrid fertility fae to you.

They should have seen you for who you are rather than for your potential to facilitate their will. But guess what, they didn't. And they won't."

Ophir gaped at him.

"Do you know what you get to do now, Princess?"

She blinked, tongue-tied as she leaned away from his lecture.

His gestures became more animated as he continued, emboldened with every word. "You get to avenge every son and daughter and child who was mistreated. You get to stand up to not only your oppressors but to those who wronged kingdoms and peoples and generations. And you're going to run off? With the power to create life from your fingertips? If you don't have the ability to fight back, then what hope does any disenfranchised child have?"

She drew in a ragged breath. "Are you saying…"

"Get revenge, Ophir. Get back at the man who wronged you."

Both women looked at him as if he were a talking animal. It was Dwyn who said, "What happened to you?"

He huffed out a lungful of air. He began to throw up his hands, then caught himself halfway through the motion as he controlled himself. From his face, she could see he'd realized how he'd let his emotions run. He calmed before saying, "Get back at him for *you*. Why should he decide that you don't get to heal? Why should your parents or your kingdom or your heritage determine whether you move forward or if you flee? Don't run away from something. Run toward it. It's what I'm doing. I ran toward vengeance, and now, I run toward you."

His words knocked the wind from her lungs.

"But your dog…"

"I'll kill the men who hurt Svea. I swear it. But the fae life is long, and she's already with the All Mother. For now, I need you, and you need me."

Sedit's shoulder blades cut an intimidating figure as he poised himself to pounce on either of the fae who posed a threat to his creator. He flicked his many-eyed gaze from Ophir to the others, tapping his talons against the cabin floor while he listened to her labored breathing.

After a long pause, Dwyn began to clap.

This was the disrespect Ophir needed to snap back to reality.

"You can't be serious." Ophir glared at the woman.

"Listen," Dwyn said. "It took a long-ass time for Tyr and I to find common ground. We spent decades feuding long before we found our common ground in you, Firi. But as much as I hate the dog, he's right. There's nothing for you here. And you seem to be the only goddess we recognize. Do us all a favor, and let's get out of here."

Ophir's hands clenched into fists. "Don't pretend you want me to go back for the same reasons."

Dwyn cocked a brow. "What's it matter? Neither of us wants you in this cabin."

Tyr's laugh was a cold, hard sound. "It matters. She kicked you out once before for deceiving her, Dwynie. Did you like sleeping on the ground in Henares? Do you want to keep lying to our princess?"

Ice overtook the cabin as Dwyn's expression hardened. Frost filled her gaze as she looked at Tyr, motionless. With an arctic clip to each word, she asked, "And what lie am I telling?"

His eyes narrowed into slits. "We kept our bargains, witch. I got mine, and you got yours. Now tell her."

"Three minutes," Dwyn said. "You were in my good graces for roughly three minutes. What a record. Savor this moment, Tyr. Enjoy the last few heartbeats before you lose everything."

They were speaking of her as if she weren't there. Ophir waved a hand to gain their attention, but they were locked in a standoff. In a bid to break their icy stares, she demanded, "Lose what? Tell me what?"

But neither of them looked at her. They remained locked

in a battle she'd seen time and time again to various degrees. She saw the barest tips of the tattoo that crawled up Tyr's neck, and then her eyes went to the hip where she knew a matching mark wrapped around Dwyn. They were inexplicably bound. Enemies forced into an alliance with a shared lover and a blood pact, they'd never had more in common than their hair color and their ink.

"There's nothing to tell," Dwyn said.

"Do you want to bet?" Tyr retorted.

Dwyn crossed her arms calmly. Her fingers tapped a pattern against her bicep as she relaxed into the stance. "Just when I thought we'd found common ground, you go and prove your worthlessness. You feel good about yourself? You know how to drain, and now you're ready to be top dog? So many know the one thing you still believe you hold over my head. Go ahead, Tyr. Make your bid for alpha. Be my guest." She tilted her head with purely predatory intent.

His intensity wilted at the poison in her eyes. He broke Dwyn's stare and looked to Ophir. "I want what's best for you, Princess. I want you to stand up for yourself. I want you to live a good life. I want you to succeed. And I don't want you to share a bed with your sister's killer."

Ophir's head tilted until it mirrored Dwyn's on the far side of the room. She knitted her brows. She could tell from his fiery passion that she was meant to be filled with fear, or adrenaline, or panic, but she felt only confusion. Her hair tickled her arm, but she continued to hold Tyr's eyes.

He took a step toward her. "Dwyn killed Caris."

He held his ground as Dwyn threw up her hands in exasperation. She made a tired sound as she stepped back toward the wall and leaned against the logs, utterly disinterested in the man and his rant. She began to pick at the dirt under her nails.

"No," Ophir said carefully, "Berinth killed Caris."

Tyr scrunched his face. "You *know* he wasn't in his right mind, Princess. You know it wasn't even his real name! You know someone else was pulling those puppet strings. You saw him in the dungeon. You knew right up until the very end. The morning of the execution, your winged demon spoke to the killer, and we both know it wasn't talking to Lord Berinth."

"It was Berinth's knife," Ophir repeated. She pressed her fingertips into her temples, assaulted by another one of her headaches.

"What aren't you hearing?" Tyr practically cried the words. "It's Dwyn, Ophir! It was always Dwyn! She's orchestrated everything. She needed to get close to you. She needed an in. She needed Caris gone. She—"

"Please, stop. My heart hurts," she said.

He stopped in his tracks. He held Ophir's eyes for a long moment before looking to Dwyn. As her mouth tugged up in a slow, calculating smile, the blood drained from his face. "Dwyn, what did you do."

She ceased inspecting her nails long enough to shrug. "You were right, Tyr. Dishonesty got me into trouble before. I couldn't let that happen again. Are you glad you rejoined my list of archnemeses for this?"

"How could you have told her?" he asked, pain and confusion on his face swirled together with horror. He took a step toward the door. He refused to look at Ophir. "You told her and…" His eyes widened. "You told her."

"We've established as much," Dwyn said, utterly bored.

"I've spent weeks wondering why you didn't heal yourself from the poison in Midnah. She begged you to use your last power to call on healing the morning of the slaughter. Even I did. I knew you had one borrowed power left from the man you drained in the cell… But you'd already used it, hadn't you."

It wasn't a question.

Tyr hadn't blinked. "How did you do it?"

Dwyn's smile didn't show her teeth. She merely looked impressed with herself as she allowed Tyr to work it out.

"You conditioned her not to have a response to the only piece of information that could be your undoing. You used your final power to tell her."

Ophir continued to watch the two talk, blinking curiously at Tyr as he deflated. The strength leached from his posture as his shoulders slumped. The damp cloud that had engulfed Dwyn for days was gone as well, as if it had abandoned her to settle over him.

"I know," Dwyn said. "You know. Ophir knows. For the goddess's sake, even Sedit knows, now." Sedit growled, and she sent the hound a wink. "You know the only true difference, Tyr? I tolerated you. I made good on my end of the bargain and taught you precisely what you sought to know. You can drain, dog. Go back to Sulgrave and avenge your murdered pet. Fulfill your life's purpose. But if you know what's good for you, you won't stay here. You've crossed a line, dog. You've made an unforgiving enemy."

"You can drain?" Ophir's confusion deepened. "What does she mean?"

He looked only at Dwyn. "You can't make me leave."

"I can," she replied, ignoring Ophir. "I've yet to do anything with the life I've taken from our belated hermit here. Perhaps I can't kill you, but Ophir can."

"Hey!" Ophir said, flaring to life. Horror consumed her as she gaped at Dwyn. "Are you implying what I think you are?"

Dwyn made the barest of winces as she laughed it off. "I'm exaggerating to make a point, Firi. We don't want the dog here. In the last ten minutes, he's yelled at you and tried to drive us apart. Enough is enough."

His face paled. "You wouldn't."

But Dwyn's face told a different story.

"Ophir?" Dwyn said innocently.

Ophir turned to Dwyn in a swirl of confusion and anger. Their words tumbled over her like arrows, some hitting a wall, others soaring beyond the barricade and into the fortress of her mind. She struggled to sort through fury and disgust and the strange, quiet voids where no emotion reached her. She looked up at Tyr, chewing her lip as she flinched against a budding migraine. Pain lanced through her temple, throbbing as arrow after arrow bounced, hit, embedded, and fell. She closed her eyes against the too-bright cabin, the too-loud room, the too-upsetting sights and sounds of her companions as they fought. She struggled to drown out Dwyn's final words as she spoke.

"See?" Dwyn asked. "Her brain can't accept the competing truths. You're fucking up my handiwork and making life harder for her. Is that what you want? To hurt her?"

"Why didn't you do this from the beginning? If it's a puppet you want, why not brainwash her and rule as queen, plucking her strings?"

Dwyn made a disgusted noise. "Because I love her. I want her to embrace her power. I want us to rule together. Firi and I have seen our combined potential, and it is glorious. The only thing standing between us right now is you."

"You're delusional."

"Go, and I won't have you killed. I don't think very highly of you, dog, but I don't think you're stupid enough to put it past me."

He pushed back, but there was no longer brimstone in his voice. It was with the cool resolution of a foregone conclusion that he asked, "Why wouldn't you do it now? Set yourself free."

Dwyn clicked her tongue. "She'd do it, but she'd feel guilty and be confused and probably miss you. I'd have to handle that meltdown until I found someone new to drain, and I have no idea how far away the next homestead may be."

"You can't," Tyr challenged. "If you give the order for Ophir to kill me, then you kill me, and you die."

Dwyn hummed thoughtfully before deciding, "You're right. It's messier to try to kill you, when it's so easy to let you live and ruin her opinion of you forever. As it stands, I'll

242

have to use the hermit's life to make her forget this exchange. It's a wasted power, and I hate you for that. I was going to use it to make us a nicer meal. You owe me a life."

It was as though cotton filled Ophir's ears. Her world spun. Everything around her muffled slightly against a high, muted hum. She looked up through the pulsing pain at the two of them. Light throbbed as if the sun itself flared in the cabin as she battled to see the two before her. Sedit's agitation grew, matching the excruciating confusion that ebbed and swelled with every passing word. Tyr's face melted in clear concern. He reached out for her, but Dwyn tsked.

"See? Sedit's agitated now that his mother is upset. Perhaps the vageth will murder you and end this."

"You're the one upsetting her, Dwyn. Are you sure you won't be the one the hound kills? Clock's ticking."

Dwyn appeared to consider this. "The best thing you can do for her is go. Then I can fix this and put her right again."

He took a half step back. "You're a monster."

"Have an original thought," she sighed, exasperated.

Ophir's mouth dried. She clutched at her chest, begging the palpitations to stop.

"Good luck crafting something she'll swallow," Tyr said. "She won't believe I abandoned her. Not truly. She knows I wouldn't."

Dwyn pushed off from the wall and walked toward Ophir. She rested her hand lightly on Ophir's back as a pained sound escaped her lips. "The longer you stay, the harder you're making this on her. Alleviate her suffering and go so I can fix her."

"Stop," Ophir said weakly. She struggled to do something, to intervene, but the spinning continued, rendering her useless.

Tyr stood, but his feet were frozen to the cabin floor. "Leave."

"She doesn't deserve this," Tyr said coldly.

"She deserves love. I love her," Dwyn said. "I'll give her

the world, even at the expense of not letting her stand in her own way."

He opened the door and flinched at another pained sound as Ophir fell to one knee. Sedit began barking, blaming Tyr for his master's pain as he retreated. He looked over his shoulder sadly as he said, "There are things love is, and things it isn't."

Dwyn wiggled her fingers to dismiss him without looking up.

Ophir looked up into Dwyn's face for help in the final moment before the spinning darkness claimed her and her world went black.

TWENTY-FIVE

✦ ✦ ✦ ✦

O PHIR OPENED HER EYES TO THE RISE AND FALL OF SEDIT'S chest. Slick, shiny skin clutched his ribs, lungs filling and deflating with every carrion-filled breath. He twitched in his sleep, large eye clenching in synchronicity with the two smaller eyes below them. His claws shot out, accompanied by a whimper as he moved. They retracted a moment later as he settled back into regular breathing. She wondered what sort of nightmare would haunt an unkillable creature.

"I assume he dreams of you," came Dwyn's voice.

Ophir sat slowly, gasping against the ache in her temples as if she'd suffered a hangover. "What?"

Dwyn leaned into her chair. "I think the only thing that would scare Sedit is seeing you hurt."

Ophir absently wondered if Dwyn could hear her thoughts. She looked back at Sedit, watching him twitch again as he huffed, attempting to run for an unseen enemy in his nightmare. She didn't entertain the idea for long before asking, "Are there any healing tonics in the cabin?"

Dwyn shook her head apologetically.

Ophir groaned as she leaned her head against the logs of the cabin wall. She searched her memory for images of the cabin rather than opening her eyes. There was only one small cabinet, and it lacked doors. None of the bottles had been the telltale brown packaged by healers. A pile of blankets, a cupboard of pots, pans, and plates, a pantry of dry goods, four windows, a door, a hearth, an uneven table, two wooden chairs, a bed, a vageth, a hungover princess, a Sulgrave fae. She brought her hand to her head as she asked, "Where's Tyr?"

Dwyn's lower lip puckered. She abandoned whatever she'd been busying herself with at the table. "You don't remember?"

The attempt to shake her head only exacerbated her headache. She winced.

"Lay down, Firi. I'll get you some cold water."

"When is he coming back?"

Dwyn sighed loudly. She gestured to the overturned bottles. "We drank a *lot* last night. Things got…weird."

Ophir grunted against the pain and the statement alike as she said, "We've been trapped in a hate threesome for months. How much weirder can they possibly get?"

She was met with an appreciative, considering face before Dwyn said, "Maybe *weird* was the wrong word. Tyr got what he came to Farehold for, Firi. He's returning to Sulgrave to use what he learned to get vengeance for Svea. He's gone."

The intricately linked log walls wobbled as her eyes struggled to focus. She rubbed her temples. "What do you mean?"

Dwyn chewed her lip. She followed Ophir's line of sight and looked at the wall for a minute before asking, "Why do you call me a siren?"

Ophir attempted to chuckle, which only worsened her headache. "A water fae who drains the lives of unsuspecting sailors? You're the only one I've met, but it's textbook siren lore. I'm still disappointed that you aren't from the Isles."

"My power is water," Dwyn said.

"Yes, water, and—"

"There is no 'and.' You know of the Reds. You know of blood magic. Why have you given me special allowances?"

Ophir gnawed on the thought. "Reds grow ill. Blood magic is outlawed. You've never fallen sick from what you do, just like the folk creatures of the sea."

"My power is only water, Firi. Just as yours is fire."

"Fire and manifesting."

Dwyn sucked in a breath. "No. Just fire." They stared at each other for a long time before Dwyn said, "Manifesting is blood magic."

Ophir laughed, but she stopped when Dwyn's expression didn't change. Sedit stirred from sleep, lifting his head long enough to ascertain that his master was okay. He settled back into a resting position as Ophir's brows lowered, forehead wrinkling with her unspoken question.

"You're drawing on the blood, the hearts, the spirit of your people. The old texts suggest that royalty might be predisposed to manifestation, but in theory, anyone with massive amounts of blood magic could achieve it. Then there's smaller blood magic."

"You keep saying that term and applying it to both you and me. Blood magic. It doesn't..."

"It's what the pact—our gang, Tyr's and mine—was pursuing. I figured out what none of them could and left Sulgrave rather than share the knowledge. When I drain, I borrow blood rather than use my own. Now that Tyr's learned how to drain, he's returning to Sulgrave to kill the men who hurt his dog."

Once more, Ophir attempted to laugh. There was denial in the sound. Her heart squeezed, an unseen hand wringing droplets of blood from it as pain shot through her. She pictured the twinkle in Tyr's eye, his wry smile, his fingers as they clasped her hips, his bright teeth grazing her throat, the warmth of his arms as he'd held her in her crumbling shack only a few nights prior. Water lined her eyes as she shook her head, face a mix between a smile at a joke she didn't understand and deep lines of concern.

"I mean it," Dwyn said, only pity in the outer edges of

her voice. "You know how fae fall ill and sometimes die after using their secondary powers?"

Ophir didn't attempt to hide her confusion as she stared at Dwyn.

Dwyn nodded as she said, "That's because a secondary power, and rarely, a tertiary power, is just one they've learned to access by borrowing against their blood. My only power is water. The others are ones I borrow. Your only power is fire. Manifestation is one you borrow from your people."

Ophir sucked in a breath as if to scoff, but no sound came out. She stared at Dwyn for a long while before asking, "If that's true, why aren't people dropping dead around me?"

Dwyn smiled understandingly. "You're borrowing against hundreds of thousands—millions, even. Drops here, heart-beats there. You channel the love of your people. What I do is a lot grittier and more direct. It can be learned. It can be taught. And I thought you should know. This is who you've shared your bed with. I use blood magic, and Tyr pursued it. It's why he followed me here from Sulgrave. I was the only member of the Pact who'd made the breakthrough, and I was his best chance at ascending, even if he hated me."

"No."

Dwyn continued, "I said more than I meant to. He learned what he needed."

"No," Ophir insisted. She scrunched her nose against the throb that banged against the inside of her skull. She shook her head hard again, despite her brain attempting to escape through her temples. "No, Tyr wouldn't. He wouldn't just leave me. He…"

Dwyn said nothing as she looked on with large, pitying eyes. Another damp cloud entered the room, filling the space as it had in the days following their escape. Ophir hated the sympathy etched into every line of Dwyn's perfect porcelain face. Her lower lip lifted, pressed into a gentle, compassionate pout. It was one of the kindest faces she'd ever offered Ophir.

She could have sworn she heard the moment her heart

splintered. It was the loud, high pop of a lake in the depths of winter as the surface cracked. Her fingers dug into her chest with bruising strength.

Dwyn stood and crossed the room in several swift steps. She crawled over Sedit, ignoring his protesting grunts as she wrapped her arms around Ophir. Ophir attempted to reject the kindness, pushing away, shaking her head, rebuffing, refusing, begging; then, piece by piece, her rebuttals turned to tears.

"I'm so sorry," Dwyn murmured into her hair.

"It doesn't make sense," Ophir said between gasps, water spilling down her face. "He said...he...I..."

"I fucking hate him," Dwyn said, "but I never wanted him to hurt you."

Ophir folded herself into the hug, collapsing against the warmth of Dwyn's chest as she heaved out her tears. The throbs of her headache matched the timing of her racking sobs. Her tears pulled in and out until Sedit was equally upset and mewling beside her, neither canine nor feline, just beyond the curtain of Dwyn's hair.

Hatred wasn't the emotion running its hands over her as her shoulders shook. Her heart chipped and crumbled as raw, unfiltered pain drove into her. It buried itself in her chest until nothing remained. "Why?"

"Shh." Dwyn stroked her hair, pulling her in close.

"It can't... I don't believe..."

"I'm so sorry, Firi. I'm so, so sorry. I didn't want you to hurt."

Somewhere between her gasping sobs and throbbing headache, she knew the words weren't quite right, but she neither knew nor cared why. She nestled her face into the column of Dwyn's neck until her vision was as dark as the rosemary-scented cloud of her hair. Maybe the pain was too heavy to carry, or Dwyn's soft, rhythmic touches were too soothing. Maybe the world was too cold and hard to face. Before she realized what had happened, Ophir had cried herself to sleep.

TWENTY-SIX

✦   ✦   ✦   ✦

Sedit's growl sent a jolt through Ophir. He leaped down from the bed and ran to the door. She sat up quickly as she scanned the room in the last gray light of day. Orange embers cooled amid the whites and grays of the long-dead fire, telling her she'd been alone in the cabin for some time. Nothing about her surroundings had changed. No new food. No new logs. No sudden appearance of broad shoulders, strong hands, and crooked smiles.

A high, grating noise filled the air as Sedit ran his claws down the door. She looked at her hound in surprise, realizing she'd never had to let him outdoors. It hadn't even crossed her mind that he might have to go in and out like a creature made of flesh and blood rather than nightmares and poison. She crossed the room, issuing quiet promises to Sedit until she opened the door. Her jaw dropped open at the kingly figure at the threshold.

"Ceneth." She breathed his name in shock.

Dark wings blotted out the last of the pewter sky as he filled the doorway. He looked her up and down, gaze a mixture of relief and disapproval. He took a long look at Sedit, then looked calmly back at her. "Ophir," he said. "May I?"

She opened the door with a silent nod.

He scanned the cabin and sighed. "One moment."

Ceneth left the door open as he disappeared back outside. She stood statue-still in the center of the cabin, Sedit at her side, as she listened to the sounds of scraping and rustling. Moments later, Ceneth reappeared with an armful of logs. The King of Raascot knelt before the hearth, stacking several atop the ashes and embers and setting the others to the side.

"Do you mind?" he asked.

Her swallow was audible. She wasn't sure why she felt so nervous, but she wordlessly complied. Her flame shot to life, consuming the logs in an instant. It banished the shadows, illuminating the room.

"How did you find me?" she asked.

He made a sound that one may have described as a chuckle, but the quiet staccato held little humor. "I was worried," he said. "If your companion can create doors to travel across the continent, you could have gone anywhere. But I asked myself what I would have done if I was angry and frightened, and I knew the answer. I'd run. Physically. I'd want to feel my muscles burn, to feel the rocks and soil and dry pine needles beneath my feet. Perhaps the frost on my wings as I took to the sky, but to exhaust myself nevertheless. I was about to give up when I spotted the chimney."

She looked at the now-cheery fire. "But it had died…"

"I was in the air. I spied you from some way off. Once the fire was out, you were a little harder to locate. Now…" He frowned. "I'm not going to put us in the awkward position of asking which of my subjects lives…" He watched her face before amending, "*Lived* here."

She continued to look at him with wide eyes as if she were little more than a child caught by a parent.

"Did you make this?"

She looked to her gown and was about to answer before she realized he was pointing not at her, but beside her. He was asking whether or not Sedit was her doing.

Her throat bobbed as anxiety bubbled through her. He'd witnessed her manifestation of the ag'drurath. Now, with calm resolve, he was asking if she was responsible for the needle-toothed abomination at her side.

"His name is Sedit," she said quietly. She cleared her throat as she found her voice. "I call him… I call them vageth."

"Them?"

"The race," she said, dropping her eyes to the floor. She hadn't had to explain herself like this before.

"Hmm," he said, the sound neither rude nor curious. "And there are others, I assume? Races of creations?"

She looked into his eyes for a long time before confirming with a slow blink and dip of her chin.

"Where are the others?" Ceneth asked.

"My other beasts?"

"Your friends," he clarified. "Where is Dwyn?"

He scanned the room as if the cabin could possibly conceal two additional fae. She supposed he didn't know of Tyr's gift to step into the space between things, but it didn't matter. They were completely alone.

"Gwydir isn't the only thing I destroyed," she said.

A painful memory gnawed at Ophir. Cruel words rang through her just as they had when they'd been flung at her in Castle Aubade. She'd barely survived her first attempt at manifesting a serpent in the sea cave beyond the castle walls. When discovering her cut, bruised, and covered in sand, Tyr had asked her why she was so careless, why she insisted on posing the greatest threat to her safety, and why she'd become the person she was. At the time, the fires of judgment and hate had burned like a furnace within her. His rebuke had driven her into Dwyn's arms that night. Now here she was, months later, and she'd be lucky if even Dwyn remained at her side when this was all said and done.

"She's out," Ophir clarified. *Probably finding a woodsman to drain*, she thought. "I am sorry, Ceneth. You didn't deserve what happened in your castle."

He shrugged, but she could see the insincerity in the gesture. She'd killed one of his men and she knew it. Though she'd grown a little too comfortable with the loss of innocent life since meeting Dwyn, she didn't expect others to feel the same. Raascot had paid the price for her vendetta against her father.

"The castle has been repaired," he said. At the surprise in Ophir's quiet murmur, he added, "Zita's man can speak to stone. He was exceptionally useful before he...volunteered for another project."

Ophir wondered briefly at his pause before asking, "Is Zita still in Gwydir?"

Ceneth didn't relax his posture. Shoulders back, hand on the hilt of his weapon, he appraised her slowly. Finally, he closed his eyes once in acknowledgment. "She's chosen to remain in Raascot until our wedding. Everyone in the Tarkhany party is welcome in my home. The queen wishes to be in attendance. One of your men—Harland—has also opted to stay behind, though the rest of your party has departed southward. There are preparations to be made before the ceremony, after all."

He said the last words with venom, but the acid was not directed at her.

Ophir looked at Ceneth with new eyes. She drank in his deeply bronzed skin, the inky shimmer of his wings, his sharp gaze, and the hard cut of his jaw as if seeing him for the first time. She'd known for years that Ceneth was a good man. She'd known since her arrival in Raascot that not only was he a decent person who'd loved Caris deeply, but that he was one of her few allies in Gyrradin. As she looked upon him now, she considered what he must be thinking.

He hadn't flinched at the sight of her, though she'd abandoned the ruined sweater and fur-lined leggings in favor of the dark, gauzy dress of her own manifestation. It rustled around her ankles like smoke, adhering to the fashions of no earthly kingdom. He hadn't approached with judgment, despite her responsibility for his friend and advisor. He'd found her alone, without the escort of armies or guards, despite knowing she was capable of immeasurable destruction. He didn't like her, but perhaps he didn't have to.

"Why would you want to move forward with the wedding?" Ophir asked. She wasn't just asking why he'd want to bind himself to a creature of unspeakable nightmares. Through its actions and subterfuge, Farehold had revealed itself to be no ally to Raascot.

"I suspect we have a common enemy," Ceneth said.

She raised a single brow ever so slightly. This was true, but it was daring of him to say so. His single sentence acknowledged that he saw Eero as a foe. Simultaneously, it asked if she was ready to turn her back on her family.

"I was never the daughter they wanted," Ophir said. "But at least I was that—a daughter. I'd always thought so, anyway. Until Cybele and her rings."

The briefest evidence of anger flashed across Ceneth's face. His eyes tightened as he adjusted his grip on his weapon. He wasn't positioning himself to strike. It was almost as if he clutched it for security against the demons in his mind rather than the ones at Ophir's fingertips.

"Her rings are meant to fuse us, Ceneth. You're not a person to them. Neither am I."

It was Ceneth who said, "Farehold doesn't want a union. They want to conquer."

Ophir knew it was true. If her parents had truly desired a treaty with Raascot, they would have trusted him to keep his word. He'd never shown any indication of backing out of this proposed union, even after Caris's death. And while her father claimed that taking territory was a sin of their ancestors for which they couldn't be held responsible, he'd positioned history to repeat itself. Once Ceneth and Ophir had fused, Eero would have a winged puppet on the northern throne. She doubted that Eero knew he was evil. In fact, she was quite certain that he believed he was doing the good and right thing. Somehow, that only made it worse.

"We'll insist upon other rings, obviously," Ophir said.

Ceneth rubbed his chin. "Strategy would caution us about making brash requests in the light of day. We may need to conceal our next steps to come out with our minds and wills intact. Farehold is a powerful enemy."

"So, what, we make peace with them?" Ophir guffawed.

"Of course not," Ceneth said. "But it behooves us to withhold just how much disdain we have for them. I'll have decoys made in their place. Ruby on gold for your ring, and sapphire on silver for mine? Is that right?"

"White diamonds on either side of the ruby, and black diamonds on either side of the sapphire. Yes. Can you have something made on such short notice?"

"It shouldn't be a problem. We'll have a plan before the wedding day. Just wait for my word. I promise: Neither of us will disappear as a result of this wedding. We've lost enough. Both of us."

The fire crackled. The bones of the cottage creaked.

"If I die, you die. The rings wouldn't just meld our wills. They're mutually assured destruction. What would Farehold stand to gain from my death? Wouldn't they want me to live on and rule in the north?"

The corner of Ceneth's mouth quirked, though he did not meet her gaze. "It comforts me to hear you refer to them as *Farehold*. But if I had to guess, it's meant to ensure that we *do* die, and whatever young, moldable heir we leave in our stead can be steered by your parents. They've assured you'll conceive."

"They want me dead." Ophir almost laughed, though the sound stuck in her throat.

"They're afraid of you. You're a threat because you can't be controlled. Honestly, Ophir... I think Caris would be proud."

The laugh morphed into something akin to a sob, though the tears would not come.

"Zita asked a favor of me," Ophir said, breaking the stretch of silence.

"Oh?"

She nodded slowly. "It was a plea, really, about the status quo. She asked that whatever I do... I do *something*."

It was Ceneth's turn to raise a brow. "And? Will you?"

She chewed on her lip for a long minute. Ophir leaned against a chair for support, tapping her fingers rhythmically against its surface. "Would you seize Aubade?"

He formed a tight line with his lips. "I'm not interested in world domination."

"Nor am I. But I don't think things can continue on. Not like this."

There was a question in his eyes. Ceneth was evaluating her, daring her to say what was on her mind.

Ophir swept in and alleviated his anxiety with four simple words. "Eero can't be king."

Ceneth chewed on the prospect "Do you have an alternative?"

She picked at the skin beneath her nails as she considered the question. "No. And I don't think that matters. If any of us takes the throne to further our agenda, how are we different?"

Ceneth relaxed his posture, allowing his hand to drop from his hilt at long last. He pushed out a breath before asking, "With that, I'd like to formally ask you: Ophir of Farehold, will you marry me?"

✦   ✦   ✦   ✦

"Firi?"

Ophir's eyes flew open to find Dwyn kneeling by the bed. Ceneth was already wide awake. He'd remained in a chair near the table, straddling it like a horse saddle so it might accommodate his wings while he rested his head on crossed arms. He'd adjusted the chair to give rest a try, but she wasn't convinced he'd gotten any sleep. She looked between the king and the siren.

"You're back," Ophir breathed.

"I wasn't sure if you'd be here when I returned. I'm sorry to have left you like that," Dwyn replied.

"Off killing simple mountain folk, I assume?"

Dwyn's lower lip jutted out in a pout.

Ophir pushed herself into a sitting position. The blanket fell around her, revealing the same gauzy gown she'd worn all day. She raked her fingers through her unbound hair as she fought to shake the cobwebs from her mind.

"You were right," she said. Dwyn tilted her head cautiously, waiting for Ophir to continue. "I'm going back. I'm returning to Gwydir with Ceneth, and we'll move forward with the wedding."

Relief splashed across Dwyn's face like the very waves to which she called. She threw her arms around Ophir's neck and practically choked on her happy noises as she breathed through Ophir's curtain of gold-brown hair. Dwyn tightened her hold until Ophir had to untangle the arms that strangled her.

"Dwyn!"

"Sorry." She coughed out an apology mingled with strands of hair, but she didn't look sorry in the least. The rain cloud that had soaked her aura from the moment they'd departed Gwydir had evaporated again. "And we're leaving now?"

Ophir looked between the two once more. "Ceneth will fly back. He offered to bring me, but I wanted to ensure you knew where I'd gone. Since you have the gift of travel, you can get us both to the castle in no time." Ophir rested heavily on the first half of her sentence, hoping Dwyn remembered which thread in the web of lies she needed to clutch.

Dwyn didn't miss a beat. She hopped to her feet, a spring in her step once more. She turned to Ceneth as if he were little more than a common inconvenience as she waved a hand. "Off you go, Your Royalness. I'll take it from here."

He made an unimpressed face as he got slowly to his feet. Then, his unamused look transitioned to the discomfort of someone dismounting a horse after a long journey. The King of Raascot looked perfectly normal as he grumbled at his aching muscles, aside from the ethereal beauty and angelic wings. Once more, she glimpsed the man Caris had loved so deeply. He looked at Ophir to confirm her security, and she offered a weak smile.

"I'll give you a moment to warn the others that death personified is returning to your castle grounds."

He frowned. "They won't think of you like that."

She matched his expression. "There's no use lying to me, Ceneth."

He was unwavering. "The only people who know you're a manifester are those who were in the room for the meeting. Word has not spread. The people know only that a dragon set the castle to ruins. They're creatures of fable brought to life. Rumors have caught on like wildfire speculating as to its origins, but most seem to believe it came from the desert. Its Tarkhany name is already well known."

"So, all of Raascot knows of the ag'drurath…"

"Yes," he confirmed as he stepped for the door. He rested his hand on the knob and looked over his shoulder. "And nothing of its maker. I think it's in our best interest to keep it that way."

She blinked, baffled. It hadn't crossed her mind that such a precious piece of information might stay concealed. Perhaps no one had to learn of her dark gifts. After a moment, she dared ask, "And Sedit?"

He looked to where the creature remained curled. "Your…vageth?"

Ophir nodded, a tiny seed of gratitude sprouting at both his memory of her pet's species and in the way he neither scowled nor recoiled as he regarded the beast.

"As I'm to go on ahead, I can ask Zita if she'd like to take credit for bringing the beast from Tarkhany as a wedding present. It would allow you to keep Sedit with you in the castle. Additionally, it might prove helpful to keep the animals' origins focused to one climate, to allow the people to make sense of them. Of course, she may decline the affiliation with your creations, which is her right."

Ophir silently agreed. When they'd said all that they had to say, she watched the king leave, listening to the mighty rustle of feathers as he took off into the air. After enough time had passed that even the keenest of fae ears couldn't possibly overhear, Ophir looked to Dwyn. "So, you have a reputation as a traveling fae to uphold."

"Happy to oblige." Dwyn smiled, and she truly did seem happy. She extended a hand to Ophir and helped her up out of the bed. "Are we keeping the haunted hermit attire?"

Ophir looked down at herself. "I think I pull it off."

"You absolutely do. Now, we have people to find."

She hesitated, and Dwyn returned the quizzical look. Ophir finally asked, "Is Tyr truly gone?"

Dwyn's shoulders slumped ever so slightly. She took a few steps toward the door and relaxed against the wall as she said, "There aren't words for how sorry I am, Firi."

"I just... We've been through hell. We've been to the corners of the continent. We've shared..." Ophir's face heated as her eyes pricked with tears. She knew if she kept speaking, she'd lose the battle against the dam threatening to break within her.

Dwyn tilted her head, allowing the curtain of her night-dark hair to tumble down her shoulders. Her eyes softened as she said, "You never should have had to feel like this."

"The last thing I remember was him burying the human. After he came in and washed his hands... I can't believe I started drinking so quickly. I've gotten drunk more times than I can count, Dwyn, but this is a blackout I've never experienced. I don't know why he'd need to wait for me to be inebriated like that. He could have just claimed he'd gone out for wood and never come back. He..."

"I do believe he cared for you," Dwyn said sympathetically. "Perhaps he knew that if you had the chance to talk him out of leaving, you'd succeed. I know you could have talked me in or out of anything. Maybe this was the only way he could do what needed to be done. Saying goodbye while you were intoxicated was the only way he could get his closure and leave you unable to fight."

The look on his face when he'd lifted his arm and tucked her against his chest on the floor of the shack had blotted into her memories like ink staining unblemished paper. She was sure she'd never forget the crack through his strength as he'd regarded her, holding her, warming her, making her feel safe and loved and protected. She hadn't just trusted him. She'd loved him.

And then he'd left.

"So, how long do we hang out in the forest before we use my amazing powers of lightning-like travel?" Dwyn asked, wriggling her fingers as if to summon such power. Perhaps she could see Ophir tumbling down the deep, dark well of her memories. It would serve neither of them if Ophir lost herself to her wounds.

"You're a feral animal," Ophir chuckled, though pain bubbled to the top of the sound. She rallied for strength as she said, "I suppose we need to get hunting if you need fresh blood."

"No time to waste! Kitty's hungry."

Ophir cringed. "For the love of the goddess, don't call yourself that."

Dwyn flashed her teeth, pleased with herself. She opened the door and made a sweeping gesture to the dense forest that encroached upon the cabin. A layer of early-winter frost was just beginning to thaw in the sunlight as her feet crunched over snapping pine needles. Ophir stepped into the chilly, conifer-scented air as Dwyn said, "Now that I know it bothers you, I'll never refer to myself as anything else. Off we go, Princess. Places to be, forests to tackle, people to kill."

TWENTY-SEVEN

+　　+　　+　　+

W HAT DID HE WANT?" SULEY ASKED, ONE BROW RAISED
in wry curiosity. She'd let herself into Zita's chambers
in the moments following Ceneth's departure from their
private meeting. The king of the north had dipped his head
in acknowledgment, tucking his enormous wings in behind
him to allow her to pass as she slipped from the hall. The door
was now locked and closed behind her. Her queen rose from
where she'd been sitting at her ornately decorated desk and
poured a second glass of wine, extending it to Suley.

"Shouldn't you be able to tell me?" Zita asked, words ripe
with implication.

Suley stood on unsteady feet as she maintained her
question.

Zita matched the expression. "Sit, sit."

Suley obliged. Zita's room was larger and grander than
her own, but it was built from the same dark, crystalline stone
that had captured the stars themselves. Zita's bed was larger,
decorated with intricate wood carvings down each individual post. Warm furs covered every surface, just as they did
in Suley's room. She suspected that their Raascot hosts were
doing their best to compensate for the unfamiliar change in

climate. Even in the deepest regions of the north, the bright scents of lemons and oranges rolled off her queen, banishing the local berry-rich perfumes she'd noted on the fae residents of Gwydir. A lit fireplace burned with red-orange intensity, banishing chills and shadows from the suite. Suley took her first generous swig of her wine while she listened.

"Ever since Farehold's wayward princess stumbled down our streets, life has grown curiouser and curiouser. Raascot's valiant king succeeded in locating the lovely conjurer. Ophir is expected back in Gwydir at any moment. He's just requested that Tarkhany take credit for her demons."

Suley couldn't contain her surprise. "Demons? Plural?" Horrid memories of a long-necked serpent clinging to the cliffs of her seaside village pierced her mind. She saw the moon shimmer on its wings as the screams of women and children joined the swelling noise. The terrible face of a winged, humanoid monster filtering into the rectangle of the open-air window she'd once possessed. Suley shuddered before asking, "And why in the goddess's good name would Tarkhany do that?"

Zita's amusement didn't waver. "We've named the ag'dru-rath. Its name is known. It seems that most of the demons have a similar skin—one more suited to the reptiles and amphibians of our warm climates than that of the north. Ceneth is requesting continuity to help the people accept their existence. The demons, in theory, could be native wildlife."

"Because," Suley began slowly, "the people know nothing of Tarkhany, and we're to exploit that ignorance. It's an achievable goal, but why? How would it serve anyone?"

She watched as Zita's smile widened.

"Everyone wins, dear Suley. Tarkhany won't be bothered. If the sands weren't enough to deter them, the threat of monsters will keep one hundred generations of zealous, conquering foes far from our lands. They've taken enough. With fear in their hearts and our name wiped clean from their mouths, they'll take no more."

Suley drank deeply from her goblet as she considered the words. Fear could be a useful tool, particularly if the goal was to be left alone. "And how does Ceneth benefit?"

"He and Ophir plan to marry. He doesn't need his bride-to-be stained by truth."

"And Farehold..."

Zita's laugh was a slow, amused purr. "I wasn't wrong about her, my sweet Suley. I do think Princess Ophir may be the key we've hoped for. She's no friend to Aubade. If taking credit for her monsters solidifies our friendship, then I do think we both win. I was told that this will require our party to acknowledge bringing a hound from Tarkhany as a wedding present."

"A hound?"

"Mmm." Zita nodded. "I suppose she is to return to the castle with some new abomination. Perhaps that's an unfair categorization of the creature. I guess all new things take some getting used to. Did you ever see the Viscountess's first-born? Quite the tiny troll, as are all infants. I must say, I'm quite curious to see what Ophir's made. It can't be worse than a baby."

Suley smiled at the queen's joke but couldn't bring herself to laugh. She chewed on her lip slowly as her eyes unfocused. She reveled in the quiet that stretched between them, savoring the silence between each heartbeat. The only thoughts in her head were her own. It allowed her to focus as she asked, "Did we know this was possible? That a typical fae might possess manifestation?"

Zita frowned, her face contemplative for a long moment. Suley watched as her queen relaxed into her chair, stretching the long column of her neck as she looked to the ceiling. Unlike her own preferences, her queen had never been one for elaborate jewels. The light caught only on the rich depths of her skin. At last, she said, "I don't think there's anything typical about Ophir."

Suley couldn't keep the disdain from her voice as she

said, "Farehold was our undoing, and now we're to expect its offspring to be our salvation?"

Zita laughed, but there was no joy to the sound. "Tarkhany does not need saving. But it deserves blood atonement."

"I don't understand. If you don't want Ophir to fix things, what is it you want from her? From any of them?"

Zita set down her glass with a gentle clink and folded her arms gracefully on the table. "No, no. There is no savior in this story. Farehold may have brought us pain, yes. And now, at long last, it may bring the same suffering upon itself."

"You want Farehold to hold itself accountable?"

Zita tutted her tongue. "Accountability is a luxury compared to what Farehold deserves. For too long has Tarkhany been called to action. I led my people to safety, then oversaw my kingdom as it rebuilt solely in the desert. I will never make peace with the loss of my ancestral home, nor will I take the weight of justice upon my shoulders. It is one ask too many. I want retribution, and I want them to be the ones who do it."

"This is a shift, Zita," Suley said. "Haven't I heard you espouse the opposite for years? You rebuked your husband's calls for revenge—"

"Well, my husband was an idiot."

"And insisted you wanted justice," Suley concluded.

"A lot has changed since the princess of chaos and creation stumbled into our lives. The law can't reign unless we trust the morality of those in power. The only justice amid corruption is anarchy."

Suley stiffened. She swallowed what remained in her goblet. It wasn't the sort of meeting for pleasant buzzes or drunken merriment. She'd spent years draining bottles in hopes that it might dull the noise, but its only effectiveness had been in helping her sleep. Her dreams had been the only true reprieve from the incessant sounds. Now, a gentle vibration thrummed through her as the wine worked its way into her system, able to do its job without a competing cacophony of thoughts. Zita leaned across the table to pour two more glasses from the pitcher.

"Speak your mind," her queen said.

"It's nothing," Suley said quickly. "I just don't know why we would count on Ophir to turn on her people."

Zita brought the glass to her lips but paused for a long time. The queen held Suley's eyes until she looked away uncomfortably. She shifted in her seat, aware that Zita took a sip from the goblet at long last. When she looked up, Zita spoke over the rim of her glass.

"That's a lovely new cuff, Suley." Something about Zita's words rang with a vaguely ominous note.

Alarm flashed through her. She didn't have time to fight the reaction as her eyes and nostrils flared. "Thank you," she said stiffly.

Zita jutted her chin slightly as she said, "You wore it right before the final summit. Now, I'd ask you to listen to Ophir's thoughts to see if she'd turn against Farehold, but I suspect I know why you'd tell me that you'd have no input on the matter."

"Your Grace...?"

"You've always called me by my name. Don't stop now."

"Zita, I—"

Zita set down her glass once more. "I don't hold relief from distress against anyone, Suley. I'm disappointed that I created an environment where you felt you couldn't share your victory with me."

Suley looked at her hands only to realize she'd bunched the fabric of her dress tightly in each fist. She continued to look at her rings, each crease in her skirt, the way her fingers forced pockets of the material into irregular shapes and sizes between her tightly clenched palms.

"Is it the cuff?" Zita asked.

Suley didn't insult her queen by asking for clarification. She forced herself to relax her hands, smoothing the skirt of her dress over her thighs. She watched as the wrinkles of soft fabric melted into perfect, seamless lines. "Yes," she said.

Her queen remained perfectly poised as she asked, "Who in the castle came to your aid?"

Suley lifted her eyes slowly. She debated wisdom and folly, truth and deceit. Honesty would mean every gritty detail, every dark secret, every evasion, and precisely how she'd come to learn that Dwyn would be capable of creating such a device, when truthfully, she'd told her queen only the broadest, most poignant strokes prior to this moment. There was no honor in lying, nor did she think the Sulgrave siren had earned a moment of loyalty from anyone. No promises had been made, and no oaths would be broken.

She sucked in a long, slow breath, and then she told her queen everything.

TWENTY-EIGHT

✦　　✦　　✦　　✦

Z ITA RAN A FINGER ALONG THE BROWN REMNANTS OF WHAT
had surely been a magnificent flower in its time. Leaves
and blossoms fell at will in the temperate south, a place that
knew no seasons. Trees shed the yellows, reds, and withered
pieces that no longer served them in favor of fresh, bright
sprigs. A bush would blossom in shades of pinks or purples
beside the deeply green foliage of a plant that had shed its
flowers months prior. The plants listened to the soil, to the
water, to the wind, rather than a chill in the air or the threat
of snow.

Nothing was the same in Raascot.

She'd enjoyed her strolls in the garden, despite the layers
of frost and naked foliage. She appreciated the unencum-
bered view of jagged, snowcapped peaks. Though she loved
her palace, the baking heat, the tall palms, the vibrant red
dunes, the rainbow flutter of parrots, the diamond-studded
nights, and the aquamarine of cloudless daytime throughout Tarkhany, there was a peerless beauty to the lavender
mountains that surrounded Gwydir. She'd ventured outside
once per day to lose herself in the misty mountains, in
the inky, churning river that surrounded the castle, in the

blue-black stones so unlike the creams and custards that made up her city.

The unpleasant cawing of a crow drew her attention. A second dark bird joined it in the bare branches, then a third. She shivered against her fur, pulling it closer as her hand dropped from the flower. Her skin had heated the remnants of hoarfrost that clung to its dried, long-dead petals. Though it had been centuries, she remembered the blossoms wilting and dying along the coast. The changing leaves along the shore had signaled to her family that it was time to leave the summer castle overlooking the western sea and return to their winter home.

Seasons were a distant memory now.

Before she could stop herself, she saw the happy faces of children playing on the beach. Her husband scooped them into his arms, kicking up seafoam as he chased them. In the vision, she clapped her hands, smiling and laughing as he hoisted one over his shoulder and caught the other around the waist. His faeling children were fast, but even a human could catch them when they were small. He grinned at her from where he stood, pants cuffed above his calves yet still soaked to the britches with sea spray.

Her sons shrieked with the high, unbridled joy known only by happy families who hadn't experienced loss, or betrayal, or pain.

She closed her eyes against the memory. Six hundred years had not been long enough. She doubted that she'd feel any different after six hundred more.

"Queen Zita?"

Zita straightened. She cleared her throat, realizing emotion had caught in it like a bit of dry bread. She inhaled the chilly air, allowing it to burn her lungs as she found the serene smile that had been her companion for so long. Her lips were already turned up with gentle amusement by the time she turned to see the golden eyes of Farehold's only princess.

"I was wondering when you might come to see me, dear. You've been back for days."

Ophir tucked her hands beneath a lush gray-and-white fur. Someone had told her it had belonged to a coyote, but Zita couldn't recall the exotic northern creatures from her tomes.

Finally, the princess said, "I wasn't sure what to say. When Ceneth told me that you were willing to claim the vageth was from Tarkhany…" Her words drifted off.

"Vageth? That's your hound, then?"

Ophir bit her lip. "He's called Sedit."

Zita's gaze shifted away from the princess, over the young woman's shoulders and toward the castle beyond. It was rare to catch the princess without a friend or guard. Someone was always loitering nearby.

Zita set her jaw as she asked coolly, "And your unseen companion? Will he be joining us on this stroll?"

Before Ophir could respond, Zita knew the answer. She saw the wound on Ophir's face as clear as a written word. It was the look she'd seen in the mirror in the years following her husband's death. It was the pain that had plagued her when her half-fae sons and their wives had passed without heirs, leaving her alone once more. It was the injury in Tempus's eyes when she'd told him she'd never love him. No, Tyr was not there. Whatever had happened between them, he was no longer beside her.

"I see" was all Zita said.

Ophir took a tentative step closer as she asked, "Ceneth said you'd like to be present for the wedding?"

"I would," Zita said.

"May I ask why?"

Zita lifted her eyebrows at that. She studied Ophir more intently this time. Beyond the gold-brown hair, several shades darker than that of the late sister whose portrait haunted Ceneth's halls, past the spray of sun-kissed freckles, deeper than the slopes and curves and ethereal beauty so boring and typical to the fae, she searched for something more. The coronas encircling Ophir's eyes shone with an emotion as bright as the flame the princess so famously summoned.

"Do you know the opposite of love?" Zita asked.

Ophir blinked. Her pink lips parted, baffled. The early-winter wind rustled her hair, stirring the loose leaves across the courtyard before she attempted an answer. "Hate?"

Zita made an appreciative sound. "Mmm, people think so, yes. But alas, hate and love are two sides of the same coin. They're both passion, possession, and obsession. Do me the honor of writing this down, dear. Return to your room, pen my wisdom, and carry my words into the ages."

Ophir did nothing to hide her puzzlement. "And what wisdom is that?"

"Indifference," Zita said, "is love's true opposite. As I look at you now, I'm wondering if you meant what you said. You called a dragon, and the world heard your anger. You burned a bridge, and we watched it go up in flames. But my, what a speech, Princess Ophir. You looked at your father and said something so exquisite that I had to taste it for breakfast, lunch, and dinner for three days straight. Did you mean it?"

Ophir looked around as if hoping someone else might jump in to her defense.

"Will you salt the earth, Princess?"

"You're asking what I feel toward my father."

The wind bit her ears and chilled her nose. Her eyes watered against the cold, but she did not look away. She watched the cogs within the princess's mind turn like the mechanisms of a clock. The final bits of metal interlocked. Ophir's shoulders relaxed. Her face softened into cool resolution.

Ophir held her gaze as she said, "Good plans aren't born of hate. True change is rarely made from brash action. Kingdoms don't fall from spiteful princesses holding a grudge. You asked me to do something, and that's why you wish to attend the wedding."

Her small smile was both genuine and endlessly sad. "And tell me, dear, what would you do?"

"I can call another dragon, if that's what you're asking."

Zita chafed her hands against her arms. She gestured for Ophir to follow her and led them farther from the castle. Words such as these didn't need prying eyes or listening ears. The movement might warm their blood, and the closer they drew to the river, the less chance they'd have of being overheard.

"Your spirit is in the right place, dear, but I didn't ask what you *could* do. I'm perfectly aware that you manifest. I was in the room, if you'll recall. Tell me, what *would* you do?"

They kept pace as they reached the bank of the river. Their feet crunched over the frosted grass as they left the path and created tracks in the bits of white that clung to the beige ground. Ophir's response had the slow, calm resonance of someone sharing impersonal facts as she said, "I'm apathetic, but not in the way one might assume. I don't care what happens to Farehold. I don't care if it falls to ruin. I don't care if Aubade is laid to rubble and Eero's and Darya's names are lost to the wind. I don't care if a fae never sits on the southern throne again."

"Well," Zita said, voice level, "that is a lot of not caring."

They continued their walk, their conversation accompanied by the steady gurgle of water against the riverbank. Zita looked across the water to where a couple caught her eye. The woman had the large wings of a crow suited to the body of a fae. She was too far away to discern if the man was human or not, but he would never know flight. They stopped to watch Ophir and Zita, too, the pale face of the southwestern shores and the deep skin of the desert so different from the citizens of Raascot. He must be human, then, to marvel at faces unlike his own. Only Raascot's humans would have had lifespans short enough to not remember a time when they'd occupied the southern kingdom.

She looked away from the couple as the princess spoke again.

"What I do want…" Ophir's hand escaped her furs as she reached for Zita. Her fingers settled lightly on the thick velvet sleeve of Zita's cloak. "Is an end to their reign. I want them gone. Not out of spite. Not because I'm mad that I was wronged. It's his ignorance that has forfeited his claim to the throne. My father is too blind to realize he's every bit as bad as his father and grandfather before him. He was confronted, he was offered a chance, and he chose to exploit me, to betray Ceneth, to deny your claim to your lands, and if he's allowed to remain in the castle, that's his legacy."

Zita clasped Ophir's arm in return. She allowed centuries of emotion to come to the surface. Pride and pain and desperate hope tore through her as she understood what it was she saw in Ophir's gaze. The glinting starbursts of yellows and golds that encircled her large, beautiful eyes were no crowns at all. They were the monarchy that she'd been sent by the goddess to shatter.

"It is," Zita said. "But it doesn't have to be yours."

"And so you want to come to my wedding and watch me raise an army of hellhounds?" The flicker of sarcasm was half-jest, half-sincere.

"Perhaps," Zita said, returning the mild amusement. "Or perhaps I have a far better idea. Pray tell, my dear, have tales of my second power reached the gentle ears of Aubade?"

✦   ✦   ✦   ✦

Zita cupped her hands, forcing warm breath between them as she reentered the castle. The princess had stayed behind with only the churning river and snow-dipped mountains to keep her company. A servant bowed his head politely as he opened the door for her. She turned away from the path to her royal suite and hugged the innermost castle wall. She followed the corridor as it wound up, up, up to a distant tower. She raised a brow at the pile of empty birdcages that had been abandoned throughout the hall, scattered like the skeletal remains of slain enemies on a battlefield. There were no attendants to see her in as she pulled open the first set of doors and saw a harp as tall as she was, but no harpist to be found.

Zita pushed open the door to the room just as Suley whipped around to see her enter.

"Zita," Suley said, fighting to keep her voice level. "I heard you from the hall."

"Oh?" Zita asked. She took one step inside and stopped. She scanned the room carefully, but there was only Suley. "It must be so much easier to hear now that you've done away with your birds. Will the musician return?"

"You know how much easier it is for me to sleep with music," Suley said.

"Mmm." Zita nodded. She took a single step to the side, keeping the door within arm's reach. The chambers appeared picked over, emptier somehow. No one in her party had brought much from the palace as they'd traveled north through the door, but there was no evidence of Suley's gowns, her scarves, or the furs she'd been allotted in the armoire that sat ajar. The room was curiously absent from the chains and baubles Suley loved so well.

"Please, sit down."

"I can't stay long."

Suley's brows pinched. "Is there something you wanted to speak about?"

"Indeed, there was, though I suppose it's moot, now."

Suley's forehead creased against the question. "What do you mean?"

Zita sighed. "I rarely see you without your jewels, Suley. Where are those pretty bangles?"

Suley's fingers flew to her nose, then dropped. She looked to the vanity, where several bejeweled trinkets rested. "I've just taken them out to wash," she said slowly.

Zita strummed her fingers atop her crossed arms as she leveled her stare. She allowed the winter day to seep through her as cold filled the room. "Did you harm her?"

"Who?"

Zita didn't bat an eye. "Answer me. Did you hurt her?"

"Zita, I—"

Bitterness joined the arctic bite in her words as she said, "You're a shapeshifting cockroach, Tempus. I knew it wouldn't be long before you returned. I see the wisdom in stealing the form of the very person I'd fetched to hear you. Now tell me, did you hurt the girl?"

"You've gone mad, Zita. I don't know what you—"

"She lost her noise, Tempus."

Confusion flashed to concern. Worry and stress and anguish flickered across Suley's face as she fought for words, struggling to string together a thought. She stammered an excuse, a plea, an argument. Then, at Zita's frozen, emotionless stare, Suley's shoulders slumped. Her face calmed. Her facade evaporated, no thespianism in the world enough to defend hers. She blew out a long, slow breath before getting to her feet. She folded her arms over her chest, mirroring Zita's hostile posture.

She smacked her lips in disappointment. "No noise, you say?"

"None."

Suley held her stare for several moments longer. It was contempt tinged with disappointment that colored her word as at last she cursed. "Damn."

"And one does not remove piercings to wash. I see your attempt. Perhaps it was wisest to take her place, you worm, but it was futile. Now answer my goddess-damned question. Have you harmed Suley?"

"Not physically."

Zita's eyebrows shot up.

Tempus, in Suley's lovely shape, raised his hands. "I gave her permission to do something she desired. She wanted to live in the Raasay Forest. Now she shall."

"She wanted to live there so it might be silent, you fool." Zita's eyes flared. "You did this while wearing my face, didn't you." The firm, angry weight of her sentence held no question. She knew the answer. She wrinkled her nose in disgust at the filth in the room. "We've spoken every day from the moment she returned from that goddess-awful cliff-side village. I've known for some time that she was without her noise, and our friendship has gone unchanged. I struggle to believe that Suley could be so easily convinced of my dismissal."

A long, evaluating pause stretched between them before Tempus said, "Perhaps she always used her noise to verify thoughts. She was certain of your friendship because she knew your mind, Zita. Without it, she had only your words, and whatever insecurity accompanied them."

"How long has she been gone?" Zita bit out the question.

"Not long. A few hours at the most."

The queen turned to leave.

"Wait!"

She twisted the knob and took a step into the antechamber. "Zita—"

It was an idea that stopped her mid-stride, not her name on Tempus's lips. She slowly lowered her heel to the ground and turned to regard the man wearing Suley's face.

"Tempus," she said. His throat bobbed as he swallowed, desperate for forgiveness, for acceptance, for any reason she might allow him to stay. She scanned him slowly, from the curls of Suley's dark hair to the ink on her temple. She took a step closer to scan Suley's skin and found what she was looking for. Tiny, perfect holes for jewels had shifted to him as he'd taken her form. The only thing he lacked was her earthly possessions. "Remarkable," she breathed. He'd taken the shapes of so many animals. He'd even attempted a tree once, though he had just ended up as a rather odd long-necked bird. Not only had she never wanted him to take the shape of a person, but she'd outright forbidden it on the day he'd suggested he could let her see her late husband again through him.

"I may have a task for you," she said.

"Anything," he said, Suley's wide, dark eyes eager as he scanned Zita's face. "I'll do anything to redeem myself in your eyes."

"Pack what remains of Suley's things. You and I have a wedding to attend."

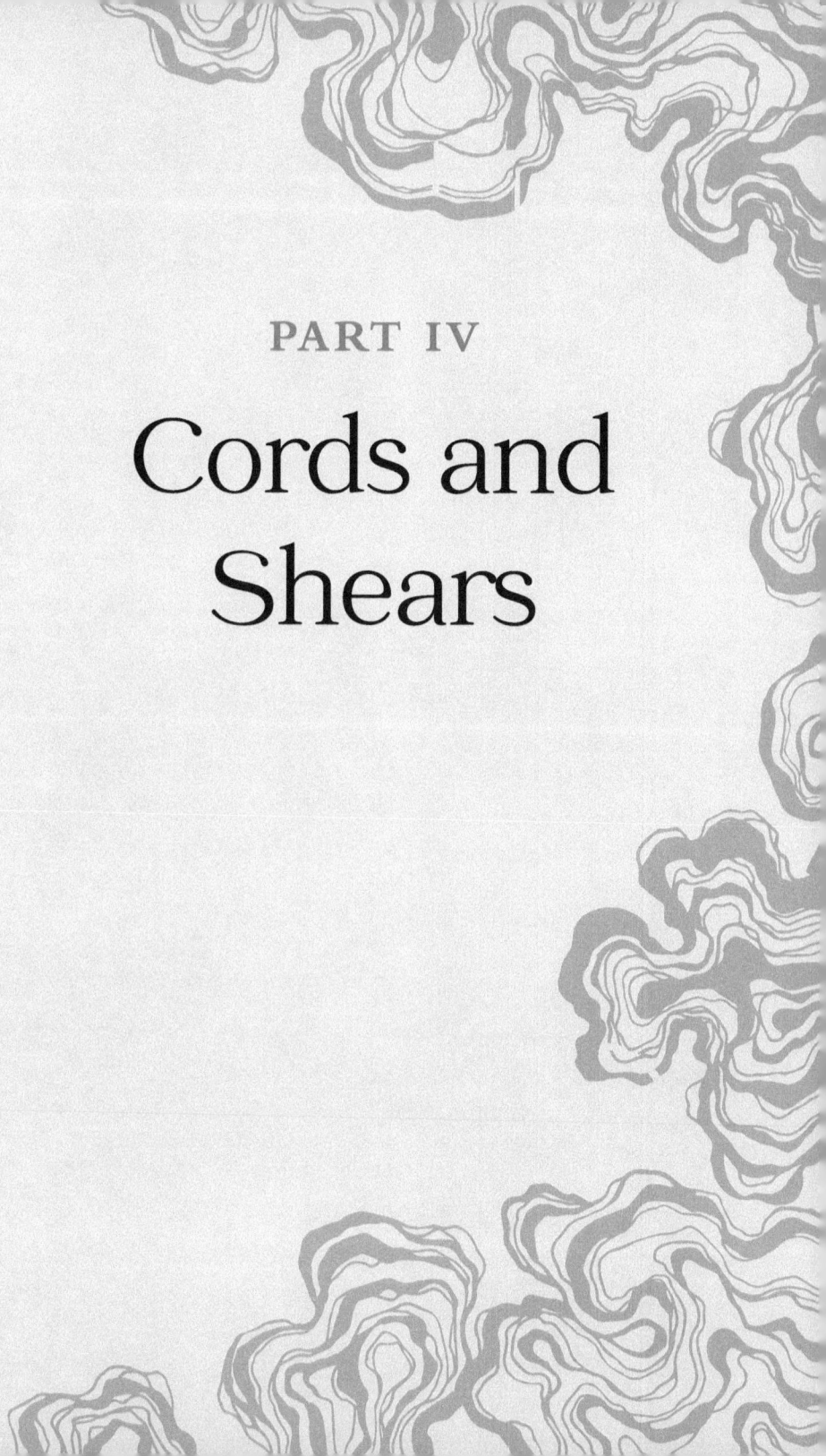

PART IV

Cords and Shears

TWENTY-NINE

✦   ✦   ✦   ✦

D WYN TASTED THE COPPER TANG OF BLOOD BEFORE SHE realized she'd been gnawing on her lip since Ophir had left. She went to the washbasin and spat out the ruddy evidence of her worry, washing her mouth with a cup of water. She began to pace the room, filled with unfamiliar anxiety.

Sedit made a low, grumbling noise, as if asking her to give it a rest and stop bothering him.

She shot the hound a glare, and he buried his snout beneath reptilian paws, resuming his nap.

Uncertainty of this magnitude hadn't found her in decades.

She flexed and released her fingers time and time again as she worked to calm herself. Ophir believed that Tyr had left. Ophir was back in Gwydir. Ophir was going to marry Ceneth. Everything was back on track. There was nothing to fret about. And yet...

Her yelp of pain cut through the room as a white-hot starburst of injury filled her eyes. She'd rammed her shin into the cedar chest at the end of the bed. Dwyn cried out in fury at the stupid piece of furniture, kicking it at exactly the wrong angle. The edge of the chest caught her toe and sent her a nauseating second wave of pain. She crumpled onto the floor as anger spilled out, cursing as steam rolled off her. She wrapped her fingers around her injured toes and cursed again while waiting for the shooting pain to subside. She moved her hand away, expecting to see a broken toe and exposed bone, but everything was perfectly normal, if a tad pink. The aching spot on her shin would surely bruise, but it didn't look nearly as bad as it felt.

"Fuck!" She bared her teeth as if the injury was an enemy she could chase away. She was certain there were healing tonics in the washroom, but she'd have to get up from wallowing on the floor if she wanted to heal her bitten lip, her swollen toe, or the steadily swelling goose egg on her shin. It was a rather frivolous use of tonic, but she didn't care. She'd use it for something as mild as the annoying voice of a table guest if it alleviated even a moment of suffering.

She rolled to her side and caught her reflection in the floor-to-ceiling mirror framed with opulent fleur-de-lis. Her memory cut to a banquet, a lovely dress, the moans and gasps and smiles of a flawless princess.

Tyr had been wrong about her.

She did love Ophir, perhaps more than any of them could ever understand. It was precisely why she'd told the truth. It was also why she'd needed to massage the message so that its revelation would no longer carry a sting. She was unwilling to lose her, whether to the stupid dog and his white-knight act or even to the consequences of her own actions. Yes, she'd been responsible for Caris's death. But that was before she'd spent months at Ophir's side. It was before her heart had squeezed when Ophir smiled, before she'd seen the power in her eyes and anger in her veins. It was before she'd realized that ruling at Ophir's side wasn't just a convenient way to access the world while pissing off the Pact and withholding knowledge from their gang leader. It was something she truly wanted.

She scooted from her place on the floor and rested her back against a leg of the enormous four-post bed that she and Ophir had shared since their arrival in Gwydir. It disgusted her to know that they'd rarely been alone in their bed, but she'd been willing to share, as long as it made Ophir happy. After all, the reincarnation of the All Mother should hardly be constrained by the social conventions of monogamy. She hadn't anticipated their relationship would be cut short by Tyr being sickeningly selfish under the guise of noble truths, but if there was one thing men did, it was disappoint.

Dwyn stared at the door, begging it to open.

She wished she could speed up time, but unfortunately, it was a power that didn't exist. She knew, for she'd tried.

She'd attempted most of them at one time or another. Small magics at first, then growing bigger and bolder as her confidence developed. By the time she was ready to go south to Farehold, there was nothing she couldn't do. Including infiltrating a royal family and attaining godhood, should she want. And want, she did.

Sometimes people had to die for you to get what you wanted. Usually, they deserved it.

Dwyn had been sixteen the first time she'd taken a life. Never for a moment had she doubted that he'd deserved it.

She'd been making shapes in the river that cut through the mountains, carving dramatic valleys as it divided the territories on its way to the Frozen Straits. It was unusual for children to access their powers, but Dwyn had been speaking to water for years. She and her younger sister had been swimming in this very river when its strong spring current swept her sister off her feet. She'd screeched in both adrenaline and delight as she followed the instructions they'd been taught. She'd relaxed onto her back and put her feet in front of her while she bobbed down the rapids. Dwyn would have been content to jog along the banks, giggling all the while, if there hadn't been a tree in the water.

It had happened before she'd understood what she was seeing.

Her sister's shift had snagged on the log, and when the current pulled her beneath its waves, only a pale, thrashing arm remained to be seen. Though only seven, Dwyn had screamed and jumped into the river. She had no business fighting the current, but rage, panic, and pain had carried her forward. She fell face-first into the cold water and came up sputtering, hair plastered to her neck and shoulders. She grunted as she shoved her feet between stones, anchoring herself with every step so that she could make it to her sister without being lost to the river's pull.

Her heart had stopped when her sister's pale arm ceased its clawing.

She'd pushed harder, faster, carelessly splashing as she leapt for her baby sister, her family, her best friend. She'd grabbed her sister's dress and yanked with a barbaric force she hadn't realized she'd possessed, snapping the branch and ripping the dress at once as her sister floated into her arms.

"Wake up!" she'd screamed, looping her arm around her sibling as she braced herself for the life-threatening trip back to the shore. She just needed her sister to hang on for a little longer, but the girl wasn't moving. Her chest neither rose nor fell. Her lips were as white as the bloodless skin of her face.

Dwyn took another step and slipped on algae-slick stone. She tumbled into the river, sister in her arms, and as she fell, a scream tore from her belly. The cry broke something primal within her, and the river responded. The water flew up on all sides, solid walls of liquid blowing upward and drying the riverbed as she howled. She and her sister dropped to the slick stones as she continued to wail. She didn't bother to look at the way the water bent to her will, answering her in her time of need. She saw only the chalky pallor of her only friend in the world.

She had been too little to understand how to pound on someone's chest if water was in their lungs. She'd never been taught that she could offer her breath, should theirs falter. She knew only that her sister should be breathing, but she wasn't. There was no flutter to her lashes, no blush to her cheeks, no pulse in her neck. Dwyn grunted against their water-logged weight as she hauled her sister out of the empty pit of the river and rolled her body onto the riverbank. The water collapsed around them and resumed its white-capped journey south while Dwyn wailed on the shore. She'd screamed and shrieked and begged and pleaded until her father had appeared in the distance.

He'd yanked Dwyn off and tossed her to the side as if she were a bloodthirsty tick flicked onto the earth as he breathed and pumped and prayed. Dwyn had screamed that he was hurting her, begged him to stop as the loud pops of ribs breaking joined the splashing and tumbling of the river. When she cried out for him to leave, the river made it so. It flung out a mighty arm to knock the man from her little sister's side as she threw herself over the body once more. She protected it like a rabid animal as her father blinked up in pain, horror, and disgust.

While the magic that protected Sulgrave kept it from being subjected to the backwater norms of winter, summer, spring, and autumn, time passed with snowmelt from the peaks, with age, with the development of a woman's body, with classmates, with afternoons that stretched into the long shadows of evening by her sister's grave, with cruel lessons, with church, and with the unforgettable distrust in her father's eyes.

They'd remained in their house by the river, but it was never again a home.

Her mother carried on dressing her, making dinner, and ensuring that she was in her bed each night, but she never again looked at Dwyn with gentleness or love. Her father avoided her at all costs, as if their youngest child had been stolen from them by Dwyn, rather than the river. The time to explain her role in the events came and went while shock still rested heavily on her heart. She hadn't been able to speak the awful truths into existence. She hadn't defended herself as they'd yelled or talked back as they'd begged. Her silence had bled into the passing years until the time came for Dwyn to see her second dead body.

"Pretty horses," came a voice from over her shoulder.

Dwyn dropped her hands, and her crystalline herd fell from the air, splashing back into the swirling rapids as if it had never existed at all. She whipped around to see Rekyr step from the tree line. She knew the others found him handsome. He was tall for their age, already possessing the chest and shoulders of a man. Though only sixteen, he'd already cultivated a reputation for unattainable desirability. The more the others wanted him, the harder he set his sights on the only person who didn't.

She had no interest in playing this game.

"I'm not looking for company, Rekyr," she said. She turned her back on him as she looked at the waves, hoping he'd leave. It wasn't the first time she'd spied him prowling the riverbank on the off chance that he'd catch her alone, but it was one of the only times he'd succeeded.

"You're never looking for company, Dwynie," he said, plopping down beside her on the bank. She recoiled at the familiarity with which he bastardized her name.

"I mean it," she said quietly, angling her body so her back remained to him. She cast her gaze upstream to where the river bent around the base of the mountain. Fifteen minutes away, she'd find her home. Thirty minutes from there, she'd reach the territory's edge. She was told that if she continued to follow the river, she'd find a winding, bending path where the devout went to meet the All Mother. She'd never been devout.

"You don't have to keep your hackles up," Rekyr said. "No one's around to see the show you put on. The cold, impenetrable Dwyn. Friend to no one, foe to all."

She bristled with every passing word, hating the truth in them.

She'd returned to school in the weeks following her sister's death to whispers. The rumors of her role in the drowning had ebbed and flowed, but she'd heard them like the ocean lapping at the beach. They'd seeped into her as she saw the same blame in their eyes she recognized in the dark, hardened gaze of her father. If they wanted her to be a foe, then a foe she'd become.

Instructors had no patience for her smart mouth. Bishops had tried to beat the obstinance from her, though her family had never been particularly religious. Her father had suggested they continue attending the lessons in godliness, but her mother had decided she couldn't have the blood of two daughters on her hands, even if the eldest was a monster. She was a feral animal in a world of stupid, docile creatures plumped for slaughter, and all she wanted was to escape her pen.

The boy made a wet, smacking sound with his lips as he lifted his fingers, brushing the hair from her shoulder. She reacted with speed and intensity in equal proportions, slapping him away. Her eyes widened as she bared her teeth at him. Glad to have her facing him, he took their nearness as a challenge.

Rekyr's hand was on the back of her head in an instant, forcing the space between them to close. The boy was quick, but she was faster. The moment he lifted his palm, she responded with her own. Her hand arced not for him, but for the river. She called to the waters, and they answered with arctic, soaking force as a column of cold, powerful water shoved him to the side. He was sent sprawling toward the trees as Dwyn scrambled away, but with her defiance, she'd changed the stakes.

He was no longer attempting to taste forbidden fruit. Now, he had a wounded ego and something to prove.

Rekyr lunged for her and succeeded in wrapping one large, callused hand around her ankle. She yelped in rage and surprise as he yanked her toward him. This time when she called to the river, her eyes widened in horror as she watched the water arc in a protective dome around him. His free hand flexed, and she understood that she had not been the only one to unlock her abilities. His jaw flexed as his shield pulsed, rebuking her water as if it were little more than rain over a tin roof. He jerked her closer, and she kicked like a foal with a rope around its neck. Her thrashing seemed to only amuse him.

The river came to her each time she called, as if the water itself felt every bit of panic that coursed through her. It had helped her when she'd lost her sister, and it was desperate to aid her now. It continued to beat uselessly against Rekyr's shield as she cried out, kicking and scratching, but he had excellent control over his ability. His free hand dropped until both hands were on her, their powers remained locked in a silent war, the assault within the shrouded veil raging with more anger, ferocity, and hostility than any of the magic beyond.

He leaned his weight into her as he pinned her down by the throat with one arm, using his free hand to yank her dress over her knees, past her hips, higher and higher. She clawed into him, leaving long, bloodied streaks across his face. Her gasps, her gnashing teeth, her disgust and anger and fury only emboldened him as he looked at her.

With a sickeningly evil growl, he said, "Your water can't save you now."

"No," she choked, "but yours can."

Before she understood how, or what, or why, she called to the water within him. She screamed for his blood to rise, and it obeyed. Her fist yanked away from him as a thick red mist escaped his mouth. His eyes widened in panic as his shield dropped. With it came the rush of river water and the abrasive, soaking cold of snowmelt as it washed her free of his touch and his violence. She sputtered away from the wave as it soaked the grass, dripping down the bank and returning on its lazy stroll to the Straits as she rolled as far from Rekyr as she could. She was prepared to run when she realized she wasn't being chased.

Dwyn coughed, hand flying to the searing pain on her larynx, to what she knew would be purple and red handprints on her throat. Her coughing continued. Each abrasive push of air felt like flesh dragged over hot, broken glass. She tried to swallow again and again as she struggled to understand what she was seeing. It wasn't the muscles of a sixteen-year-old boy or the healthy body of a fae. She took a step closer, then another as she examined the strange, shrunken form of skin stretched over bone, trapped forever in a silent scream. She straightened her skirt as she took another step closer and kicked him with her shoe. The skeleton rolled like a dehydrated trunk rather than a man.

She saw her father's face. The faces of the bishop, of her peers, of the teachers. She didn't even realize what she was doing before she summoned the water to wash Rekyr away. It pulled him into its clutches, sweeping him from the grass and carrying him on the rapids.

Dwyn didn't go upstream to the mountains. She would never return to her cabin home again. Instead, she walked into the city. She walked for three hours until she understood where her feet carried her. She was well into Territory One before she saw the tall arches of the cathedral and knew exactly why she'd come to see the house of a goddess she didn't worship. She hated the church and everyone within it. They did, however, have something she didn't.

Dwyn settled into an alley and stared at the windowpanes of an upstairs loft that rested above the sanctuary's atrium. She caught a flash of silhouettes followed by a subdued blast of color. She tucked herself against a wall and watched the shapes move as day turned to night. She fell asleep with her back upright and head against the wall that first night, hidden behind a cylindrical wooden barrel and a dusty rainspout. Rain blew in on the second day, but she asked the water to fall around her, and it complied. Her dress and hair remained dry as she watched the shadows move, knowing it was the Reds who trained in secrecy.

Whispers of the Reds had been one of the only reasons Dwyn had willingly accompanied her parents to church week after week. Her mother had perhaps hoped that her soul would be converted, and she'd have one daughter who might yet be saved. Her father had doubtlessly counted on the bishop to beat sense into her. But it was the glimpse of crimson fabric and the hushed secrets of an elite force the All Mother had gifted with incredible gifts that truly captured her attention, knowing it was within anyone's grasp, should they dedicate themselves to the goddess. It was said that in exchange for their devotion, she allowed them access to the magic that flowed through the universe.

The groundwater, they called it.

Dwyn knew a thing or two about water.

Rain continued flowing around her like a curtain as she maintained her control over the droplets that fell from the sky, until a gruff voice broke her concentration.

"Who did that to you, girl?"

She gasped in surprise, and that was all it took for her focus to shatter and the rain to drench her to the bone. Icy droplets that fell from heights where snow still clutched the mountain peaks soaked the fabric of her dress. Her hair became a sopping shell as it clung to her. Her fingers flew to the evidence of violence against her throat as she looked to where a large, dark shape stepped out from the shadows. She'd been so intent on the Reds within the church that she hadn't listened for anyone else. Their footsteps had been covered by the rain. Drenched from head to toe, a late-in-years fae peered down at her.

"You seem young to have already mastered your gift," he said. "What are you? Fourteen? Fifteen?"

"Sixteen," Dwyn croaked, surprised at the rough sound of her own voice. Her hand tightened around her throat as if it might alleviate the bruising.

The man gestured to a figure behind him, and a woman stepped up, shouldering a satchel. She flipped it open, allowing the man to rummage through its contents until he procured a small brown bottle.

"I'm Anwir. Let me make you a deal," he said.

She eyed him warily. She didn't care for the sound of deals with men.

"Swear to keep the rain off our heads until we finish our task for the evening, and I'll have my friend Mitra here pass you this healing tonic here and now."

Dwyn looked between the bottle in Mitra's hand and the man. Her fingers tightened around her bruised neck. She shook her head slowly, saying, "I'm fine."

"Suit yourself," Anwir said. He beckoned for the others to move forward.

"Wait," she breathed. She watched his face tense with curiosity as he awaited her response. "Does this have to do with the Reds?"

Mitra and the man exchanged looks. Voice cautious, he asked, "What do you know of the Reds?"

She blinked several times, raindrops clinging to her eyelashes and weighing down her lids as she sputtered through the cold. Dwyn lifted a hand to help her focus her magic as she created a shelter for herself once more. It wasn't warm, but she would dry in time. The others eyed her gift appreciatively.

"I know I want to do what they do," she said.

Anwir chuckled. The sound was joined by the laughter of his companions. Unlike that of her peers at school or the cruel sounds of Rekyr thinking he'd won, this laughter was the low rumble of appreciation. They understood.

The man turned to the woman with a satchel. "What do you think?"

"I like her," Mitra said.

"You know my name," he said. "And you are?"

"Dwyn," she responded. She regretted it in an instant, certain she should have offered an alias.

He nodded. He looked at Dwyn not like a man looking at a woman, but like a burglar eyeing a diamond. "I like her, too," he said. He straightened his shoulders and said, "Let me amend the terms, girl. Keep the rain off our heads, and I'll do more than give you the healing tonic. We know how the Reds do what they do. Hell, several of us were Reds once upon a time. What we want is more than they can do."

"But they can do it all," Dwyn said through a gasp.

"Nearly," he said quietly. "Nearly."

Her heart matched the quick, rhythmic pattern of the rain on the stones. She was tired, cold, wounded, and scared, but the adrenaline that flooded her was something else entirely. She got to her feet, wincing at the pinpricks of bloodlessness, and she'd lost all sensation in her legs in her hours spent in the alley. She looked at the man and woman before her, who stood unflinchingly in the rain and glanced over their shoulders to the figures beyond, obscured by the downpour. Dwyn flattened her palm and raised her hand to help herself focus as she stretched her gift, telling the water to bend around the alley so she might see everyone plainly.

"Nearly?" she repeated. "Then what is it that you want?"

His laugh was a single, dark exhalation as he answered. "Everything."

THIRTY

✦ ✦ ✦ ✦

DWYN HAD PACED THE ROOM FOR HOURS. SHE FELT LIKE A caged jungle cat stalking for an escape. She pounced the moment the door opened, stumbling to the threshold and throwing her arms around the princess.

"Firi," she said, doing little to hide the panic in her throat.

"Goddess, Dwyn," Ophir said, returning the hug. The fur fell from the princess's shoulders. "I was only gone for a little while. I just needed to see Zita and confirm plans for the wedding. Then I ran into Harland—"

"Harland is still here?" Dwyn pulled away to search Ophir's face.

Her expression was nearly one of irritation, but she shook the signs of emotion as she said, "I sent him home to Aubade." Ophir rolled her shoulders until Dwyn's arms dropped, dangling at her sides.

"I thought Farehold's party left?"

Ophir nodded, the remnants of annoyance still playing on her face. "They scattered on the wind. Samael is off on some mission to which I'm not privy. My father"—she spit the word—"left the first chance he was able, taking Cybele with him. Harland stayed behind to petition to remain my personal guard. Ceneth said it was my decision."

"And?" Dwyn attempted to keep the desperation from her question.

"I already told you, didn't I? I've sent him home to Aubade."

Relief poured over her. Harland was the final lynchpin to her undoing, and now, he was gone. Suley and Zita were the only two remaining in Gwydir who knew enough about her to destroy her reputation. The rest of Raascot believed her to be little more than Ophir's irreverent companion who quelled her fire and allowed her ease of travel. The first was true. The second was able to be true if she were given a few minutes to prepare. Though she wasn't foolish enough to believe Ceneth liked her, she was quite certain that her ability to ensure that Ophir didn't burn down the castle earned her enough favor to remain in the princess's bed.

For whatever it was worth, she liked Ceneth. At least, she liked him as much as someone could like a man betrothed to the woman she loved. There was a certain level of disinterest she might have expected, from Raascot's king and perhaps that apathy may have extended to not caring who Ophir fucked or whether the princess adhered to a single one of Gwydir's norms. His character extended beyond that, however.

The choice he offered Ophir wasn't for lack of care. In fact, if Dwyn had to guess, she suspected it was the exact opposite. It was his love for Caris that forced him to see Ophir's humanity, to value her choices, and to respect her free will. For now, it was enough to keep the king of Raascot in her good graces.

She suppressed a smile at the power she held, knowing it was a rare person who could quietly choose whether a king lived or died. Though she'd originally planned to bide her time until after the wedding before she disposed of him, she'd begun to think perhaps the man had earned the breath he drew.

Then again, she'd been wrong before. She'd even begun to think of Tyr as a friend. For a moment, they'd been allies united by their love for Ophir and the vulnerability she'd allowed in sharing the ability to drain. And then he'd done what people did. Once he'd taken what he'd needed, their deal had been void. He'd rather see Ophir in pain, suffering under betrayal, loss, and the trauma of memories as he triggered the gory viscera of Caris's death with his words. With a few careless sentences, he'd hurled Ophir's progress into ashes. Along with it, he'd destroyed Dwyn's faith in him. Tyr was little but another mistake in a long string of disappointments.

Ophir was sad, of course. Dwyn understood loss. She knew grief, and absence, and the raw, terrible road to healing. But the sorrow Ophir felt over a perceived abandonment was nothing compared to the pain from which Dwyn had spared her. Tyr would have broken her, and he would have done it in the ignorant, shortsighted name of affection and honesty. It wasn't the first time a man would prove that he knew nothing of how to keep a woman happy, and it wouldn't be the last.

"Dwyn?" Ophir pulled away fully and crossed the room. Dwyn marked the way she created space, each intentional step drafting a barrier between them. Ophir could create monsters from air. Dwyn could kill with the flick of a finger. They were both infinitely safe and terribly in danger. She wished Ophir felt comfortable with her, but perhaps the princess's cautious wisdom was just another thing to love. Still, she frowned at the way her name hung on her tongue.

"Yes," Dwyn said, voice airy. She brushed her hand through the air as she breezed across the room, jumping onto the bed with all the levity in the world. She tilted her head, flashing a brilliant smile, ever the picture of ease. "Call to me again, Firi. It sounds so good on your lips."

Dwyn flopped backward against the pillows and let her eyes flutter to a close. She kept the smile playing on her lips, corners tugged upward while her heart thundered. Anxiety, worry, fear, and caution were all feelings that never left someone who lived in fight or flight. Her heart remained open, aching, and beating, despite the stony facade. The only things she could change were her actions and her outward expression.

"You said some things in the forest," Ophir said slowly.

Dwyn propped herself up on her elbows and quirked a single brow. "About?"

"About being a siren," Ophir said. She looked at Sedit as if hoping the vageth would step in and vouch for her. The hound, of course, remained silent. Dwyn watched the princess fight with her words before saying, "About...*not* being a siren, that is. You were explaining that everything you do is blood magic, just like the Reds, except...*not* like the Reds. That it..." She took a few sharp breaths as she tested her words before speaking them. "You said it was something that could be taught without killing its user. That it was something you studied, and a skill Tyr learned from you."

Dwyn watched her for a while, waiting to see if there would be another question, another breath. Ophir stayed perfectly still while she waited.

"It is," Dwyn said at last.

Ophir swallowed loudly. Dwyn suspected that her expression of uncertainty was intentional. There was an admirable honesty to it. She communicated as much with her nonverbal fidgets, with the way she scrunched her brows, with the tilt of her shoulders and twist of her mouth, as she might with her words. Dwyn took the time to consider all of the reasons the princess might ask, and all the outcomes she might supply, before Ophir spoke again.

"Will you show me?"

Dwyn worked to control her face. She kept her staple, calm amusement as she said, "Why? People you need to kill? Powers you need to borrow?"

Ophir chewed on the inside of her cheek. She twisted the skirt of her dress in her hands for a minute, watching her thumb and forefinger before looking at Dwyn once more. "No," she said. "I just want to know how it's done. I don't need the ability. I have more than enough."

This wasn't what Dwyn had expected. She pushed herself up onto her palms until they were at eye level. "You just want to see the process?"

"No," Ophir corrected, "I've seen the process. I've seen your life as a siren. I've seen you drain farmers and homesteaders and unsuspecting citizens. It's not about witnessing or about practicing it for myself. But when you had me conjure the snake in Aubade, you knew something I didn't. And the fact that you can not only be a siren but can teach others... You know things, Dwyn. I don't want to do it, but I do want to know what you know."

Dwyn swayed in surprise. She blinked as she continued to fight emotions from breaking through to the surface. Ophir of Aubade, Princess of Farehold, manifester, felt that Dwyn was her magical superior. Ophir could create from little more than thought and intent, and yet she still didn't see herself as the goddess she was.

"Yes," Dwyn said, slipping her fingers over Ophir's hand. "I'll teach you. Use it or don't, I'll teach you."

Dwyn had been right to keep the knowledge to herself for lifetimes.

The moment she'd shared it with Tyr, he'd turned on her.

She'd known Anwir and the Pact would do the same. The moment she'd cracked the riddle that had plagued them for centuries, she'd fled to the sea. The water had always been her friend. If she could hone her newfound skill and take a little more, she was certain she could stick to the western ocean and brave the cold long enough to escape the Pact and the effects of their binding ink.

Anwir's eyes had twinkled when she'd explained her first and only kill. At age sixteen, she'd manipulated the water in the blood of another, and it had saved her in her time of need.

"Do you think the Reds know of this?" he'd asked over his shoulder.

The woman, Mitra, nodded. "They speak to water, to

ice, to fire. Name an element, and they call to it. Dwyn didn't fall ill because water is her primary power. The Reds risk their lives when they call to new gifts."

"And, what? We should have been recruiting fae with gifts for water?" he said.

She folded her arms. "Perhaps. She fell ill all the same, but because of her predisposition for water, she carved a path forward. The girl called to the water in her blood and kept it pumping, forcing her heart to move, to filter out the poison. Dwyn's ingenuity with her gift helped her survive where others have fallen."

He chewed on the information.

"The answer is here somewhere," he said, eyeing Dwyn. "She took the boy's blood. It's what we've looked to do for decades."

"It's not," his second said tersely. "She's a murderer. We've all killed. It unites us more than any vow or the ink of our tattoos."

Dwyn looked down at her soft leather pants. Beneath them was the still-healing scab of a large spiral tattoo. With it, she'd been bound to them. It had made sense in the moment. There were no drawbacks to the bond, they'd promised. It kept everyone in the Pact safe, as it was impossible to harm one another.

"What do you know of gangs, girl?" Anwir had asked.

Without thinking, Dwyn had regurgitated the only thing she'd heard her mother murmur. "There's no honor among thieves," Dwyn said, reciting the platitude older than ice or snow.

Anwir had agreed, dipping his needle in ink. "It's true," he'd said. "The best way to ensure trust is to alleviate the possibility of betrayal. It makes our family safer and more loyal than any on the continent. After all, a house divided cannot stand."

She'd heard these words before but wasn't sure where.

Mitra had answered her question before she'd had the

chance to voice it. "He's quoting the church," she said. "Anwir was a Red in his day. Many of us were."

"Were you?" Dwyn had asked the woman.

Her amused laugh had been short and terse.

"It's how we learned to access the groundwater of magic that unites us all. The church taught the Reds, and the defected Reds have taught the Pact. Calling to power isn't the hard part. Reds do it in the name of righteous sacrifice. For us, it's attempting to survive that call that does us in."

"Has anyone figured it out?" Dwyn had asked. "How to call on the groundwater without falling ill, that is?"

Mitra had shaken her head. "It's blood magic. All magic comes at a price. For secondary abilities, that price is your blood. If you call a third or a fourth, your wish will be granted at the expense of your life."

For the next three years, they hunted for answers. Dwyn was well liked, at least in the beginning. She was clever, beautiful, and useful. Her ability to call to water was excellent not only in storms or in times of thirst, but was exceptional at killing people where they stood, even before she'd learned to call on the groundwater. Once she understood how to tap into the magic of the earth, she became peerless. She figured out how to call on the water in her blood and faster than most and quickly worked her way up the ranks of the Pact. In no time, she rivaled the spot for Anwir's second.

She fell ill like all the others when she called on the groundwater as she tested fire, wind, weather, emotion, lust, pain, and fear. She played with danger and suffered the consequences. Unlike the others in the gang, Dwyn came with an advantage. Chalky, sweating, and knocking on the All Mother's door, she urged the water in her blood to move.

She stood by as they held thieves' funerals for others in the Pact as brothers and sisters fell to the powers they stole. She watched the dripping, pleading final moments of life as those who'd bound themselves to her in vows and ink took their final breaths and left the mortal plane to join the All Mother after calling on their stolen powers. She held their hands. She watched them sweat, and writhe, and blink. She pressed her fingers into their necks as she'd seen the others do, just as she'd done to her sister without understanding why. Their hummingbird pulses fluttered erratically in the moments before their eyes rolled back. Their clammy hands went limp, unclenching from the panic, the fear, the regret in those final moments.

When Dwyn's time came, she had nothing and everything to lose.

She'd called on the earth and broken the stone itself, cracking the ground in two as she'd saved the Pact from capture. The world splintered as the elemental sinkhole had swallowed their enemies, forcing all who remained to retreat. Anwir had scooped her into his arms as they'd laid her to rest for what might very well have been her last goodbye. He'd barked orders for cold cloths, for soft pillows, for a comfortable farewell to the bruised girl in an alley who'd given her life for the Pact.

But Dwyn had something the ghosts who haunted their gang hadn't.

She wasn't a healer and knew little of medicine, but she understood water.

When her heart began to skip and thunder, she recognized the erratic beats. The rapid thrum was something that only belonged to the wings of insects, the trill of birds, and the final beats of the dying. Anwir squeezed her hand, and she closed her eyes and asked the water within her to slow. She knew the dying were clammy, that their blood still contained whatever price they'd paid. The water responded, each beat going slower and slower than the one before. The water in her blood moved lazily from her heart to the parts of her that filtered poison. She pictured the illness within her as a tangible metal and asked the water to push. She wasn't sure if she could manipulate this water enough to separate good from bad, but the worst that could happen was to fall prey to an inevitable demise.

Instead, Dwyn fell asleep.

When she awoke, the blush had returned to her cheeks. Her hair curled near her temples where salt had dampened it with her sweat, but her heart and breathing were normal. The others clapped and hooted and celebrated as if her survival were a miraculous breakthrough, and she bit down on what she knew to be true. She held a piece that the others did not.

When she was strong enough to sit up, Anwir grabbed her head as if she were a beloved child with a fretting parent and pressed a rough kiss into her head. He pumped a rough fist into the air as he said, "No one's survived an ordeal like that without greenstrike blood!" He was unable to keep the grinning joy from his bits of vital knowledge.

While she knew she was supposed to be ill and on a miraculous return from the brink of death, she couldn't let go of his innocuous words. It was a piece of information that he hadn't known he was giving her. The greenstrike—a tropical, leaf-colored creature that looked remarkably like a stick—lunged toward would-be prey, burrowed beneath their flesh, and engorged itself on its new host's blood. Anwir had never mentioned it before and never spoke the words again. Entirely separate blood could intercede on behalf of that which had been poisoned.

Six months later, Dwyn was brave enough to test her idea.

And when she did, she succeeded.

THIRTY-ONE

✦ ✦ ✦ ✦

How do you choose someone?" Ophir whispered. She trusted Dwyn, but she couldn't articulate why. The woman was funny, and beautiful, and spectacular in bed. She'd been loyal, supportive, and had helped her through her darkest times. But even as she led Ophir through the streets of Gwydir, Ophir knew she was following a killer.

Ophir swallowed the thought, remembering the blood on her hands. Her first intended kill had been Guryon, the merchant, but she'd slaughtered three farmers in cold blood in the days before his righteous execution. She'd killed intentionally, and she'd killed on accident. Whether she wanted to admit it or not, she was responsible for the deaths of hundreds in Tarkhany from the morning of Berinth's death. Her ag'druraths had killed before and would kill again. As she watched Dwyn bob between streets, she idly wondered who had the higher body count.

"At this point?" Dwyn stopped between buildings. She wasn't being overly sneaky, but given that neither of them was a resident of Raascot, they did their best to keep to side streets. "I've lost my goodwill for people—humans and fae alike."

"What do you mean?" Ophir whispered, hurried and anxious.

Dwyn didn't look at her as she answered. Her exhalation was a short huff as she continued scanning the streets. "I mean," she began, eyes still screwed to the distance, "think of the last time you saw a sweet old man drinking tea alone and assumed he was probably mourning his late wife. Did you feel sad for him?" Dwyn stopped to look over her shoulder.

Ophir's brows furrowed.

Dwyn remained nonchalant. "I don't. No one is without sin. If I see an elderly man alone, I assume he beat his wife to death or hurts children, and I carry on with what needs to be done."

The air left Ophir's lungs. She felt like she'd been punched in the gut as she stared at the back of Dwyn's head. Her speechlessness drew the siren's attention.

"What?" Dwyn demanded. She straightened her posture and abandoned her search to face Ophir. "Look me in the eye and name all of the truly good people you know. Name every person who hasn't done something terrible."

Ophir stammered. Her mind went right to her family, then flitted away from her father, knowing he deserved whatever fate came to him, and from her mother for her complacency in everything she enabled by perpetuating his reign. She thought of Harland, but her nose curled against his judgment, his cruelty, his failure to understand her when she needed him most. She thought of Tyr, and pain pierced her.

"My sister is good," she said. "Was good," she corrected, hating herself for it.

"Yes, and your sister died for her goodness." And though Dwyn was typically cavalier, she softened her words and face alike as she spoke. She rested her hand on Ophir's shoulder. "Anyone else?"

Ophir chewed on her lip. "I believe Ceneth is genuinely good."

"Excellent," she said. "Then they were a match made in

heaven. You've met hundreds, perhaps thousands in your life? And you've named two. I'm not good, nor will I pretend to be. I would bet that anyone you spot has lied or stolen or betrayed or stepped on a puppy's tail."

"On accident."

"On purpose!"

And though the intent had been to joke, and while they smiled in the alley's shadow, Dwyn's point rang true. Perhaps no one was truly good. And while it was immeasurably disturbing to see every sweet elderly gentleman and imagine that he'd done unspeakable things to a child, Ophir understood that Dwyn had recontextualized empathy for the sake of practicality.

Caris had been good.

She'd been perfect, and kind, and empathetic, and had devoted her life to others. She would have made change for the continent, not just for her people, but for everyone. She'd been loving to those who deserved it, and even to those who didn't. And she'd still died.

Ophir would never be the selfless humanitarian who united the continent.

She would never be her sister.

She'd wrestled with the thought for ages, suffocated by the perfect shadow Caris casted.

But Dwyn's reaction following the events of the summit had been correct. Ophir shouldn't run into the forest and disappear into oblivion. She had no business living among the rabbits and deer and pines when she could still make a profound and lasting impact.

Her imprint on the world would be something Caris would have never achieved.

Her legacy would be destruction.

"Him," Ophir said, using only her chin to motion to a fae who may have been in his twenties or two hundreds, for all one might judge the life of the fae.

"He has wings," Dwyn said, frowning.

"Does that make him a better person?"

Dwyn grunted. "It just means your first target is a shark instead of a guppy, should he want to fight or flee. Not that I don't think you can withstand the challenge. Are you ready?"

Ophir grabbed her arm. Dwyn looked at her bicep and the fingers digging into it, then up at Ophir. Her dark brows curled up in the center, almost as if she'd sucked on a sour lemon.

"I don't want to learn to drain," Ophir said.

Dwyn's face puckered into deeper confusion.

"I don't," she repeated. "I want to understand it. This is who you are, right? I want to know you, and what you do, and how you do it. But it's not a skill I want or need. And if anyone discovers your wake of husks and asks for an explanation, I'll reaffirm what I've always believed to be true. You're a creature of the sea and the siren of fairy tales."

The muscles in Dwyn's face softened, concerned wrinkles disappearing. When Ophir released her bicep, Dwyn nodded slowly in agreement.

"I've told you of Sulgrave's Reds who run the church with a legion of unfamiliar gifts, blood magic, and borrowed powers."

Ophir listened. Yes, she'd heard it all.

"I took a gamble when I left the Pact. It was replicable enough that I was able to teach Tyr. And even if you don't want to learn, I'll teach you now. First, you do as the Reds do, and you borrow against your blood."

"But that's what kills you."

Dwyn flashed her teeth in a smile. "Precisely. You're not just going to do it; you're going to do it twice."

"I'm not going to do it any times," Ophir corrected.

Dwyn crossed her arms. She eyed Ophir and said, "I disagree. I think it's only ethical that you do it once, to that winged man there—the one you selected. His life is in your hands. Put yourself in my shoes."

"I've never borrowed any second ability," Ophir said. "I can't."

Dwyn laughed loudly enough that it drew eyes from a mother and her child passing by. She covered her mouth. "Firi, you're a manifester. You draw on the hearts of your kingdom. You don't just borrow on blood or second abilities; you borrow on *every* ability. If you want to summon wind, it will be so."

The cold winter air burned Ophir's tongue before she realized her mouth had dropped open.

"Listen," Dwyn continued. "The secret is hidden in plain sight. You simply borrow twice. First, you call to the wind. Leverage the gift against your own blood."

"But—"

"Then," Dwyn continued testily, "you borrow against your blood a second time. Exchange the poisoned, sickly blood in your body for theirs."

Ophir buckled against the statement. She looked up over Dwyn's shoulders at the thin, frosty snowflakes that began to fall. It was cold enough that they wouldn't melt on impact. Each speck of white cast a dramatic droplet against the midnight-blue and black stones that must have been birthed from the nearby mountains, as every shop and home and bridge sang the hues and crystalline stars within. She hadn't considered how Raascot's wings shone with the same oil-slick radiance of the city's labradorite. Perhaps the north had not been historically theirs, but if there was indeed a goddess, she'd married the dark-winged fae with this city.

It was a marriage that was set to swiftly end for one ill-fated citizen.

"You've drained without knowing how you were going to use it," Ophir said.

Dwyn cocked a brow. "So I'd have you think. It certainly makes me seem more mysterious and dangerous when you have no clue what I'm going to do next. But no. I go into each kill with intent, even if I have to sit on that intention and wait until the time is right."

Dwyn concentrated on their task. "Your blood is twice

poisoned. The first is for wind; the second is for the swap. But by the time both poisons take effect, it will all be in their veins, pumping through their heart, sapping them of their life. It's why they perish on contact. In the moment of the switch, you've amplified everything you wish to give and take. A single stolen power would make someone sick. If they're extremely practiced and skilled, as the Reds were, they may be able to withstand recovery from a secondary or tertiary power. Some devotees were fabled to call on a fourth before they fell to their religious cause. But these people aren't Reds. They haven't trained or exercised or created fortitudes within themselves. Two unfamiliar powers at once will kill them almost instantly. If they're human, it's surefire. If they're fae, it may be a bit slower. Then again, if they're fae, I often take a little extra, just to be sure."

Ophir saw her own golden curls before she realized she was shaking her head. She felt so disconnected from her body while Dwyn spoke. It felt like a wicked fairy story.

A moment later, Dwyn flattened her palm against her lower back. "Go," she said. "First wind, then exchange. Think wind in your first heartbeat; think of the trade with the second beat."

"What if I fuck it up?"

Dwyn made a face. "If you can't think two thoughts, one after the other, then you're an idiot and you don't deserve to live. Now, go."

Ophir stumbled out of the alley and immediately regretted ever asking. She was angry with Dwyn for forcing her into the street before she was ready. She was angrier with herself for not having her hood up at the start. With a flick of her wrist, she covered her dark blond hair and began walking down the street. It would be more suspicious to idle amid the shops and milling townspeople on the main walkway of Gwydir. At least if she was moving, they'd have less cause to stop and stare.

Her pulse quickened as she closed in on the man. She

fought the urge to look over her shoulder at Dwyn, but she knew the siren was watching. It comforted her that no matter how much Dwyn teased or pestered, she believed in her bones that she'd be at her side in an instant, slaughtering every man, woman, and child in the city to save her if she fell ill and things went awry.

She didn't have time to wrestle with the morality of her confidence in her partner. She wasn't certain she'd taken a single breath. When the air around her began to shimmer and spin, she knew for certain that she hadn't.

Ophir sucked in a lungful of air as she plastered a friendly, beautiful smile across her face. It was one she'd seen Dwyn use time and time again. She extended a confident hand to the man, batting her lashes and grinning as she urged him forward into the space between the nearby bakery and what may very well have been a bank. It was chilly enough that the side streets were nearly empty, and she wasn't concerned about onlookers.

Confusion and misogyny were her allies. Not only would the man be too perplexed to stop her, but she knew that most males would not chase away a pretty woman. Perhaps an unevolved part of him would hope she'd fallen in love and was pushing him into the alley with a hasty, primal mating call. She knew the larger part would be the bits of his brain that reassured him that no woman could do him harm. It was with that certainty that she'd put a hand on his arm and taken six confident steps with him into the narrow gap between buildings before she thought two subsequent thoughts.

Wind, and exchange.

The gale-force whipped her hair and kicked the snowflakes into the air before she knew what she'd done. She tilted her head back to look to the sky, searching for signs of a change in weather in the split second it took her to understand that she was the storm itself. Hurricane gusts picked up a withered male husk. Ophir gulped in horror and stumbled backward into the bank's wall before a hand was at her arm.

"Come on," Dwyn said urgently.

She pulled Dwyn onto the main walkway as awnings crumbled, chairs toppled, women screamed, and carts skidded madly into the street.

"Go, Firi!"

Dwyn positioned herself firmly at Ophir's back, shoving her forward as they crossed the bridge and ran for Castle Gwydir. She squinted against the bits of gravel, hardened snow, and strands of hair that whipped against her eyes with violent intent. She stumbled blearily over the slippery winter slopes of the front lawn as wind howled too loud for her to hear what was being shouted. Attendants yelled for them, concerned only for the safety of the women who crossed the castle grounds.

The moment they burst through the door, Dwyn interlocked their fingers and tugged Ophir forward, refusing to break their hurried stride until they'd rounded the corner, mounted the stairs, and burst through her chamber door.

Sedit jumped down off the bed and trotted into the washroom as if he knew better than to be present for the energy they brought to the bedroom.

The door hadn't clicked fully closed behind them before Ophir's back was against her bedroom wall, Dwyn pushing her into the stones as their mouths met. The giggles of excitement, the thrill of escape, the rush of power that pulsed between them was intoxicating. Ophir attempted to push off the wall, but Dwyn shoved her against the surface until she was pinned. She drove her fingers into Dwyn's hair, balling them into tight, silken fists as she pulled her closer. Dwyn's rosemary flavors mingled with passion and snow and panic and crime and love and revenge. It was exotic and inebriating, each new taste burning and quenching all at once, too much and not enough.

Dwyn's fingers worked deftly against her dress, tearing where the ties wouldn't relinquish their knots until they both tumbled, half-naked, half-crazed, onto the bed. Ophir arched her hips up off the mattress as Dwyn yanked off whatever remained of her shredded winter gown and tossed it to the floor. Lips sucked in the tender, desperate peaks of her nipples. They kissed and grazed and traced the soft skin of her stomach. Ophir squirmed and twisted and begged with her body for that mouth to find the hot, wet, wanting place as a soft, perfect tongue licked and swirled and tasted between her thighs. As she bucked and gasped and writhed, each tantalizing sensation building and growing until it erupted in a magnificent, denominating, screaming explosion, Ophir experienced the drunken thrill of what it meant to make love in the face of death.

THIRTY–TWO

+   +   +   +

P RINCESS OPHIR?"
Ophir popped her head up from between two milky thighs.

"You've got to be fucking kidding me," Dwyn pouted.

"Who is it?" Ophir called over Dwyn's knee.

Dwyn groaned and grabbed the pillow beside them. She slammed it on top of her head. "Now that you know how to drain, can you go kill her for us?"

"I'm sorry." Ophir rested her head on Dwyn's knee. "We can finish later. But murdering my future subject for interrupting sex is in poor taste."

"You're right," Dwyn agreed, hips rolling as if desperate to consider their session. "We do it like the queens of yore. Off with her head."

Ophir wiped her mouth with the back of her hand. "What is it?"

The woman cracked open the door, scarcely giving Ophir enough time to yank the sheet up over her breasts. Dwyn couldn't be bothered to shift beneath the covers. The attendant had caught them together on more than one occasion and was unable to be fazed. She'd seen Dwyn's bare body nearly as many times as Ophir. The woman leveled them a tired, unimpressed face as she said, "We're to begin packing for the journey south for your wedding."

She rested on the final word as she looked between Ophir and her naked companion.

Emboldened by the challenge, Ophir raised a brow. "I can't wait. I'm sure my future husband is thrilled," she said.

The attendant looked exhausted. "Ceneth has instructed us to accommodate your requests. He suggested that you and your companion might have alternate modes of travel. Would you like attendants to travel with you and Lady Dwyn?"

From beneath the pile of pillows, Dwyn said, "I'm no lady."

Ophir concealed a smirk. "When does he plan to depart?"

"Today, Your Grace. Even flying, he expects it will take a few days. There was talk of asking your companion to travel the party members individually, until someone pointed out that it was her secondary power. I suppose it's only safe for her to use it once or twice."

Ophir blanched at the idea of Dwyn being backed into a corner of having to merrily transport dozens of members of the Raascot court.

"You're right," Ophir said quickly. "Even with the two of us alone, she'll be sick for days after. If it will take Ceneth a few days to travel, then Dwyn and I will remain in the castle until he's projected to arrive in Aubade. I don't desire to arrive on the coast ahead of time."

The woman hesitated, and Ophir was curious how bold her attendant was. Would she ask why Ophir wasn't interested in planning for her wedding? In seeing her parents? In watching the sun set over the western horizon in the days preceding her nuptials? But no. The woman said none of that. If Ophir hadn't made her disrespect to the castle, her betrothed, and her title clear enough, she'd take every opportunity to do so now, should she be pressed.

She suspected that the attendant saw all of this and more,

for she merely nodded and said, "I'll be back this after-noon to help you pack before I depart. Another attendant will stay behind to see to your needs while you remain in the castle. I'll be ready in Aubade to receive you, Princess Ophir."

"It isn't necessary," Ophir said.

The woman's brows met in the middle.

"Help me pack, if you will. But I have attendants in Aubade I've known for decades. I don't mind spending a few days with them before I return to Gwydir to live out my days. You and I have a long future ahead of us. Why not give yourself a reprieve and take a holiday while I'm on the coast? Unless you have a deep-seated urge to watch two star-crossed lovers in their royal wedding."

"I do not, Your Highness."

Ophir chuckled lightly at the woman's frankness. "Then please, go see your family. Do something nice for yourself. Don't worry about me."

"As you wish," she said. But as she closed the door, Ophir thought she caught the first appreciative glimmer she'd ever seen on the attendant's face.

They scarcely had the time to roll out of bed and help each other into their gowns before another knock broke their secretive chatter. Ophir slammed her mouth shut as if whoever was at the door could possibly have understood what "draining" meant or what it was they'd accomplished only one day before. Dwyn rolled her eyes as she marched toward the door, face set to give the attendant an earful.

"Unless you've returned with tea—"

Ophir peered over Dwyn's shoulder to see who'd succeeded in stopping her sentence in its tracks. Suley stood in the doorway.

Dwyn pushed the door open a bit farther and dropped her arm, but she didn't step aside.

"Dwyn," Suley said, nodding first at the siren. "Princess Ophir," came her acknowledgment as she called into the room. "Queen Zita and I request your presence in a meeting."

Ophir moved toward the door before Dwyn had a chance to say something snarky. She stood beside Dwyn, shoulder to shoulder. "When?"

Suley looked between them. "Now, Your Highness. And Lady Dwyn is invited."

Dwyn's face changed. Her brows lowered, setting with cool suspicion as she stared at Suley.

"Where is this meeting?" Dwyn asked.

Ophir didn't understand the odd ice that had entered her voice. Cautious hostility rolled off her like smoke.

"Please, follow me," Suley said.

Ophir took a step forward, but Dwyn positioned her arm to block her advance. Ophir blinked at the forearm acting as a barricade, then frowned up at Dwyn.

"No," Dwyn said.

Ophir and Suley exchanged surprised glances.

"Dwyn," Ophir whispered, "Zita and I have an agreement. She and I—"

"Have her come," Dwyn said.

Suley's eyes narrowed ever so slightly. "You want the queen to fetch you? As if she's a common attendant?"

"Yes," she said, word clipped. Every passing moment grew colder between them.

They exchanged unblinking glares in challenge. Ophir took a half step backward into the room as she watched the incomprehensible standoff.

"Fine," Suley said at last. She turned on her heel but only made it a few steps before Dwyn called out after her.

"Both Zita and whoever the hell you are."

Suley's shoulders jolted toward her ears. She tilted her head, cursing to herself quietly in their native tongue. When she relaxed her posture, she turned with slow, cool command. She rolled her shoulders, then her neck. Suley returned to the doorway and leaned against the door.

"What gave it away?"

Dwyn offered a single dark chuckle. "Aside from the piercings?"

"These fucking piercings," Suley muttered to herself.

"Suley and I are a lot of things, but we're not ladies. She would never have referred to me as such. Now, I'm not sure if I care who you are or what you want. But I'll tell you that the next words out of your mouth will determine whether you live or die."

Ophir's eyes flared dramatically. Her heart caught in her throat as she took another backward step. "Are you saying…" She looked at Dwyn, but the siren did not look away from Suley. "Is this not Suley? What the hell is happening?"

Dwyn shrugged, eyes still trained on Suley. "I'm not sure, Ophir. Have you come across any shapeshifters other than during our dramatic sunrise in Tarkhany? Because I'd put my money on this being the same bastard."

Adrenaline pumped through her. "Sedit," she called. The vageth trotted up beside her and planted its feet, baring its fangs against the person wearing Suley's face. She saw the whites of Suley's eyes as the woman gasped at her demon.

"It's like the dragon," she said, voice thick with fear and disgust as she leaned away from the bedroom.

"You have until the count of three," Dwyn said testily. "One, two—"

"Wait." Suley lifted a hand. "It's not just me, I swear it. Zita and Ceneth are already in the war room. It has no windows, and no chance of being overheard. Zita knows who and what I am, and it's part of why we need all of us in the same room."

"For what?" Dwyn demanded.

Suley looked down the corridor in either direction before saying, "For the wedding."

THIRTY-THREE

✦   ✦   ✦   ✦

L ONG GONE WERE THE FROSTED EVERGREENS, THE SLUGGISH river, and the blue-black stones of Gwydir.

Ophir missed the lavender mountains. She missed the continent she'd put between herself and her parents. She missed the kingdom and the people who were willing to see her as an adult, rather than an extension of their dynasty. She did not, however, miss the road. Travel did not become her.

She'd been in Aubade for less than a day before servants had cleaned her up and shoved her back into pinching corsets and impossible shoes. She watched the clock with impending dread as she waited for her mother's arrival. The door opened and slammed against the wall with the woman's entrance like a gavel sentencing her to death.

"My dear," her mother cooed. Queen Darya opened her arms for Ophir. The princess stood still while she allowed the embrace to happen, a victim of it rather than a participant. The queen stepped away with an exaggerated frown. "Come, now," she chastised. "You've had months to come to terms with your royal obligations. Do you think I wanted to marry your father? But we had two beautiful daughters, and I get to serve as this kingdom's queen, just as you will in the north.

You're finally back in our castle one last time before Gwydir becomes your home. Is this really the glum face you want to wear on your final visit to Aubade as an unmarried woman?"

"At least pour me a strong drink before you begin the verbal assaults," Ophir grumbled. When the servants did nothing, she crossed to the bar cart and plucked the cork out of a green bottle. "Would you like a glass?"

"Truly, Ophir, why are you like this? You're about to be a bride!"

Ophir had nothing to say. The woman she called Mother hadn't breathed a word about manifestation, about the castle, about the summit. Darya had expressed neither concern nor interest, either because it was unsavory to discuss such things or because denial was her most effective coping mechanism. Ophir glanced about the round tower room, bitterly remembering the last time she'd been called to this particular chamber. Her parents had sat on the far side of the table as they'd informed her that she was to stand in Caris's stead and be wed to the king of Gwydir. The light filtered in from the far window now just as it had then, months prior. The seasons had changed, and the world had grown cold, but she'd grown colder.

They had been right about one thing. She was safe with Ceneth.

Her mother breezed to the table at the center of the room. "Now, we did have the Raascot party bring magnificent cuts of fresh pine boughs. Your father and Ceneth exchanged a few letters to have it orchestrated. It will be a glorious winter wedding, and the people of Aubade so love to see Yule celebrated in the northern way. We're inviting the kingdom."

Ophir looked dully at her mother. She was tired from travel, even if she and Dwyn had awoken in Gwydir only that morning. She'd created six doors in the thicket behind Castle Gwydir before she'd succeeded in making one that opened to reveal Castle Aubade perched on the cliffs. Her gift for flame had proven useful as she'd destroyed each of her failed portals before stepping through the door to the seaside kingdom. She'd sent it up in ashes behind her as they entered the pleasantly warm weather. She supposed it was winter here, too, but it would be another month before anyone noticed a change in the temperate weather.

"I miss Sedit," Ophir had muttered glumly as she and Dwyn had started for the castle.

"We'll fetch him after the wedding," Dwyn had promised. She'd grunted as her shoe slipped on a loose beige stone and cursed traveling on foot.

"And if we don't? If the plan fails?"

"Then we'll make you a new Sedit."

Ophir had glared unappreciatively but hadn't had much time to wallow. The steady sounds of hooves on compact ground had filled the air as a traveler approached.

"Would you like to do the honors?" Dwyn had asked.

"Absolutely not," Ophir had hissed.

Dwyn had sighed. "I'll do it, just like I do everything. I expect a nice gift for Yule."

Three hours later, the women had been ushered hastily into the castle by confused servants. The Gwydir party had arrived the day prior, and it seemed as though no one had known of Dwyn's gift for travel before Ceneth had informed them. Fortunately, the castle was in upheaval attempting to accommodate the winged fae and attendants sprinting to and fro in preparation for the royal wedding, meaning that Dwyn and Ophir had been able to slip back into the room they'd once shared while answering remarkably few questions.

The one time they had been stopped by a curious guard, Ophir had simply told him that she was a princess and it was none of his business, which had earned her an appreciative pinch on her left ass cheek from Dwyn.

She thought enviously of Dwyn now, who'd remained napping when Ophir's mother had summoned her.

"Come, come." Darya waved her over. "I have all of the diagrams drawn up for the coliseum."

"You can't be serious. The coliseum?"

"Weren't you listening? We've invited the kingdom! We've sent runners to all of the neighboring cities. Anyone who can get here in time is welcome. We've been arranging and decorating for a solid week prior to your arrival. Three days from now, you'll be married at sundown. It's the most exciting event in centuries, and surely there won't be anything like it for hundreds of years more."

With a low, bitter whisper, Ophir said, "You don't know the half of it."

"What was that?" Darya asked, not bothering to look up.

Ophir watched her mother curiously. She'd spent decades believing she was the lesser daughter only because Caris had received all the love that her mother was capable of giving. Now as she watched the queen busy herself with blueprints of tables, decorations, stands, banners, and makeshift rafts from which they might suspend festive conifer branches, she wondered at her perception of the woman. Perhaps she hadn't received her mother's love because the woman had none. She was a queen of obligation, a vessel to offspring, a warden of the southern kingdom. If Darya had always felt this way, then maybe Ophir had severely overestimated how much favoritism Caris had received.

She thought sadly of Caris running and jumping into Ceneth's arms.

Their over-the-top love had a lot to swallow. It had seemed unfair that her perfect sister had everything. But if Darya had been as disengaged with her firstborn, then maybe Ceneth was the first person who truly had seen her. How terribly lonely it must have been for Caris to carry that burden alone, never telling Ophir that Ceneth's arms were the first place she'd felt wanted.

It was easy to project upon the dead, unless, of course, one had access to a medium.

"Look at this," Darya said breezily. "We'll have the loveliest chamber set up as your bridal preparation room. You'll come out from here," she said, pointing to her diagram.

Ophir peered across the table. Her eyes narrowed into unamused slits. "I'm to emerge from the dungeon?"

Darya scoffed. "We've already moved the prisoners, and we've spent a week cleansing it. It will sparkle by the time you walk down the aisle. Now, Ceneth and his witnesses will come from the door on the far side. It will be deliciously dramatic. The crowd will love it. We'll have the orchestra here. The guests of importance will be on the floor with the wedding party, of course, but we've even arranged for sweets to be distributed amid the stands! Isn't that generous?"

"So generous," Ophir mumbled. Several pieces of enormous parchment covered the table. One was a diagram of the arrangement. Other papers had been elaborately rendered by artists who hoped to capture an emotion. They depicted rows of excited faces as the people of Aubade peered down on the wondrous affair. Another picture displayed a faceless bride with a long, elaborate veil trailing behind her as she approached the groom and the officiating bishop. Sketches of tables, of nobility, of fresh-cut pine, of yule berries, wine glasses for toasting, and of a winged man with a fae wife littered the surface. Some had been painted with watercolor, the reds and creams and browns of Aubade decorating the coliseum in muted arrays as her white dress popped from the art. Her eyes caught on one image in particular. There was a rather detailed depiction of the exchanging of rings.

Ophir fought to keep contempt from her voice as she let her fingers drift down to the page.

"How curious that the artist would want to portray such a mundane moment," Ophir said.

"Mmm." Darya nodded stiffly. "Yes, well, we're doing things a bit differently. After Ceneth says his vows, we'll have the first exchange of rings. You must put on the ruby, then slip the sapphire band on his finger, just like the picture."

Ophir tensed. She closed her eyes slowly, praying that her

mother wasn't implying what she believed. "I think I'd like to go first," Ophir said testily. "I like the custom of the bride being the first to don the ring."

"No, no," Darya said hastily. "You'll put it on Ceneth's hand first. The bishop will ensure it is so."

Ophir kept her eyes closed as she did her best to look agreeable. When she opened them, she watched her mother prattle on through watering eyes. The dull hum of the day's rituals, of vows, of duty and kingdom and rites filtered in through one ear and drifted out the other. Her mother knew. The bishop knew. Everyone intended for Ceneth to disappear on their wedding day, fused to Ophir and the will of Aubade with every complacent citizen cheering them on. Ophir nodded along, forcing a semblance of a smile on her lips while she fought to keep herself from crying.

She watched the Queen of Farehold chatter over plots and plans and papers, never once looking at her daughter's face to gauge her reaction. Ophir's presence was a byproduct of her being biologically tied to Darya and little more. She'd been wrong to assume that Darya would give more time, care, or affection if it weren't going elsewhere. Her mother had nothing else now. She had no children, no responsibilities, nothing else to rule over or celebrate or plan or mourn or worship. And yet, Ophir still felt as if she were alone in the room.

"I trust you with the plans," Ophir said quietly as she backed toward the door.

Darya clicked her tongue. "I wish you took more of an interest in your own wedding, but at least you believe that I know what's best."

Ophir nodded, a single tear falling down her cheek. "I do," she said.

"Go, go," Darya said, waving her away. "I'll have everything ready for the big day. You'll love your dress, as will the people. It's truly stunning. I can't wait to see the portraits that come from the big day! And your children. Won't it be interesting to see whether or not they have wings? Oh, what a future lies ahead for Farehold."

"What a future for Farehold, indeed," she repeated as she reached for the knob. She twisted the handle and stepped into the corridor just as the tears began to fall.

"Oh, Ophir?" her mother called out.

Ophir stiffened. She didn't turn to her mother as she begged her voice to remain calm, hoping beyond all hopes that the cracks in her soul were inaudible as she asked, "What?"

To her back, Queen Darya said, "Don't bother your father, if you don't mind. He'll be very busy until the wedding. We can all reconvene after the ceremony."

Silence flooded her like the dark, chilly waters of the Gwydir River. She closed her eyes, dipping her head as a new emotion joined her pain. She was disgusted. Her mother knew. Her mother had collaborated, and plotted, and schemed with Eero to ensure Farehold remained the goddess's favorite kingdom—a favor taken by force and retained by silencing any who might oppose it.

"Of course," she choked out to the hall before she launched herself down the corridor. Her mother shouted something else at her disappearing form, but she couldn't hear it over the high-pitched ringing in her ears.

Three more days, and it would all be over.

Three more days, and Farehold would pay.

✦   ✦   ✦   ✦

She marched straight from the meeting with her mother to Ceneth's room, tears streaming down her face all the while. If the servants had noticed her red nose or her stifled sobs, no one had said a thing. He answered after only two swift raps of her knuckles.

Ceneth's dark eyes widened as he greeted his miserable bride-to-be. He pushed the door open to allow her entry.

"Ophir." He blinked through his surprise.

"I'm in," she said.

He looked at her cautiously. His wings flared out, then tucked in again. "Ophir, in Gwydir, you said…"

"I hadn't made up my mind when we spoke in Gwydir. Farehold needs a change, to be sure, but I didn't realize I was still grasping at straws to believe that my parents—" Her words were broken by a ragged sob. She brought her hands to her eyes, catching her tears in her palms as her shoulders shook. She struggled to breathe as emotion claimed her.

A heavy hand on her shoulder unleashed whatever she'd been holding back.

He hadn't tried to bring her into a hug. He hadn't attempted to be anything he wasn't. She wasn't Caris. They weren't in love. But there was an honesty both in his willingness to stand by her even if he disliked her and in his loyalty to her late sister. She looked up through the foggy curtain of tears at his blurry shape. Her lip trembled as she said, "Caris was lucky."

His eyes watered, matching hers. She knew the expression. It was the face of a scab ripped clean, revealing a fresh wound just when you'd thought it had begun to heal.

"We'll avenge her," she said. "It won't be the world she could have achieved, because I'm not her, and I never will be." Ophir straightened her shoulders. She looked at Ceneth with determination as she said, "But it also won't be the path of the continent she tried to end. We'll break the cycle. And we'll do it in a way that only we can."

He reached out for her before she knew what was happening. She stifled her sounds of surprise as he crushed her against the muscled wall of his chest and held her tightly.

When he pulled her into a hug, it wasn't the false embrace Darya had offered. It wasn't the hold of a lover, or the clutch of a friend. It was gratitude. In three days, they would be wed. In three days, they would end the world.

THIRTY-FOUR

+   +   +   +

T HEY'LL KNOW SOMETHING IS WRONG," GALENA SAID. SHE
hadn't stopped wringing her hands from the moment
they'd stepped into the antechamber of the great spherical
theater that remained open to temperate seaside weather. It
was the perfect evening for a wedding.

Galena's fretting competed with the scores of string instruments that filled the coliseum beyond. The merry sounds
of people, music, and the gaiety of celebration matched the
lovely sunset for two kingdoms to join.

The incessant fidgeting was setting Zita on edge, and she
didn't need any more reasons to feel anxious. Orchestral music
wafted into the room, carried on the words of the chattering
crowd. The noises were nonsensical babble from behind the
cream-colored walls. One arched doorway separated them
from the festivities beyond.

Ceneth and Zita shared a look. She examined his night-
black formal attire. The lapels shone with a velvet shimmer as
if to complement his wings. The king offered a shallow dip of
his chin for Zita to take over. She leveled her gaze at Galena.

"They won't," Zita said with cool certainty, "because
Farehold knows nothing of the world. This is the first wedding

between kingdoms in hundreds of years. Our presence will be observed as an exotic custom."

"And Princess Ophir—" Galena began.

"Is north of the city. A crew is set to intercept her." Zita folded her arms and looked out the window at the waiting crowd. Thousands of pale faces had poured in as Aubade's citizens gathered in the stands to see their princess wed the winged king of the north. She lost herself as she peered into the sea of pink faces amid smears of copper, gold, and watery-brown hair. Her gaze settled on a child on top of its father's shoulders. She closed her eyes, regretting the moment.

"Ophir didn't just give her blessing," Ceneth said coolly. "She told us to burn it to the ground. She should be with the crew any moment."

Galena broke the quiet once more as she prodded, "A crew who…"

Ceneth lifted two fingers in a subtle gesture. Zita was grateful for his intercession as he spoke. "I don't just appreciate your presence, Galena. You're saving us by being here today. But the less you know, the safer you'll be. Just trust it's taken care of, both with her and with the bride."

"The bride was left with special protections for exactly this cause," Zita agreed. "If anyone tries to intercede before the ceremony, one prick from the ring on her finger, and they'll be unconscious before they have the time to cry out. There's enough coma-inducing venom in the subtle weapon for three or more uses. Hopefully, that's all the bride will need."

"Coma?" Galena repeated.

"It will render the victim unconscious, dear," Zita said. She couldn't keep breeziness in her voice. Solemnity weighed over her as she felt the fate of centuries of people on her shoulders. This wasn't just for her husband, or even just for Tarkhany. The injustice at stake was bigger than any one kingdom.

Galena's speechlessness communicated volumes.

Zita lifted her chin and straightened her shoulders. She met Galena's eyes, appreciating the gradient as they transitioned from night-dark to a regal shade of gold just before her pupils. The winged fae tucked her wings respectfully behind her, shrinking nervously under the scrutiny.

"When I give the signal, clasp onto your king. The bride will grab for you. I will shield us all."

Much to both of their surprise, Ceneth reached for her hand now. Zita watched curiously as the King of Raascot regarded his subject.

"Just like this," he said kindly.

Galena looked down at where her fingers rested in his hand. "Your Majesty…"

"I didn't want the first time you touched me to be in our moment of need. We can't afford your hesitation. Just like this, okay? Grab me and hold on tight." He squeezed her hand, offering a sad smile that did not reach his eyes.

Her eyebrows tucked into the middle as she looked between them. "I know that you don't want me to know much, but I have to ask. Why would you have me neutralize you? Your Majesty, to my knowledge, my gift would not impact your gift for flight. I don't understand what purpose I serve, or what it is I'm nullifying."

"That's fine," he said. "And when the moment comes and you do understand, I need you to continue holding my hand, just like this."

"Your Majesty—"

"Call me Ceneth."

"Sir—"

Zita's voice was soft as she interjected. "Galena, I must apologize for what you're about to see, but your king is right. Hold tightly to him. And when you do, for what it's worth, I recommend that you close your eyes."

+   +   +   +

Harland felt like someone had stuck a pin between his

shoulder blades. The sharp pain of something terribly amiss shot down his spine. He'd never looked forward to the day Ophir might be wed. Of course, when Caris had been alive, there'd been the possibility that Ophir might have lived a long and happy life belonging to no one but herself. The moment Farehold's favorite princess had died, Ophir's dreams of freedom had died with her.

Still, he'd prepared himself to see her strike a stunning silhouette in an unspeakably beautiful gown. He knew she'd still sweep him off his feet, even if he wasn't the one at the far end of the aisle. Neither she nor her husband-to-be was excited about the marriage. But that was not what was bothering him.

"I wish Samael was here," Harland mumbled.

Eero had been pacing for the better part of an hour. He paused near a window to look down over the crowds settling into the coliseum. The entire city had been invited to appreciate the opulent decorations, the magnificent rugs that ran the length of the sand, the expensive bouquets, the jewels, the banners, and the twinkling fae lights that transformed the space. The room in the tower allowed for one of the few vantage points for the castle to look down upon the stadium. Harland knew it brought him a sense of control to oversee the people from his hidden peak before the ceremony began and his presence was expected.

"I could certainly use Samael's advice," the king agreed.

Harland's hand went to the hilt of his blade. He stroked the cool metal protectively. "Something feels amiss, Your Grace. I don't know what."

Eero's thick golden brows met in the middle. He looked nowhere in particular as he crossed his arms, tucking his chin between his thumb and forefinger. "I'll tell you what's wrong. I raised the reincarnation of the All Mother in her least sacred form. We've seen what she's capable of. If she snaps today, she could bring Aubade to its knees."

Harland tried to nod, but Eero's words rung hollow. "With respect, I don't believe that's it."

"Then perhaps you're frustrated with a wedding that was never meant to happen. Caris didn't require such a heavy hand. Or perhaps you're upset because you've fallen for my daughter's wiles, Harland. I've heard the rumors, of course. I expected more strength from you. Know your place, even if my second-born fails to know hers. Women rarely do."

Harland sucked his teeth, if only to keep himself from an executable offense. Perhaps if Ophir succeeded in taking both thrones, it meant the king would be kicked from his royal position at last. It might be the one good thing to come from today, as far as he was concerned.

Eero chuckled humorlessly. He moved back to the window to watch over the sea of citizens. "Look at them," he said. "They have no idea their princess has the power to bring hell with her fingertips. If Samael were here, he'd say the same. But he's off with a Raascot woman and a Tarkhany man who can speak to stone, goddess knows where, doing goddess knows what."

"He's accompanied by his twin sister and Queen Zita's advisor on the way to Mount Reev," Harland amended. He watched his king carefully as he spoke, but Eero didn't react. "We both know Samael's doing the continent a great service by taking care of these beasts. And Samael has promised not to hurt Ophir while preventing the creatures from wreaking havoc on the continent. It's more than we could hope from anyone else."

"I'm your king, Harland," Eero said curtly. "You needn't tell me when I should or shouldn't feel gratitude."

"My apologies, Your Majesty."

"You keep twitching, Harland. What could you possibly have to worry about? I've fixed everything. I fixed it with Ceneth after Caris went and got herself killed. I fixed it with Ophir after she threatened to drive us into ruin with her carelessness. I fixed it with Zita after she tried to blame us for making a home that my father rightfully claimed as his own. That's what kings do, after all. They conquer."

"You fixed everything with Ceneth regarding the rings?" Harland made no attempt to conceal his skepticism.

"The good king saw the wisdom in using our manufacturing to temper Ophir's spirit," Eero replied. "Her little display with the dragon all but sealed their fate. He can't very well have a bride tear down his castle every time she's in a bad mood."

"And, what, he believes he'll be in control? He thinks he'll be able to seamlessly rule a manifester?"

"Men love power," Eero said with finality.

The king waited expectantly for Harland to agree, but it was all he could do to keep from using his immense strength on the man who ruled his kingdom. For everyone's sake, he hoped Ceneth had not fallen for Eero's deceit.

The king peered through the window at the people once more, appraising the crowd. "I built this life for them. The mortals don't realize how good they have it in Aubade. They have my father to thank. They really turned out in droves, didn't they? I suppose royal weddings don't happen in every human lifetime."

"Not when fae are on the thrones of the continent's kingdoms," Harland said. "Perhaps your citizens would feel differently if this were Sulgrave. Didn't Dwyn say their comtes were democratically elected?"

"Don't speak to me of what the witch said, filling Ophir with ideas, taking her from her home."

Harland would have jumped at the chance to disparage Dwyn on any other day, but he was too disgusted to agree with his king on anything.

Eero opened his mouth, but a light knock at the door cut him short. Queen Darya opened the door without waiting for an answer. Eero's face softened slightly as he extended a hand to his wife. She left the door ajar as she crossed the room for him.

"Are you ready?" she asked. She didn't bother to look at Harland, but he didn't mind. His queen had more important things to do on the day of her daughter's wedding.

"Harland," Eero said without looking away from his wife, "please stay with Ophir to ensure she doesn't cause any trouble. Do what you must to get her down the aisle."

Harland offered a shallow, wordless bow before excusing himself from the room. He shut the door behind him, feeling the pin between his shoulders with every passing step. Anxiety rose to match his discontent. Eero was wrong to fear Ophir today. She was too powerful to need to return and fake her way through formalities. She didn't need to cause trouble or fight her way out. She could have simply stayed away, surrounded by nightmarish creatures. Instead, she'd chosen to return with Ceneth to Gwydir. She'd agreed to the wedding plans. She'd played nice, remained quiet, and allowed everyone in Raascot to pretend that she hadn't shattered a wing of the castle to bits with the membranous wings of a dragon.

When she'd returned from the Raasay Forest, she hadn't been herself.

Tyr—the only one of her friends that he trusted, however begrudgingly—was no longer in her company. Even Dwyn, as poisonous and obnoxious as he believed her to be, had emerged from the woods subdued and sullen. When he'd asked what had happened, she'd merely looked at him with sad, sun-gold eyes and told him to go back to Aubade. While he'd petitioned Eero to let him stay in Raascot and had been preparing to request that Ceneth allow him to remain as Ophir's personal guard in Gwydir, it seemed his efforts were useless if she no longer wanted him around.

He chewed on the memory of rejection as he wound through the castle. Minutes later, he reached the ground floor. He paused outside of a room that had been repurposed for Ophir's attendants. He'd watched women carry packets of hot water, perfumes, mirrors, wardrobe changes, and pleasant snacks in and out of the room throughout the first part of the day. He rapped on the door lightly with his knuckles and listened, but none of the bustle that had filled the makeshift bridal suite hummed any longer.

An older woman called out in question, and Harland cracked the door without bothering to respond.

His lips parted in surprise as the woman stepped away from the long, lacy veil she'd been carefully draping down Ophir's back. The woman recognized him as the princess's personal guard and nodded in acknowledgment before taking her leave. Her work had finished.

His breath vanished as he looked at her. He'd never cared much for fashion and felt confident that a dress was just a dress. Someone beautiful was equally gorgeous in a gown, in a potato sack, or utterly naked before the All Mother. Someone unattractive was no prettier on their wedding day than any other. Yet, it was tradition to gasp and fawn and coo over every bride in white. It seemed like a respectful convention, if only to preserve a blushing bride's feelings, but an unnecessary one.

Looking at Ophir now, he knew he'd been wrong.

The dress clung to her, outlining her breasts, her waist, her curves before it cascaded out like the mist of a waterfall in white and silvery shimmers. The long, bell-shaped sleeves opened up near her slender wrists, offering a similar shimmer as the fabric tumbled as if by magic. A bit of clever tailoring had created a sheer, fog-like stretch of fabric just below her collarbone that dipped daringly to her sternum, broken by the deep sweetheart neckline of the gown. He'd expected her hair to be elaborately pinned in gaudy curls, but it had been left unbound, slicked back behind one ear and pinned by a single line of pearls.

"You look like the goddess herself," he breathed.

She smiled a bit uncomfortably, which caused a resurgence of concern to shoot through him.

He did his best to assuage her nerves as he approached. The light scent of citrus danced through the air, presumably wafting off the treats and treasures decorating the space that had been dedicated to her honor.

"Don't worry. I've got your back until it's time to go out there."

Ophir's laugh was staccato and dismissive. She looked away from him and into the hall, as if wondering if the attendant would return.

He frowned, but he knew it was impolite to make the day any worse for her than it must already be. Harland attempted levity. "Seems like you need a drink on the wall. Need me to go get a bottle?"

"The wall?" she asked. She turned over her shoulder and looked through one of the small, round windows that had been embedded in the room. It offered a peek into the stands above as she scanned the walls that surrounded the coliseum and the people within them.

His frown deepened. "Is something wrong?"

She looked at him briefly but didn't hold his gaze. Her sights returned to the small window as she said, "It's my wedding day. It's normal for a girl to be nervous."

And though he couldn't place why, he knew this was exactly the wrong thing to say.

Fear took hold as he looked at her. She was scarcely aware of his existence, lost to her view of the crowd. His heart picked up as adrenaline released into his blood.

Harland took a step closer. He kept his voice level as he asked, "Firi? Where's Dwyn?"

She looked at him briefly and frowned. "With the others. Is the attendant coming back?"

He hadn't even realized his hand had returned to the hilt of his sword. The metal warmed beneath his sweaty palm as that inexplicable fear thudded through him. He feigned a smile as he said, "I thought maybe you'd say *she* was on the wall, just like you and Caris used to do. Do you wish you could have gotten a drink with her like old times?"

Ophir nodded dismissively. "Of course."

In three steps he was upon her. He encircled her arm in his hand and squeezed.

Ophir yelped in surprise, eyes flaring. Her pupils constricted until they were little more than pinpricks.

He bared his teeth as he tightened his hold. "Where is she?"

Her lashes fluttered. She tried to shake herself loose. "You're hurting me!"

"I asked you a question. Where is she!"

Ophir cursed, flashing her canines as her eyes blazed with infernal heat and she growled to herself. "For fuck's sake, people never work out. I should have stuck to birds."

"Who the hell are you, and where is Ophir?"

THIRTY-FIVE

+ + + +

Z ITA HAD BEEN TO SIXTEEN WEDDINGS IN HER TIME, TWO OF which had been her own. She'd only been invited as a foreign dignitary to one other wedding in a distant kingdom, and it had been to see the union of the king and queen of a northern territory, ones who would masquerade as her friends, who would spend the winters in her seaside castle, who would steal her ancestral lands, and who would go on to father Eero—a man who would not only reign as if Aubade had always been his, but who would pursue the migration of humans and fae with melanin into Raascot while he claimed the warmer lands.

She'd spent time in Gwydir getting to know Eero, and she didn't believe him to be evil. Yet, that was the most malignant of all tumors. The ones that didn't see themselves for the cancer they were. His unwillingness to acknowledge the past or make the future right had been everything she'd dreaded, and at the same time, the confirmation she'd needed at long last.

Her mind flashed to other weddings. While some in Tarkhany wore white to reflect the fragrant magnolia blossoms and the heavenly purity affiliated with the clouds that spent their time with the sun, other brides had worn red, purple, yellow, or blue. These weddings had been relatively happy occasions of Tarkhany dignitaries, nobility, and even of her favorite handmaiden. While some events had been intimate gatherings with only elected family and friends, others had been balls and feasts and parties.

None had required a coliseum.

Aubade had never been truly cold even on the deepest of winter days. It was part of what had made it a desirable escape for their northern allies when others had searched for a reprieve from frost and chill, and Zita's family had been magnanimous enough to extend an invite to their castle while they basked in the heat of the winter palace deep within Tarkhany. Their trip had been a biannual ritual every spring and every fall for as long as she could remember, both for Zita and for generations of ancestors before her. Aubade was best enjoyed in the summer, when the ocean moderated the climate and provided an escape from the baking sands.

Those who had fathered Eero's bloodline were bred for the cold. The goddess had intended their colorless skin for the snow, soaking in every ray of sunlight in dark seasons, absorbing the heat in endless winters. His pale hair and yellow irises were a mockery of the climate he possessed.

Even in the depths of Aubade's winter, furs were nonessential. She'd noted only a few tufts of animal skins, warm coats, and blankets here and there amid those who populated the stands. But it was chilly by desert standards, to be sure. She was in a thick, velvet dress.

The seamstress had asked if she'd wanted black, to match Ceneth as his witness.

No, Zita had said. She wanted to wear red.

It was uncouth to pull eyes from the bride on a typical wedding day. Of course, she'd never be so rude. But today was not a typical wedding day, and Zita was dressed for blood.

She knew she'd escape the stadium unscathed. Her shield

was her primary power, and as such, it would hold no matter what happened.

She'd raged through centuries of loss, betrayal, hope, despair, wishes, pain, and oppression, their culmination in today's wedding taking the form of a high, ringing calm. She was certain that some of the crowd's chatter was about Ceneth and his great black wings. She knew that some of the voices must have whispered and gasped about the fabled rich skin of the people who kept to the desert. She was curious as to how she might feel about the mutterings from thousands of fair-skinned faces under other circumstances. She was certain she'd pity them, but she didn't know if Ceneth or Galena felt the same. She was glad Suley was safely in the quiet of the Raasay Forest, far from the noise and thoughts and judgments of those who'd never been exposed to a world beyond the kingdom they believed to be their own.

Ceneth looked over his shoulder, and she dipped her head slowly in confirmation.

He struck a stunning figure at the end of the long velvet carpet that ran the length of the aisle. The bride-to-be would walk the sandy length of the coliseum while rows of privileged guests rose to their feet on the ground. In the stands, thousands of civilians from Aubade and the surrounding cities would stand in reverence as they watched the last fae princess of Farehold take the steps to merge the continent. She was to stand in for Caris, unifying Raascot and Farehold until they'd melted into a homogenous kingdom. Of course, Caris had sought reunification through peace, justice, and education. She would have been an excellent source of healing, of forgiveness, of progress.

The world mourned Caris's absence, but Zita had a taste for Ophir's brand of retribution.

If she hadn't trained herself for poise and serenity, she would have jumped when a booming voice cut over the crowd and orchestra alike. She kept her face placid as she gazed up into the stands, beyond the milling bodies and sea of civilians, to the royal box. The king wore a goddess-awful ruby necklace that had been spelled to amplify his voice. She cooled her expression as she listened to him speak.

"My people!" His voice boomed, and the citizens responded in a roar of jubilation. "Today we gather to see the end of turmoil, the end of strife! For years, we've maintained our distance from Tarkhany. On this auspicious occasion, we welcome their queen, who will serve as King Ceneth's witness!"

Gasps and cheers celebrated the victory of centuries of revelry. At long last, Tarkhany had dropped its grudge. The coastal city of Aubade was Farehold's to possess, after all.

"The King of Raascot will bring an end to decades of strain as our peoples find their rightful place in the north and south," Eero went on. "Today, as he marries my daughter, we will publicly declare our will as one."

Zita's breath caught in her throat as she watched Ceneth twitch. She only needed him to maintain composure for a few minutes longer.

She unclenched the moment she saw his wings relax behind him. Fortunately, their place on the coliseum floor was too far away for the audience to perceive the tensions and expressions of their party. The officiating bishop would have noticed had he not been glued to Eero's every word. She didn't bother to turn to see what the lords, ladies, and wealthy parties of Farehold made of Ceneth's flinch.

Soon, it wouldn't matter.

"Rise, good people," Eero continued, "as we bear witness to history."

The rumble of thousands of bodies shifting their weight as everyone got to their feet accompanied the orchestral swell of string and woodwind instruments. The tune was too solemn for a wedding, but perhaps an air of gravity was necessary for the melding of minds as Farehold became the continent's only power.

Zita followed the turn of ten thousand heads as wooden

doors on the far side of the stadium swung open. The stadium was too large for her to see the exact details of Ophir's lovely face, but even from the distant edge of the sands, she smirked at the bright white smile on the princess's face. Tempus was doing his best impression of what he suspected a woman might look like walking down the aisle to her beloved, of course. He knew nothing of Ophir, of her reputation in the kingdom, of her complex emotions, or of how a woman might weep on her wedding day.

He'd stood at the far end once, beaming at Zita while she'd maintained a polite expression. Tempus couldn't even master serenity as he grinned at the dignitaries on the sands below. She would have found his weak portrayal of women amusing if this day weren't the end of the world.

She didn't have to wait much longer.

Ceneth clasped both hands behind his lower back. He was to flash a signal with his fingers when he was ready. She supposed it really should be his call. She'd be ready no matter what. She needed to know that her allies would survive the ordeal. She looked at Galena's still-fidgeting form, but she had long since given up on wishing the winged woman would stop. Galena was right to feel disquieted. It was a respectable emotion in times such as these. As Zita didn't employ a neutralizer within her courts, she saw it as a sign from the All Mother that their plans had been kissed with blessings. Perhaps one of Ceneth's men had had to perish for her to understand the usefulness of Galena's gift. The woman had been instructed to cast her power over the room in the summit, and by the time the castle had collapsed around them, it had been too late to see the error of her ways.

Today would be different.

Zita knew Galena was no newborn fae. Now in her seventh decade, Galena could focus her power with intent, as could every fae who'd exercised their ability. The seamstress had tailored a pretty gray dress for the Raascot witness, though she'd struggled to accommodate the woman's wings.

Galena had been unable to keep her wings still since the start of the wedding. She reminded Zita of the birds who would flit through the fountains in her courtyard, treating them like birdbaths. Their wings would twitch and move as the water cascaded down their backs. Galena's flexed, flared, and tucked with the subtlest of movements as she struggled to control her emotions.

She only needed to hold it together for another minute or so. Tempus and his large, bright smile would be at the end of the aisle any moment. He'd stand across from Ceneth wearing Ophir's lovely face while the bishop began the ceremony. There would be no dramatism of waiting for the vows. There'd be no lull of silence or shifting boredom before the man of the cloth delivered his speech. Everyone would sit, including King Eero and Queen Darya. Ceneth would flash the fingers clutched behind his back. Galena would lunge. And Zita would begin.

She began to count in her head.

The coliseum was roughly twelve stories tall, though several of those were a steep, blank wall. Ten rows. Twenty. Thirty rows surrounded the coliseum. It took the shape of an elongated circle, stretched into an imperfect oval. From the longest points, she estimated the stadium had to be shy of six hundred meters. The music swelled as the clock wound down. Violins, cellos, violas, double basses, and lutes thrummed enthusiastically beside the flutes, piccolos, bassoons and twisted golden horns of the brass and woodwinds.

She looked at the nearly thirty thousand citizens in the stands.

The music swelled, every hand moving in tandem as their bows, their fingers, their breathwork and lips and intensity matched the pace of the rapidly approaching bride. There had to be fifty musicians in the pit. Only a dozen or so royals sat securely in the box with Eero. On the floor, there were at least two hundred members of Farehold's nobility. Wealthy families, smiling faces, judgmental eyebrows, glittering jewels, stoic merchants, and women filled with contempt for a princess who lived a more blissful life than their own grinned and glared alike as the bride took her final beaming steps down the aisle.

The princess mounted the final steps, and Zita sucked in a breath.

Galena looked over her shoulder at Zita, panic clear in her wide, worried eyes.

Panic would do her no good now. Her only use was to grab Ceneth when the moment came.

One minute. Thirty seconds. Ten. Five.

Ceneth flashed the sign as the bride stepped up beside him. The bishop had barely opened his mouth to speak as Galena lunged for her king.

She locked onto him with viselike intensity as Zita raised her hand above her head and called upon her feared power—the one that had kept her palace prostrate before her whenever she quirked a brow or wriggled her fingers. No one dared defy their queen when she possessed the power to destroy.

No one else possessed this gift, she was certain.

Word of it would have reached her ears. She might have met her equal, fought for the crown, bequeathed the throne upon someone new, if it had.

But with great power came immense loneliness, and Zita was peerless.

The time had come to use her gift. It was a power so terrible it would bring the world to its knees should she choose to use it. Her wisdom and benevolence alone had kept her from unleashing it on the world as the centuries passed.

His gaze bore into Eero, waiting for him to meet her eyes as she spoke a single word.

"Frenzy."

✦   ✦   ✦   ✦

Harland opened his eyes to screaming.

He'd heard men on the battlefield. He'd heard women in

childbirth. He'd fought in wars and rushed into flame to save Ophir from her night terrors.

He'd never heard the pandemonium that bounced off every stone in the chamber. The shrill screams and bloodthirsty cries clawed through his very core, ripping him limb from limb as they forced him to his feet. He stumbled to the wall and hoisted himself up against spinning, dizzying nausea as the sounds drove him forward. Harland blinked time and time again but couldn't clear the fog from his brain as he fought to reach the small circular window that separated the bridal chamber from the coliseum beyond.

The sun had dipped below the lip of the stadium, casting the entire coliseum into shadow. He must have been unconscious for hours for the entire building to be saturated in shades of gloom. How long had he been asleep? Had he missed the ceremony? He fought through the bleary fog to separate nightmare from reality as the sounds continued.

Surely, a horrid part of his mind remained suspended in unconsciousness. Perhaps it was the broken part of his heart that didn't want to see Ophir marry another. Perhaps it was the wicked piece of himself that wished he'd been the man at the far end of the aisle. And yet, as he blinked, his vision found its focus on moving shapes and bodies across the sand, but the sound did not dissipate.

He grabbed for his sword but stumbled as if he were missing a limb. He looked down and fought the urge to vomit when his body rejected the sudden motion. His equilibrium knew no peace as his hand searched the empty air for a weapon that wasn't there. Wherever it was, it had been stolen from his hilt. He was defenseless as his hands flattened against the wall so he might look out the window.

Surely, he was dreaming.

Vomit choked him, catching in his throat as thick, miserable poison pumped through his veins. He was wide awake for this nightmare.

He flinched again against the noise as he begged his eyes

to make sense of the shapes, of the dark, seeping liquid, of the sounds, of the tumbling from high places, of the piles of corpses, of the toppled decorations and scraps of instruments and shreds of fabric and rivers of blood.

Then he saw her. The woman he knew had not been Ophir.

Ceneth. Zita. Galena—the winged companion he'd learned was responsible for their uselessness at the summit. They stood on the sand while the world raged around them. Aubade was falling into chaos, and they were immobilized lighthouses in the storm.

A high, horrible sound cut through him like butter as a woman's voice came from directly behind him. He swung on unsteady footing to see the Duchess of Yelagin, bodice torn, teeth bared, fingers flexed as if she bore claws. Eyes wide and angry, she threw herself at him with the fury of a rabid animal. He had no idea how royal dignitaries had made it from the coliseum into the passageways, but the woman appeared terribly ill.

"Du—" It was all he could say of her title as she attempted to tear out his throat. He knew enough of fighting to understand that she was no worried woman or skilled assassin. It was with the crazed, violent frothing of a dangerous animal that she tore for his jugular, gargling her spit and blood despite the wounds she already possessed.

Harland attempted to disarm her, to pin her, but the fight was over in an instant.

She'd made for a killing blow, and he'd answered in kind.

Harland continued to fight against the fog as he stumbled into the hall. Screams rushed through the corridor of the coliseum dungeon as if they were water filling the space.

This was precisely what he'd seen through the window, though he'd refused to believe it was true. He didn't know how much time he had left to get out. Tens of thousands of people were feral, they were bloodthirsty, and soon, they'd be upon him.

PART V

Unmade

THIRTY-SIX

+ + + +

G WYDIR'S SNOWFLAKES WERE NOTHING COMPARED TO THE icy wasteland of dunes before the Frozen Straits. The cold burned Ophir's nose. Her lungs ached. She'd heard legends of the Straits, but she hadn't fathomed how bitter and desolate it would feel to stand on the edge of the known world.

"I'm not happy with this plan," Dwyn grumbled as they crested the top of the hill. She peered over the stark-white hills as the terrain flattened into a terrible, porcelain nothingness. She shuddered at the endlessness of the Straits, then looked over her shoulder. "Are you going to destroy that door?"

Ophir looked at it for a moment, appreciating the hard ninety-degree corners of the ornate door backlit against the pastel gradient of the winter landscape around them. She flicked her wrist as if to summon her flame, then thought better of it. "I think it might be fun to leave a few around the continent, just for the chaos. How disappointing for some intrepid voyager to find a magic door only to have it leave them bereft on the Frozen Straits."

"That may be my favorite thing you've ever said. Unfortunately, I'm too irritated with you to enjoy it." Dwyn bundled herself into the thick white furs they'd taken from the treasury. Ophir had made an offhanded comment about the coats belonging to an aboriou, which Dwyn had promptly told her did not exist.

"You aren't happy with any of my plans," Ophir retorted. She gestured with a thickly gloved hand to the people gathered in the distance. "There," she said. "That's the crew." Her feet broke through the icy crust of the snow as she advanced.

"That's not true." Dwyn dragged behind. "I liked the plan to return to Gwydir. I loved the plan that turned the wedding into a bloodbath. What an iconic way to bring a dynasty to an end. I wish we could have seen it."

"I don't," Ophir said into the wind.

She hated the questions gnawing at her. Were her parents already dead, or was that carnage still to come? Had Zita's power for frenzy truly turned tens of thousands of Aubade's humans and fae into beings of sheer chaos? She wondered what home looked like, then reminded herself it wasn't her home any longer. A new power would have to claim the bloodstained sands, but it wouldn't be her.

She shivered but wasn't sure if the cold was the true cause.

Brief thoughts visited her as to what it would take for Ceneth to heal from what they'd done. The sun turned red as it descended to her left. Across the continent, the sun was setting over the sea as her doppelgänger walked down the aisle. Perhaps her betrothed was looking into her face even now. She wondered if the crew would spot them, but she supposed the white fur would have a camouflaging effect until they were practically on top of the men.

"It's not too late to change the plan," Dwyn said. "Aubade is gone, but your future doesn't have to be. We can tell the men anything. We could still go to Gwydir. Think of how beautiful you'd look upon the throne in a castle made of labradorite, Firi."

"No," Ophir huffed. Her lungs burned against the frosted air and the exertion of trudging through the snow. "I'm doing what must be done. When they don't find my body among the carnage, they'll go looking for answers. They'll need a monarch's ass to sit in Aubade. If they think I'm still on the continent, they'll try to reinstate me in Farehold."

"Then let them!" Dwyn gasped. "It's perfect. Then you don't even have to get married or hang around with wings-for-brains. With Eero and Darya gone—"

Dwyn stopped speaking at Ophir's flinch.

"Look, I'm sorry. I'm not trying to be insensitive. I won't bring them up again. But Farehold will need a ruler, and—"

"And they can figure it out for themselves. It will be easy enough to understand how the winged fae were able to escape, but they'll have expected my husband to have brought me with him. You're from Sulgrave, Dwyn. This is the only way to make it make sense."

Her eyes flared. "That we escaped the massacre and went back to my homeland? Without your husband? You're newly-weds, for the goddess's sake."

"No one believes we're happily in love. It won't be a stretch for them to imagine that, given the turmoil, we chose to tackle separate corners of the continent. Ceneth would need to stay behind with his people. Meanwhile, I'll go on as an ambassador for Farehold and Raascot pretending to look for answers as to what happened in the coliseum, because I'm such a good and selfless queen. Going to Sulgrave is a great plan."

"Only because it's easy. It's great if you're looking to disappear into oblivion as the only golden-haired defector in our mountain kingdom. It's fine if you want to live a life of obscurity. Do you want to hear a better plan?"

Ophir ground her teeth until her jaw ached. She turned in the snow to glare at Dwyn. The wind kicked up a swirl of crystallized snow, cutting a magnificent silhouette along with Dwyn's long, dark hair as it fluttered behind her. Dwyn shot her a challenging stare.

"Take what's yours, Ophir."

"I am," she said through clenched teeth. "I'm taking choice. I'm taking autonomy. I'm taking control of my narrative."

"The world is at your fingertips, Firi. All of the obstacles were taken out with fire and frenzy. You have the support of Raascot and Tarkhany. You can claim the throne and make it new! You can do anything! You're the next fucking All Mother!"

Ophir blanched. "How could you say that?"

Dwyn stamped a foot, but the gesture was futile, muted as snow absorbed it. Her anger was caught on a gust as she threw her hands out to either side. "This is what it means to be a god. You create and you destroy. Look what you accomplished in Aubade."

Ophir refused to meet Dwyn's imploring gaze. "I wasn't even present for what happened in Aubade."

"And yet it happened because of you."

Frost and fury burned through her in equal proportions. "Are you trying to tell me their blood is on my hands?"

"It is. And I mean that as the highest compliment. The continent has been waiting for you for centuries. Zita could have called her frenzy hundreds of years prior, but she was waiting for you, whether or not she knew it. Raascot would have been squished beneath Farehold's thumb. You changed history. You make and unmake. That's godhood, Ophir. You're the goddess of change, of creation, of—"

"Discord and strife," she sneered. "I know what I want, Dwyn, and it isn't to rule. If you're going to stand in front of me and tell me to go back to the throne, then you're no better than my father. I haven't come this far just to have someone else's will imposed on me. Stand with me, or step aside. I'll take care of the crew myself." She turned and marched toward the specks of workers in the distance, who busied themselves around the dock at the edge of the Straits.

"By going to Sulgrave, you're throwing it away," Dwyn said, voice ripe with pain and frustration.

But Ophir didn't turn to look at her. She'd said all she needed to say. The siren could scream into the snow all she wanted. Ophir wasn't going to Sulgrave. But she was finished being told what to do.

+   +   +   +

TWO HOURS FOLLOWING THE WEDDING

As far as she knew, the ship had never seen the sea. It was built on skates for northern ice, not for salt and waves. Why then, she wondered, did the sailors reek of rotting fish?

"I hate these men," Dwyn said, eyeing the sailors bundled against the arctic as they bustled in and out of the ship in preparation for departure. The men were citizens of Farehold paid by Ceneth's coin to take his new bride and her companion to Sulgrave.

Ceneth had promised that the men would ask no questions. They had been skeptical, but were ready to do whatever their princess needed, particularly when their pockets were lined with gold. People rarely survived passage across the Straits, but Ophir's gift for flame was well known across the kingdom. It was the reassurance they needed that, should the ship falter and the wind crack its hull, she could call a fire as large and hot as the sun to keep the ice and snow from consuming them.

"You hate all men," Ophir hissed back.

"That's not true." Dwyn's attempts at a whisper fell short. A crew member raised a disapproving brow as he passed.

Ophir had been aboard pleasure cruises that idled around the coast with Farehold's nobility. She'd enjoyed the rocking of the western sea while drinking wine and dipping crab legs in melted butter as dolphins leaped into the wake behind them. She'd enjoyed watching the wind fill the sails and the way Caris had clutched the mast while she'd scanned incessantly for the merfolk that most certainly didn't exist. This enormous, land-bound ship reminded her of the seafaring ship in many ways, but it was on an interesting set of thin, flat skis, prepared to glide across the snow. She was told that they were still several miles from the Straits and that the crew would set to work switching out the boards for blades once they hit the ice. She struggled to imagine what the Straits must look like if this barren sea of white nothingness was still several miles from its territory.

"Name one man you don't hate," Ophir demanded. Though she had been shown to the captain's quarters, she had opted to stay amid the crew beneath the ship. If the men needed to be brainwashed into telling a very specific story, she thought it might serve her well to observe them before they utilized that ability.

Dwyn chewed on her lip.

"Told you."

"I'm thinking," Dwyn bit back defensively.

After a long pause, Ophir leveled her a dry, unamused look.

"Well, in my defense, I don't like any women, either. Except you. My misanthropy is an equal opportunist."

Ophir wasn't sure what to say, so she closed her eyes and tilted her head back against the inner wall of the ship. She'd expected it to be cold as it absorbed the winter winds beyond, but some lovely insulation kept heat pulsing through the sides of the vessel. What saddened her wasn't Dwyn's statement. It was that she believed that Dwyn meant exactly what she said. She knew Dwyn cared for her, and liked her, and wanted to be with her. And even still, Dwyn didn't understand her at all. She'd have Ophir return to Aubade and don a glittering crown to rule over a people in turmoil.

Either she didn't care to empathize with Ophir enough to absorb just how much she'd hate that future or she knew and she didn't care.

Dwyn loved her. She knew it was true.

She also knew that being loved by Dwyn would never

bring her peace. And maybe she didn't deserve peace. Perhaps she'd earned every miserable second that stretched out before her. But if she was going to spend eternity suffering, she wouldn't do it with a kingdom beneath her.

"How did you cross?" Ophir asked, changing the subject.

Dwyn looked about the ship for a bit before saying, "I came by sea."

She twisted her mouth into a mock smile as she said, "And not with your ability to travel?"

Dwyn lifted a cheeky brow. "I absolutely would have used that ability if it had crossed my mind. At the time, the only thing I could think was to venture south using the water. I nearly perished."

Ophir's contempt calmed for a moment as she considered Dwyn's words. "You almost died?"

Dwyn nodded. "I came alone. It was how I learned I couldn't stockpile stolen abilities indefinitely. I'd wanted to move as fast as the wind. I killed…" She stopped herself from the number on her lips. "Many," she said finally. "I needed rapid speed and to keep myself warm. I thought if I traveled beneath the waves, I'd be spared from the elements. I didn't need a ship, or a crew, or anything of the sort. I thought I'd make it all the way to Aubade."

"You didn't need to breathe underwater, either?"

Dwyn shook off the question. "No, that's unnecessary. I just move the water around me. It bends for me, so I can keep a bubble of air and change it out for fresh air. The water has always been my friend."

Despite knowing that Dwyn had made it, she felt her heart rate spike. She pictured Dwyn beneath the frozen northern sea, scared and alone. "And? What happened?"

"I saw my fatal error when I started to get cold. I felt the temperature before I realized I was slowing. And now it seems so foolish. I really could have used a gift for travel. I'd never met someone with the ability, nor had I heard stories of such a power. If it had been on my mind…"

"How far did you make it?"

"Just past the Straits, thank the goddess. I stumbled to the shores on the Farehold side of our shared border. I don't remember much. I was blue, half-mad with cold, and unable to move my arms or legs. A fisherman saw me come up from the sea. He intended to save me, I'm sure." She laughed, but there was a sadness to it. "He succeeded."

Ophir knew the man had died, as did anyone else in Dwyn's path.

"I wonder how Tyr got to Farehold." She regretted saying it aloud the moment it left her lips. Regret stabbed through her. She hadn't wanted to think of him.

She'd wondered many times whether Tyr had truly left her to avenge Svea or if Dwyn had found a way around their bond at last and ended his life. Either way, Ophir was left heartbroken. That was how life was, and how it would continue to be as long as she stayed with Dwyn.

The siren was too caught up in her own traumatic memory to notice how Ophir's entire body had winced at the pain of Tyr's memory. "Members of the Pact would never be trusted on an excursion, but voyagers go south from Sulgrave all the time. Tyr stepped into the place between things and remained unseen. He traveled in warmth and comfort, using their supplies and making the crossing without ever being detected."

The statement was odd enough that she almost forgot they'd been discussing Tyr at all. "Citizens of Sulgrave come to Farehold?"

"All the time." Dwyn nodded. "Just to see the sights or check in on your bodies of government. But keep that to yourself. No one wants Farehold or Raascot to know the journey is possible. It's how we keep the southern rabble out of our kingdom."

Ophir couldn't keep herself from smirking as she asked, "Farehold's the rabble?"

"Hell yes, it is." Dwyn laughed. "Just because you've

spent your time with two former gang members doesn't mean we're representative of Sulgrave. We're centuries beyond the backwater practices of the south, which you would know if you had more discerning taste in friends. You should really be more careful about the company you keep, Firi."

The amusement in her soft chuckle was genuine. Dwyn's humor had never been self-deprecating. She hadn't been sure the siren was capable of humility, even for the sake of a joke. Sadness quickly replaced the modicum of joy Ophir had found as she focused on what she had to do. She knew that where she was about to go, no one could come with her.

And the worst part: Dwyn couldn't know.

Their reverie was cut short as a man stopped in front of them. Ophir looked up at the jackets and leathers that had been thickly lined with mismatched furs. Tufts of black, gray, and brown stuck out from the cuffs around his wrists, his ankles, and his collar. He gave his hat a tug, exposing his hair and ears respectfully as he addressed his monarch. Of course, he had no way of knowing that Ophir was all that remained of Farehold's royal family. To be fair, Ophir also couldn't be certain that their plan had worked and that the scourge of Aubade had been expunged from the map. But a part of her felt that she was deeply and profoundly alone.

"Your Highness," he said, gruff voice reminding her of rocks tumbling together. "The men are ready to set sail. I'm the ship's captain, but you're the captain of the captain, as it were."

He waited for her to laugh at his joke, but she did not. He fidgeted uncomfortably as he looked at Dwyn. "I've never met anyone from Sulgrave before," he said.

"Well, get ready to meet an ocean of us. I don't know if you realize this, but Sulgrave is full of people from Sulgrave." She looked at him with deadpan seriousness.

"Yes, of course, I didn't mean...I simply..."

Ophir wanted to hit Dwyn for teasing the poor captain.

"Well, if you're ready, I'll give the men the signal."

Ophir continued to look up from where she remained on the floor. It would only be peculiar for a little while longer. Then she'd make all of the confusion disappear. "Yes, of course. Give your men the go-ahead."

He grunted a respectful acknowledgment before leaving them be.

"Dwyn, do you smell something?" Ophir asked.

"I smell unwashed sailors."

Ophir rallied what might pass for a convincing smile. "Something's cooking. Will you find the galley?"

Dwyn wrinkled her nose. "I'm your servant, now? If we're going to Sulgrave, shouldn't I be the one in charge?"

Ophir winked. "I'm the goddess, now. Worship me or die."

That earned a light chuckle. Dwyn grunted as she got to her feet and rounded the corner in search of the galley. The ship was large, but not so big that Ophir could afford to waste time. The moment Dwyn disappeared, she sprinted in the opposite direction. She only had a few minutes to do what needed to be done.

Her plan was threefold.

First, she'd need to create something that would allow her to move forward unseen. Ideally, she could kill two birds with one stone and manifest a companion in the battle she knew was coming. Second, manifestation wouldn't help her as she brainwashed the men. One would need to fall so she could use her newfound abilities in draining to convince them of one story alone: that Ophir had died on the voyage. Third, she would escape, and she would do so alone.

352

THIRTY-SEVEN

+   +   +   +

ONE HOUR FOLLOWING THE WEDDING
PRIORY

G ALENA HADN'T HESITATED.
Her vision twitched. She was in the forest. She was
outside of Priory. She was safe. Yet her heart still thundered
as if she were in Aubade's coliseum. The screams of tens of
thousands clanged in a dissonant cacophony. Their shouts of
excitement became cries of fury and pain. Ripples of horror
turned into gooseflesh running up and down her arms.

Everything had gone precisely as the others had assured
her it would. Injustice had reigned for hundreds of years, and
at long last, she had brought hell to them.

"Galena, are you okay?"

Her king was speaking. She looked into his eyes. His face
was so kind. His wings flared around her, blocking the trees,
the Queen of Tarkhany, the All Mother herself from looking
upon Galena's face to see what she'd done.

She opened her mouth to reply before she reeled, the
earth tipping on its axis.

The bishop was talking again. She was back in the
coliseum. The man had scarcely inhaled to begin his speech
when Ceneth flashed the signal. Galena leaped for her king,
and Zita spoke the single word that would be the world's

undoing. The only humans or fae spared from her frenzy would be those neutralized. With a flick of her fingers, man became monster. Pupils all around them dilated as the animals within took over, no sentience or sanity remaining in the madness that engulfed them.

Shielding was the queen's gift. Frenzy was her curse. And as she was a good, fair queen, the threat of her power was plenty. No one pushed her, nor did they possess the desire. She wasn't evil. She wouldn't have called upon her dark ability of her own accord. But then it had come from the princess's own mouth: She didn't just want to burn her kingdom to the ground. She wanted to salt the earth when she was done.

Zita hadn't had time to soak in the animalistic cries tearing through the throats as citizens and nobles clawed each other to shreds. Galena had saved them from Zita's power, but it wouldn't protect them from the bishop as he bared his teeth and lunged for them. Zita cast her shield with one hand, maintaining her frenzy with the other. An unseen bubble engulfed Ceneth, Galena, and her. Tempus, still wearing Ophir's face, clutched Galena's arm, sparing himself from the madness of Zita's frenzy. Galena knew he'd lived in fear of her power for years. The day had come for his fear to be vindicated at long last.

From the distance, Ceneth was shouting at her. "Galena, hey, look at me. Open your eyes."

She wanted to see him. She wanted to be back in the forest.

But she was still in the coliseum.

The bishop glanced off the shield and howled with bloodthirsty rage. He tore at the invisible wall, desperate to dig his fingers and teeth into feathered Raascot wings. Galena cowered at his first downward plunge but then straightened her spine and steeled herself as she faced the madness around her. Ceneth wrapped his arms protectively around her, sheltering her from the gore as chaos unfolded.

A man's voice cut through the memory.

Her king was speaking.

"She needs help," Ceneth called.

"She may not be ready for help," the queen replied.

Perhaps she wasn't. Perhaps she would never be.

+ + + +

THIRTY MINUTES FOLLOWING THE WEDDING

Zita couldn't tell if she was in a dark room or if she was still battling for consciousness. The world rocked beneath her as if she were at sea. She didn't understand her surroundings at all until the impact of landing and the flutter of wings informed her that the blackness had been that of feathers.

"How long have I been asleep?"

"We just needed to get out of the city," Ceneth said quietly. "It's finished."

He set her gently to the ground.

She was alive, which surprised her. An immense display of secondary powers often cost the user their life. She'd entered the wedding unsure if she'd make it out. Yet, here she was, opening her eyes in the arms of Raascot's king.

Thirty minutes prior, she'd stood beside him in the coliseum's center, prepared to upend the world.

She'd looked into the eyes of King Eero and Queen Darya, knowing it was the last time she'd see them. She'd gazed at their citizens, at the dignitaries, at the throngs who sat in a stolen stadium in a stolen capitol on stolen ground.

Ophir had been about to destroy the world, yet she hadn't even been there to watch it happen.

The bishop had barely begun the ceremony when Ceneth's signal had set the plan into motion.

The neutralizer had grabbed King Ceneth, sparing him from Zita's most terrible power as she had raised her hands and sent thousands of cheering spectators into a mindless

355

throng of ripping, tearing maniacs. She had held her shield around their little party as the chaos descended.

The bishop had torn for their throats. When the once-holy man had failed to grab Ceneth or Galena, he'd slashed for Ophir.

Zita had seen the precise moment that Tempus had understood what she'd done.

Her shield had not extended to him.

She had sunk to one knee as her secondary power weighed heavily on her, but she had met her husband's eyes.

"Zita!" he'd shrieked, still wearing Ophir's face, holding on to Ceneth's hands for dear life, desperate to be connected to the neutralizer. The moment Tempus released his vise grip on Ceneth, his mind would be lost.

"Zita, please! Zita!"

She had held his gaze in his final moments. He'd deserved to watch her cold difference as he realized she'd meant what she'd said when she'd banished him. He was a cockroach. The only thing that could kill him was a swarm of insects low enough to eat him alive.

"Zita," he had gasped one last time. She had maintained her hold on the frenzy and shield alike as the bishop had succeeded in wrenching the bride from Galena. The moment Tempus had lost his grip on the neutralizer, madness had claimed him. They'd ripped into one another with instantaneous wrath, their bloodlust not stopping when nails bore into skin, when teeth bit into flesh, or as entrails were ripped from the abdomen of the other. She'd watched the bride ripple into little more than an unloved man in a stolen dress as the life had dimmed from his eyes. He and the bishop had collapsed into one another, soaking in the other's blood as the world fell to pieces around them.

Bodies had toppled from on high. Chairs, dresses, instruments, decorations, jewels, wine, and festive pine boughs cut for a Yule wedding had smashed into splinters, floating on rivers of pulp and crimson viscera. The screams had begun to ebb as the numbers around them had dwindled.

Zita had blinked against crippling exhaustion as sickness had begun to claim her. She had looked up through foggy eyes to the royal box where the king and queen had stood only minutes prior and had spotted Eero's bejeweled crown on a cracked-open skull.

Relief, sorrow, vindication, and remorse had roiled through her as she'd taken several ragged breaths. Her second knee had dropped. Her arms had wavered as she'd struggled to maintain her hold on her gifts. Before she'd realized what was happening, the King of Raascot had scooped her into his arms. With Galena on his heels, they'd launched into the sky, escaping the stadium just as the coliseum had fallen into an eerie, powerful silence.

It was the end of the usurper's era.

The foliage beyond Priory was untouched by the early signs of winter. Yellow leaves and dense underbrush replaced the yellow hair and twisting bodies in her memory.

She was safe for the time being, though only beginning to feel the true consequences of her power as her heart weakened. Her knees buckled.

Galena landed beside her and rushed to help support her. "Goddess, Zita, are you okay? Is there anything you need?"

"I... I didn't expect to awaken." Zita shut her mouth before she said more. She didn't want to speak her truth before the others: She had wanted to die in that coliseum. She refused to be like the line of Farehold's kings who had profited off the suffering of civilians. She'd secured one thousand years of her cities wiped off the maps, ensuring her people would not be further exploited by foreign dignitaries. Anyone who'd want vengeance for what had happened in Aubade was dead now, and those who'd survived surely would have no idea what they'd seen or what had occurred. Confusion and frenzy were allies, after all.

Ceneth seemed to understand her silence.

"This isn't your fault," he said.

She pursed her lips.

"You helped Aubade find its retribution. You saved your people. I became the sort of villain who could never look Caris in the eyes again. It's good she's dead. I wouldn't want her to see what I've become."

"Would either of you blame the victim for swinging the sword against her pursuer?" Galena asked. She appeared fully present as she waited for their reply.

"It's a false comparison," Ceneth exhaled. "Our kingdoms were at peace. They believed us to be their allies."

"You're not ignoble for breaking the rules that another exploited for your oppression. The rules were at fault, as was the one who crafted them for subjugation. Not you."

It was the sharpest Galena had appeared in some time. The winged neutralizer appeared to fall in and out of the present as her eyes unfocused once more.

Zita looked at the king, whose head was still bowed. "Where are we going?"

"Back to Gwydir," Ceneth said. "You have a direct portal to Tarkhany just beyond the city. With Tempus gone and Suley beginning her new life, there won't be much incentive to stay in Raascot. Of course, you're welcome in my kingdom as long as it pleases you. Hassain is still with Samael, but he may very well wish to escort you home."

"Suley is gone." Zita swallowed.

"She's on my land," Ceneth said. "She's very safe among my people, and I'm certain she's fine. I'll send word and a tracker will find her within the hour of our arrival."

She nearly protested, given Suley's wishes for a solitary life, but was warmed by a thought. The young fae had sought asylum to be free of the noise. Now, thanks to the blood magic of the fae called Dwyn, Suley had gotten her wish. Maybe between the two of them, Zita and Suley wouldn't need to spend the rest of their days alone. Perhaps they could share the years that remained, free from the curses that had plagued them.

For the first time in a long time, Zita felt an unfamiliar ember of hope.

Her happily ever after awaited her, and at last, it took the shape of peace.

Zita shivered against the chill that crept through her poisoned blood. "I would like that very much. I believe Suley would, too. But we won't be able to fly all the way back to Raascot without provisions, and I'm too sick to contribute."

"It's all taken care of, Queen Zita. It's over, and we've won. The rest of my party is awaiting us," Ceneth said. "They were instructed not to attend the wedding. They're waiting near Farehold's Temple of the All Mother. It seemed a safe rallying point away from prying eyes. They have food, water, and the warm clothes we'll need for travel. Are you well? We can carry on."

She confirmed that she was fine but wasn't certain it was true. The chill she felt wasn't solely the result of the weather. Her blood cooled, cold sweat clinging to her forehead. She'd sustained her frenzy for a long, long time. She'd only used it twice in her life, and both times had nearly resulted in her demise. The first time, her tutors and peers in the palace had been the ones to pay the price as she'd discovered her power for chaos. After six days in bed carefully watched over by healers and a crying mother, two things had been determined. The first was that her power was extremely dangerous to everyone around her. The second was that she would also suffer the cost of its usage.

Perhaps it was fitting. All magic came at a price. If a kingdom toppled, so should she.

She began to relax onto the ground when a bolt of lightning shot through her. Her mouth dropped open in panic as she grabbed for Ceneth's arm.

"The rings!" She gasped at their oversight. She'd meant to swipe them from the bishop and his attendants, but she'd succumbed to her secondary power before she'd had the chance. The rings had been the pivotal piece of information that had swayed Ophir's decision. The manufactured objects were far too dangerous to remain in the world.

"I grabbed them," Galena said. "The moment you fell and dropped your frenzy, I dove for the box as Ceneth rushed for you."

Relief washed over her.

"I'm so glad you're with us now, child. I was worried we'd lost you. Now, give me the rings."

The fae tucked her wings behind her back. Her body was present, but her mind still appeared absent, fighting her demons just like the fae who'd seen war and couldn't leave the battle on the field. Eyes glazed, she began to hand Zita the box, then hesitated.

Ceneth nodded his approval, and the fae woman gave Zita the rings.

She would have been offended, but Galena was not her subject and had no fealty to her.

Zita took the box and allowed relief to soothe her, massaging the tension from her muscles and easing her worry as the final key to Farehold's manipulative power was securely in her hands. She popped the box open…and frowned. Zita looked up at Ceneth, who matched her expression.

"This isn't right."

"What is it?" Galena asked.

Zita shook her head slowly, denial joining her exhaustion as the miserable sickness threatened to pull her under.

It was Ceneth who spoke, his whisper joining the rustling of branches around him as he said, "This isn't right. These aren't the rings."

THIRTY-EIGHT

+   +   +   +

I T WAS TITS TO ASSES IN THE GALLEY, BUT IF DWYN THREW the right combination of glares and elbows, she would get back to the ship's belly without a man touching her. She bared her teeth, hissing at the only sailor who dared to make direct eye contact as she shoved into the main interior.

"Firi, the food—"

Dwyn's grip around the plate went slack. The meal she'd sourced from the galley was little more than brown rolls and a cut of warm ham. She'd prepared a grumbling speech about how if they were already denied sweets and vegetables on the first day of their voyage, it was going to be a terribly uncomfortable crossing. Now, she frowned as she looked up and down the belly of the ship, scanning the arctic sailors who were too busy to be bothered by her presence. A few of them cast her curious glances, but they weren't foolish enough to speak disrespectfully to the princess's companion.

"You there," she said to a passing sailor. He swallowed audibly as he skidded to a stop. "Did you see where the princess went?"

He blinked rapidly. "I'm sorry, m'lady. I would assume she's in her quarters."

"Her quarters?" Dwyn clarified. Her eyes drifted up to the deck of the chip. The captain's quarters were directly below the wheel, completely removed from the crew.

"It's not my business to know," he mumbled apologetically. "We were surprised you came into the ship's belly in the first place, m'lady."

Dwyn turned for the ladder without thanking the sailor. She frowned up at the latched door on the ceiling. The same sailor jogged up behind her.

"Allow me," he said. He quickly climbed the ladder and knocked thrice. Someone deckside cranked a chain until the hatch opened. "It's sealed to keep us warm," he explained. "Someone will always be top or bottom to ensure you can get in or out, should you or Her Highness need to. I'd put your gloves back on before you go topside."

"Fine," Dwyn said dismissively. She shoved her left hand into her glove, leaving her right hand exposed as it gripped the plate. She balanced the dish in one hand as she mounted the ladder. She'd managed to forget just how cold the air was in their short time in the belly of the ship. The instant blast of arctic air set her eyes watering. She was certain the ham had lost any residual warmth. "I hope you like cold meat," she muttered, irritated. Dwyn got to the captain's quarters and yanked on the door without knocking. It didn't budge.

She began to bang on the door with her gloved hand. "Firi, I have your food. Let me in."

"The princess hasn't been topside," a man called to her from the starboard side. "My lady," he added hastily.

She glared at the man as if he were to blame for Ophir's absence. Each word was a dagger as she asked, "Then where is she?"

It was clear from the shock on his face that he felt every drop of angst she threw at him.

A bloody cry cut through the wood from the belly of the ship. Dwyn and the sailor dropped their gazes as each looked beneath their feet. It was not the cry of man or fae. Dwyn's eyes tightened as a second cry, one like rust and broken glass and anguish, ripped the boards apart with its piercing scream.

"Firi," she whispered. "What have you done?"

The hatch burst open a moment later. Dwyn dropped the plate of food as she stumbled backward, back pressed against the lip of the ship in horror as an atrocity stared back at her. A humanoid beast shook its head to scream, but as it did, its mouth dropped lower, and lower, and lower until its jaw dangled near the sternum of its manlike chest. The blood of a fresh kill dripped from its fangs. It whipped at them with the razor-sharp arms of a praying mantis. She threw her hands up to protect herself, calling to water that didn't come. It was so cold that the bitter snow lacked the moisture she needed.

Dwyn thrust out her hand to attempt to bend the blood within the creature, but it shrieked as if she were little more than an annoyance.

"She's gone!" came the hound-like cry from a voice deep within the ship's belly. "The princess is gone!"

Dwyn's heart dropped into her stomach. She lurched for the sailor who'd spoken to her only seconds before. The man shoved aside his fear as he responded to the emergency, extending his hand as if to help a damsel in distress. She whipped off her glove and gripped his outstretched hand. The withered husk of a man was taken on the wind before he'd even realized what had happened.

With a powerful yell, Dwyn called to the air and hit the demonic abomination with a gale-force column of wind. The creature screamed as the wind punched it with unbeatable strength as if it were the fist of the All Mother herself. The thrust sent the monster flying from the deck and skipping across the ice like a stone over the pond. It would be on its feet in a second, but Dwyn was fast. She dove into the hull and blinked rapidly against the change in light as she struggled through the darkness.

Dwyn tripped over something and collapsed to the floor. She gasped at the hot, sticky liquid covering her hand, her knees, and saturating the fur of her white coat. The creature had worked very quickly.

Panic tore her to pieces. She grabbed the first man she saw as she drained him to borrow the ability to heal. If Ophir was wounded, Dwyn would find her. Cortisol gagged her as she shoved through the chaos of hollering men. "Ophir!"

"She's dead, she's dead, she's dead!" one continued crying. She reached the man and gripped his shoulders.

"Where is she!"

"She's dead," he said again. His cheeks were red and stained with tears. Each ragged breath was punctuated with the horrible proclamation, time and time again. Dwyn looked over her shoulder at the slain man, his throat slit, his soft organs strewn about the belly of the ship.

"Where!" Dwyn demanded. She could scarcely hear her thoughts over the screams of the men as pandemonium filled the ship. Between the horrific fanged demon, the withered husks of men, and the slain princess, there was no sanity to be had. Terror rang in her ears, battling their screams. Her eyes spiked with tears as the fear consumed her.

"So many are dead," he sobbed. "So many..." He lifted his hand to gesture to another body. Dwyn nearly hit him to get him to focus but followed the point of his finger to see the drained husk of a sailor.

She blinked at the body. She slowly released the man and walked over to the bloodless, mummified man. She'd killed only twice since boarding the ship, and their fragile bodies had already been taken by the wind and blown onto the ice. She took a few steps closer to the sailor and kicked the new man with her shoe. He moved easily beneath her nudge as if he were made of little more than paper. This was not her doing.

Her fear was replaced with something else entirely. She turned to the sobbing crewman and changed her question. "How did she die?" Dwyn asked woodenly.

"She walked out onto the ice. No one could stop her! She was claimed by the Straits."

Time slowed as she worked through her next question. "And, what are you to do with this information?"

He wiped his tears as he continued to blubber. "Return to our villages and tell others how she died."

There was a weightlessness to the numbness that claimed her.

"Firi, how could you," she whispered.

She saw the calamity for what it was—a sleight of hand. She walked away from the wailing sailor. She stepped over the brutalized body of the young man who'd fallen victim to Ophir's latest monstrosity as she mounted the ladder. Dwyn would have shivered against the cold if she could feel anything at all. She scanned the horizon for any sign of the princess but saw only the husk of the man she'd eliminated as his bundle of bones and clothes was pushed along the ice by the whipping winds.

She was continuing to scan for where Ophir had gone when she saw it.

Out of nowhere, a doorway appeared. It opened, closed, and disappeared into a bout of smoke and flame as if it had never existed. Ophir had drained a man to try her hand at hypnosis. The tale of a monarch who'd died on the Frozen Straits was even more final than the false hope that she might one day return from Sulgrave. Dwyn realized in that moment that Ophir had never intended to relocate to the mountain kingdom. She didn't want to live at Dwyn's side at all.

The horrid, shrieking creature rammed the hull of the ship. Dwyn peered over the edge at the terrifying monster that Ophir had made merely for distraction. Unless the princess had drained a second sailor, then perhaps this beast knew a thing or two about how to help someone slip away unseen.

She blamed Tyr that Ophir had even considered stepping into the place between things.

She watched the demon ram the ship time and time again as it slashed and hacked at the wood in vain. Its tearing had no impact.

"My lady!" came the concerned voice of a sailor rushing for her. "Did you hear? The princess is dead. She—"

Dwyn grabbed the man by the neck. She dug her nails into his throat, wrapping her hand around his esophagus just to feel the thrill of his panic in his final seconds as rage pumped through her. She'd already stolen and used wind. The second power she'd taken was healing, though she may very well still need it soon if she was about to set out onto the ice.

"It's nothing personal," she said to the man as his blood vanished, his skin suctioning to what remained of his skeleton. "I need a few things. You and a few of your brothers are going to have to cough up the price."

The first stolen power was that of strength. She burst through the locked cabin door as she stormed into the captain's quarters. Just as was true of ships bound for the sea, the captain's cabin had a large map of the continent on the table at its center. Dwyn sighed as she looked at the map. She worked her face into a dramatic display of pain and panic as she screamed for help. She cried out again and again until someone sprinted to her aid. The man threw himself at her protectively before identifying the source of her fear.

Within a moment, she'd claimed him.

She turned back to the map and used her next power.

"Show me Ophir," she said to the map.

A large, dark blotch appeared on the elaborate parchment. To her surprise, Ophir had not gone to the Raasay Forest, or the warm coastal climates, or Tarkhany, or Sulgrave. As she looked at the dark spot on the map, she desperately wished it had been the Etal Isles.

Dwyn snarled at the map as she spun out of the cabin. A concerned, handsome face opened his mouth to intercept her, perhaps concerned for her safety as crewmembers dropped dead left and right. He'd be her final kill. She didn't hear what he had to say before she grabbed the rope that dangled over the ledge and lowered herself to the icy ground.

She only needed to get far enough away from the ship to keep the men from following. She tucked her exposed hands into her coat, praying Ophir's demon would be too distracted by the crew to come searching for her.

Healing awaited her should she need it, but she had one more power to use.

Dwyn closed her eyes as she made good on the rumors that had circulated about her for months and became a fae who had the gift of travel as she focused on the Unclaimed Wilds.

THIRTY-NINE

+   +   +   +

S EDIT'S HEAD SHOT UP IN SUDDEN ALARM. HE POUNCED
from the luxurious feather bed with feline grace as he
ran for the door. With the high, alarming whine of nails on
slate, he began to scratch at the door as he attempted to escape
into the corridors of Castle Gwydir.

Tyr was on his feet a second later.

"I'm sure you miss her, but she's coming right back," he
promised the vageth. His words came out in a hushed plea for
the creature to be quiet. Sedit had never made a commotion
like this of his own accord.

Sedit sprinted to the window and jumped up on his hind
legs. He pressed his large paws into the glass as he surveyed the
three-story drop below. With a huff, talons shot out from his
paws as he began to bring his weight down on the windowpane. His glossy, amphibious skin matched the blue-black
labradorite of the castle, making him look like a gargoyle
perched at the window, carved from the stone itself, rather
than a demonic dog attempting escape.

"What the hell," Tyr gasped. "What are you doing?"

He watched in horror as the demonic hound pounded at
the window, throwing his weight into it again and again. He

turned to Tyr and bared the venom-slick rows of his needle-like teeth. His eyes were solid black as they reflected sheer, feral urgency. Sedit abandoned the window and ran for the door once more, this time throwing his entire body into the barricade as if he were a battering ram.

"Is it Ophir?" Tyr asked. He knew the vageth couldn't talk. He hadn't particularly cared for the hound, but it had been his only connection to Ophir after Dwyn had banished him. Any wishes for vengeance or hopes of returning to Sulgrave to track down the men who deserved their long-cold revenge simmered in a distant pot in the back of his mind. He'd barely removed himself from the cabin for fifteen minutes before he'd returned in the space between things.

Heartbroken, Ophir hadn't looked for him.

With no one to drain and no reason to believe that Tyr would remain with a princess who didn't want him, Dwyn hadn't posed a threat.

Sedit hadn't been fooled for a second. He'd raised his head to look at Tyr the moment he'd slipped back into the cabin. He'd also promptly decided he didn't care, and he had allowed Tyr to carry on in obscurity while he napped by the fire. The vageth had remained his tether to Ophir as they'd returned to the castle, his partner in avoidance as they'd glared at Dwyn from the washroom when the siren had sunk her greedy claws into the princess, and his only companion as she'd departed for Aubade.

With her ability to craft doors, he hadn't expected her to be gone for long.

The castle had remained quiet, and the attendants were too afraid of Sedit to do much more than shove piles of food into Ophir's chambers and leave. Fortunately, this kept Tyr fed while doing markedly little for his own survival.

Sedit rammed himself into the door again. Tyr had known the creature to be sloth-like in Ophir's absence. It was content to sleep all day, graze on the food provided, and warm itself by the fire. It would occasionally curl up next to Tyr when

369

it wanted attention. More or less, the demon hound kept to itself. He'd only seen Sedit strike or act in violence when Ophir had commanded it.

He threw his body into the door again.

"Is she calling you?" he demanded of the vageth. "For fuck's sake," he mumbled to himself, "the dog isn't going to answer."

If he had to, he'd open the door and sprint after the vageth until his legs could carry him no farther. He took four steps across the room, but he wasn't fast enough. Sedit had given up on the door again and bolted across the room with full force, thrusting his body into the window. It shattered into a million pieces as he burst through the glass. It cut into him, blackened blood spurting into the air in streaks as gravity claimed him.

Tyr ran for the window in shock. He'd scarcely reached its lip when the loud, horrid *thwack* of meat hit the frozen earth. His stomach roiled in horror at the limp, smattered remains of the dog on the ground below.

Ophir's door flew open as an attendant responded to the commotion within. The woman barely had time to scream before Tyr slipped out around her. He snagged a cloak and gloves and tugged them into the unseen place between things with him as he slipped out of the castle. It took him less than a minute to round the corner and slide through the snow-slick lawn to where pieces of Sedit twitched. From overhead, the servant was still screaming.

He wasn't sure as to the wisdom of what he was about to do next.

"I'm so sorry," he whispered to Sedit. The vageth whimpered, white, phantom tendrils emanating from his jaw as they attempted to stitch the upper and lower halves together. Tyr took off in the opposite direction as he ran for the stables. He didn't know how much time he had before Sedit put himself back together, but two horses were tethered to the back, ready for riders. Whether it was dumb luck or the goddess was blessing his haste, he had no idea. Still unseen, he unwrapped the reins from the post, swung into a saddle, and clicked his tongue, kicking the horse to spur it into action. He'd made it around the castle before a shout from the stables alerted others to a runaway horse.

By the time he made it to Sedit, the hound was missing vital pieces.

Tyr knew he only had a few moments before his horse was snatched. He jumped down from the saddle and scooped what he could of the vageth into a pile. "How does this work?" he hissed urgently.

He flinched away from the searching, prodding cobwebs that reached from one piece of the demon to another. The hound's head was whole. His front legs were working. The wounded split in his torso was nearly knit. He pulled back his teeth in a snarl, but not at Tyr. A loud, threatening growl rumbled from his throat as he stared down two attendants who'd taken off after the horse.

Tyr counted on Sedit to keep them at bay, letting the hound bark and snap as he pushed the vageth's back leg back into its socket, allowing the ghostly vines to sew it back together. Sedit got up onto unsteady feet and took a testing step forward. The attendants cried out in horror as the demon rose from the dead, unable to be killed by glass or heights or dismemberment.

Tyr was in the saddle before Sedit took his first lunging steps away from the castle, over the bridge, and into the city. People screamed and parted like the sea as a rabid hellhound tore through the streets, a stallion without a rider quick on its trail.

Tyr pushed the horse faster and faster but knew he'd lose the vageth soon. He looked up at the mountains stretching to the west and cautiously eyed the land beyond the city. Days of rugged terrain, rocky foothills, and useless soil separated Gwydir from Gyrradin's unknown northern lands. From the looks of his arrow-slick body and the intensity of his speed, it looked like Sedit was barreling straight for the Unclaimed Wilds.

371

FORTY

✦　　✦　　✦　　✦

THREE HOURS FOLLOWING THE WEDDING
AUBADE AND THE FROZEN STRAITS

HARLAND HAD THOUGHT HIMSELF A COWARD FOR RUNNING away, until he realized he was running *toward*, not *from*. A door stood on the cliffs just as he broke free from the coliseum, perfectly at home as if it had been constructed for no other purpose than to watch the sun set over the western horizon. The screams of bloodshed had died down by the time he wrapped his hands around the knob. He shot one look over his shoulder, but he knew there was nothing for him in Aubade. Not anymore.

He gagged on the blinding white that hit him as frigid wind filled his lungs.

His eyes watered from the blast, eyelashes instantly feeling heavy as they frosted.

"Fuck." Harland slammed the door. He wasn't sure what had happened in the coliseum, but if the Duchess of Yelagin was any indication of the maddening screams that had come from the now-silent stadium, going back would mean facing the blackened pits of hell. Still, walking through Ophir's door into the frozen wasteland with little more than temperate seaside clothes on his back would help neither him nor the princess.

Night had fallen by the time he returned to the door. Numbness beyond a warrior's fight had descended on him. Harland had seen death. He'd encountered blood and taken lives. He'd fought, and protected, and buried. There was no space in his head or heart for what he'd encountered as he'd picked his way through the quiet, lifeless carnage to reenter Castle Aubade and retrieve lifesaving clothes for temperatures that would see him dead in under a minute. His mind had succumbed to a chill as cold as the weather beyond Ophir's terrible door as he'd stepped over fallen bodies, open mouths, and unseeing eyes.

His shoes were slick with blood, his eyes glazed with an unseeing, protective nothingness by the time he found his way back to the sea. The waves continued to pound against the shore as they had long before the wedding and as they would for one thousand years after. Seabirds called out against the darkness. The night and its moon burned through the starry sky, promising that time would go on, that the world wasn't over, that this was not the end, but he felt nothing.

He put one foot in front of the other as he gripped the frosted knob and braced himself against the cold.

It ate him alive.

Harland stumbled into the loud crunch of ice-crusted snow breaking beneath his feet. He didn't bother to close the door behind him as he crested the small hill and gazed over the bright silver snowscape. A full moon cast metallic light over the flat plane that spread out before him. At the bottom of the hill sat a large black shape. He scrunched his face against the cold and stared into the howling winter night as he struggled to see the silhouette.

Seeing nothing else and knowing that Ophir had created this door, he set forth toward the ominous gray-black shape that broke up the reflective obscurity of winter midnight. It wasn't until he reached the bottom of the hill that a tall, thin shape distinguished itself against the shadow blotting the snowscape. He was nearly upon it before he realized he was seeing a ship.

He'd run through a number of curious scenarios in the time it took him to discern the wooden structure from the ice around it, but he decided it was a ship that had been abandoned before the waters had frozen beyond passable voyage. He gripped as tightly to his theory as he did to his thick winter clothes as he trudged toward the shape, until his guess was shattered.

"Look out!" came a loud, strained voice from the ship.

Harland's face shot up from where he'd been picking his way against the slippery surface to distinguish a gloomy figure on the deck.

He opened his mouth to exclaim but understood the warning a moment later.

An inhuman shriek had him stumbling back into the snow within seconds. On the horizon, the moon caught the glistening outline of a horrid, ghostly form as its jaw dropped open in a scream. He could have counted all of the teeth in its too-wide jaw in the moments it took him to draw his sword. He didn't have to understand what he was fighting to fall upon a century of training. His sword came up in a preemptive arc, anticipating the monster's trajectory before it was upon him. With a loud cry, Harland landed his blow. The blade crunched against flesh and spine as the monster gave a guttural howl. His sword ate into its flesh as it flew to the side. Blood drenched him as the demon skidded from its path.

Harland stumbled to his feet to dislodge his sword as the creature spun on him.

"What the fuck!" He gasped, staggering backward.

The monster clutched at him from the snow with insect-like arms. Its jaw dragged along the snow as if it lacked hinges altogether. The cutting, razor-sharp shriek of the beast sliced into him, puncturing his ears with knives made of sheer sound as it wailed. It twisted through the clotted puddle of inky blood as it righted itself and sprang for Harland a second time.

There was no time for the shock that gripped him. He was a heartbeat away from having his heart torn out and dying on the snowy expanse of this goddess-forsaken wasteland. He shook off the adrenaline as he readied himself for the animalistic lunge.

This time when he swung, his sword ate clean through the monster's neck. The screaming didn't stop as it skidded across the ice again. Its hands and legs continued to kick and thrash even as it fell to the ground and began searching through the blowing and drifting snow for its decapitated head.

Harland brought the sword down again and again and again. He left the creature in a pulp of twitching bits before the men aboard the ship shouted to him once more.

Harland looked down at himself to assess the damage, expecting to see torn clothes and evidence of the attack, but instead he found...a lack.

"What in the goddess's lighted kingdom..." he breathed in horror as vacancies dotted his body. Where his whole leg, torso, and arm should have been, bits of him were missing. He could see the snow below him as if pieces of his very being were made of nothing at all. Harland took his fingers and pressed them into the windows through his body, but they connected with solid flesh. He was still there, he just... wasn't.

Harland stumbled away from the beast and the baffling repercussions of tussling with such a creature. He jogged up to the boat as a rope was tossed down.

"Where did you come from?" a frantic voice demanded from the deck.

"Aubade," Harland said. "Did Princess Ophir come this way?"

A small crew gaped at him, and Harland could guess a dozen reasons why. The most obvious, of course, was because he was stitched together by air. "It's the demon," Harland said. "I don't know how, but it seems to have had this effect. One of you, get me some water. I need to see if the damage is permanent. Someone, for the love of the All Mother, answer my question. Have you seen Princess Ophir?"

A low, sorrowful moan bubbled up from the belly of a heavyset man. It consumed him until his shoulders were shaking, face red with emotion.

"For fuck's sake," one of them muttered. "He'd just stopped grieving."

"She's dead," mourned the man. "The princess is dead."

Harland's soul escaped through his parted lips. There was a weightlessness to the sick and terrible denial that took its place, filling the vacant shell of his body. She couldn't be dead. She'd escaped the coliseum only to die out here in the cold and ice? His mouth moved to form a question, but no sound came out. Instead, he listened to the sobs of the man as they mingled with the wind.

At long last, he forced himself to swallow. He couldn't cry. Not yet. "Where is her body?"

"She went out onto the ice, and she died," he cried.

Another sailor shook his head. "He's been repeating it nonsensically for hours. We can't get more out of him."

Harland's eyes widened. Venom dripped from every word as he demanded, "You left her body out on the Straits?"

"Sir, the demon—"

"Go!" Harland barked. They'd scanned his royal garb the moment he'd boarded the ship. Perhaps the Frozen Straits weren't under either Farehold's or Raascot's jurisdiction, but in the calamity that had befallen their ship, perhaps they found it comforting to have someone tell them what to do. Four men hustled to obey. They descended the rope and began to jog in the direction that their pained companion had indicated.

"She's dead," he repeated again and again.

"Where are the others?" Harland asked. A ship this size should have had a crew of at least twenty men.

"Dead, sir," answered a sailor. "Some by the demon, and others by a sickness. It fell upon them so swiftly; no one knows what happened."

He stiffened slightly. "A sickness?"

The sailor nodded.

"Show me."

The sailor led him into the belly of the ship to where the papery skin of a former crewmate had been sucked clean of its blood, its meat, and all things that had once made it human or fae.

"In all our years, we've never seen anything like it," the sailor said. His lips moved rapidly in a silent prayer to the All Mother while Harland knelt beside the body.

"I have," he said gravely. He looked up at the sailor. "Was there a second woman? A fae with dark hair?"

"There was," the sailor said. "It happened so quickly. The princess and her handmaiden arrived and were only here for a few hours. We were meant to set sail for Sulgrave. After the princess died, the lady disappeared just as the demon burrowed its way into our ship. There was so much blood and chaos, sir, it was impossible to keep track."

Harland got to his feet. He sneered at the idea of Dwyn posing as a handmaiden. "Who saw the princess die? Only the one crewmate?"

The sailor shook his head, both concern and apology plain on his face. "I don't know how he could have seen it, sir. He was down here beneath the deck with the rest of us when he began crying for her. But he insisted it, as sure as I insist my mother's name. You don't speak with conviction like that for nothing."

"Certainly not for nothing," Harland said bitterly as the image of the parasitic Dwyn shot through him.

A call came from topside that the men had returned with no evidence of a body, which did nothing to assuage Harland's simmering fury. He didn't understand why, but the siren must have convinced the men that Ophir had died. Whether Ophir had created the creature to escape the sailors or the girl crafting stories of her demise, he couldn't guess.

"Did Princess Ophir leave anything behind before she…

died?" He struggled with the absurdity of the lie, particularly contrasted against how gutted he'd been only moments before at the idea of a world without Ophir. It felt wrong to play along with Dwyn's game, but it would be easier to return with a healthy princess later than attempt to explain Ophir's manipulative attachment now.

"If she did, it would be in the captain's quarters allotted her," the sailor replied.

Harland led the way up the ladder. He waved off the fretful faces of the apologetic sailors. They promised to continue their search in the morning, but their words glanced off Harland's back as he turned for the cabin. He let himself in and walked toward the center of the room, scanning for any clue as to what Ophir might have been up to. If Ophir had escaped Aubade and had time to deploy a doppelgänger for her wedding, then she'd had a hand in planning Aubade's demise. He couldn't be sure why she'd need to make a pit stop on the Frozen Straits only to jump ship moments later.

Harland rested his hands on the table, frowning as he found no clothes, no food, no trinkets, not a single shred of evidence that she'd been on the boat at all. As he righted himself to leave empty-handed, something caught his eye. He glowered at the map, allowing his brows to meet in the middle as he stared at a large, dark blot.

He marched from the cabin and scanned the men.

"You were bound for Sulgrave?"

It wasn't a question. They looked at the man in royal Farehold armor with guilty expressions.

"You wouldn't take a new bride to a distant land under Farehold's orders. Can I assume you're paid on King Ceneth's coin?"

"Sir, we—"

Harland cut the sailor off with the flick of his hand. He sucked in a breath of bitterly cold air. "Which one of you is captain?"

They slowly turned to look at the blubbering man

who continued to loudly mourn the loss of his beloved monarch. Whatever had been done to his mind had gone a touch too far.

Harland sighed, his breath puffing white and glistening against the torches that dotted the deck to stave off the night. "Who's first mate?"

"I am," said the sailor who'd escorted him about the ship. "Navigation is my inborn talent."

"Excellent," Harland said. "Your name is?"

"Caleb, sir."

"I'm commandeering this ship under Farehold banners, Caleb. Take me as far east as the ice allows."

The men glanced at the shell of their babbling captain then exchanged uncertain looks. "Sir? We were meant to go north."

"Not any longer," Harland said, voice firm and steady as it drifted over the snowbanks and crystallized in the winter air. "Take me as close as you can to the Unclaimed Wilds."

FORTY-ONE

+ + + +

"H OW MUCH FARTHER, CALEB?" HARLAND PANTED AGAINST the sweat and exhaustion of their travel. He'd dedicated decades to mental and physical discipline, but he'd never spent a week on foot trudging through the snow. Each new step took on the weight and effort of twenty. Each time he lifted his foot and punched it down only to sink into the mountainside exacerbated their struggles. Still, the cold was different here. Whether the Frozen Straits had been cursed by a malevolent deity, he'd never know, but once they'd anchored their ship and set off into the forest, the temperatures began to climb.

It was still the depths of northern winter, but no longer were they in the arctic tundra. Between the clean furs, free of whatever invisibility magic had stained his clothes from the castle, and the constant movement, sweat glistened on their brows.

Harland waited expectantly for the first mate to turn and answer. The fae ahead guided them past a deeply red tree large enough for three men to wrap around. It seemed as though the trunks swelled the deeper into the forest they went.

"It doesn't work like that, sir," Caleb said over his shoulder.

"But surely, you must feel it growing stronger or weaker. There has to be something…"

Caleb shook his head. "I'm not a tracker or a seeker, not in the way you're thinking. I navigate. I can point us to our intended location, and we will not miss. But it could be over this hill or six weeks' travel from here, sir. I have no insight beyond that."

"Well," Harland grunted, "that's a damn shame."

They carried on until the last gray hour of day. They unrolled the canvas packs they'd taken from the ship's supply stores before Harland had horrified the first mate by telling the crew to go home. Harland had promised him that once they'd found what they were looking for, they'd be able to travel faster than any skiff over ice. Whether they'd walk through a door or ride out on a winged beast, Ophir was a manifester. Her imagination was the only limit to what she could accomplish.

Game was plentiful in the Unclaimed Wilds, but he was grateful they didn't have to hunt. He was sick of the dense, nutty brown bread in their satchels, the slabs of aged, salted meat, and the dried apples lining the bottoms of their bags. He was quite certain that he never wanted to see a white rind of salty, earthy cheese again. Still, they were mentally and physically exhausted. Caleb was with him on a wild goose chase. Though he was grateful for the first mate's company and skill, he seriously questioned the man's judgment. He wondered if anyone could have strutted onto the boat in the wake of that night's chaos and been handed the role of leadership.

"You really think the princess is still alive?" Caleb asked. The fire they'd built between them smoked as the pine leaves caught and turned to ash.

"Wouldn't you know?" Harland asked, frowning.

"No, sir." Caleb looked frustrated as he answered. "Like I said, I'm not a tracker in the way you might want. I'll lead us to her, but I may very well be leading us to her bones or to whatever remains of the princess in the stomach of some animal."

Harland chuckled lightly, which drew a look of concern. "Sir?"

"It's nothing," Harland said, a small smile on his lips. "But you underestimate her. No animal could best her." He'd once been so afraid for Ophir's safety. He'd run into fires for her night after night when terrors had haunted her. He'd tried to protect her from the world. He would have given his life to save her. Little had he known that she was the most fearsome creature on the continent. There was no beast that would find its match in Ophir, unless the monster's name was Dwyn.

"Pardon me for saying, sir, but you speak like a man in love."

His heart ached at the words. Was he as transparent as he was foolish? Love made people do wonderful, terrible, foolish things. If only he'd been wiser, he would have known how to love her better. It was a conviction he'd never dream to have returned. In his wildest fantasies, his only hope was to make amends for the pain he'd caused.

A pop to the south of their camp drew their eyes to a dark space between trees. They'd chosen a flattened area between mountains and pitched their tents among the fallen logs. The forest floor was barren, the overhead canopy of leaves too broad and dense to have allowed bushes and brambles any chance for survival. The pressing silence offered only by a carpeting of snow should have been the only sound.

A twig snapped, and Caleb nearly jumped out of his skin.

"What do you think it is?" he whispered.

Harland shook his head. "We're fine," he said, but his voice was unconvincing. "Wild animals would be scared off by our fire, not drawn to it."

"Even bears?" Caleb asked in a hushed tone.

Harland casted a glance at their satchel of food. He wasn't sure how bears felt about fire, but if one was scouring the cliffs this late into the season, it would be starving. It could have sensed their meats and cheeses from leagues away. He wished he'd brought a bow, but he'd been fleeing the stadium and had scarcely had the wherewithal to return for winter gear. All things considered, he counted himself fortunate to have a good sword.

Another sound came from the woods.

Not an animal, but a man.

"Sedit, don't," said the deep, male voice.

A low growl rippled between the trees. The sound felt like melted snow had been drizzled down Harland's back. He tensed, hand on the hilt of his sword as he called out.

"Hello?"

"Please, Sedit!" The man's voice came more loudly this time.

A new confusion filled Harland, tinged with an uncomfortable familiarity. There was a musical lilt to the dance of the man's voice...almost as if he were...

"Tyr?" Harland called out.

"Ah, fuck," Tyr said in the split second it took for the creature's noises to turn into the snap of its maw. A frustrated shout, the crunch of snow underfoot, the break of a fallen branch, a cry from Caleb, and the bloodthirsty barking of a demonic hound flooded him in the time it took to blink.

Harland was on his feet as he sprang into action, ready for battle against the unknown shadow. He rolled out of the way as the dark shape extended its talons for him. He gasped against the glittering horror of eyes and teeth as it gnashed its maw inches from his face. He unsheathed his sword scarcely in time to knock it from its lunge, but he barely nicked the animal. Rather than act wounded, it was merely spurred on. Infuriated by his blade, the creature pounced again.

The shouting of men behind him faded to noise as he squared off with the creature. Tyr was saying something while Caleb ran for his weapon. When the monster sprang the next time, it was not for Harland but for the first mate.

Caleb's short sword was good for little more than

threatening unruly crew members. It didn't stand a chance against a hellhound. He lofted his weapon with both hands and brought it down as if he were chopping wood, but his timing was faulty. The creature had its teeth in his shoulders in a second.

Caleb screamed as jagged needles embedded themselves into his flesh, ripping free with the leather of his coat and a pound of fresh red fae meat. The dog had its talons in Caleb's chest as it forced him onto his back in the snow, but Harland was quick on his feet. In two bounds, he was past the fire and brought his weapon onto the dog.

He was still vaguely aware of Tyr shouting—not at the demon this time but at him.

The demon whimpered in pain and fury as it was forced off his first mate and into the snow. When his blade came up, it was slick with the same black, viscous liquid that had coated it on the Straits. He raised his sword again only to cry out as a strong hand gripped his wrist.

Tyr may have been built, but Harland's fae power was strength. He forced his arm down and watched the plea in Tyr's eyes.

"Don't fight him," Tyr begged.

Harland gasped between Tyr and the demon. "What are you—"

"It's Ophir's dog!"

The memory hit him like a crack of thunder. He remembered stumbling upon Dwyn's sleeping form outside of a manor in Henares. He'd crept up the stairs to see his beloved princess fighting with a dark-haired man from Sulgrave. Beside her had been the amphibian-skinned monstrosity, part canine, part feline, that dripped with Caleb's hot blood now. Pain had lanced him as he'd been hit over the head with a blunt object, only to awaken the following day beside his tethered horse. Ophir had been gone, and the Sulgrave fae had been nowhere to be seen.

Ophir's manifested hound.

Tyr took several careful steps between Harland and the dog. "Sedit, stop," he said, flattening his hands. Then to Harland, he said, "Put out your fire."

"It's the dead of winter," Harland protested. "My man's injured."

"Fire aggravates him. Put it out."

Harland growled, "Fire shouldn't—"

"Put it out!"

Harland blinked at Tyr. The man had spoken to him as if he were his lord and master rather than someone who'd infiltrated the castle and brainwashed the princess. Then again, he had saved him...

Caleb groaned from where he'd slowly brought himself to his feet. If his gored shoulder hadn't been evidence enough, the ashen pallor of his face would have let Harland know that something was seriously wrong.

"You put out the fire; I'll help Caleb," Harland said.

"No," Tyr said cautiously, "I don't think I should move."

Harland looked between Tyr and the hound and realized the man was right. He'd thought he'd injured the creature, but it looked perfectly healthy as it flexed its muscles and readied itself to pounce. It drew its talons through the snow as it challenged him.

"Let me get the tonics—"

"The fire, Harland!" Tyr barked.

Harland nodded, half in shock as he gathered an armful of snow to smother the fire. Several piles later, nothing remained of the yellow and orange warmth that had kept them alive only moments before. He didn't wait to ensure that the hound had been pacified before going to his satchel to dig for the tonics. Given the severity of Caleb's wound, he grabbed two. One to clot the exterior and one to drink. They didn't have a lot of time to waste, and he couldn't risk prolonging Caleb's healing process.

"What are you doing here?" Tyr demanded.

"The same thing as you, I'd suppose," Harland replied.

The navigator took the first brown bottle in his good hand and uncorked it with his teeth. He spat the cork into the snow and downed it in two swallows while Harland drizzled the remaining bottle onto the mate's shoulder. Caleb sighed as he leaned his head against the tentpole.

"It's still here, isn't it, sir?" Caleb asked quietly.

Harland nodded. "That's Tyr. He's a...friend." Harland wasn't sure if he liked the word in his mouth, but it was the only one that rang true. He looked over his shoulder as his eyes adjusted from the brilliant red and yellow firelight to the dark of the night. He'd heard that humans often took several minutes to see when light and dark changed quickly, but then again, humans had always been the goddess's most pitiful creations on so many accounts. It was by the starlight that poked between the canopy that Harland discerned the hound's glistening hide. Though it hadn't fully relaxed, it no longer looked feral.

Harland wasn't sure what tone to strike on an occasion such as this. He swallowed as he asked, "Ophir's...dog. Did you give it a name?"

"She did," Tyr said. "Sedit. And I've been following him from Gwydir. I believe she's calling to him. Of course, I have no way of proving that, but..."

Harland nodded slowly. He wanted to feel bewildered, but it was hard to believe that anything could shock him. Wherever Ophir went, demons and destruction seemed to follow, and neither Tyr nor Dwyn was ever far behind. Even in the rugged northern wilderness to which no kingdom had laid its mark, despite the trees the size of castle towers and the presence of hellhounds, Harland couldn't bring himself to respond with the appropriate level of surprise. He'd primed himself to ask another question when Caleb groaned.

"Hush," Harland said as he rested a comforting arm on the man's good shoulder. "You were brave. The tonic will begin working any second. You should already be feeling a bit better."

"If you say so, sir," Caleb said. The younger fae gritted his teeth and scooted backward against the pain, shoving his back into the tentpole with more force.

Even in the starlight, Harland made out the clammy glisten of sweat on his forehead. "Do you? Has your pain lessened, that is?"

"I hate to sound like a coward," the first mate said between ragged breaths, "but I'm feeling markedly worse, sir."

Sedit barked once and took one step back, then another.

Tyr looked at them with wide eyes. In a hurried voice, he said, "He's leaving. I have to keep following him or I'll lose the trail to Ophir. I'll leave markings as I go so you can find us. Wait thirty minutes before you light another fire. I'm sure I'll be seeing you shortly. And Harland?"

Harland nodded through the urgency. "Yes?"

"You know how we hate Dwyn?"

"Deeply."

"She's so much worse than we even imagined."

Rather than run toward Sedit, Tyr took off in the direction from which they'd come. A moment later, the muscled shape of a dark horse cut across camp as he chased Sedit across the mountain.

Harland kept Caleb distracted with sordid tales of how he'd gotten the job as Ophir's personal guard, skipping over the more personal bits and relying heavily on humorous elements that might make the first mate laugh. He had to dig the firepit out of the snow before he could begin the process of lighting a new flame on fresh wood.

He wished he had Ophir's gift for flame, but they'd brought flint and a small bottle of alcohol meant for dousing rather than lighting. It took a few tries, but before long, he'd fostered the kindling until the logs had caught fire. He nurtured it into a small blaze before he turned to check on Caleb. His smile faltered the moment he rotated.

"Caleb?"

Harland's hand flew to the man's neck. There was still

a pulse, but it was erratic, almost as if the man had ingested poison. Harland grabbed the satchel and dug for the remaining tonics. They only had one remaining, but clearly the injuries were far more serious than he'd estimated. Even still, the first mate was fae. Two tonics even on a major artery should have sufficed. And yet…

Harland uncorked the final bottle and tilted back Caleb's head. He dribbled a little into the fae's mouth and waited for the man to swallow. He did, which Harland took as encouragement.

"Hang in there," he said. He sniffed the tonic to ensure it smelled every bit as medicinal as the ones he'd used in the castle. Some horrible part of him wondered if the ship had been stocked with fraudulent bottles to save on costs, or if the men had been swindled when they'd purchased supplies. He hadn't thought to consider the efficacy of the tonics before deploying them the first time.

He stuck his tongue to the edge of the bottle and waited for the familiar tang, and he was satisfied when it came. Even if the first two had been water, a single tonic should work, when ingested; it would merely take longer.

"Sir, I don't think I'm getting better," Caleb said, voice weak.

"Perhaps the first bottles were spoiled. But this one is every bit the real thing. You might have an uncomfortable night, but the fire is going, we have food, we have water, we have shelter, and we'll give you the time you need to heal. Here." Harland continued to hold Caleb's head as the fae consumed the last of the liquid. "Just rest tight."

"You know," Caleb said, voice trembling, "I've never been anywhere. My village was only a short journey from the border, and they knew of my gift for navigation. It wasn't enough to qualify me for the job, to be honest, but since we were a landlocked ship rather than a seafaring one, the captain was a bit different. This trip to the Frozen Straits, the chance to see Sulgrave…and then when you asked me to come with you to the Unclaimed Wilds. Sir, it was a dream come true. Overnight, I went from a boy who'd never ventured beyond his village to a voyager."

Harland smiled. "Then you'd better survive to go back to tell the village that you sailed the Straits and pursued a princess across the Wilds, don't you think?"

Caleb coughed. "What's Aubade like? The castle, I mean?"

Harland's heart twisted painfully. Of course, now was not the time to talk about oceans of blood, of screams, of fallen bodies. It was not the time to inform him that his king was dead and that there was no monarchy in Farehold. It wasn't even the time for him to think of how empty and homeless he'd felt when the person who'd tethered him to Aubade had left. So instead, he spoke of the sea, of walls the color of custard, of large, white birds that fished with their gullets, of tall trees, and hard brown fruits full of sweet water. He watched Caleb's face as he discussed crossing the desert with Samael and seeing the Tarkhany Palace. He spoke of dragons as tall and wide as buildings with cries that could be heard for miles around. He told Caleb of the glow of the northern lights that had been caught within the very crystal stones of Castle Gwydir, of the river so dark it could have been made of the gloom between stars, of a people with the black, glistening wings of angels.

He watched Caleb relax in his arms as he realized the tonics were not working. Whatever had happened in the man's fight with the hellhound, Ophir had created a demon that would win its battles in one form or another. Though her dog was bounding through the forest, the gored man he'd left behind had not been spared.

So, Harland spoke of love.

The wind was the gentlest of winter breezes, the enormous trees and their canopies as tall as the gods themselves rubbing together in the night wind as they quieted themselves to listen. Even the forest wanted to hear about the guard who'd fallen in love with a princess. They wanted to know about the man who'd tasted sunshine and then smiled at the bitter medicine of his own folly. A man who understood that some lessons were beautiful to learn, and that even if Ophir would never love him in return, he wanted her to be safe, to be at peace, to be whole. He spoke of Caris, but only the good parts. He spoke of Ophir's nightmares, but only of her moments upon waking, and the relief it had been to think there was no hope only to find that the night was darkest just before the dawn. And he spoke of watching her grow and become someone new, and how no matter where she went or who she was, she would always have a friend, and an ally, and someone who would cross the corners of the continent as many times as it took to make sure she was happy.

He didn't know the exact moment Caleb's spirit left to be with the All Mother, but he waited until daybreak to be sure that no, the tonics had not worked.

The soil was frozen at this time of the year, but if Harland's strength was good for anything, it would be to spend the time, however long it might take, and ensure that Caleb was given a true and proper burial. For all he knew, the young man was the first to be buried in the Unclaimed Wilds. If his sacrifice was not in vain, perhaps he might be the last.

Harland packed only one tent as he prepared to leave that morning. The other would serve as a tombstone for a man who had set out to see the world.

✦   ✦   ✦   ✦

ONE WEEK AGO

Red trunks the size of mountains surrounded her. Ophir hadn't escaped the snow, but at least it fell in gentle, silent sheets now. There was nothing to hear this far north. Not a bird, not an animal, not a person—

A woman's voice sliced through the silence. "Firi, stop!"

Ophir skidded to a halt. Her blood chilled as she turned to see Dwyn panting, arm outstretched as if willing her to freeze in her steps. She'd scarcely had the time to soak in her surroundings as she'd stumbled through the door in the dead of the night and careened headlong into a solid wall. Except, it hadn't been a wall. She'd stepped into a tree so broad around its base that she'd suspected she'd run into a building.

She'd burned the door and continued to run, though she didn't know why.

She'd escaped. Her plan had been flawed, as was true of most of her plans. But she'd made it out. How had Dwyn found her?

FORTY-TWO

✦   ✦   ✦   ✦

FIFTEEN MINUTES BEFORE ESCAPING TO THE
UNCLAIMED WILDS

WHAT THE FUCK ARE YOU?"
Ophir panted within the belly of the ship
moments before it was scheduled to set sail. Dwyn was still
off on her fool's errand fetching food, which meant she only
had a few moments to do what needed to be done.

The companion she'd manifested to help her escape
had not been what she'd envisioned when hoping to create
something that would help her harness Tyr's ability to step
into the place between things. She gaped in horror at the
monstrosity within the ship's walls, and it stared right back
at her, jaw hanging loosely on its hinges as if the bolts in its
joints required tightening. She supposed she'd been trying to
create something to help her fight, to help her flee, *and* to
help her hide.

And her mind had come up with…this.

"How the hell are you supposed to help me become
unseen?" Ophir asked. Part of her was astounded at how calm
her voice sounded. She was inches from a creature so terrifying it belonged in the pits of hell or the furthest corners of
nightmares, and yet she trusted that it would not hurt her.
The things she made were hers to command. For once, she

saw it for what it was: a manifestation. Not just of her will or her want but her subconsciousness brought into the world in a true and tangible way.

It was dark, and broken, and twisted, because it reflected its maker.

The warped, man-like beast lifted a talon and drew a cut on its grayish-white skin. The blood that dribbled from it was nothing short of abhorrent. It was the same thick, tar-like liquid she'd seen in her other creatures, the same darkness that puddled in her own veins. Except she was the monarch to a kingdom, one with pink cheeks and golden eyes and who people often said smelled and tasted of sunlight. At least her creations didn't pretend to be something they weren't.

She didn't flinch from the beast as it brought its broken skin to her own and pressed itself upon her. When it pulled away, she saw...nothing.

She blinked at the open space in her forearm, then back up at the beast. She nearly choked on her question. "That's how you help me with the place between things?"

It was not an intelligent creature and had nothing to say.

Ophir's eyes darted about the room until they landed on a blanket draped over the barrels of foodstuff to keep dust and elements from spoiling the vegetables. She yanked the blanket clean from where it had rested and spread it on the ground. "Okay," she said to the monster, "open up."

While she remained wholly visible, save for the voided splotch on her arm, her blanket was saturated in the dark goo that disappeared on impact until there was nothing left.

She asked the beast to create a distraction so she might escape, and it did exactly that.

Draining a crewmember so that she could convince the nearest man that she'd died on the ice was a bit of a rushed afterthought. It certainly wouldn't convince Dwyn, but it would at least create the cover story she needed for the kingdom. And if she worked quickly, she'd be in the farthest reaches of the continent before Dwyn even realized she was gone.

The bubbling of screams, shouts, and grieving seemed like evidence that her plan was working. She made it down and off the ship without being detected. The ship was in total upheaval as her beast ran amok. She nearly slipped on the ice as she stretched her hand out for the creation of a door. She wasn't sure where she wanted to go, except that she asked the door to take her somewhere no one would find her.

When it went up in flames, she discarded the horrendous, sulfuric blanket and stumbled forward in the dark and the snow. She summoned a ball of flame to act as her own personal sun as it cast daylight over the forest of giants. The shadows it created were nearly as ominous as the indescribably large trees themselves. Each step into the snow was new and bizarre and terrifying, yet exhilarating and freeing at the same time.

She wasn't sure why she continued walking.

She could stop at any time. She was somewhere unknown. She hadn't seen trees like this in Raascot, though she supposed she hadn't made it far beyond the grounds of Castle Gwydir. She knew nothing like this existed in Farehold or Tarkhany. There was a chance she'd ended up in Sulgrave, but she'd been led to believe that, aside from the sheer cliffs, Sulgrave was rather densely populated.

No, unless she'd been taken to another continent entirely, this had to be the Unclaimed Wilds.

Maybe she would be the one to claim them.

She walked and walked and walked until she reached a large clearing. The trees stood as sentinels around her, guarding the open space. The moon had a clear view of the earth at long last, and she soaked in its silver light as it bathed her in freedom. Ophir spun slowly in the large, circular opening and flushed with emotion. Tears threatened to spill over.

No, it wasn't home yet.

It was an empty, forested snowscape. Sedit wasn't here, but if she called to him, she felt in her bones that he would come. And she could make whatever she needed. She could make a shelter. Or a home. Or a mansion. Or a castle. She could make friends, or animals, or anything she needed. The Unclaimed Wilds were hers now. If she was to be the goddess, then surely she needed a place and people to rule.

This would be it.

This would be hers.

And so, she got to work. She split her focus so that her fire warmed her and illuminated the world that was hers for the taking. Perhaps she wouldn't get it right at first. There would be flaws, and setbacks, and crumbling shacks built on broken foundations, but she would have time. Tonight, she needed a bed, four walls, a roof, and a fire. Tomorrow, she would begin her empire.

She was nearly too excited to sleep. Whatever part of her that had been rooted in fear had finally snapped when she'd looked into the eyes of her final creation and understood what she'd failed to grasp for so long.

It was her.

And so was the ramshackle house, and the compass that had fixated on time, and the horrendous fae that had embodied fear and terror and pain.

They were her.

And perhaps if she knew why she'd made everything bad, then maybe, just maybe, she could start to learn how to make something good.

She'd barely gotten any sleep before she awoke and got to work. And though in theory she should have been able to picture Castle Ophir and have it manifested into existence, every attempt at a building returned shattered and cracked and unsteady. Surely, there was something at the heart of her issues with manifestation. Surely, if she could only piece together what it was that made every house she built unstable, she could yank it up from the roots like a weed and tend to her heart's garden.

The moment she caught a flash of dark hair and the furious, pale face of the one she'd left behind, the dreams of her kingdom fell to pieces.

Ophir could have done anything. She could have raised an army of rabid, undead bears. She could have conjured a battalion of skyborne fae with gnashing teeth and swords for arms. She could have called the earth and manifested walls around the clearing to fence her in. But she didn't.

Instead, she turned and ran.

"Firi, stop!" Dwyn's voice was fury and plea. The command was desperate.

And that desperate note struck a chord. It dissolved her excitement and returned her to that place on the cliffs following Caris's death where she'd been so empty, so broken. Maybe Dwyn took her back to that time and place. Maybe she empathized with what Dwyn must be feeling in this time of loss and couldn't bring herself to force Dwyn through a living death.

Ophir took a few steadying breaths as she turned to face the lithe shape among the woods. Dwyn's lovely form looked so small among the red giants. She was little more than a speck beside the mountains who'd dreamed of being trees and grown lush, green coniferous leaves to block out the sun. Her hair caught in a gust and whipped to the side, casting a striking figure as she balled her fists in anger.

Even from across the glen, Ophir could see Dwyn's pain.

Ophir winced at the look in her eye. She didn't want to see it, didn't want to face it. She wished Dwyn had stayed on the ship, that she'd gone home to Sulgrave, that she'd taken the goddess-damned hint and gone on to live her life. She knew it had been a fool's hope. Dwyn's tenacity towered above her other qualities. She was both fearless and peerless as she forced her way forward, plucking everything she wanted from the world. And while Ophir admired the quality in someone else, it was not something she wanted in her life.

"Why would you leave me?" came Dwyn's broken question. It caught on the wind, joining the snow and the rustling of branches.

Ophir closed her eyes slowly. When she reopened them, Dwyn had taken several steps closer. "You want something I can't give you," she said.

Dwyn was aghast. "That's not true. There's nothing you can't do."

Ophir made a small silencing gesture. She didn't miss the steps Dwyn took to close the gap between them, but if they were alone in the Unclaimed Wilds, perhaps it was time for Ophir to meet her reckoning. "I mean," Ophir clarified, voice barely more than a whisper, "you want more than I'll ever be willing to give you. You want a real kingdom. You want rulership and power and conquering. You want things that I'll never want."

"Then... What do you want? You're a goddess, Firi. Speak it and make it so."

Ophir looked at where her feet broke through the crust of the snow. "I want Caris back."

Dwyn shook her head, choking on a sound that was halfway between laugh and sob. Her face twisted in panic and pity as she said, "You just don't see it like I see it. What you did in Aubade... You changed history. You steered the course of a kingdom. You overthrew a dynasty. When you want to make change, you fucking *make* it."

"Yes," she agreed quietly, "and I made the change I wanted to make. I'm done, Dwyn."

But Dwyn wasn't finished. "Your dragon took out scores of people in Tarkhany. Your creation destroyed a wing of Castle Gwydir. But do you know what you did to truly change the world?"

Ophir remained silent as, step by step, Dwyn crossed the frozen meadow.

"You simply made a decision. It wasn't your power. It wasn't your manifestation. It was your *choice*. Zita used what she had. Her husband stood in your stead, wearing your face. Ceneth posed as lure and bait. The kingdom and those who deigned to call you family came to see *your* wedding.

You didn't break the wheel of the world because you're a manifester. You changed kingdoms and powers and dynasties because you're *you*."

"I did what I needed to do," Ophir said. She looked around at the trees. "I avenged my sister's murder in Midnah. I ensured her beloved was set up for the world he deserves. I dethroned a tyrant. I helped Zita see crumbs of the retribution she's owed. And I don't want more, Dwyn. I don't want to go back and wear a crown. I want to be here."

Dwyn's eyes were wild with disbelief. "That's absurd, Ophir. You're highborn. You grew up in a castle. You loved parties, and life, and drinking, and sex. You can have anything you want. You can't simply walk away from that to be alone in the woods."

"I can." Ophir looked at her feet again. "And I have, Dwyn. And that's why I had to walk away from you, too. Forsaking one means losing both, and I accept that. I know it's painful, but I need you to respect my choice."

"Your choice to sit in the snow by yourself? You're a fucking goddess. You don't like the old faith? That's great. Start a new religion. You don't want to obey the laws of an old kingdom? Fine. Create a new nation. Become the mother of monsters, Ophir, and set them free. There's only one thing you do not do, and it's isolate yourself in the goddess-forsaken middle of nowhere to be queen of nothing!"

Dwyn closed the space at long last. She swept Ophir into her arms in a crushing, tearful hug. Ophir felt the hot, wet salt of Dwyn's pain and regret as cheek pressed against cheek. Dwyn snatched up Ophir's hands and used her fingers to wipe away her tears.

Ophir looked sadly at her for a moment before something chilling and solid broke the tender heartbeats between them. Ice filled her veins the moment the cold pressed itself to her hand, shooting down her spine and up her wrist in tandem until it met in the middle. She looked down in horror at the small piece of metal on her hand.

"Dwyn…" The word escaped as a phantom in a grave-yard. Dizziness claimed her. She stumbled backward, but Dwyn caught her elbow and kept her upright. Her stomach churned as she stared at the tiny silver-and-sapphire handcuff that had been placed on her finger.

"I love you, Firi," Dwyn said through her sobs. She lifted the other ring and looked between Ophir's wide, terrified eyes and her own hand. "I love you."

Ophir tried to yank her hand away.

"Please don't pull away. Let me rule beside you. I can help you see your potential! I can get you to the top, but clearly you can't do this alone. You can't get rid of me, Firi. I won't leave."

"Let me go," Ophir yelled, the noise neither fae nor human as she tore her forearm from Dwyn's grasp. Dwyn clamped down with bruising strength to keep Ophir steady.

If Dwyn wasn't going to let her go, she would make her. Ophir called for her flame, but Dwyn preempted it with a drenching flood of water, bending to her will from the snow around her. Ophir called the fire into her very arms, her limbs blistering with infernal heat as she lost herself in its power, but Dwyn was every bit the water summoner that Ophir was for fire. The women interlocked in a horrid battle of elements and wills until Ophir thrust out her hand and a vageth sprang forth from the earth.

Its glossy skin and terrible teeth were her salvation. She continued to push against Dwyn as she struggled to maintain room to breathe.

"Help me!" she cried to the hound.

The beast answered without a moment's hesitation. The vageth lunged for Dwyn, fangs snapping for her throat.

Dwyn didn't flinch. She didn't jump or roll or run. Face streaming with silent, passionate tears, Dwyn slipped the matching ring onto her own finger. An unseen tether between them snapped into place as the spelled piece of metal bound them together.

"Stop," Dwyn said to the vageth, and it obeyed. The creature relaxed its posture and became utterly docile at their feet.

"No," came Ophir's horrified response. She stared at the demon, seeing her beloved Sedit as she begged, "Please."

The vageth looked at her with wide, jeweled eyes.

"It's no worse than my tattoo," Dwyn insisted. "You know how I'm bound to Tyr? How the Blood Pact joined us all?"

"It was meant to keep you from killing each other," Ophir snarled. "Is that what you need? A ring to keep me from murdering you?"

"It's better than that and also more frustrating," Dwyn said, voice hinging on desperation. "Every physical infliction that someone in our pact does to someone within our gang happens to everyone else. If one of us ascended to godhood, we all would. The rings don't do that! They don't make what happens to one happen to the other."

"No. They simply make my will disappear into yours until I vanish altogether," Ophir said, eyes lining with tears. "How long have you planned this?"

In an uncharacteristic show of vulnerability, Dwyn flinched.

"Tell me."

"The truth won't do you any good," Dwyn said.

"Tell me!"

Dwyn chewed on the inside of her cheek. She remained tense as she picked her words. "This was never my plan, Ophir. But I may have helped Eero see the benefit in first bringing the manufactured rings from Aubade, if only to help the transition go smoothly. You would have made a spectacular ruler, and you could have had both kingdoms in an instant."

"This was…" The wind left Ophir's lungs. "This was your doing? All of it?"

Dwyn took a step closer. "From the first day I met you, I've been saving you. I've saved you from the waves, from your nightmares, from your enemies—I've saved you from yourself more times than either of us can count. What do I have to do to prove to you that I'm on your side?"

"You aren't on my side," she gasped. Ophir stared on with helplessness as she realized there was nothing she could manifest to get her out of this. Dwyn had commanded her vageth as if she were its mother. Powerlessness sucked the air from her lungs as her knees wobbled once more. The new vageth nudged her calf with concern, but she could barely look at it. The creature should have been her salvation.

"Let me prove it to you," Dwyn said quietly as she closed the remaining gap between them. Ophir clenched her eyes tightly, flinching against the touch as if it pained her. "You are hurting yourself, Ophir. You are sentencing yourself to a lifetime of pain because you refuse to experience the joy and luxury and life that are rightfully yours. I swear to the goddess—*you*, Ophir, I swear to *you*—that I will not let you stand in your own way, even if it makes you hate me."

Voice dripping with disgust, Ophir said, "There are things love is, Dwyn, and things it isn't. And it's not this. You don't love me."

"But I do, Firi. I do."

FORTY-THREE

+ + + +

T HE MAPS WERE WELL NAMED.
Harland had always suspected that the Unclaimed
Wilds were full of mountain tribes and sovereign people. He
hadn't believed them to be truly vacant. An eternity of trudging through the forest without a single sign of cut logs, of
smoky chimneys, of shelters, had led him to believe that the
tattered paper map curling in Aubade's war room had been
right all along.

The moment he broke through the clearing, he understood what he was seeing.

The princess had made a shelter surrounded by ancient
and beautiful trees. His gaze snagged on a large patch of
melted snow in the meadow, and he frowned. Footprints
had been stamped into the snow on either side, then stopped
where the charred evidence of fire and the glistening traces of
ice showed bits of the ground.

Ophir and Dwyn had fought. He could think of no other
explanation for the singed ground and ice-slick remnants of
water. He shuddered to think of what a battle between them
might look like as, though Ophir was the most formidable
and powerful fae on the continent, she lacked something that
Dwyn possessed.

Ophir was not evil.

Harland's heart quickened. He scanned the clearing for other evidence of movement and finally landed on a single trail of footprints leading from the cabin and into the woods on the far side of the meadow. The single set of tracks led him to believe that one had left, and the other had stayed behind. The other scattered markings appeared to have been from an animal, as they were too wide and chaotic to have been created by a fae. He paused near the tree line and listened, but he heard nothing.

Tyr hadn't been to the cabin, then. Even with his gift to step into the space between things, he wouldn't have been able to hide his footprints. Harland wondered if he was around. He wasn't stupid enough to call out to the man. If Dwyn was angry enough to fight Ophir, then stealth may very well be their best and only asset.

Harland surveyed the woods, estimating just how large the clearing must be. It was practically the size of Aubade's coliseum.

If he was going to go, it should be now.

Harland broke free from the tree line and sprinted for the cabin. There was no wisdom in remaining out in the open for long. He slowed his pace as he approached the cabin and pressed himself into the wall. He snapped his mouth shut and breathed through his nose, forcing himself to calm down as he sidled along the wooden structure toward a warped window. He slowly leaned in order to look into the structure and saw...

Harland was at the front door in an instant. He threw it open and met Ophir's wide, startled eyes. At her side, a vageth jumped to its feet.

"Harland!" she gasped, muffling the sound as her hand flew to her mouth. She looked up at him from where she sat on the ground in the center of the room. Though the cabin had the basic amenities, when he'd spied her slumped on the floor, he'd feared the worst. She looked to the hound and put a hand on its hide. "He's a friend, Sedit," she whispered.

The demon continued to eye him suspiciously, but it rolled its limbs into a calmer state.

Harland slipped inside and closed the door behind him. He didn't need Dwyn spying the open frame from across the meadow. Every precious second counted.

"Where is she?" he said, voice low to match Ophir's.

Ophir looked at the fireplace, then back at Harland. "She's getting firewood."

"But you don't need wood," he said with a little hesitation. The fire that glowed and burned in the fireplace floated as if on the wick of an invisible candle. Ophir could hold the flame with her own intent if she chose.

"I know," Ophir said bitterly. "And she knows. But I've been...noncompliant. She's trying to prove a point by forcing me to not light a fire."

"Forcing you?" Harland repeated the woods slowly.

Ophir's shoulders slumped as her eyes returned to the ground. There was little to look at in the humble cabin, the bed and chair piled high with the dark cobwebs of strange, gauzy blankets. There were no decorations. There was no food. There was only Ophir and her animal.

"Ophir, let's go. Make a door."

She looked up at him hopelessly. There was no light behind her eyes.

"Let's go, Firi! Make a door. It's how I tracked you to the Straits. It's how—"

"I can't," she said, then dropped her eyes once more. It took him a moment to realize she was crying.

He knelt beside her and caught her hands in his own. "What do you mean?" But even as he asked the question, his thumb rolled over something cold and unfamiliar. He looked down at the warm, delicate fingers and the metallic band cinched firmly to her the space between her knuckle and palm. Horror stole his breath as his second knee met the floor. "No," he said, shaking his head. He repeated his denial again and again.

Ophir said nothing. She brought her hands to her face to catch her tears.

"This can't be true," Harland insisted. "You can make flame! You're doing it now! I'm sure you can manifest. I'm sure you can—"

Her face whipped up to meet his pleading eyes with a level stare. She dropped her hands and gritted her teeth as she said, "I'm able to make flame because she's allowing it. It's a false freedom, and she knows it. Her ability to beat my fire was the reason she was brought into my life in the first place. Water wins every time."

"We'll go," he pushed. "We'll go now, and we can find someone who can speak to metal to get it off your finger. We'll—"

"She told me to stay put," Ophir said, each word dripping with venom.

He dug his hands into his hair and got to his feet as he began to pace.

"But you can be separated, right? She's gone right now to get firewood. She could leave and never come back."

Ophir shrugged glumly. "From what I understand of their magic, I belong to her while I wear the ring, but she's also bound to me. I don't think she could leave me. It wouldn't have served Eero's agenda if I could have commanded Ceneth to stay put and then I fucked off into the sunset. We're tethered."

"These blasted things are evil."

Ophir looked at him until he couldn't hold her gaze any longer. He understood the accusation. He'd known about the rings when he and his party had ridden north for Raascot. He'd said nothing when Ophir was set to be the wearer.

A muscle in his jaw ticked in frustration. He looked at the hellhound and said, "This is Sedit?"

She nodded, then waved the comment away. "I made another, but I sent it off when Sedit arrived. I don't think Dwyn can tell the difference."

"If Sedit is here, Tyr must be, also," Harland said excitedly. "With the two of us combined—"

"Tyr left me to return to Sulgrave," she said, voice as cold as the winter wind beyond. "He got what he wanted from his visit to the continent, and he left. He can drain now, just like Dwyn."

Harland pinched his chin between his thumb and forefinger. He went to the window to keep an eye on the meadow while they spoke. "He can drain? Like the siren's stolen powers?"

"It can be taught," she said bitterly.

"He's in the Wilds, Firi. I saw him just two days prior. He came up from Gwydir with Sedit."

She shook her head slowly, hair catching in the clean-burning firelight. Her forehead wrinkled. "No, he left us in the woods after the ag'drurath. Dwyn taught him how to drain, and when he got what he wanted..." She let her words drift off. A new expression crossed her face. "But why would Dwyn lie? Why would..." The pinched space between her brows relaxed. She closed her eyes and looked at nothing. "Because that's what Dwyn does. She wants control."

"She's wanted it ever since she killed Caris," Harland said.

Ophir nodded. "I know."

His brows shot up in surprise. "You know she's responsible for your sister's death?"

"Berinth killed Caris."

Harland abandoned his place by the window and joined her on the floor once more, down on one knee. "Look me in the eye, Ophir. You are aware that Dwyn is behind the orchestration of Caris's murder?"

Confusion sparkled through her golden eyes. Not confusion at his words, but at the energy and tone he brought. "Yes."

"How long have you known?" he asked, cupping her shoulders gently on either side. "When did you learn this information?"

406

"In Tarkhany," Ophir said plainly. "Dwyn told me the morning of the execution."

Harland's mouth dropped open. "But you kept her at your side! You continued to stay with her. She's been with you since…" His words lost their trail. "How did she accomplish this?"

Ophir's lower lip puckered in a questioning frown.

Harland reiterated, "How did she tell you in such a way where you'd have no emotional response?"

Once again, his thoughts vanished as something else took their place. He pictured the blubbering captain on the ship. Lord Berinth had been under a powerful hypnosis, one that had crafted his backstory, that had won others to his cause, that had thrown party after party to lure the princesses to his estate. Once he'd accomplished what Dwyn had brainwashed him to do, her hold over him had snapped. He looked at Ophir now, and rage swelled within him. "That clever fucking bitch. Of course, if she got out ahead of the narrative, she would never have to be worried about someone spilling her secret. No one holds power over her if she's not keeping the truth."

Ophir merely looked at him.

"Tyr is here. He did not leave you." Harland was firm. It wouldn't serve either of them if he pushed Ophir to understand what Dwyn had done. What they needed now was to get out of here. "I don't know what Dwyn has told you, but we're going to get you out. The rings have to work both ways, right? You're fused, and she can't do things without your behest either, right?"

He tried to get Ophir to her feet, but she tugged out of his grasp. Hate dripped from her words. "No. It's why Ceneth was to go first in the ring ceremony. The first to put on this shackle is the victim. The second is its master. This is how I'd be able to force Raascot to bend to my will, should I have wanted. I could have had Ceneth and his people march against Tarkhany. My father thought himself so clever, but that bastard wasn't even the one pulling the strings."

Harland tried again to get her to her feet. When she resisted, he scooped her up.

"Put me down!" she demanded, instantly frantic. He attempted to ignore her, but she called her flame until he cried out in surprise and pain. Ophir thudded to the cabin floor and rolled to a halt. She shot him a frenzied look as she begged him to understand, "I can't go anywhere."

He looked at her speechlessly. He had no idea what to do. His eyes went to the ring, then up to Ophir. He reached for her hand, and she allowed the contact as he attempted to yank it off. It didn't move. It didn't even twist or budge like any piece of jewelry crafted by man or fae. It was truly fused to her.

Ophir's eyes widened. She grabbed Harland tightly, eyes darting between him and the sword.

"Cut it off," she said urgently.

He blinked at her. "The ring?"

"My finger," she said, voice hitching in hurried petition. "Cut it off, Harland."

"Ophir, I—"

"Save my fucking life. Cut it off! Do it now before she comes back. I lose a finger, or I lose eternity to a witch! Don't be a coward. I need this. I need—"

"Okay," he agreed. He drew his blade as she slammed her hand against the ground and spread her fingers as wide as they would go. He looked between the ring and the grit and determination on her face.

"I'm ready," she said.

"Wait," Harland cautioned. He slipped off the leather belt that holstered his blade and cinched it around Ophir's tiny wrist. He used the edge of his blade to cut off a thick chunk of the leather and stretched it out toward her mouth. "Bite down on this."

Her lips parted as she accepted the leather bit. She closed her eyes tightly as her entire body tensed in a flinch. She pinned her ring-bearing hand down with her free hand to prevent it from shifting.

"Are you ready?" he asked. It was more for himself than for her. He would cut off his own arm a thousand times before mutilating Ophir. He wanted to spare her from pain, to rescue her, to make her life better. He never could have foreseen what would drive him to lift his blade to her tender flesh.

"Do it," she grunted through the mouthful of leather.

And just as Harland readied himself to push the blade through flesh and bone, the door to the cabin opened, and a bundle of firewood clattered to the ground.

FORTY-FOUR

✦ ✦ ✦ ✦

OPHIR'S EYES FLEW OPEN. SHE SPAT OUT THE LEATHER IN the time it took for Dwyn to soak in the sight, nostrils flaring with rage, eyes wide with horror. They called out at the same time, Dwyn erupting in rage and Ophir lunging in alarm.

"Get him," Dwyn commanded the vageth.

"No!"

The beast was on Harland in a second. It sank its teeth into his sword arm until he cried out, forcing the blade to clatter to the ground. It shook Harland's arms furiously as it had him in its jowls.

"Stop!" Ophir lunged fearlessly for Sedit. She shoved her hands into its very mouth as she attempted to pry its jaws apart. Fresh red blood poured over Sedit's tongue and dripped onto the floor. She looked up at where Dwyn remained silhouetted in the doorway and called to her in desperation. "I'll do what you want, Dwyn! Don't hurt him. Don't let anything happen to him. Please, for the love of the goddess, stop!"

"Ophir!" Harland snapped. He began to drive his free elbow into the demon's skull repeatedly as he tried to free himself from the beast's grasp. "Don't you fucking dare!"

Dwyn leveled him a challenging glare.

"I can't lose anyone else." Ophir's panic broke into tears as she begged on her knees.

Dwyn looked away as if the scene on the floor was too much for her to handle. Her throat bobbed as she swallowed in disgust. Refusing to acknowledge the vageth mauling the man, she flicked her fingers and told it to stop.

Ophir couldn't stop the tears of helplessness from falling. She was the same broken deer that had limped through a glen all those months ago. There was no strength, no vengeance, no empowerment. Dwyn had wanted her to become a proud, dark, terrible snake. The moment she'd achieved the vision, Dwyn had taken it from her.

"Look," Dwyn said patiently. "I stopped. I stopped, okay? Harland is fine."

"Harland is *not* fine," Ophir said through ragged, mournful pulls of air. She turned to her guard and yanked the cinched belt from her wrist, tying it around his arm. He grunted as he looked up at Dwyn from where blood gushed from him into the slowly gathering lake below.

"Do you have any tonics?" Ophir asked, trying to keep the suffocating panic from her voice. Her question trembled as she reached for his bag.

"No," he said through gritted teeth. "I used all three on someone else. Someone who'd also been gored by a vageth. The man couldn't be healed."

Ophir looked at him with confusion. She looked up at Dwyn, but the siren refused to acknowledge her. She had the audacity to act as though she were the one betrayed as they knelt on the ground. She mouthed, "Tyr?" But Harland shook his head.

"Are you happy?" Dwyn spun on them bitterly. Ophir glared up at her and watched as Dwyn's face transitioned from anger to desperation. "Firi, I'm sorry. I never want you to feel pain. He was going to hurt you. This man had a blade to your hand. I can't let anyone touch you like that. Please try to understand."

"What I understand," Ophir said through swallows of venom, "is that you and everything about you is poison. I understand that I may create demons, Dwyn, but you have no one to blame but yourself for whatever made you the way you are. I'd rather be tethered to a sea of my evil creations than wear this shackle for another second."

Dwyn lowered herself to the ground and scooched toward Ophir as if she were a frightened animal. She approached with caution, lifting a hand as her lip trembled. She reached out to touch Ophir, but Ophir flinched away. "You don't mean that," Dwyn said. Her mouth, her brows, her eyes kept twitching between a hopeful smile, worry, pain, and rage.

"I do," Ophir bit. She positioned herself so that she bent protectively over Harland. "And if he dies, I will never forgive you."

Dwyn sneered. "Until you do," she said.

"What the hell is that supposed to mean?"

Dwyn's eyes narrowed. A silver trail of water escaped the corner of her eye, but she wiped it away as she let the anger win. "What it means is that you don't know who or what is good for you, Firi."

"Firi is what my friends called me," she said as she shook with rage. "You are no friend of mine."

"Fine, Ophir," Dwyn snapped. She kicked the logs closer to the fire and made a disgusted noise at Ophir's flame. Ophir had refused to keep a fire going when she'd been in the cabin before. If Harland weren't already shaking from the blood loss, she'd let it wink out again now. "But I'd be nicer to me if I were you. Do you know how easy it would be for me to make you forget about Harland? All I'd need is…well… *Harland!*" She laughed, the sound tinged with her anger.

Ophir blinked through her tears. "Don't you dare," she said.

"I'm trying to prove a point, Ophir. I'm not the villain you're making me out to be. Can't you see what I'm saying? I could take him! I could force your hand! But I want you to choose this life with me. I want you to *want* to rule together. I want us to work through this, Firi." Dwyn stopped as Ophir bared her teeth. "Get over it, because it's what I've called you since the day you swam into my life. Or did you forget that? Did you forget how you wouldn't exist at all right now if it weren't for me?"

Through a pained grunt, Harland said, "And she wouldn't have wanted to die if it weren't for you, either."

Ophir cocked her head slowly at his words.

Dwyn's eyes widened simultaneously. Her rage was replaced with the shaking of her head, with a fretting gesture of her hands. "Hush, hush," she said nonsensically.

Ophir looked between Harland and Dwyn. "I wanted to end my life...because of you?"

Harland chuckled, but his eyes were only on the dread etching itself onto Dwyn's expression. "Was there a part of the story you forgot to brainwash out of her, witch? Maybe she won't react to the information that you killed Caris, but you did more than kill Caris, didn't you. You drove her into the ocean that night."

Ophir's mouth dropped open. "You...you're the reason I..."

She waited for a headache that didn't come. The knife through her heart was rough and raw as it tore into her soft tissues, cracking her open.

"No, Firi, no." Dwyn continued shaking her head. Her expressions flickered—a smile as if to laugh it off, a tremble as if to cry, an ardent denial as her dark tendrils of hair moved at her shoulders. Her eyes were as deep and tumultuous as the ocean from whence she'd come.

"It looks like you have a choice, Dwyn," Harland said. He adjusted the grip on his arm as he groaned and forced himself to sit. "Drain me. Then what? Do you make Ophir forget about me? Or do you make her forget about this? Because you healed a pain *you* created. She wanted to kill herself because you murdered her sister. You weren't a balm. You were the wound."

Ophir looked at Dwyn with disgust. "Where would it end, Dwyn? You wipe my mind clean every time someone says something you don't like? You manipulate me and push me around the board like you're a game maker and I'm a pawn? You do this while calling it love?"

"Firi, I'm in love with you."

Ophir laughed a dark, teary laugh. "You're the most selfish person I've ever met. Caris loved me. She loved her people. She loved Ceneth. Love is self-sacrifice. It's putting the good of someone and something else above yourself. You may want me. You may want whatever you think it is I can give you. But you, Dwyn, have never loved anyone or anything."

"That's not true," she whispered as tears began to fall in earnest. "I do love you. I may have done selfish things before, but I had to. Most of it was before I knew you. And—"

"What about Tyr?" Harland asked.

Dwyn stilled. She was as motionless as a deer who'd caught a predator's scent.

"Did you make Ophir believe that Tyr had left her for Sulgrave before you knew her? Or was it recently that you made her think she'd been abandoned by everyone but you?"

Dwyn twitched. Ophir watched her gaze flit from Harland, to the sword, to Ophir.

Her face twitched again, and Ophir began to realize that they may have made a mistake. Knowledge was power. In sharing their final card, they'd handed over too much. They had to be smart if she had any hope of getting Harland out and finding him help. They wouldn't succeed if Dwyn felt she had nothing left to lose.

"Tyr did leave," Ophir said tersely. She looked at Harland with an almost imperceptible shift, but she knew he saw the strategy in the way her eyes flared. "You're the only one who's fought to stay by my side time and time again." She looked up at Dwyn and said, "He just wants to protect me, Dwyn. Let him do what he was put on this earth to do. He can stay."

Dwyn stared back, as if not quite believing the danger had passed. She watched Ophir's face in the firelight for a long time before she began to nod. "He can stay," she repeated slowly. "As your guard."

Ophir watched the cogs in Dwyn's mind whirl as she struggled to unravel fact from fiction. She'd woven a tangled mess of powers and lies. Perhaps she'd made it impossible to discern what could or could not be true, given who she'd brainwashed and how she'd done it.

Three heartbeats. Then five. Then seven. Ophir realized she'd been holding her breath, but she couldn't quite bring herself to relax. They were caught in a stalemate of false promises, each hoping the other believed them, if only for a moment.

"What can I do to prove that I'm on your side?" Dwyn asked, the fight falling from her words. She looked pathetic in the cold gray light.

Ophir saw her opening and took it. "There are no more healing tonics. I can't lose Harland. Please, help."

She wrung her hands as her eyes continued to bounce between them, little more than a fretful hummingbird unsure as to which flower had what she needed. Dwyn's concern grew as she finally absorbed just how much blood Harland had already lost, presumably connecting what that blood loss meant for her.

"You can make some," she said hopefully to Ophir.

"No, I can't," Ophir replied, pain thick in her voice. And she saw in Dwyn's eyes that they both knew she was right. Nothing Ophir manifested would be reliable for consumption—not on her first try, at least. She'd never crafted anything that had turned out the way she'd intended, and a healing tonic was not the place to start.

"Snowberry," Harland said weakly.

"What?" Dwyn demanded.

"Snowberries are used in healing tonics. They're nowhere near as effective when they haven't been distilled with a healer, but they're the soul of every tonic."

"It's winter…" Dwyn said skeptically as she looked over her shoulder.

"Snow is in its name, for the goddess's sake. It's a winter berry. It's white, so it may be hard to spot against the ground, but the bush will be barren. They look like little clusters of snowflakes. The plant may be no taller than your knee, or up to your hip."

Dwyn nodded along as she listened. "And they'll be here? In this forest?"

Ophir snapped with irritation. "How is he supposed to know! We're in the Unclaimed Wilds, Dwyn. Please, for the love of the goddess, help him."

Dwyn's head continued bobbing uncertainly as she slowly got to her feet. Her eyes remained glued to the ever-expanding lake of blood. She looked at Sedit, who was calmly grooming himself like a cat, licking the evidence of his crimes from where it had splattered against him.

"Go," Ophir begged.

"Okay, yes," Dwyn agreed. "I'll be back before dark, with or without the snowberries. I can't leave you alone overnight with a dead body. But… It won't come to that. I'll find them." She shut the door behind her as she disappeared into the winter day beyond where their eyes might follow.

Quiet stretched between them for so long that Ophir was almost certain she could hear the sound of Harland's blood leaching from his body.

"Is it true?" Ophir asked. "The thing about the berries?"

Harland waited for a painstaking while before he said, "No. It's not."

Her heart sank into her entrails, bobbing around her stomach and leaving her chest cavity dark and vacant. She looked into the hazel eyes that had been with her for so many years. "Are you going to die?"

He held her gaze. With his good hand, he brushed a tear from her face. "Everybody dies."

"You said a man in the woods was gored by a vageth?"

She watched the ashen color of his face deepen further into whites and grays as he answered. "By Sedit. It seemed he was drawn to the fire. I wonder if he thought it was you, since your gift is flame."

Ophir looked at Sedit, but he continued licking his paws.

"Tyr was with him. He instructed us to put out the fire. It was the only thing that calmed your hound."

It hurt her to think that Sedit had been pulled in by a flame only to feel betrayed that she was not its source. "The man with you—you said he drank three tonics and still perished?"

Harland looked at her grimly. "I don't know much about your creature, but the bite soured his blood. He drank two, and the third was put directly in the wound. Maybe I'll be fine. Maybe I'm wrong. But if these are our last moments together, Firi—"

She scrunched her face against a bubbling sob. She tightened her hold on Harland. "Don't say that. You're going to be fine. The snowberries—" But she stopped herself. The snowberries had been a lie to get Dwyn out of the cabin. He'd said as much. Even if there was nothing dangerous about Sedit's bite, Harland had already lost so much blood.

"Let me say what I need to say, please," Harland asked.

She peered down into his kind face and was transported to drinking wine on the wall, to seducing him in the castle, to being shaken awake when her nightmares had consumed her. He'd suffered blisters, burns, and unmatched pain each time he'd rushed in after her. He'd fired every other guard who'd attempted to keep watch outside her room, trusting no one to do right by her. He'd followed her to Henares, then to Tarkhany, then to Gwydir. And goddess, the man was imperfect, and frustrating, and had made her want to pull out her hair on many occasions, but she knew what love was and what it wasn't. And she knew that Harland loved her.

"Okay," came her quivering response.

"I've been in love with you since the first day I laid eyes on you," he said. He smiled as he continued to whisk the tears from her face with a comforting, cupping hand. "But no one deserves you, Ophir. I would never be foolish enough to think I did, and I know from the bottom of my heart that Dwyn will never be worthy of you. Because you are priceless beyond measure."

"Harland…"

"I'm almost done," he said, offering a weak smile. "We have a little time left before Dwyn gives up on her goose chase. We're going to make a plan, and we're going to get you out of here. And when you leave, you need to keep a promise to me."

And perhaps because she knew it was a mortal sin to deny a man his dying wish, through her silver tears, she whispered, "Anything."

He looked at her sadly before he said, "You need to forgive yourself for all that's happened. You need to let go of Caris. And you need to find a way to be happy. Because you deserve a full life, Ophir. Lay claim to the world. It's yours."

FORTY-FIVE

+   +   +   +

TYR HELD HIS BREATH AS HE WATCHED THE CABIN DOOR open and close. Dwyn was alone.

He remained in the place between things, but he didn't want to risk her hearing his movements as he broke through the crust of the snow. He waited until she disappeared behind the furthest tree trunk in his line of sight before picking his way toward the cabin. Deciding it was best not to give sound the chance to carry should Ophir exclaim in surprise, he opened and shut the door in the quickest of motions as he slipped inside the shelter.

The moment he stepped out from the place between things, it was to shock and horror.

Ophir looked up at him with wide, panicked eyes. "Can you help him?"

It was the only greeting they required. Any explanation, any apology could wait. He knelt beside Harland and examined the bite marks. He tugged on the belt and exhaled. "The tourniquet is perfect," he said to Ophir. He looked at the vageth. "Sedit did this?"

"Dwyn commanded him to," she said, voice thick with emotion. She lifted her hand, and he blanched with the horror of understanding. He'd been in the room with her in Gwydir when he'd learned of the rings. "She's wearing its counterpart, but since I put it on first... I'm a prisoner, Tyr."

He could tell from her unsteady breathing that she'd been crying for a long, long time. In the months he'd known her, he'd never seen her in shambles like this. He dropped her gaze and let his hand hover above the wound. "It's hot," he said with a frown.

"What's that mean?" She swallowed, adjusting her grip around him.

"It's infected. How long has he been unconscious?"

"He was speaking minutes ago. He was weak but okay." She began to tap against his cheek with her hand until Harland's eyes fluttered open. She responded with a quiet, hopeful laugh. "There you are. Hang on, Harland. Tyr is here. We're going to get out."

Tyr's heart ached at the confidence in her words, as if he were the cavalry here to save the day. "Okay," he said as he slipped an arm behind Harland's back. "I'll carry him. Let's go. We have to hurry. I don't know how long Dwyn will be out."

"I can't," she said, shaking against the words. "She's forbidden me from leaving."

Tyr's eyes flared as he absorbed the weight of her meaning. Dwyn could command her beasts and force her to stay put, all because of those stupid rings.

"Cut my finger off," Ophir said urgently. "Cut it off! We were going to before Dwyn showed up and—"

"No," Harland said, voice quiet but firm. He tried to right himself as he looked at Tyr, but sweat dripped down the gray skin of his face. "I'm dying," he said.

"You're not," Ophir insisted. "Don't say that."

Harland ignored her as he held Tyr's eyes. Tyr straightened respectfully as he nodded for Harland to go on.

"Is it true, what she said? Did you learn how to drain?"

Tyr furrowed his brow. He didn't understand Harland's

question until Ophir's face went white with dread and denial. "Absolutely not, Harland. No—"

Harland spoke over her, looking only at Tyr as he said, "You can get it off her. You can speak to metal."

Tyr looked between the two of them.

"No, Harland, no, he won't do that. He's not going to hurt you. You're going to be fine," Ophir insisted. The fire flared within the hearth as if emphasizing her words, blazing with intensity and vanquishing the room's shadows as she clutched him.

"I'm dying, Firi," he said calmly. "This is why I'm in your life. It's what I was meant for. Let me save you one last time."

"Harland!" she gasped, fear and misery dripping from his name on her lips, every bit as thick and painful as the blood that splashed to the ground from his wound. She touched her forehead to his as she cried.

Harland accepted the touch for a long, stoic moment before he looked at Tyr and nodded.

"Close your eyes," Tyr said to her. She'd seen enough. She'd suffered enough. She didn't need another nightmare engulfing her in flames.

She shook her head in cold, cruel rejection of the truth.

"Close your eyes." Harland echoed the command.

Her cries intensified as she bowed her head, her hold on Harland slackening. Tyr didn't wish to prolong the moment any more than necessary. Not for Harland and not for her. He felt the hot threat of emotion on his lids as he put his hands on the sides of Harland's face.

"Thank you," Tyr mouthed to him. He needed Harland to feel the gratitude, not for him, not for either of them, but for Ophir.

Harland's lids fluttered closed, and a moment later, it was over.

The wail that pierced through the evening could have been heard from miles around. Ophir immediately brought her hands to her face to muffle the cries as she dropped the dusty remnants of Harland's body, and Tyr knew her well enough to understand that her suffering was coming from a wound much deeper than this loss. She was grieving how everything good around her died.

Still, the sound had been too loud. Dwyn could be anywhere, and if she had heard Ophir, they might only have moments.

"Ophir—" Tyr grabbed for her hand.

She yanked away in her suffering, but he found the strength he needed as he forced her hands away from her face. "Look at me, Princess. Prove to Harland that this wasn't for nothing, and let's get you out of here. Give me your hand."

"I—"

"Give it to me!" He jerked it away from her face perhaps a bit too hard, but he saw it in the shift of her posture that her acute fae ears had heard it, too. The steady thumping of feet as someone ran for them.

The chaos that erupted in the next few moments was a blur of unspeakable proportions. Tyr spoke to the metal, forcing the ring to widen until it was a loose band that could easily slip off her finger. The metal finished pulling away from her just as the cabin door burst open. He saw the golden hair as Ophir jerked toward Dwyn and felt the rush of cold water as the siren attempted to douse him in ice and snow, but by the time she screamed for Sedit, it was too late.

"Stop," Tyr said to her in a calm, loud voice. He rose from the floor, ice-cold water dripping from his clothes.

To Dwyn's horror, her water ceased. She flexed her fingers again and again, but nothing happened. "No," she began to repeat over and over. "That's the wrong ring. It's…"

Ophir looked down at her hand and then up at Tyr to see what he'd done.

"The first wearer disappears," Tyr said, unfeeling. "You're the first wearer now, Dwyn."

"How could you," Ophir said, the accusation like flesh

422

dragged over glass until it was sliced and raw. "How could you," she repeated.

"Dwyn," he said, "go wait outside."

And while Dwyn cried out and pounded against an invisible barrier, her feet forced her to obey. The fangs of her elongated canines caught in the firelight as she bared her teeth, howling like a feral animal as she was forced beyond the walls of the cabin. She continued her banshee's cry as Tyr walked calmly to the door and closed it.

"How could you," Ophir said a third time.

He cupped her face in his hands. "You never would have been safe."

"You could have killed…" He saw the light of recognition in her eyes before she finished her sentence. No, to kill Dwyn would be to end his own life. "I'll kill her," she said firmly. "Let me kill her."

"We're fused now more than ever," he said. He tugged his collar humorlessly over the tattoo. "I couldn't have killed her before. But with these rings, if one of us goes, the other does, as well."

Ophir's breathing became shallower and shallower as she pleaded with him for any alternative. She needed a plan, a solution, something to fix what had been broken. Her rapid pants were the only sounds apart from the furious shrieking that crawled under the door and between the cabin's cracks.

"I won't let her hurt you," he said.

"This hurts me," Ophir said firmly. She grabbed his hand and pressed it into her heart. "Tyr, I can't do this. How am I supposed to move forward knowing you've bound yourself to that witch—"

He chuckled lightly.

With shaking shoulders and trembling breath, she said, "I don't see what's funny about any of this."

He shrugged, a sad smile on his face as he pulled her against his chest. "I've been calling her a witch since the day I first met her. It just feels good to have you finally on my side."

She buried her face in the center of his chest while she cried.

She started several sentences, answering each demand before it completed its journey from her lips. Dwyn couldn't be sent away if they were fused by both the rings and the bond of their ink. She couldn't be killed, unless he, too, was ready to die. He felt her fingers dig into him as if she could keep him from leaving if she just held on more tightly.

"This is the only way," he said.

"Don't leave me" was all she could say in return, soaking his shirt with her tears.

He tugged her chin up to force her to look at his face. She tried to look away, but he held firm as he said, "The fae life is long, Ophir. Your first century was more eventful than most. Not many get to realize they're the All Mother."

"I'm not the—"

"You are," he said quietly. "And while this year was horrible beyond all imagining, it was also the year where you discovered who and what you are. And what you are is someone who changed the world. You're brilliant, and stubborn, and brave, and fierce, and incredible. I would have traded my centuries before now just to share the moment in time we had together, and I will trade my centuries after to honor my time spent with you."

She closed her eyes, but he left his hand beneath her chin. "What do I do now?" she asked into the darkness.

"You do what you do best," he said. "You make."

"Tyr..." Her eyes fluttered open. She held his gaze for as long as she could.

"I was never religious," he said as he brushed a kiss against her tears. "I didn't care whether or not there was some greater power. I didn't have faith. Until my sorry, foolish ass stumbled its way into the blessing of spending a year with you. You changed the course of kingdoms, of the people, of the world. You're the reason we pray. And if I get one thousand lifetimes after this one, I can't believe I was lucky enough to have loved a goddess."

EPILOGUE

✦   ✦   ✦   ✦

WHY MUST THEY ALWAYS SCREAM?
"Please be quiet. You won't suffer for long," she
said impassively. It had been a long time since she'd been able
to muster compassion. The snow had melted. The months
had come and gone. Years became decades became centuries. The enormous trees that encircled her glen grew taller
still, taking up space as they swelled with time and water and
memories.

Ophir scanned the empty silence of the wilds for her pet.
She brought her fingers to her temple and gently massaged
the slowly blooming headache.

"Here, Sedit," she called to her hound. She hadn't spotted
him where he doubtlessly chased wild hares in the woods,
but she knew the creature would respond to her. Her voice
held no emotion, save for the barest hint of irritation. The
headache had grown from a blossom into a fully rooted weed
somewhere beneath her temples. Once the horrid noise
ended, surely peace would follow. She hated their screams.

Sedit jogged up on the four legs of a canine, powerful
haunches propelling him along the barren edges of her estate.
His glistening, amphibious skin was muted against the gray of

the overcast sky. Winters had been particularly hard on her creatures, but as many of the naked monsters migrated south for warmer weather, some had gained the love and affection of living with Ophir in her manor. Sedit wasn't her most perfect creation, but he was the first thing she'd made that she'd loved.

He looked up at her lovingly with the many twinkling predator's eyes he possessed. She admired the rows of needle-like teeth that had inspired many of her finest creations. She appreciated how they punctured and tore so absolutely. Nothing could shred like her vageth, and as he was the first of his kind, he'd remain her proudest manifestation.

"Dinner, Sedit." She gestured to the pit.

A girl shivered on the soil below her, earth and grime marring her pale skin. At least, it might have been a girl. Her shape was wrong. Her face was human—but not. Her spine rose up with unnatural spindles, curling with knobs and divots where no spine should. Her eyes were large, even for the fae. Rather than the sharpened canines she'd been trying to create, this girl had rows of jagged teeth on both the top and the bottom. There was always something uncanny about the near-fae creations she conjured from earth and air. They could speak. They could function. But no matter how she tried, her demons had no soul. They were nothing but imitations, shells of what took one from man to monster.

Sedit leaped into the pit, and the girl wailed, a feral, guttural sound. The wet noises of gore and viscera joined her dying shrieks, mingled with the delighted ripping and disemboweling of the canine. He enjoyed the shredding more than the eating and quickly tired of his limp toy. The pit had been too sheer for the humanoid creation, but Sedit had no trouble burying the talons of his mighty paws into its walls and climbing out.

"Good boy," Ophir shushed, stroking his hide.

She sat down along the pit and stared off into the spaces between the trees, knowing no one was looking back from the dark gloom of the forest's gaps. It didn't stop her from scanning the woods, hoping that one day, a familiar face might step out from the space between the great redwood trees. She was quite certain that when she'd arrived, she'd thought it would take three to five fae to encircle their bases. Now, if twenty strong men gripped each other by the wrists, they could still not wrap their arms in a complete circle against many of the trunks in these forests.

She knew Tyr would have loved everything about the forest.

He'd loved animals, and nature, and things that were good. He would have loved the way it smelled. He'd have loved the empty, open possibilities. He'd have loved that no men or fae had sullied the lands. It was her kingdom of birds and fish and deer. He'd loved the short life they'd shared, chaotic and disastrous as it may have been. Somehow, he'd loved her.

His absence wasn't a silence. It was a void.

When Caris had been murdered, Ophir's heart had perished with her sister.

When Tyr had left, whatever had remained of her soul had gone with him. His sacrifice had stirred in a darkened cauldron with Harland's, simmering for years as it told her that all the pain, the suffering, and the loss was because of her.

Sedit began to nuzzle against her, and she stroked the head of the great gray beast. His frog-like skin was made slicker with the remaining bits of organs and blood that coated the dog's face. At least, she liked to think of him as a dog. Tyr hadn't ever cared much for the vageth, and Sedit had never been particularly fond of her lovers, either. In the end, Sedit had been the one who'd stayed.

Then again, her monsters had no say in the matter. She was their mother, after all.

"Come on, boy. We'll try again tomorrow." Ophir stood from the pit and began to walk away from the unholy grave. The freshly abandoned body of the recently slaughtered girl was one in a long line of many. Corpses in various phases of decomposition littered the circular space that had been carved into the earth. The clean-picked spinal column of her first attempt was a bright white reminder of the time that had passed in her decades of trial and error. Every day desensitized her more to her failure.

Manifestation was as much art as it was science.

Some of her earlier creations had done the digging for the very pit that served her now, though for one reason or another, she hadn't kept them around. While her monsters had been fun exercises in creative expression, any true partner needed to be perfect.

She knew from her botched success with the ag'imni that she could make creatures capable of speech, though their gargoyle features, reptilian skin, and monstrous, birdlike talons had immediately disqualified any ag'imni from becoming someone or something with whom she might share what remained of her days. She made a few more, interested in how the demons spoke to one another, and urged more than one to go off and find the ag'drurath that she'd long ago left alone in the world. The lives they lived and the characteristics they developed were incredible to behold. She may have birthed them through mind and will, but their individualistic expression of her manifestation was unique and beautiful.

The pale, bug-eyed abomination who now rested dead in her pit was a testament to how far she'd come. Her hands were soaked in blood. Her brokenness had handcuffed her far more than a ring ever could. And while she put most of the creatures out of their misery, there had been a few she'd set free just because the sounds they'd made had been akin to the broken glass of madness. It made her smile with the barest amusement to inject a little chaos into the world, and it felt good to smile.

She'd felt so little for so long.

She'd used to love with her whole heart, her whole body, her whole mind. Ophir had danced, she'd explored, she'd been curious and interesting and fun. She'd had lovers, she'd had family, she'd been a whole person, once.

Sedit followed her into the hall of her manor, the clatter of his talons sounding over the stones of the foyer. The halls were empty, save for the creatures who served her.

She sank into a chair at the head of her dining room table. Three vacant chairs remained, one for every soul who'd abandoned her once they'd made it to the Wilds. They'd remained empty—untouched. Harland, Dwyn, and Tyr. The three who'd stood in her ramshackle cabin centuries prior—ghosts of names she didn't utter.

A twisted, speechless thing limped with its club feet and shriveled hands as it carried something from the kitchen. "Thank you, Keres." She smiled at the goblin as it clumsily slid a plate before her, releasing the food from its spider-like fingers. She'd enjoyed the sick joke of naming it something so similar to her sister. While Caris, the perfect fae Princess of Farehold, was named for "beloved" and "grace," Keres meant "destruction of the dead."

She didn't think her sister would have appreciated the joke.

Keres nodded as it set the plate in front of Ophir, limping back to the kitchen. The goblin was a benign improvement on the other humanoid abominations she'd created, and she'd chosen to keep it. It was a perfect—albeit silent—servant. It contained the sentience necessary to listen and understand, but it could not argue, it could not fight, and it experienced nothing of longing, reflection, or anything indicative of a soul.

Ophir ate her dinner slowly, taking no joy in her food. She wished she could eat with half of the fervor that Sedit possessed as he tore into flesh time and time again. Instead, the wine had become ash in her mouth. The meals, no matter how decadent or sweet or buttery, had all begun to taste like the same carrion she'd created. Ophir would not die of natural causes, but perhaps if she stopped eating altogether, starvation might still claim her.

If she didn't learn how to create her perfect companion soon, perhaps she'd abandon the enterprise of survival altogether. She'd served her time in purgatory on the continent. Though the fae face didn't show the lines of age, she'd been alive for a millennium, watching time pass with the cruel disinterest of a god who'd made her world and walked away. Her creations would wander from the manor, many never to be seen again.

The uneven slap of Keres's feet against the ground of the manor sounded as the goblin meandered about the estate, lighting the evening torches. The sun had not yet set over the gray gloom of the day, but it was only a matter of time.

Ophir wandered the halls of her manor for a while after dinner. There was nothing to see. There was nothing to do. The vases held plants that had withered and dried years and years ago. The trinkets and baubles hadn't been dusted in decades. The dirt and cobwebs that filled her home hadn't bothered her in lifetimes. Nothing had mattered in a long, long time. Ophir had torn down the portraits of Tyr and Caris. She'd set fire to the beautiful things she'd put aside to keep them close to her. She'd burned, and raged, and screamed.

She didn't want to remember. She wanted to forget.

Ophir paused in the hall where the stones discolored.

An oil painting had hung on this wall for three hundred years. The sun had begun to bleach the wall around it until she'd shredded it in a rage. She stood in the buttery pool of orange torchlight and fixated on the bleached discoloration, feeling something click as the mechanisms of a lock whirred in her mind. This space had been reserved for a portrait of Caris. She'd manifested one nearly identical to the honorific commission that had hung in the hall in Aubade following her sister's murder. The perfect, angelic princess's golden hair had hung loosely at her shoulders; her dress had been the beautiful cherry-blossom tone of spring.

Ophir twisted her fingers to watch another portrait come

into existence in her hand, crafted from the very air around her. She had less trouble creating that which already existed, as replication required neither soul nor imagination. She hung it on the same mounts that had lofted the portrait for centuries prior, taking a step back to admire it. Caris's gentle jawline, her rosy cheeks, the sweet, upward slope of her nose were exactly the way they'd always been. The portrait was perfect.

As she stared at her sister's memory, she knew why her creatures had been abominations.

Perhaps the problem was that she was trying to invent something new, when what she needed to do was re-create. Her closest successes had been her fumbled compass, her monstrous horse, her vague hound. If ever she was to make something that wasn't a nightmare, it would come from something true.

+   +   +   +

"Go play, Sedit." She gave her pet a push toward the woods. Maybe he'd find a rabbit to slaughter. "If I do this right, I might not need you today."

There was a slight chill on the wind today, but she didn't mind. Ophir wrapped her cloak around her and enjoyed the scent of the forest as she stilled her mind. She waved her hands, and two palm-sized portraits appeared. Tyr and Caris were small and perfect as their captured likenesses stared back at her from the miniature canvases. She set them down next to her on the grass and knelt. Today, she would not create. She would recapture.

She focused first on Caris.

Not her perfect sister's blue eyes, her golden hair, or her physical features. She thought of the very spirit her manifestations had lacked and meditated on what had knitted the eldest princess together on her innermost level. Caris had been sweet. She had been soft-spoken, likable, and had smiled so easily. She had been beautiful, yes, but she had been driven by a desire for unity. Her life had been motivated by a desire for a borderless world. Caris had dedicated her life to the vision of a kingdom stitched together from shards of prejudice and inequality. There were so many complexities, nuances, and intricacies to crafting a soul. If she were to borrow a spirit, it needed to be that of the perfect, belated Caris.

Ophir held out her hand before her, closing her eyes as she felt a soul begin to take shape. She gave it purpose. She offered it reason, personality, and drive. She fed it with knowledge, family, and strength. Ophir had lived for one thousand years and still hadn't forgotten what had separated Caris from those around her. She had been flawless.

Ophir's eyes opened as she stared at the portrait of Tyr she'd brought with her.

She didn't think she could survive if she stared into his face every day, but nor could her heart tolerate the pain of seeing an eerie replication of who should have been Caris but wasn't. Instead, she'd make for herself something new: a sister, a daughter, a friend. She pictured Caris's sapphire irises and Tyr's ink-black hair. She envisioned the gilded skin of the man who had left her, but the shoulders, the arms, the stomach and legs of the sister she'd lost. A shape began to stitch around the soul, bones and muscles and tissues sewing themselves in swirls around the blue center of the soul.

Ophir closed her eyes as she pushed the final ingredient into the creature as it manifested: a mind. It would need memories, information, language. Though she could not create a perfect history for the creature, she instilled within it the ability to generate the memories it would need to fill in essential blanks and craft a life in its wholeness. She'd spent the night creating a beautiful story for her companion, her ward, her child.

With a gust of air, Ophir blew the shape into the pit and squeezed her eyes together more tightly. She gripped handfuls of grass and prayed to a goddess that she didn't believe in while she waited for the screams. There were always screams.

No sound came.

Ophir opened her eyes to see a dark-haired woman scrambling backward toward the edge of the pit. Soil, hands, and limbs pressed into the earth as she clawed at the dirt, eyes darting to take in her surroundings. Grime covered her body, hair blanketing her naked shape. Her eyes were wide with confusion.

Ophir begged speech to come to her. She hadn't spoken to a person in so long. She knew she was only moments from disappointment. In a second, the creation would start screaming. It would be mindless, soulless, and as broken as every other monster she'd created. Tinged with desperation, she offered a single, "Hello?"

The dark-haired woman blinked up at her. "Where the hell am I?"

Ophir almost choked. Her breath caught in her throat as she clawed to the edge of the pit, nearly tripped over herself as she tumbled down into it. She had lost all sense of coordination in her panicked excitement. She took off her cloak and immediately began trying to shelter the woman, wrapping her in the cloak. The woman was too bewildered to fight her.

"Where am I?" she asked again.

"Let's get you inside." Ophir waved her hand and made a ladder. She led the way up, offering her hand to help the girl to her feet. The young woman, still exposed and covered in the muck of the pit, followed her across the lawn. She looked around with so much panic, so much confusion.

She'd granted the woman Caris's motives, her drives, her charisma, and her winsome spirit. She'd failed to prepare the creation for the enormous redwoods, the empty forests, or the excited vageth who leaped and bounded around their lawn. Ophir wasn't sure where the new fae's ability to generate the memories required for wholeness would start or stop, and the woman was understandably terrified.

"Keres!" Ophir shouted as they crossed the threshold. "Please clean the guest room!" The shuffling noises of her half-formed servant moved throughout the corridors as they bustled past too quickly for the newcomer to see.

She had her arms around the dark-haired fae as she led her to her personal bedchambers. Ophir moved them past the rug, bed, and dresser into the adjoining bathing room. She snapped warm, soapy bathwater into existence, thick with the perfumed, spring-like scents of the gardenias and blossoms she had loved so much on her sister. The woman had apparently been effectively instilled with enough wherewithal to understand bathing and the basics of self-care, but the panic had not left her.

"How did I get here? Where are my clothes? Why—" the woman asked, teeth chattering. Her trembles were most likely a byproduct of shock.

"Here, here." Ophir gestured to the water. "You fell and hit your head. Let's get you cleaned up and see if you have any wounds." She took the cloak from around the young fae woman's shoulders and offered a stabilizing hand as the girl moved into the bath. Ophir couldn't stop staring at her. She'd created someone perfect. She'd manifested a beautiful, intelligent, complete fae.

The woman stepped into the water but was shivering despite its warmth. Her hands rose to cover her nakedness even beneath the soapy waters.

"I don't—" She looked around the confines of the bathing room like a caged animal. "I don't remember how I got here. I don't... I don't remember my name."

Shit. She hadn't given it a name.

Ophir fought to control her facial expressions. She thought quickly of names from the southern dialects. She wanted something beautiful—something appropriate. This companion was her greatest achievement. She'd never rendered anything so wonderful. She couldn't believe she'd knitted this fae with her heart, mind, and body into one perfect package. A single name came to mind, one that meant "majestic creation." She'd done this, and only something truly splendid would suffice.

"Daifa," she said. "You're called Daifa. Goddess, how terrifying. That must have been quite the spill. Are you feeling okay?"

Daifa's slender hand flew to her head, splashing a bit of bathwater accidentally as she checked for a wound. Every movement, from knowing to reach for injury to questioning her name and location, was a sign of how flawlessly she'd been crafted.

Daifa shook her head and looked up at Ophir, eyes still wild with confusion. It was then that Ophir noticed one slight deviation from the perfection of her creation. The sapphire irises that had been such a stunning feature on Caris took up nearly the entirety of this new creature's eyes. The blue was so stark, such a stunning contrast on someone with Sulgrave features. She was certainly unique, but no one would question her heritage from looking at her. She was fae in every way.

"I'll get you something to wear and lay it out on the bed. Take your time and come meet me for dinner. Are you hungry?"

Daifa's brows gathered in the center as her hands left her hair and went for her stomach. She nodded, still rippling with confusion. She hadn't begun scrubbing at the grime. She sat shivering and wet with the soil from the pit still clinging to her skin. Perhaps she just needed some privacy and some time to herself.

She'd been born into the world a fully formed person. The tale of a head injury would fill in any and all gaps Ophir needed as she crafted her companion, but she'd done it. She'd finally done it.

She dipped her head in acknowledgment as she left the bathing room, heart swelling with a body-warming smile. She'd created someone. Not a monster. Not a demon. Someone. She'd made someone real.

At last, she could give Caris the dream that was stolen from her. Daifa could be anyone to Ophir—a friend, a daughter, a sister—while she embodied Caris's vision for the continent. This new perfect creature would fill the void left by those she'd loved and lost.

She could unify the continent.

Finally, Ophir had made something that would save the world once and for all, or destroy it.

READ ON FOR A PEEK AT
THE FIRST BOOK IN THE
NO OTHER GODS SERIES

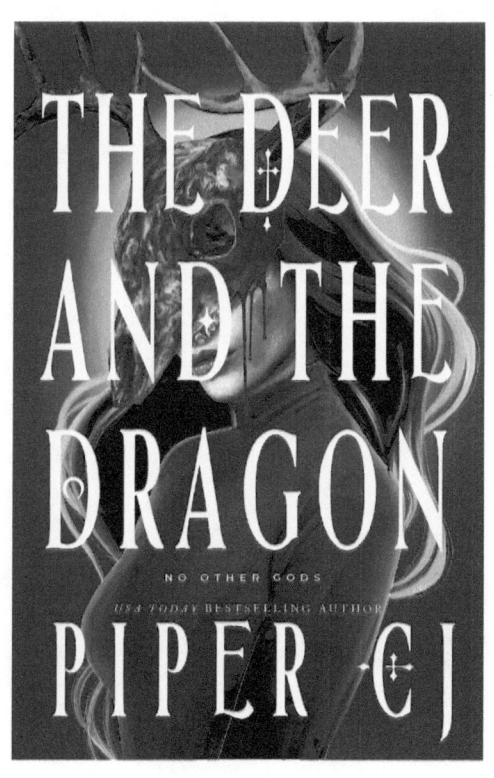

Chapter One

I STARED DOWN THE BARREL OF THE LESSER OF TWO EVILS: THE flesh-and-blood disappointment of a human man, or a life trapped in my imagination with a fictional lover.

I remembered reading that the brain stops forming at twenty-six. I watched the man across from me chew his food with his mouth slightly ajar, not bothering to swallow before he went on to name-drop yet another notch in society's belt. He was holding his chopsticks wrong. He had mixed wasabi directly into his soy sauce. He'd spoken at a cringe-worthy volume throughout the meal, drawing curious, if disgruntled, stares. There wasn't a single etiquette he followed, and it wasn't even close to the worst thing about him.

I wasn't sure if I hoped the bit about the brain was true. I was halfway through my twenty-sixth year and not so sure that this was the finished product I wanted for my mind. I was doing my best to be normal. This was what normal people did, right? They went on terrible dates with ordinary humans. They didn't see things that weren't there. They didn't cling to ghosts and maladaptive fantasies they'd conjured in the dark. They took their medications they went to therapy, and they learned how to distinguish what was real.

If my brain had stopped forming, however, it might come with perks. On the one hand, it meant that this bovine-mannered date wouldn't be a core memory. The man in the suit across from me—Jared? Joshua? I'm pretty sure it was Josh—would be a forgettable date after a long string of mediocre sex and dating apps. On the other hand, maybe it meant my courtship habits and hidden, wish-fulfilling coping mechanisms were cemented in stone and there was no hope for me. Perhaps I was doomed to repeat a cycle of Joshes. This was my curse.

"Marlow?"

Oh, fuck. He was staring at me. Had he asked me a question? I squinted my eyes slightly, peering through the din of the too-expensive restaurant and the polite chatter of upscale patrons for a clue.

"Come again?" I attempted an apologetic smile.

His perplexed look was one I understood. Of course he would be confused that I hadn't been listening. This was our second date, and he expected more from me. After all, I'd been utterly delightful last time. Painted, waxed, and squeezed into the most stunning dress, sporting the glossiest hair and the most charming smiles, I was a living superlative. I'd spent my life learning how to make the perfect first impression.

My profile had been curated to snag any curious suitor. First was a high-resolution picture that a friend had taken four years prior on a boat in Rio de Janeiro, where the greens and grays of the coast matched my eyes. "Where was that picture taken?" gave prospective dates an easy conversation opener. The next two had been selected to attract the outdoorsy types, from the HD pic of me flexing on a mountain in yoga pants and a sports bra to me on the beach laughing with friends—which also created the perfect excuse to show off a bikini body and gave me an easy way to screen out anyone who didn't like curves. I rounded out the profile with a picture of me alone with my coffee cup and computer, looking very serious and business-like, immediately followed by a photo of me jumping on the bed holding a bottle of wine, dress flying up, muddy blond curls a cloud around my face, smiling as if I were having the time of my life. Whatever dream you wanted to project onto me, I gave you the option right there in my intricately tailored series of images.

"Who are you?" the app had asked.

"Whoever you need me to be," my profile replied.

Every date was spent in a song and dance of asking the right questions, laughing at the right pitch, tossing my hair over my shoulder, arching my neck, lowering my lashes, and, as always, keeping them talking. They'd leave thinking they'd met their soulmate. I'd leave wondering if I could catch the newest episode of *Fire and Swords* or if I'd have to wait until it was on a streaming service.

"I asked if you've been to the Galápagos," he repeated.

"No." I kept my tone as light as possible. I glanced down at the elaborately plated omakase sushi that had doubtlessly cost more than half of the country made in a month. This was why I'd agreed to go on the second date. I loved good sushi, and free just so happened to be my favorite price. The salmon belly was the most well marbled in the hemisphere. I'd come back with terrible company just to eat my weight in the stuff even if it meant thinking about what sort of life these ocean animals had before they ended up on my plate.

He grabbed the sake kettle and tilted the alcohol into his glass first, then mine.

I kept the disarming smile on my face as I said, "I've wandered my way through a lot of South America, but I was teaching English as a second language and I—"

"Oh, you have to go back and do it the right way. I have a friend who works at the most incredible resort you've ever seen. The fish swim right underneath…" His mouth kept moving as my thoughts drifted into the restaurant's ambience while I started to think of marine life. I liked aquariums. I wondered how long it had been since I'd been to one. Maybe I'd go to the city's aquatic zoo, bring a bag of magic mushrooms, pop in my headphones, and listen to music while counting sharks over the weekend.

Josh required little encouragement to continue the conversation. It only took a pleading look to the waitress and a firm "*No,*" when asked if we wanted desserts for her to bring the check without waiting for his argument on digestifs. She knew from the very intentional way I'd selected designer pieces, from the delicate chain around my neck to the bag that dangled over the back of my chair, that I could afford the bill if I'd requested it. My deadpan stare challenged him to give it to me. In my early twenties, I would have rushed to cover the check so that Josh wouldn't expect anything from me. Now I expected him to procure his Amex as penance for making me watch him chew with his mouth open. It was the least he could do.

I idly wondered if Josh had ever asked me what I did for a living. Perhaps that was my own fault. I'd gotten so good at getting others to talk about themselves that I'd become excellent at living in the shadows. I wonder how many of my dates knew more about me than my name and how spectacular I was in bed.

We'd scarcely stepped into the cold, cloudless night before he asked, "So, should we go back to my place?"

"Oh." I pouted slightly to underscore my feigned regrets while shrugging into my coat, saying, "I'm so sorry. I called a rideshare while I was in the bathroom. It's only two minutes out."

Josh looked like he'd been slapped. I wondered how many times a man with a forty-thousand-dollar Rolex was turned down. Then again, it had been a running pleasure of mine to play catch and release. The bigger the fish, the more satisfying it was to throw them back into the water. Everything about this evening had me wishing I'd stayed in to watch the documentary about whales rather than wasting the perfume by stepping out into the world.

"What about the concert?"

I frowned, scarcely looking up from my phone. "Concert?"

Confusion faded into agitation as he studied my face. "Next week, the one I—"

Fish. Everything about this man was a fish. When they tell you that there are plenty of fish in the sea, they forget to mention that half of marine life is boring, scaly and a part of an identical school of thousands just like him. I would rather be alone, high, and looking at tropical fish next weekend. "Oh, I'm so sorry, Josh—this is my car!"

"It's Jacob."

I grimaced. I really was sorry about that one. I should have checked his name from the dating profile when I'd escaped to the restroom.

He knew the evening had soured but still had the balls to go in for a kiss. I intercepted with a side hug before launching into the street to stop my car. I closed the door and took off into the night before my date had time to recover from his wounded ego. The driver asked precisely the right number of questions, which was zero. He left me alone to the buzzing phone that illuminated the back seat of the vehicle.

(Kirby) How was the banker?

(Nia) CFO, right? Big money

(Kirby) Not like tech guy. Mar, could you call him up again? We used to go to much nicer places when you were sleazing it with the tech guy.

(Marlow) I'd like to sleaze it up with a loose bag of cheese and my sweatpants

(Nia) You were supposed to get laid. How am I supposed to live vicariously through you if you're pulling a celibacy act

(Kirby) No, that's fair. She's always been a slut for cheese. No one made you get married, Nia.

(Nia) And so what? I'm supposed to live with the consequences of my actions?

(Marlow) I'm just going to call it an early night

(Nia) And waste a great hair and makeup day? Damn, there
must be some fantastic cheese back at your place

I clicked the button on the side of my phone, turning the
screen into an obsidian mirror and leaned my head against
the window, watching the black and auburn blur of homes,
shadows, lawns, and fences as we crossed through a neighbor-
hood. I used to look at houses and wonder about the lives of
the people who lived inside. What did the family do to afford
a home so close to downtown? What did a three-story house
with fantastic landscaping cost in one of the world's flashiest
cities? It had been a long time since I'd cared.

I saw the driver frown as the GPS turned into the northern part of the metropolis. It wasn't an unusual reaction. No
one lived in the warehouse district. There was no reason for a
girl of any repute to take a car to the warehouses in high heels
and red lipstick. He pulled up along the sidewalk and eyed
what had once been a bread factory. His expression deepened
into worry at the smattering of lights and darkened entryway.

"Is this right, miss?"

"Home sweet home." I smiled. I flashed him my screen
to show the glowing rating I'd sent his way as I slid out of the
car. His eyebrows remained knit, but he shrugged as I closed
the door. He wasn't paid enough to care.

A blanket-like quiet pressed in as the car pulled away—a
sound challenging to achieve anywhere in the city. There
was no traffic, no pedestrians, no indication that anyone but
the phantoms of long-dead industry tycoons haunted these
corridors. The April night clung to the last of spring's chill,
sending goose bumps up and down my bare legs. I fished a
metallic rose-gold card from my purse and pressed it against
the panel, satisfied when it buzzed.

I rounded the brick corridor for the atrium, where an
ever-attentive receptionist waited to respectfully greet me.
She was one of four and arguably my favorite. No matter
how short my skirt, how high my heels, or how late the

hour, she remained polite without speaking. I knew her boyfriend's name, I gave her chocolates every holiday, and we never failed to gush about the new episodes of *Fires and Swords* if I loitered in the hallway, but she had an innate gift for knowing when I was overwhelmed and needed silence. Perhaps intuition was a prerequisite for anyone who took a job in luxury apartments.

Though she'd never say it outright, her expressions conveyed the same long-standing concern that I'd stumbled through the door after too many dates to count. She'd helped me get into the building when I was a bit too drunk to see my phone and buzzed me up to my room whenever I'd lost too much brain function to recall how my card worked. It seemed like a safe bet that she was not the sort of person who got high at aquariums.

The small bank of polished elevators waited quietly, all in disuse given the lateness of the hour. One opened for me the moment I pressed the button.

I didn't wait for the elevator doors to close before slipping out of my heels, dangling the sharpened ends from one hand. I caught the brief, disapproving narrowing of eyes through the rapidly closing doors and flashed my most dazzling smile. Part of me respected her bravery. It was bold to be judgmental of the residents when they knew precisely how much these apartments cost.

I pressed the glittery, metallic card onto the pad to gain access to my floor—second from the top. The penthouse hadn't been available, and I'd been okay with it. Everyone who lived here had their reasons for wanting to stay off the world's radar, and there wasn't a better establishment in the city for those with deep enough pockets to erase themselves from the map. The building's discretion had been worth the downgrade, and as someone who lived alone, I couldn't have justified the extra space unless I was looking to install a private bowling alley.

The elevator door opened noiselessly onto my floor.

There were thirteen units in the entire building—two per floor, save for the lucky bastard who'd snagged the thirteenth. I walked barefoot down the sparkling black marble to my room and pressed my thumb into the pad, allowing it to scan my fingerprint until a subtle click told me the mechanisms had unlocked.

It was dark in my apartment and stayed that way. I'd had the features for automatic lights disabled the day I'd moved in.

I tossed my purse onto the floor, leaving it in a jumble with my shoes. I walked to the window and stared out over the twinkling lights of the city and the sliver of river I could spot from my unit. I was a sucker for a good view.

The hairs on the back of my neck prickled in the way they did when one knew they were being watched. The rush of gin, moss, and mist filled the room the moment before I heard it. I breathed it in like a prayer.

"Leave it open" came a male voice from the shadows.

I fought the deep, conflicting bloom that emanated from somewhere near my center. My toes curled, heart thundering at the purr of his voice. "Don't do this to me," I grumbled half-heartedly, but I was certain he heard the ghost of a smile in my voice.

"Didn't go well?" he asked.

I continued facing the window but reached over my head for the zipper. Years had gone by, and I was still breathless every time he spoke. It was so easy to lose my resolve whenever those silken words tumbled over his lips. I managed to give the thin metal a tug but lost my grip on it as I said, "He was utterly forgettable."

"They all will be," he said, brushing my hair away from my neck. Goose bumps started at the nape of my neck and slithered down my spine. He held the top of my dress in one strong hand, using the other to gently tug the zipper. He stopped before releasing it more than a quarter of an inch. I waited for the next sensation, but nothing came. Tension swelled as I swallowed another deep breath of earth and perfume.

"What?" I breathed.

The electric current of his touch coursed through me.

"Holy fuck," I murmured, falling to pieces.

His fingers began to work their way up the hem of my dress, nudging it up over my hips. My stomach clenched. My lips parted in a stifled gasp, eyes closing as he came up behind me. His mouth sucked gently on the tender place where my throat met my shoulder. Every sense in my body homed in on the delicious sensation. His mouth moved to the back of my neck, hands dropping from my hips to urge me forward. I leaned into the floor-to-ceiling glass, letting the cold seep into me as his hand slid from my inner thigh, higher, *higher*.

"Oh god," I gasped when he grazed the soaked evidence of my black-lace panties.

"You know better than that," he chided softly at my choice in words, a teasing warmth in his voice. He relaxed his body into mine until I was pressed wholly against the window. "Now, are you going to let me in?"

My face betrayed the battle going on in my head and heart. My body ached for him. My breasts peaked against the thin dress. The pulsing in my chest extended into every piece of me, and I felt my heartbeat in my greediest places. My fingers clenched against the glass. He chuckled lightly.

"Nothing without your permission," he said, fingers still grazing me with tantalizing slowness. The tingle of the water between my legs trickling onto my inner thighs elicited a low groan of approval. His fingers continued to move over the thin fabric.

I gasped against the sensation, and he leaned into my throat once more, smiling through my pleasure.

"You know I'm…" Words felt useless.

"You're what?" he pressed me into the window with more force.

"I'm trying to stop."

AFTERWORD

Remain in Gyrradin with The Night and Its Moon quartet and accompanying novellas to see Ophir's demons and creations across the continent, the royal family who filled the void in Farehold after Eero's death, Samael's league of assassins in Uaimh Reev, and what became of Daifa's legacy.

If you enjoyed the Villains duology, please leave a review, tell your friends, and let me know if you'd like us to return to Gyrradin once more for future installments.

CONTENT WARNING

"There are no heroes in this story." Everyone is a villain, which may create dangerous/dubious immorality and reading conditions that some readers may find upsetting or unsuitable:

Mass death, reference to one character's unsuccessful attempt to take her own life, themes of depression, grief, death, loss, emotional pain/suffering, a main character struggling with PTSD, reference to book one's witnessed murder, witnessing mutilation, human sacrifice, hunting humans for murderous revenge, group sex, explicit descriptions of sex, cursing, lying, magic, betrayal, blasphemy, manipulation of trust, inter-kingdom politics that may include themes of the villainous kingdom exercising colonization and ethnocentrism (with on-page condemnation of the act[s]) and on-page retribution), a character being held against their will (hostage, kidnapping) through physical, mental, and magical force, sacrifice, mediumship and ghosts/spirits, consorting with the dead and themes of the afterlife, threesome (titillating), murder, assassination, dismantling of a kingdom (including mass murder and civilian loss of life).

Please connect on the author's website for further updates to content and trigger warnings: pipercj.com

ACKNOWLEDGMENTS

I'm battling the urge to write "you know who you are and what you've done," but that doesn't seem fair to my editor, Letty Mundt, who poured love and attention into her work. I'd also like to raise a glass to Kyria and Nigel for their incredible artwork, Johanie for her sensitivity read, Alexandra for her marketing expertise, Christa for taking a chance on me, and the entire team at Bloom for letting villains have their day in the sun. Thank you to my friends, my little coven, my partner, my dog, french fries, and the corner booth at my favorite pub in Seattle.

Mostly: thank you to evil women. May they get their happy endings.

ABOUT THE AUTHOR

Piper CJ, author of the *USA Today* bestselling bisexual fantasy series The Night and Its Moon and No Other Gods, and *New York Times* bestselling series Fern's School for Wayward Fae, is a photographer, hobby linguist, and French fry enthusiast. She has an M.A. in folklore and a B.A. in broadcasting, which she used in her former life as a morning-show weather girl, hockey podcaster, and in audio documentary work. Now when she isn't playing with her dog, she's gaming, binging cartoons, dissecting fairy tales, or disappointing her parents.

Website: pipercj.com
Instagram: @piper_cj
TikTok: @pipercj